# TAILSPIN

## Novels by Sandra Brown

*Seeing Red*

*Sting*

*Friction*

*Mean Streak*

*Deadline*

*Low Pressure*

*Lethal*

*Mirror Image*

*Where There's Smoke*

*Charade*

*Exclusive*

*Envy*

*The Switch*

*The Crush*

*Fat Tuesday*

*Unspeakable*

*The Witness*

*The Alibi*

*Standoff*

*Best Kept Secrets*

*Breath of Scandal*

*French Silk*

*Slow Heat in Heaven*

# TAILSPIN

# SANDRA BROWN

**GRAND CENTRAL**
PUBLISHING

NEW YORK    BOSTON

Copyright © 2018 by Sandra Brown Management, Ltd.

Jacket design by Anne Twomey
Digital illustration by Elizabeth Stokes
Photographs of man and woman by George Kerrigan
Jacket copyright © 2018 by Hachette Book Group, Inc.

Grand Central Publishing
Hachette Book Group
1290 Avenue of the Americas, New York, NY 10104
grandcentralpublishing.com
twitter.com/grandcentralpub

First Edition: August 2018

Grand Central Publishing is a division of Hachette Book Group, Inc. The Grand Central Publishing name and logo is a trademark of Hachette Book Group, Inc.

The publisher is not responsible for websites (or their content) that are not owned by the publisher.

The Hachette Speakers Bureau provides a wide range of authors for speaking events. To find out more, go to www.hachettespeakersbureau.com or call (866) 376-6591.

Library of Congress Cataloging-in-Publication Data has been applied for.

ISBNs: 978-1-4555-7216-8 (hardcover), 978-1-4555-7212-0 (ebook), 978-1-4555-7215-1 (large print), 978-1-5387-4687-5 (signed edition)

Printed in the United States of America

LSC-C

10  9  8  7  6  5  4  3  2  1

# Chapter 1

*9:42 p.m.*

**N**o. Not doing it."

"When I called, you were Johnny on the spot."

"But I didn't know then about the weather. It's socked in solid, Dash."

"Fog ain't solid. You can fly through it, you know. Like clouds. Or didn't your online flight school teach that?"

The young pilot rolled his eyes. "They closed Atlanta. *Closed* it. How often does that happen? It must be bad, or the airport wouldn't have been shut down the night before Thanksgiving. Be reasonable."

Dash pressed his beefy hand over his heart. "I'm reasonable. I'm the soul of reason. The client, on the other hand…He don't care the airport's shut down. He wants this box *here*"—he slapped his hand down on top of the black metal container sitting on the counter behind him—"to get *there*"—he pointed in a generally southern direction—"tonight. I guaranteed him that it would."

"Then you've got a customer relations problem."

He was called Dash, first because the few who'd ever known

his real name had forgotten it, and, second, because the name of his charter and airfreight company was Dash-It-All.

Older than he owned up to being, Dash had a potbelly that served the same purpose as a cowcatcher on a locomotive: Little could stand in the path of his stomping tread. Always under a deadline, his singular expression was a scowl.

As menacing as that glower was, however, thus far it hadn't fazed the pilot who was resistant to taking off from Columbus, Ohio, for Atlanta, where, for holiday travelers, the weather was screwing with tight schedules and well-laid plans.

And if airfreight was your business, satisfaction guaranteed, it was screwing with your livelihood.

Frustrated, Dash clamped down on an unlit cigar and worked it between his stained teeth. Smoking was prohibited in the fixed base operator. His rules. But also, his cigars. So he gnawed on one whenever somebody was giving him a hassle he didn't need. As now.

"No real flyer would get squeamish over a little fog," he said.

The pilot gave him a look.

*Okay.* Only to himself, Dash conceded that it was more than a little fog. It was the likes of which no one alive had ever seen. People along the Atlantic seaboard had awakened this morning to find their cities and towns engulfed. The fog had created traffic hazards and general havoc over the eastern third of the United States and showed no signs of lifting.

The Weather Channel was getting a ratings boost. Meteorologists were practically giddy over the phenomenon, which one had described as "biblical," and another had called "epochal." Dash wasn't sure what that meant, but it sounded grim. What the blasted fog meant to him was lost revenue.

At Hartsfield-Jackson and other major airports in a double-digit number of states, passenger flights and cargo carriers had been grounded on this Thanksgiving eve when it seemed that everybody in the nation was trying to get from wherever they were to someplace else. Dash figured it would take till Christmas for the carriers to unsnarl the mess, but that was of no concern to him.

His concern was keeping his fleet of airplanes in the air, shuttling stuff that people paid to have shuttled in the shortest amount of time possible. Birds nesting in the hangar didn't make money. He needed this pilot to grow a pair, and quick, so he could back up the guarantee he'd made to his client, a Dr. Lambert, that this box would reach Atlanta before morning.

Hoping to shame the young aviator into taking off, Dash looked him up and down with unconcealed scorn. "You could make it fine if you wanted to bad enough. Scared of the fog, or scared you won't be back tomorrow in time for your mama's turkey dinner and pumpkin pie?"

"I'm waiting it out, Dash. End of discussion."

The pilot was on the shy side of thirty. Even at this time of night, he was clean-shaven and smartly dressed in black slacks and white shirt. His eyes were clear, like he hadn't violated the FAA's bottle-to-throttle minimum of an eight-hour abstention from alcohol before flying, and also had gotten that many hours of sleep.

Dash had years of experience sizing up flyers of every caliber, from top guns to crop dusters. He gauged this one as an uptight stickler who flew by the book and wouldn't know an aeronautical instinct if it bit him in the ass. He abided by the rules no matter what. All the rules. All the time. No exceptions.

Dash wanted to strangle him.

Curbing that impulse, he tried again. "You'll be jockeying the Beechcraft. Just had it overhauled, you know. All the latest technology. New seats. Cushy as they come."

The pilot stood his ground. "When the weather in Atlanta clears, and the airport reopens—"

"A decade from now!" Dash interrupted in a shout. "If they reopened right this minute, it'd be hours before they work through the stack-up. By then your tuna fish sandwiches will have spoiled." The client had agreed to pay for a catered box lunch for the "crew." It had been delivered wrapped up all nice in a white pasteboard box. It, too, sat on the counter behind them.

In an ominous mutter, Dash added, "They'll have spoiled or been snatched."

He cast a look across the lobby toward the sofa against the far wall. The couch was an eyesore. Its turquoise-and-tan plaid upholstery was lumpy, stringy, greasy in spots, and stained with not even God knew what.

But its condition seemed not to matter to the man stretched out along it. He lay on his back, hands linked over his stomach, a years-old aviation magazine with curled pages tented over his face while he slept.

Dash came back around to the pilot. Still speaking in an undertone, he said, "We get all kinds passing through here, you know."

"I'll guard my lunch until I can take off."

Dash exhaled with agitation. "It's not like your cargo is a rodeo bull."

He had actually flown one such snorting mean bastard from Cheyenne to Abilene in a DC-3. Damn thing had bucked all the way there. The bull, not the plane, which had been a sweetheart. That was 1985, if he was remembering right. Back when he was young and wild and thin. Well... thin*ner*.

He sighed with nostalgia for the good ol' days then resumed his argument with the pilot. "All you'll be carrying tonight is this fancy tackle box."

"The airport is closed, Dash."

"The big mama, yeah. But—"

"And so is every FBO in a two-hundred-mile radius of Atlanta."

Dash shifted the cigar from one side of his mouth to the other, then held up both hands in surrender. "Okay. You win. I'll cut you in for a larger share."

"I can't spend extra pay if I'm dead."

Dash bit off the soggy end of his cigar and spat the wad into the trash can. "You're not gonna get dead."

"Right. Because I'm not flying until the fog dissipates and the airport reopens. The plane is fueled and ready to roll when we get the thumbs-up. Okay? Can we drop it?" He pulled himself up taller. "Now, the crucial question. Is the popcorn machine still busted?" With that, the pilot turned and followed the odor of scorched corn kernels toward the hallway that led to the pilot's lounge.

Dash's cell phone rang. "Hold on. Maybe this'll be your thumbs-up."

The pilot stopped and turned. Dash answered his phone. "Yeah?" When the caller identified himself, Dash held up an index finger, indicating that it was the call he'd hoped for. It was his counterpart who'd brokered the charter at a private fixed base operator attached to Hartsfield-Jackson.

"Yeah, yeah, he's ready. Good to go. Chomping at the bit," he added, skewering the pilot with his glare "Huh? Divert to where?" His frown deepened as he listened for another half minute. "No, I don't think that'll be a problem." Even as he said that, he knew better. "No PCL system? You're sure somebody'll be there to turn on the lights?"

The pilot flinched. A pilot-controlled lighting system would have enabled him to turn on the runway lights from his cockpit.

"Okay," Dash said. "Email me the particulars. Got it." He clicked off and said to the pilot, "We're in luck. There's an FBO outside a small town in northern Georgia. The client will meet you there. He's leaving Atlanta now by car. It's a two, two-and-a-half-hour drive, but he's willing—"

"Northern Georgia? In the mountains?"

Dash made a dismissive gesture. "Not big ones. Foothills."

"Is it controlled?"

"No. But the landing strip is plenty long enough for this air-craft if you, uh, set down at the very end of it, and the crosswinds aren't too strong." Reading his pilot's dubious expression, he snapped his fingers. "Better idea."

"I wait for Atlanta to reopen."

"You take the 182."

The pilot sputtered a laugh. "That bucket? I don't think so."

Dash glowered. "That bird was flying long before your daddy was born."

Which was the wrong thing to boast because the pilot chuck-led again. "My point exactly."

"Okay, so it's not as young and spiffy as the Beechcraft, and it's seen some wear and tear, but it's reliable, and it's here, and you're going. I'll gas her up while you file your flight plan. Name of the place is—"

"Hold on, Dash. I signed on for the Beechcraft, flying into a controlled airport, not chancing it in uncontrolled airspace over mountainous terrain, in pea soup, and landing on a short strip where there's likely to be strong crosswinds. And hoping that somebody will be there to turn on the runway lights?" He shook his head. "Forget it."

"I'll pay you triple."

"Not worth it. I'd have to be crazy. Up to you to head off the client and make him understand that nobody can deliver tonight whatever is in that box. He'll get it when the weather improves. I'll continue to monitor it and get on my way as soon as I can."

"You pass on this, you're history with my outfit."

"Not so. You need pilots too bad." He picked up the boxed lunch and took it with him as he crossed the lobby and headed down the hallway.

Dash swore under his breath. He'd issued an empty threat, and the smug son of a bitch knew it. He needed pilots rated for several categories, classes, and types of aircraft who could climb into a cockpit and fly at a moment's notice.

This one was an asshole, but he was a bachelor and therefore more available than the men with families. He was eager to chalk up hours that he could eventually peddle to a commercial passenger carrier.

And, truth be told, to fly into that backwoods airfield under these more-than-iffy conditions, he would have to be altogether crazy. He wasn't. He was a levelheaded pilot who didn't take unnecessary risks.

Dash needed the other kind.

He looked across the lobby toward the sofa, shifted his cigar again, hiked his pants up beneath his substantial overlap, and took a deep breath. "Uh, Rye?"

The man lying on the sofa didn't respond.

"Rye," Dash said more loudly, "you awake?" The sprawled form remained motionless, but Dash continued. "I've got a situation here. Rotten kickoff to the holiday season, and you know that's when I make half my year's income. This guy's turned pussy on me, and—"

Dash stopped talking when Rye Mallett lifted the old magazine off his face. He rolled up and swung his feet to the floor. "Yeah, I heard." He stood, tossed down the magazine, and reached for his bomber jacket and flight bag. "Where am I flying?"


*10:21 p.m.*


Rye had opted not to take the Beechcraft for the reasons cited by the other pilot, whose name he didn't know and couldn't care less about. Dash had put the Cessna 182 through its preflight check while Rye accessed a computer in one of the waiting areas. He'd gone onto a website that provided aerial photos of airports.

He'd studied the bird's-eye view picture of the Howardville County Airfield, made note of the lay of the land and how the FBO fit into the landscape, then printed out the photo to take with him.

He called flight service and filed his flight plan using instrument flight rules. He would be relying on instruments from takeoff to landing. Nothing unusual about that, but the fog was.

Wanting to get the skinny, and not from someone in a TV studio with capped teeth and cemented hair, he'd logged on to several flight-related blogs to see what the chatter was. As expected, nearly all the messages posted today had been about the fog and the hell it was creating. The pilots who'd flown in it were warning others about vast areas of zero visibility.

Typing in his user name on one of the sites, Rye had posted a question about Howardville. He'd received a flurry of replies, the first of which was, "If ur thinking of flying into there tonight, what color flowers do you want on your casket?"

Another: "Beware the power lines. *If* u make it as far as the landing strip alive, brace yourself. That bitch is a washboard."

Similar posts had followed, words of caution spiced with graveyard humor and the irreverent quipping that was universal among aviators who didn't wear uniforms. The upshot of the online conversation was that one would be wise not to fly into Rye's destination tonight.

But Rye often received such warnings, and he flew anyway.

Even Dash had seemed uncharacteristically concerned. The only thing Rye had ever seen the older man get sentimental over was a three-legged cat that had hobbled into the hangar one day. The animal was emaciated and flea-ridden. It hissed and scratched at anybody who went near it. But Dash had taken a shine to it and had fed it until it was strong enough to hobble off. Which it did one night, never to be seen again. When Rye asked after it, Dash had told him with noticeable gruffness in his voice, "Ungrateful bastard run off."

Rye had gotten a glimpse of Dash's well-hidden softer side then, and again now as Dash escorted him out onto the tarmac where the Cessna workhorse sat ready.

Dash grunted as he bent down to remove the chocks from the wheels and, after grumbling about his damned trick knee, said, "The box is buckled into the copilot seat."

Rye nodded and was about to step up into the cockpit, but Dash cleared his throat, signaling that he had more to say. He removed the cigar from his mouth and regarded the unlit tip of it. "You know, Rye, I wouldn't be asking you to fly tonight except that it's the start of the holiday season and—"

"You already said that."

"Well. And, anyhow, you're the best pilot for this type of flying."

"In lieu of flattery, how about a bonus?"

"Besides," Dash continued without addressing the mention of a bonus, "I doubt it's as bad as they're letting on."

"I doubt that, too. It's probably worse."

Dash nodded as though he also feared that might be the case. "After you make the delivery, don't worry about flying right back."

"You're all heart, Dash."

"But if you could return her by noon tomorrow—"

"Sure."

"I know that's a quick turnaround, but you don't require a lot of sleep."

Rye had conditioned himself to function well on as little sleep as possible, not only because that particular skill made him more *flexible* when it came to FAA regulations—and cargo carriers appreciated flexibility in their freelance pilots—but also because the less he slept, the less he dreamed.

Dash was saying something about the pilot's hoarded boxed lunch. "I could weasel a sandwich out of his stingy self if you want to take one with you."

"Can't stand tuna."

"No, me neither. There may be a couple of stale doughnuts left over from this morning."

Rye shook his head.

Dash worried the cigar between his teeth. "Look, Rye, you sure you're—"

"What's with the hand-holding, Dash? Are you working up to kissing me goodbye?"

Dash's comeback was swift and obscene. He turned and lumbered back into the building. Rye climbed into the cockpit, called flight service and got his clearance, then, after a short taxi, took off.

*1:39 a.m.*

When he was only a few miles from his destination, Atlanta Center cleared him for the VOR approach. Rye told the controller he would cancel his flight plan once he was safely on the ground.

"Good luck with that," the guy said, sounding very much like he meant it.

Rye signed off and tuned to the FBO's frequency. "This is November nine seven five three seven. Anybody home?"

There were crackles in Rye's ears, then, "I'm here. Brady White. You Mallett?"

"Who else have you got coming in?"

"Nobody else is crazy enough to try. I hope you make it just so I can shake your hand. Maybe even scare up a beer for you."

"I'll hold you to it. I'm on VOR/DME approach, ten miles out at four thousand feet, and about to do my first step-down. Go ahead and pop the lights."

"Lights are on."

"Descending to thirty-two hundred feet. Still can't see crap. What's your ceiling?"

"It's whiteout almost all the way to the ground," Brady White told him.

"Got any more good news?"

The man laughed. "Don't cheat on the last step-down, because there are power lines about a quarter mile from the runway threshold."

"Yeah, they're on the chart. How bad are the crosswinds?"

Brady gave him the degree and wind velocity. "Light for us, but it's a mixed blessing. A little stronger, it'd blow away this fog."

"Can't have everything." Rye kept close watch on his altimeter. Remembering the name on the shipment paperwork, he asked, "Dr. Lambert there?"

"Not yet, but due. What are you hauling?"

Rye glanced over at the black box. "Didn't ask, don't know."

"All the hurry-up, I figure it must be a heart or something."

"Didn't ask, don't know. Don't care."

"Then how come you're doing this?"

"Because this is what I do."

After a beat, Brady said, "I hear your engine. You see the runway yet?"

"Looking."

"You nervous?"

"About what?"

Brady chuckled. "Make that two beers."

On his windshield, beads of moisture turned into wiggly streams. Beyond them, he could see nothing except fog. If conditions were as Brady described, Rye probably wouldn't see the landing strip lights until he was right on top of them and ready to set down. Which made him glad he'd elected to fly the smaller plane and didn't have to worry about overshooting the end of the runway and trying to stop that Beechcraft before plowing up ground at the far end. Also, he had near-empty fuel tanks, so he was landing light.

No, he wasn't nervous. He trusted the instruments and was

confident he could make a safe landing. As bad as conditions were, he'd flown in worse.

All the same, he was ready to get there and hoped that Dr. Lambert would show up soon. He looked forward to having the doctor sign off on the delivery so he could raid the vending machine—assuming Brady's outfit had one—then crawl into the back of the plane to sleep.

Dash had removed the two extra seats to allow more cargo space. To save him the expense of a motel room for overnighters, he'd provided a sleeping bag. It stank of sweat and men. No telling how many pilots had farted in it, but tonight Rye wouldn't mind it.

The nap he'd taken at Dash-It-All was wearing off. Sleeping wasn't his favorite pastime, but he needed a few hours before heading back tomorrow morning.

He reminded himself to make sure Brady didn't lock him out of the building when he left for home. Otherwise Rye wouldn't have access to the toilet. Assuming there was a toilet. He'd flown into places where—

He saw the runway lights flicker through the fog. "Okay, Brady. I've got a visual on your lights. Is that beer good and cold?"

No reply.

"Brady, did you nod off?"

In the next instant, a laser beam was shone into the windshield and speared Rye right between the eyes.

"Bloody hell!"

Instinctually he raised his left hand to shield his eyes. Several seconds later, the piercing light went out. But the damage had been done. He'd been blinded at the most critical point of his landing.

He processed all this within a single heartbeat.

The ground would be coming up fast. Crashing was almost a given, and so was dying.

His last thought: *About fucking time.*

# Chapter 2

———◦◉◦———

*1:46 a.m.*

Pilot training, reflex, and survival instinct kicked in. Despite his blasé acceptance of almost certain death, Rye automatically and unemotionally began to think through options and react in a way that would better his chances to live and tell about this.

And he had milliseconds in which to do it.

Instinctively he eased back on the yoke to tilt the craft's nose up and pulled back the throttle to reduce his airspeed, but not so much that he would stall.

If he could achieve a touch-and-go on the airstrip and stay airborne long enough for his vision to clear, he could possibly do a go-around and make another approach.

He would like to manage it just so he could kill Brady White.

But below him wasn't wide-open spaces. If he overshot the runway without enough altitude, he would clip treetops. If he gained enough altitude to clear the trees, he would still have to get above the foothills, and he no longer trusted his ability to gauge their distance. With the fog, and purple and yellow spots exploding in his eyeballs, he was flying by feel.

Likely case: He didn't stand a snowball's chance in hell. He

13

couldn't see his instruments for the frenzied dancing dots in front of his eyes. Without the instruments, his spatial orientation was shot. He could be flying the plane straight into the bosom of Mother Earth.

And then ahead and slightly to his left, he spotted a lighter patch of fog that intensified into a brighter glow that soon separated into two beams of light spaced closely together. Looked like headlights. A parking lot? No, the road. The road he'd noted in the aerial picture of the airfield. In any case, the lights gave him some indication of how close he was to the ground.

No time to ponder it. He went into an ever so slight left bank and aimed the craft toward the lights.

*Nose up enough to clear the headlights.*

*Easy easy easy, don't stall.*

The plane sailed over the lights, stayed airborne for maybe another forty or fifty yards, and then hit the ground hard. The plane bounced back into the air a few feet. When it came down again, it did so on the left and front wheels only. Then the right gear collapsed. The plane slewed to the right, the right wing dipped, and, catching the ground, whipped the craft into an even sharper right turn, which Rye was powerless to correct.

His instantaneous reaction was to stand on the brakes, but if the wheels had been torn off or even badly damaged, the hydraulic line would've been cut, so brakes were useless.

The plane skidded off the road and into the woods. A tree branch caught the windshield. The Plexiglas remained intact, but the cracks created a web that obscured his vision all the more.

Then impact.

The Cessna hit an obstacle with such momentum behind it that the nose crumpled, and the tail left the ground before dropping back down with a jolt that made Rye bite his tongue when his teeth clamped.

He was rattled, but cognizant enough to realize that, impossibly, he was on terra firma. The plane wasn't engulfed in flames. He was alive. Even as that registered, he fumbled for and found the master switch to kill the electrical power and reached down to the floor between the seats to shut off the fuel selector valve.

Then he allowed himself time to catch his breath, slow his heart rate, and run through a mental checklist for likely injuries. The purple and yellow dots were dissipating. He could see well enough. He wasn't hurting anywhere, only feeling pressure against his torso from the yoke, which the cockpit panel had jammed against his chest.

The plane was so old it didn't have a shoulder restraint, only a lap belt. He labored to get it unbuckled, but was finally free of it. The door on his left appeared undamaged. He unlatched it and shoved it open. Cold, damp air rushed in. He sucked in a lungful and expelled it through his mouth.

It took several tries and teeth-gnashing effort, but he squeezed himself from beneath the yoke, out of the seat, and through the opening. His flight bag was on the floor in front of the copilot seat, crammed underneath the panel. It was a strain to reach it, but he snagged the leather strap and wrangled the bag free. He pulled it out of the cockpit and tossed it to the ground.

That left only the black box.

In a crash situation, the pilot was allowed by the FAA to take only his flight bag from the plane. Everything else was to be left as it was until an accident report was filed with the FAA and it was determined whether or not an on-site investigation was necessary.

But, remembering the urgency behind this cargo, he released the seat belt, picked up the box, and cradled it in his right elbow. As he backed out, he shut the door of the plane, then hopped to the ground like he'd done roughly ten thousand times over the course of his career.

Only this time his knees gave way. He went to the dirt and

was very glad that nobody was there to see his impersonation of a rag doll. Apparently he was more shaken than he'd realized.

He sat up, bowed his head low between his raised knees, and concentrated on taking deep, even breaths. He stayed like that long enough for the dampness of the ground to seep into the seat of his jeans.

Eventually he raised his head and opened his eyes. He was wrapped in fog and total darkness, but his vision was clear. No more dancing spots. He could distinguish the two fingers he held up.

He didn't realize until then that he'd been thrust forward on impact and had banged his head. Tentatively exploring, he discovered a goose egg at his hairline, but it couldn't be too bad. His vision wasn't blurred, he didn't need to puke, and he hadn't blacked out, so he ruled out a concussion. He was just coming down from an adrenaline surge, that's all.

He rested the back of his head against the fuselage and swiped his forehead with the back of his hand. It came away wet with sweat, while inside his bomber jacket he was shivering.

He wasn't too bothered by it, though. His shakes weren't anything a good belt of bourbon wouldn't cure.

Having reached that conclusion, he dragged his flight bag toward him and unzipped it. Fishing inside it, he found his flashlight and switched it on. With the black box still in the crook of his arm, and the strap of his bag on his opposite shoulder, he braced himself against the fuselage and stood up to test his equilibrium.

He wasn't in top form, but he was okay. He ducked beneath the wing and moved toward the plane's nose. The freakin' tree he'd crashed into had to be the biggest one in Georgia. It was massive. With only the flashlight for illumination, he surveyed the damage to the aircraft.

He could see well enough to know that Dash was going to be pissed.

He sat down again, this time with his back propped against

the trunk of the tree, and pulled his cell phone from the pocket of his jacket. When he saw that the screen was busted, and the phone wouldn't come on, he searched his flight bag for his spare. He didn't recall the last time he'd used it, or charged it, and, sure enough, it was as dead as a hammer. Atlanta Center needed to be told that he was on the ground, but he couldn't notify them until he got to a working telephone.

Muttering a litany of obscenities, he looked around himself but couldn't see a damn thing except fog and more fog. The flashlight's beam was strong, but instead of penetrating the fog, it reflected off it and made it appear even more opaque. He switched off the flashlight to conserve the battery. Left in the dark, he considered his situation.

If he were smart, he would sit here, maybe nap, and wait for the fog to lift.

But he was madder than he was smart. He wanted to go after Brady White and beat the living shit out of him. He'd been so busy trying to avert a catastrophe, he hadn't had time until now to contemplate why the guy would sweet-talk him to the end of the landing strip and then hit him with a goddamn laser. It had to have been a fancy one in order to penetrate the fog and impact his vision as it had.

Brady White had seemed a likable character, and a bit in awe of Rye. Not like somebody who had it in for him. And what grudge could he be carrying when they'd never even met?

But who else besides Brady White had even known Rye was flying in? Dr. Lambert. But he hadn't arrived yet, and even if he had, why would he book this charter to get the payload here tonight and then sabotage the plane? Made no sense.

Made no sense why Brady White had sabotaged him, either, but Rye was going to find out, and then teach him a hard lesson in aviation safety, which, for the rest of his natural life, he would remember. Rye wanted to inflict pain and regret in equal portions.

In anticipation of that, he looked around, trying to orient

himself. Once he reached the road, he'd be able to find his way to the FBO office. He only hoped that while thrashing through the woods in search of the road, he wouldn't stumble over a fallen tree and fracture a leg bone, or step off into a ravine and break his neck. Best to get on with it, though.

He shouldered his bag and was about to stand when out of the corner of his eye, he caught a diffused light making a sweeping motion through the woods.

So he didn't have to go in search of Brady Boy, after all. Brady had come looking for him. Like an arsonist watching the building burn, this sick bastard wanted to gloat over the destruction he'd wrought.

Well, Brady White had no idea what he'd let himself in for.

Moving quickly but creating as little sound as possible, Rye duck-walked around the trunk of the tree and out of sight. Without taking his eyes off the fuzzy orb of light bouncing in the fog, he reached into his flight bag and unzipped the inside pocket where he kept his Glock pocket pistol. He covered the slide with his palm to help mute the sound as he chambered a bullet.

He watched from his hunkered position behind the tree as a dark form materialized in the fog. White's flashlight wasn't substantial. In fact its beam was rather yellow and sickly, but on one of its sweeps around the clearing, it moved past the aircraft's tail, then swiftly reversed and spotlighted the tail number. He froze in place, one foot still raised.

Rye didn't move, barely breathed. He could hear the hand on his wristwatch ticking off the seconds. After ten, the guy lowered his foot and continued walking toward the plane but in a much more hesitant tread. He moved the light along the fuselage until it shone on the smashed propeller and nose.

Cautious still, he continued forward. The fog made him indistinct, but Rye could tell that he was dressed head-to-toe in dark clothing, the hood of his coat covering his head.

Rye's first impulse was to rush him, but he savored the guy's obvious hesitancy. Who would deliberately disable a pilot in flight from a safe distance on the ground? Only a damn coward. It made Rye's blood boil. His hand tightened around the grip of the small Glock, but he decided not to do anything until he saw what this stealthy son of a bitch did next.

When the guy reached the wing, he bent down to clear his head as he walked under it, then aimed the flashlight up at the window on the pilot's door. The angle was wrong and the beam too weak for him to see into the cockpit. He seemed to debate it for several moments, then climbed up until he could reach the door latch and open it.

It was obvious to Rye that he had expected a body to be strapped into the pilot's seat because he reacted with a start and shone the flashlight around the cockpit. Rye could see the beam crazily darting behind the cracked windshield.

The guy pulled back, gave a furtive look around, then hastily scrambled down and started walking back in the direction from which he'd come, no longer hesitant. In fact, he was moving in a big damn hurry.

"I don't think so." Rye lurched to his feet and charged.

The tackle almost knocked the breath out of Rye, so he knew his saboteur had borne the brunt of it, and that gave him a tremendous amount of satisfaction.

The flashlight was dropped and landed on the ground a few feet away from where they tussled. White reached for it, but Rye wrapped his arms tight around the torso beneath his, pinning the guy's arms to his sides and rendering his legs useless by straddling them and practically sitting on his butt.

"What's the matter, jerk-off? Did you expect to find my bloody corpse in the pilot's seat? Well, *surprise*."

He flipped him over, grabbed a flailing wrist in each of his hands, even as his right maintained a grip on the nine-millimeter. He forced the guy's arms out to his sides and flattened the backs of them against the rocky ground.

As angry as he'd ever been in his life, he growled, "I want to know just what the fuck—"

He broke off when he realized that the eyes glowering up at him were set in a soft, smooth face framed by a tumble of dark, wavy hair. He said, "Who the hell are you?"

"Your client."

Rye recoiled in shock and looked down at the chest inches from his face, which was rising and falling with agitation...and was also indisputably female. "Dr. Lambert? I expected a man."

"Well, *surprise*."

Then she kneed him in the balls.

# Chapter 3

━━◆◆◆━━

*2:01 a.m.*

Damn!" She'd missed. He had sucked in a sharp breath in anticipation and shifted his hips just enough to prevent a direct hit. Teeth clenched, she said, "Get off me."

He didn't. Instead, he secured her legs by pressing them more tightly between his. "You're supposed to be at the FBO. What are you doing out here?"

"Do you have the box? Why do you have a gun?"

"I asked first."

Their eyes engaged in a contest of wills, but he was angry, large, strong, and on top of her, all of which gave him the advantage. "Because of the fog, I missed the turnoff. The road came to a dead end at a cyclone fence. I was about to turn around when your plane swooped in from out of nowhere."

"Oh. You belong to the headlights. I flew toward them."

"*Toward* them?"

"So I could land on the road."

"But you didn't. You crashed."

"Wasn't my fault."

"No?" The instant the word was out, she realized how snotty her tone had sounded, and it made him mad.

"No, doctor. The fact is, I kept the craft from falling out of the fucking sky, which it would have done if I weren't such a fucking good pilot. It took a hell of an effort to avoid taking your head off. You should be thanking me."

"Gratitude isn't exactly what I'm feeling for you right now. Was the box damaged? What caused you to crash?"

"Someone—" He stopped, rethought what he had intended to say, then said a terse "Power outage."

"On your plane?"

"The instruments blinked. These kinds of conditions, being able to see your instruments can mean the difference between living and dying. I managed to pull it off." He continued to stare down at her with mistrust. She forced herself to hold his stare without shrinking, although he looked unscrupulous, and kept her mindful of the gun in his right hand.

"How long are you going to keep me pinned down?" she said. "You're hurting my hands, and there's a rock planted in my left kidney."

He didn't react immediately, but then he must have decided that the standoff was pointless. He released her wrists, moved off her, and stood. He picked up the flashlight she'd dropped and shone it directly into her face, staying on it until she asked him with curt politeness to get it out of her eyes. He kept the flashlight on, but angled it away from her. It provided ambient light.

She sat up, rubbing the gouge on her back. "What's your name?"

"Rye Mallett."

"Mr. Mallett," she said in a murmur as she started to stand. He cupped her elbow to give her a boost. As soon as she was on her feet, she pulled her arm free and began brushing the dirt and twigs off the backs of her hands. They were nicked and scratched. One had a smear of blood on it. She shot him an accusing look.

"Sorry," he said. "I thought you were a guy."

"It would have been nice if you'd made that distinction before coming after me. Armed. Was the gun really necessary?"

"Wasn't, but might've been."

"Do all pilots carry guns these days?"

"What other pilots do isn't any of my business."

She looked over at the plane. The damage appeared to be considerable. He'd been fortunate to walk away from the crash, much less have enough strength to overpower her and keep her pinned down. "You don't seem to have been injured, Mr. Mallett. Are you all right?"

"I'm fine."

"Are you sure?"

"I'm *fine*."

"I'm glad to hear it." With that settled, she asked, "What about the box?"

"Do you know Brady White?"

"The man who manages the airfield? I talked to him on the phone tonight. He agreed to be here when you landed, although I don't think he believed that anyone would actually fly in tonight. He said—" She broke off when a thought occurred to her. "He did show up, didn't he? He turned the lights on?"

"Yeah. He turned the lights on."

"Good. He did what he was supposed to, then."

"According to your directions." His jaw was tense with what appeared to be cold fury. His eyes narrowed on her again. "What's in that black box?"

That was a question she had no intention of answering, especially since it had been posed with such suspicion. She said, "I didn't see it in the cockpit."

"That's not what I asked."

"Your only concern should be its delivery. To your client.

Who happens to be me. Is it secured in the back of the plane? Please tell me whether or not it was damaged."

"Wasn't damaged."

"I'd like to see that for myself."

"Don't trust me?"

"You have the gall to ask that when you were the one waving a gun around?"

"Didn't wave it around. But the point here is that the mistrust works both ways. What's so bloody important that the contents of that box had to get here tonight, never mind the weather?"

She held her silence.

"Hmm? Not even a hint? Come on. What could be so closely safeguarded and time-sensitive? The secret ingredient in Grandma's candied yams?"

"This is no joking matter, Mr. Mallett."

"You're goddamn right, it's not," he said, raising his voice and taking a fractional step closer. "How come you were sneaking up on the plane?"

"I wasn't *sneaking*."

"Looked like sneaking. The hood, the—"

"I pulled my hood up because of the mist."

He held out his hand palm up, inches from her face, waited a few seconds, then said, "Dry as dust. No mist."

"It was misting when I left my car."

He waited a beat, then asked, "You're a doctor?" She nodded. "Medical?" She nodded again. "Didn't you take an oath to do everything possible to ward off death?"

"Yes."

"Did you mean it?"

She refused to honor the insult with a reply.

"Reason I asked," he continued, "when you saw the wrecked plane, how come you didn't break into a run to see to my welfare? For all you knew, I was one heartbeat away from checking out."

"I was exercising caution."

"You were creeping."

"Because I wasn't sure it was safe!" she exclaimed. "Crashed planes sometimes explode, catch fire."

"Yeah, I know."

His tone had the quality of a death knell, a warning that the topic would be better left alone. But she held her ground and said with stern emphasis, "Give me the box."

"Trade you for it."

She huffed a laugh. "I'm sorry? Trade?"

"I need a lift to the airport office."

She was about to refuse when she realized that he was, indeed, stranded. "Of course."

"Thanks."

She'd been so focused on getting what she'd come for, she hadn't thought of the other repercussions of the crash. "Poor Mr. White," she said. "You were just about to land. He must be frantic to know what happened to you."

"Oh, poor Mr. White will know what happened to me. He'll know I'm down, one way or the other."

"You should have notified him that you're all right."

"Couldn't. My phone's busted, and my spare isn't charged up. So either he's out searching for me himself, or he's reporting to the authorities that the plane and I are unaccounted for. In which case, we'll soon have hillbillies with badges poking around and asking questions, and somehow..." He dipped his knees to bring them eye to eye. "I get the drift that you had just as soon avoid that as much as I would. *Doctor.*"

The emphasis on her title didn't escape her. Neither did his pause, which invited her to confirm, qualify, or dispute his "drift." When she didn't speak at all, one corner of his lips tilted up marginally, smugly. "What I thought."

He straightened his knees and returned to his full height. "Whatever you're up to, it's no skin off my nose. But I'm anxious to meet Brady White up close and personal, and to demonstrate just how alive and well I am."

"When you blew over my car, I tried to call him but didn't have service." She took her cell phone from a coat pocket, then turned it toward him so he could see for himself that she didn't have a signal. "Cell service is unreliable up here, especially in bad weather."

"You know this area?"

"I'm one of the hillbillies." She gave him a pointed look. "I grew up here. That's how I knew about the county airport." Looking beyond him at the plane, she asked, "Are you just going to leave it here?"

"It's not going to fly off."

"Is it yours? Do you own it?"

He shook his head. "I'm only a flyer for hire."

"I see."

"No, you don't, but it doesn't matter." He continued without a segue. "If the fog clears, I'll get somebody to bring me out here tomorrow. I have to take pictures to include in my report."

"To?"

"The nearest FAA office. Depending on whether or not the agent I draw is a real hard-ass, this probably won't be investigated. No deaths, no injuries. Very little to report, right?"

Again she got the feeling that he was fishing and was curious to hear how she would answer. She fiddled with her phone to avoid looking directly at him. "I don't know anything about FAA regulations."

"I know everything."

She dropped the phone back into her pocket, then gave him a slow once-over, starting at his uncombed hair and working all the way down to his scuffed boots. His jaw was bristly. He wasn't wearing a uniform, only jeans and a battered bomber jacket. The shirt underneath it looked slept in.

There was a nickname for his sort of cargo pilot, but she couldn't recall it offhand.

Meeting his cool gaze again, she said, "I rather imagine you also know how to get around FAA regulations, Mr. Mallett."

"Lucky for you. Nobody else would've risked flying here tonight."

"Why did you?"

He just looked at her, his face a mask. Then, "About that lift?"

"Yes. If we can find our way back to my car."

"I charted the layout of the airfield. The road you were on dead-ends at the southeast corner of the property."

He turned away from her and walked back toward the airplane. He disappeared around the tree into which it had nosed and reappeared with a leather duffel bag slung over his shoulder and a padlocked black box. He gave her back her flashlight, then handed her the box. "Delivered."

She hugged the box against her chest. "Thank you. Truly."

"We'll complete the paperwork when we get to the airfield office. And I accept gratuities. Truly."

He returned the gun to its zippered compartment in his bag, then took a flashlight from it and switched it on. He motioned with his chin. "Back the way you came." He went past her, assuming the role of leader. Over his shoulder, he said, "Stick close. If you fall behind and get lost in the fog, you're on your own. I won't come looking."

She believed him.


*2:16 a.m.*


The two men who were hunkered down in the underbrush a few yards away from the wreckage waited until the pilot and doctor were swallowed up by the fog. The cold haze had helped conceal them, but it was also making a complicated situation just that much more difficult.

When it should have been so easy.

That's what the boss was going to say when Goliad called in to report this royal fuckup.

"What now?" his partner whispered.

"Plan B."

"What's plan B?"

"For me to know. Come on." As Goliad stood up, he looked down with loathing at the man beside him, whom he would gladly throttle here and now. The boss had told him to bring someone with him, someone disposable, to be the fall guy if something should go wrong. Timmy had been suggested.

Bad idea. Timmy had screwed up, and, for him, there would be hell to pay. But not until the time was right. Presently, Goliad was letting him live because he might yet prove to be useful.

Goliad had been born in the Texas town of the same name. It was the name on his baptismal certificate. The name stuck, but the baptism didn't take. His sainted mother had died clutching her rosary and sobbing over the path he'd chosen for his life. It wasn't the straight-and-narrow one she'd fervently and futilely prayed for.

Timmy had been inducted into his first gang at the ripe age of eleven after he'd slit the throat of his abusive father and took to the rough streets of Philadelphia, where he was absorbed into the thriving criminal element. Now in his early twenties, he maintained a feral, street-gang mentality.

They made an odd pair. Goliad carried a handgun but was rarely called upon to use it. His height and breadth of chest made him so physically imposing that few men would think of challenging him.

The top of Timmy's head didn't even reach Goliad's shoulder. He was small, wiry, and mean. He liked to provoke and was easily provoked. He preferred blades to bullets and never carried fewer than three knives, well concealed.

As they headed back to where they'd left their car, Timmy asked, "Are you going to tell the boss about the laser?"

"Haven't decided yet," Goliad replied, intentionally leaving Timmy to worry. But he didn't want to get a knife in the back, so he motioned for Timmy to take the lead.

"I can't find my way back to the car in this shit."

"Then I guess you'll stay lost out here in the woods and may never be found."

Timmy must've sensed the underlying threat. Mumbling about how much he hated nature and missed city life, he plowed ahead, but it was Goliad who set the pace, keeping close behind Timmy, giving him a prod whenever he tripped over something unseen or slowed down to avoid collision with a sapling or boulder that took shape out of the fog, often only inches in front of them.

"I just want to know one thing," Goliad said. "What the hell were you thinking?"

"I've got a curious mind," Timmy said in a whine. "I saw it on TV. A story telling how dangerous lasers were to pilots. Lots of them are getting zapped."

"So you thought you'd try it out on this pilot, see if it worked to make him crash."

"I just meant to mess with him some."

Goliad shook his head over the stupidity. "Where'd you get the damn thing?"

"Saw UPS delivering a package to a house. Stole it off the front porch soon as the truck drove off. Didn't even know what was in the carton until I opened it. Bonanza!"

"When was this?"

"Coupla weeks ago."

"You know, they catch thieves like that on home security cameras."

Timmy guffawed. "I know how to dodge those."

"You had better hope. Have you shown it off to anybody?"

"No. Never turned it on before tonight."

"You couldn't have picked a worse time to experiment."

"I wanted to see if it would work in the fog. Jesus, what's the big deal?"

"The big deal is that the people who hired you are waiting for what was in that airplane."

"I didn't know it would crash," he muttered.

"Well, it did. Just be glad that box wasn't destroyed."

"See? No problem. It'll look like this sorry pilot screwed up, missed the runway in the fog."

Goliad feared that it wouldn't be dismissed as lightly as that. He feared a ripple effect that could result in serious consequences for the people he was paid to protect.

After having to backtrack only once, they relocated the car. Goliad was the designated driver. Timmy got in the shotgun seat.

As Goliad reached for his phone, he made a split-second decision to be as short on details as possible. Once he and Timmy returned to Atlanta with that black box, any mishaps they had encountered during the undertaking would be irrelevant.

He turned on the speaker so Timmy could listen in and placed the call. After only half a ring, it was answered, not by the boss, but by his missus, who was much more excitable.

In a voice hard enough to chisel granite, she asked, "Do you have it?"

"Not yet, ma'am."

"The plane's not there yet?"

"Showed up about half an hour ago."

"Then what's the problem?"

"It crashed."

She gasped.

Goliad said, "The pilot was about to land, overshot the runway, crashed in the woods."

He gave Timmy a look that said he could thank him later for saving his ass. Timmy gave him a thumbs-up.

"The plane burned, it was destroyed, what?" she asked. *"What?"*

"No, it wasn't destroyed. The box made it okay."

There was a pause, an exhale, a huskily spoken, "Thank heaven."

"But the doctor beat us to the crash site." He described the scene that he and Timmy had crept up on. "She and the pilot were talking."

"He survived?"

"Uninjured, best we could tell."

"What was *she* doing at the crash site? She was supposed to meet the plane at the airfield."

"I don't understand that, either," he admitted. "All I know is, she was there. The pilot gave her the box. It's as described. About the size of a loaf of bread. Padlocked. They struck off together on foot. They were headed to her car. She was giving him a lift to the airfield office."

"So why didn't you go after them? Richard will demand to know. How will I explain this to him?"

"They had no idea we were there, ma'am. Tracking them on foot, we could've given ourselves away. It wouldn't have been a smart move."

Knowing how thin she was on patience, he used as few words as possible to adequately describe how bad conditions were. "You think it's bad in Atlanta, it's worse up here. If we came up on them accidentally in this fog and there was an... encounter...this could get botched real easy."

"It could've got messy," Timmy said, speaking for the first time. "Because he was packing."

"What's he talking about, Goliad?"

"The pilot was armed. You, we, nobody took him into account. He wasn't even supposed to be in the picture."

"Why would we have taken him into account? We didn't know he would crash!"

"True. There was no predicting that." Goliad shot an angry glance toward Timmy, who squirmed in his seat.

"You say he was armed?" she asked.

"Pocket pistol. Nine-millimeter. He's not a regular pilot. Looked worse for wear, and not because of the crash."

She didn't say anything for a while, thinking it over, Goliad guessed.

He said, "The plane going down was a setback, but the box survived it, and the doctor has it. Only a little time has been lost. We'll catch up with her at the airport."

Timmy opened his mouth, but Goliad gave a forbidding shake of his head, silencing him before he spoke.

She was saying, "Need I remind you that every minute counts?"

"We know, ma'am."

"The next time you call, I want to hear that you have the doctor in tow, with the box, and that you're on your way back to Atlanta. Is that understood?"

"Loud and clear."

"Good. I'm hanging up now. I suggest that you start immediately making up for lost time. I must go explain to my husband that you've been delayed. He won't be happy. I'm certainly not. I advise you both not to fail us." With that, she ended the call.

Timmy whistled. "She burns hot, don't she? Bet she fucks like—"

Goliad's arm sliced across the console of the car and clotheslined Timmy's neck. "Remember who you're talking about." He pressed his arm against Timmy's windpipe hard enough to make him wheeze. "Playing with your new laser," he sneered. "This isn't a game, you idiot."

Slowly he released the pressure on Timmy's throat and resettled himself behind the steering wheel. Out of the corner of his eye, he stayed aware of where Timmy put his hands. His right was rubbing his throat. Goliad half expected him to produce one of his blades with his left.

But he was gulping air and swallowing noisily. When he had his wind back, he croaked, "I was only joking."

"Wasn't funny. You work for them. Show respect for both, or this is your last detail."

"Okay, okay," Timmy mumbled. "So what now?"

Goliad started the car. "We go to the airstrip, be waiting for them when they get there."

"That's plan B?"

"That's plan B."

"You think the lady doctor will go along with us shouldering in on her?"

"She will once we tell her that we've been dispatched by Mrs. Hunt, personally. We'll tell her that Mrs. Hunt was concerned for her, driving up here alone in the fog. Mrs. Hunt sent us to make sure she has a safe trip back."

"She'll buy that?"

"She'll probably call and confirm."

"What if she still doesn't like it?"

"Let's wait and see what happens."

"What about the pilot?"

"Wait and see." He looked over at the younger man. "We're up shit creek. What are you grinning for?"

Timmy giggled. "'Wait and see' means I might get to kill somebody after all."

# Chapter 4

———❖———

*2:32 a.m.*

A freight dog. That's what they call you."

"That's one of the nice things," Rye said.

After abandoning the plane, they had trekked through dense forest, made more challenging by the fog. However, they reached the doctor's no-frills sedan without mishap or getting lost...only to be met there with another problem.

Rye had been about to get into the passenger seat when he noticed that the right front fender had collided with a fence post set in concrete. That side of the hood was buckled, but worse, the wheel was bent up under the chassis. He swore.

"What's the matter?"

He looked at her across the roof of the car. "Don't bother getting in. We're not going anywhere in this."

She'd walked around the rear end to join him on the passenger side and surveyed the damage with dismay. "I didn't realize I'd hit it."

"How could you not realize it?"

As exasperated as he, she fired back. "Something awful must've distracted me. Like a propeller in my windshield."

Cursing under his breath, he'd gone around her and set out on foot. She hurried to catch up before he disappeared into the fog.

Within a few minutes, they'd reached the turnoff she had missed earlier. A sign pointed them toward the Howardville County Airfield. The road leading to it was bumpy, narrow, and enshrouded in fog. They stayed in the middle of it to avoid veering off into the ditches on either side.

He set a brisk pace. His companion had become a bit winded, her breaths escaping as puffs of vapor. But she hadn't once complained or lagged behind. He supposed her mention of a freight dog was an attempt to make conversation, but he didn't follow up on it. His thoughts were too focused on how he was going to deal with Brady White.

Why would the asshole offer to scare up a beer or two for him, then blind him with a laser beam?

Like drones, the more sophisticated, powerful, obtainable, and affordable lasers had become, the more of a hazard they posed to pilots and by extension the aviation industry. He'd read harrowing accounts from both private and commercial pilots who, hit by one, had narrowly avoided an accident. Many feared that it was only a matter of time before someone with a laser, either a terrorist or a prankster, caused a catastrophic crash.

Rye was well aware of the threat. He'd just never expected it to happen to him. It had. He'd come to within feet of killing the doctor, and, with just a bit more momentum when he hit that tree, his crash could have been fatal.

But, unless he caught that son of a bitch red-handed with the laser, he couldn't prove it existed. If he called the cops and filed a formal complaint, it would be Rye's word against White's. Stalemate. A waste of time. A hassle that would keep him grounded for at least a few days.

Besides, he would rather skip getting local law enforcement involved and mete out White's punishment himself.

He would have to include the laser in his accident report to the FAA. It was the responsible thing to do. He would do so with reluctance, however. Agents would be all over him, asking questions, forcing him to fill out countless, time-consuming forms.

On the upside: No damage had been done to property on the ground. Even the tree was still standing. No one had been injured. No one had died. The lack of casualties would minimize the amount of red tape.

The downside: Without proof of the laser, his claim might be discounted as a lie to save face. In which case, he would have to suck it up and let the accident be attributed to pilot error.

That was the most galling aspect of this whole damn thing, and reason enough to pound the living daylights out of Brady White.

"The slang term escaped me earlier."

The comment pulled Rye out of his angry musing. "Sorry?"

"Freight dog. It just now came to me where I first heard it."

Because of the exertion, the doctor had pushed back the hood of her coat. Light from their combined flashlights limned her profile. He wondered how he could have mistaken her for a man, even from a distance and in darkness and fog. Maybe the laser had done more damage to his eyes than he'd thought. Because there was nothing manly about her. She was pure female.

Although he hadn't encouraged her to expand on the topic, she did. "Several years ago I went on a Caribbean getaway with a couple of girlfriends. One afternoon it started raining hard enough to drive us off the beach and into the bar."

"As good an excuse as any." His droll remark caused her to smile. Her lips sure as hell weren't masculine.

"These guys were gathered around a table," she went on. "Five or six of them, getting drunk and loud and rowdy, talking about airplanes and flying."

"Which island?"

She named the island, and Rye named the bar.

"You know it?"

"There's one near every airfield in the world."

"Where pilots go?"

"Gotta pass the time between flights somewhere."

"Well, they noticed us and..." She made a rolling motion with her right hand.

He nodded in perfect understanding of what she meant by the gesture. "They sprung for a round, and invited themselves to join you, and you said okay."

"We had to be polite."

He gave her a look, and she laughed softly.

"A couple of them were really cute. Anyway, one was wearing a t-shirt with a freight dog logo on it. My friend asked what that was about, and they explained the kind of air cargo piloting they did. As the afternoon progressed, stories of their escapades got raunchier and less credible, all about their maverick lifestyle and derring-do. I guess they wanted to impress us."

"They wanted to get laid."

She gave him a quick look, which caused her to stumble.

Out of reflex, Rye took her arm in a steadying hand, and, before he could stop himself, asked, "Did they?"

She reclaimed her arm, turned her eyes downward, and picked up her pace. "Not by me."

He snuffled. "No surprise there. You strike me as a lady who's hard to impress."

"I am, but what makes you think so?"

"Nothing in particular. I just figure you're too smart to be taken in by bullshit."

"Was it bullshit? Doesn't your breed of pilot fly rickety airplanes, in any kind of weather, no matter how bad, at all hours of the night, at a moment's notice, having had little or no sleep?"

"The planes aren't always rickety, and sometimes the weather's perfect. But that's a fairly accurate job description."

"Certainly a fair description in regard to tonight."

"Conditions tonight were bad. But I would've made it fine if it hadn't been for—"

"Hadn't been for what?"

He tucked his chin into the raised collar of his jacket. "This damn fog."

She looked at him with keen perception. "That wasn't what you were going to say." When he didn't contradict her, she said, "I haven't earned your trust yet?"

*Not by a long shot*, he thought. But he said, "Just wondering what's going on with you, that's all."

"Nothing's going on with me."

"Oh, you go traipsing around in the woods alone every night at about this time."

"No," she said, dragging the word out. "Only when I witness an airplane crash."

"Would you have come looking for the crash site if you hadn't been after the box?"

"Of course."

His derisive chuckle expressed his doubt. "What's in it?"

"Why do you keep asking?"

"Why don't you answer?"

"Do you interrogate all your clients this way, Mr. Mallett?"

"Just the dodgy ones."

"There's nothing dodgy about me."

"Only everything."

Initially, when she'd arrived on the scene so soon following the crash, he'd thought she might have had something to do with bringing down the plane. He no longer thought so. She wanted that damn box too bad. Since he'd handed it over to her, she'd kept a tight hold on it.

But something was out of joint. She could deny it till her shapely chest ran out of breath, but she had crept into that clearing and approached the airplane in a covert manner, and not because she was afraid it would ignite.

Of course he didn't really care what the box contained. Let it be her secret. So long as it didn't affect him, he didn't care if the Hope diamond had been heisted and she was the fence. His participation ended as soon as they signed off on the paperwork, and he got his pound of flesh from Brady White. Then it was *finis*, and he was out of there.

"Is Rye short for something?" she asked.

"No. Just Rye."

"I've never known anybody named that." After a pause, she said, "Not that you asked, but my name is Brynn."

"Brynn? Never knew anybody named that, either."

"Very dodgy name." Again she gave him that smile, and he admitted to himself that if he'd been killing a rainy afternoon in an island bar, he'd have covered her drinks in the hope of covering her. Without a stitch between them.

"You're staying here overnight, I guess."

He dragged his thoughts away from the tantalizing prospect of seeing her naked amid damp sheets. "I planned to bunk in the plane, fly back in the morning."

"Sleep in the plane?"

"Sometimes it's the only option, so I'm used to it. But now?" He raised a shoulder.

"What will you do tomorrow?"

"Depends on what the FAA agent decides. If he passes on an on-site investigation, Dash, that's the guy who sent me here, will—"

"Dash-It-All."

"Right. He may want me to stay here and babysit the plane until he can get an insurance adjuster on it. But I doubt he'll have me hang around for however long that'll take."

"Why?"

"He'll want me flying. More than likely, he'll send me to pick up another payload."

"Where?"

"Could be anywhere. Tulsa. Trinidad."

"You'll just . . . go?"

"I'll just go."

She thought on that for a time. "How long have you worked for him?"

"I don't. I freelance. But Dash uses me a lot."

"You must like each other."

He huffed. "Not a bit. We're just used to each other."

"Do you live in Columbus?"

He shook his head. "That was just the last place I lighted."

"So where is home?"

"The last place I lighted."

Obviously that wasn't the answer she'd expected, and it subdued her for another minute or more. Then, "It's Thanksgiving."

"So I'm told."

"You don't have any plans?"

He turned his head aside and looked through the fog beyond his right shoulder. Plans had been made for him. He hadn't accepted. "No."

"You'll spend the day alone?"

"More than likely."

"Maybe your friend Dash will get you back to Columbus so you can celebrate—"

"Look." He came to an abrupt stop and turned to her. She stopped and faced him. "Dash isn't my friend and won't give a damn how I spend my Thanksgiving, any more than I care how he'll spend his. I know you're just trying to make friendly conversation to fill an awkward silence between strangers, but I'm not big on friendly conversation, and I don't find silences awkward. In fact I like silences and prefer strangers.

"So stop asking me personal questions, okay? A few minutes from now, we'll go our separate ways and never see each other again. You got your whatever." He indicated the box she held under her arm against her rib cage. "I'll get paid for delivering it, I'll give you a receipt. With that, our business will be concluded. Over. So I don't need to know anything about you and your life, and you sure as hell don't need to know anything about mine."

He felt her seething anger as she turned away and resumed walking—more like marching—toward the airfield's office, which had materialized in the fog. The brick building was small, squat, square, and had little to recommend it. Its only two windows were in front and overlooked the landing strip, a windsock, and a pair of antiquated fuel pumps. Through the fog, Rye also made out the semicircular shape of a Quonset hut hangar nearby.

The runway lights blinked through the gloom. The light coming from the windows of the office was faint, as though its source was in a back room. A pickup truck was parked between the office and the hangar, indicating that the manager was still there.

Brynn approached the office with an angry energy that matched Rye's. Then she stopped and turned back to him. "When I set out from Atlanta tonight, I knew the round trip would be difficult, but, thanks to *you*, I've had more of an adventure than I bargained for, including the near loss of my life. Furthermore, you've delayed my return trip when time is of the essence.

"You never even apologized for almost crashing your plane into me, or for any of the other objectionable things you've said and done. I don't give a rat's ass about you or your life, Mr. Mallett. As soon as I sign off on your paperwork—forget a gratuity—you'll be rid of me, and I'll be *well* rid of you. I can't wait to start never seeing you again."

She pivoted on her heel and continued walking toward the building.

The putdown was deserved, of course. He couldn't say exactly why she'd gotten under his skin, but she had. It was an itch he had to terminate. So he'd reset barriers and reestablished boundaries, and he'd achieved that by behaving like a complete jerk.

It had worked to ward her off. She wasn't smiling anymore, wasn't drawing his attention to her pouty lower lip, wasn't inspiring fantasies of slippery sex during a tropical rainstorm.

All way too enticing. He couldn't get away from her fast enough.

By the time she reached the office door and pushed it open, he had caught up with her, then bumped into her when she came to a dead stop.

A man sat slumped over a desk, his head lying on it.

Shock rooted him and Brynn in place, but only for a second. Rye pushed her out of his way and rushed over to the desk. Brynn hesitated only long enough to set the black box on a chair and switch on the overhead fluorescent lights.

Rye bent over the man. If this was Brady White, he was two decades older than Rye had estimated, given the youthfulness in his voice. Blood from a wound behind his ear had formed a puddle on the desktop. Rye worked two fingers inside the collar of his plaid flannel shirt and pressed his carotid.

"He's got a pulse. Check him out." As he stepped aside to give Brynn better access, he swung his flight bag off his shoulder and unzipped it.

She lifted the injured man's eyelid to look at his pupil and turned his hand over where it lay on the desk so she could get his pulse. As she felt for it, she looked up at Rye. "How did he—"

"He didn't. It was done to him." He took the pistol from his bag. "Don't touch anything else. Keep a heads-up. Yell if you hear anything outside. I'm going to take a look around."

"Is the gun necessary?"

"We'll soon know."

Rye carefully walked around two sets of muddy shoe prints he'd noticed on the vinyl flooring and started down a short hallway. It took him under a minute to check the three back rooms.

One was little more than a closet stocked with cleaning and office supplies. There was a compact bathroom having only a commode and sink. A reception-type room was furnished with a sofa, a pair of matching chairs, and a coffee bar. Nothing was fancy or new, but everything was organized and tidy.

He looked for a back door. There wasn't one.

When he returned to the main office, Brynn had the receiver of the desk phone to her ear, holding it with fingertips covered by her sleeve.

"We assume it's Mr. White. He has a head wound. No, we believe that it was inflicted."

Rye patted down the man's pants pockets and located his wallet. In it was Brady White's driver's license. He held it up to Brynn, and she confirmed his identity to the 911 operator. "He's unconscious, but his pupils are reactive."

As Brynn gave the dispatcher a rapid description of the situation and Brady's condition as best she'd been able to determine it, Rye looked down at the bald spot on the crown of Brady's head, which somehow made him appear more vulnerable than the bleeding gash.

Rye had relished the thought of bashing this man himself. Now, he was ashamed for leaping to what was obviously a wrong conclusion about him. On the desk, beside the radio setup through which he'd been communicating with Rye, was a framed photo of Brady, a woman of similar age, two boys, and a younger girl with a missing front tooth. All were dressed in typical summer vacation clothing. Cameras and sun visors. In the background was the Smithsonian Air and Space Museum.

Also on the desk, acting as a holder for pens and pencils, was a coffee mug decorated with a picture of the Wright brothers' plane, aloft on the beach at Kitty Hawk. A shelf at eye level above the desk held a collection of books on aviation, an autographed picture of Chuck Yeager, and a model of the *Spirit of St. Louis*.

Brady White was an aviation buff. To this guy, aiming a laser beam at a cockpit would be a mortal sin.

"Pulse, sixty-two but thready," Brynn was saying into the phone. "Yes, of course, but they need to hurry. Thank you."

She hung up and said to Rye, "The ambulance could take up to ten minutes because we're so far out. And the fog." She glanced toward the back rooms. "Any indication of...anything?"

He shook his head. "Far as I can tell, nothing back there has been disturbed. Cash and credit cards are in his wallet, so it wasn't a robbery. No back door." He called her attention to the shoe prints. "They entered same way we did, came up behind him, probably while he was on the radio with me. They did what they came to do, turned off the radio, left."

"The sheriff's office is sending deputies out to investigate."

He looked at his watch. "Ten minutes? Is he going to be all right?"

"Head wounds bleed a lot even when they're not bad, so I'm not as concerned about the blood. It's already coagulating. But he's probably concussed. There's a possibility of fracture. He'll need an X-ray and brain scan."

Rye dragged his hand over his mouth and chin and muttered deprecations to whoever had done this.

Brynn looked at the footprints, one set of which was noticeably larger than the other. "No signs of a struggle. Nothing taken. What possible motive would anyone have had to just walk in here and do this?"

Rye didn't answer, but he was sure of one thing. Whoever had done that trick with the laser on him had also done this. No way in hell could the two incidents have occurred in an otherwise sleepy mountain town, within minutes and a mile of each other, and not be connected.

"The 911 operator knows the family," Brynn said. "She's going to notify Mrs. White herself. She also sent two deputies to their house."

Rye's gaze remained fixed on the family photograph on the desk. Deep inside him a vengeful anger began simmering on behalf of Brady White and his family. On behalf of Dash, too. He loved that beat-up old 182, just like he had loved that beat-up old cat.

But as soon as those vindictive thoughts began edging their way into Rye's mind, he cautioned himself against letting them lodge there. It wasn't up to him to get payback for the wrong done to the Whites, or to Dash, or to anybody. He sternly reminded himself that he was responsible only to and for himself.

Ah, but there was the hitch. He'd also been victimized by these fuckers. They had to be made to answer for trying to crash him. He was in this damn thing whether he wanted to be or not.

Feeling the pressure of obligation settling over him, he pushed his fingers through his hair, then ran his hand around the back of his neck where tension was already collecting.

"One of the deputies will stay with the Whites' children." Brynn had continued talking, unaware of the turbulent nature of his thoughts. "The other deputy will drive Mrs. White to the hospital."

Only half hearing her, Rye murmured, "My worst nightmare."

She looked at him with surprise. "Hospitals?"

Absently, he shook his head. "Involvement."

# Chapter 5

———◦《◉》◦———

*2:41 a.m.*

Delores Parker Hunt entered the master bedroom and was dismayed to find her husband lying on the bed outside the covers, dressed except for his shoes. There was a pillow beneath his head, but he was wide awake.

As she approached him, she said, "I envy your ability to relax."

"Relax? Hardly. I only yielded the pacing contest to you. You were doing enough for both of us, wearing a path in the carpet while wearing me out just watching you."

Nudging his hip with hers, she sat down on the edge of the bed. "This should rejuvenate you. Goliad called a few minutes ago."

"Why you and not me?"

"He did call you. You left your phone in the sitting room. I took the liberty of answering it, knowing you would want to hear the latest right away."

"Well?"

She clasped his hand and squeezed it. "The package arrived. Fog or no fog, we'll receive it well ahead of the deadline."

His expression remained fixed, but his relief was evidenced by a long exhale through his nose. Only she would have detected that giveaway.

"The doctor took delivery," she continued. "Goliad is there to make certain she returns to Atlanta with it immediately."

Despite her parting shot to Goliad, she had no intention of telling Richard about the plane crash, the pilot, et cetera. These unanticipated bothers would only anger him, and she was angry enough for both of them. Seeing that he was about to say or ask something, she laid her index finger vertically against his lips. "Don't worry."

"Why would I worry? What could possibly go wrong?"

"I'll ignore your sarcasm, if you'll entrust me to take care of everything as you asked me to." She laid her hand on his chest and leaned down until their faces were close. "You know I'm up to the task. I would move heaven and earth."

"I don't doubt it for a moment. On my behalf, you've already made a pact with the devil."

"No," she said, stretching out the word, "I gave God the night off."

He gave her an arch look. "Del, only you would speak so cavalierly about taking over for the Almighty."

"Only I. And *you*."

Laughing, he said, "True enough." He reached up and tangled his fingers in her well-maintained, streaked blond hair. "My lioness."

"You had better believe it, mister." She pulled his hand to her mouth, growled against his palm, then nipped it with her teeth. "Claws, sharp teeth, and all."

Five minutes after being introduced to the handsome, charming, and recently divorced Richard Hunt at a charity gala, Delores had resolved to become the second Mrs. Hunt. By the end of the evening, she had abandoned her date and engaged in hot and urgent sex with Richard in the hotel elevator.

Six months to the day of that memorable evening, they were honeymooning in the Seychelles. Every day since, Delores had devoted herself to being his fiercest advocate, adoring wife, and ardent lover. He loved and trusted her above anyone else, and she made damn sure he continued to.

"I can retract my claws long enough to give you a back rub."

"Not now."

She placed her hands on his shoulders. "You're tense. I feel it."

"Of course I'm tense. There's a lot at stake here. For both of us, but especially for me."

"I don't dispute that, Richard."

A vertical line appeared between his thick brows, which were threaded with gray. She smoothed it with her fingertip, but she doubted he even felt it. His mind was elsewhere. "As soon as you get an ETA from Goliad, I want to know."

"Naturally."

"What's the new man's name?"

"Tommy? Timmy? Something like that."

"He's qualified for this type of work?"

"Goliad says he's *overqualified*."

"That could be either good or bad. I don't like having a man on the payroll that I haven't vetted myself." He was about to get up when she planted her hand against his chest and pressed him back against the supporting pillows.

"You conceded the pacing contest to me, remember?"

He resisted, but then he relented and stayed on the bed.

"The rest will do you good," she said.

"I won't rest until this is over." In thought, he pulled on his lower lip. "Goliad shouldn't have broken in a rookie on an errand this important. He should have taken someone he knew he could rely on."

"Actually, Timmy was a smart choice."

Richard gave her a sharp look.

"His tenure with us is short. Although I don't predict that anything will go wrong, if something should, we can lay the blame on the new guy who obviously didn't appreciate or adhere to our rigid standards."

After a moment's consideration, Richard gave her a canny smile. "Leaving us off the hook." She gave him a look of prim satisfaction that made his smile widen. "Sometimes I think we share the same brain, Del."

"A lot of you has rubbed off on me in the past fifteen years."

"Sixteen last month, remember? You should." He slipped his finger beneath the platinum chain at the base of her neck. "You're wearing your anniversary gift."

A ten-carat diamond glittered against his finger. No less brilliant were the tears that welled in her eyes. "*You* are my gift, Richard. You." She kissed his lips tenderly, then left the bed and started for the door.

"Please bring me my phone."

"I will when Goliad calls. In the meantime, take advantage of this downtime. I'll fret for both of us."

As soon as she had cleared the door and closed it softly behind her, she blinked back the recent tears and gave vent to supreme irritation. She checked the Cartier watch strapped to her wrist and cursed under her breath.

What was keeping Goliad from calling?

He had already been working for Richard when Delores entered the picture. The story was that Richard had found himself in need of a man to do his dirty work while keeping his own hands clean. After doing due diligence, Richard had pulled a young and hostile Goliad out of a court-mandated drug rehab program and made him an offer: If he got clean, and stayed clean, he would live lavishly and get paid handsomely to do what he'd been doing before, which, basically, amounted to being a thug.

Following their marriage, Goliad's loyalty to Richard had expanded to include her. He had never failed to do everything he was told to do, no matter how unsavory or illegal. But he was human, and therefore fallible, and, as Richard had alluded, this endeavor was fraught with possibilities for error.

To a compulsive planner like Delores, even an nth degree of uncertainty was untenable. Once a decision was made, she acted on it. No second-guessing was allowed, and she was relentless.

But people were unpredictable. Fate was fickle. Nature played tricks. Fog—for crissake, *fog*—had kept their private jet grounded, so it couldn't make a short round trip to Columbus tonight. They'd been forced to rely on another plane, another pilot, and then he had crashed! Unforeseen interferences such as that made her crazy. Chain reactions could cause a simple plan to rapidly derail. She had to trust Goliad to handle the tenuous situation, but it was hard to depend on anyone except herself.

On the end table, Richard's cell phone vibrated. *Goliad.* She clicked on and said, "Tell me you're on your way back."

"I'm afraid not, ma'am."

*"What?"* Her blood pressure spiked. "Why not? You were supposed to intercept the doctor when she left the airfield."

"We can't go near it. The place is crawling with cops."

# Chapter 6

<hr />

*2:57 a.m.*

Using the phone on Brady White's desk, Rye had called Atlanta Center to tell them that he was on the ground. He didn't tell them the manner in which he'd gotten there. He'd save that for the FAA.

Standing in the open doorway of the office, he'd looked toward the end of the runway where he would have touched down. Whoever had shone the laser at him could have been in that very spot. The angle would have been perfect.

While waiting for the ambulance, Brynn had continued monitoring the injured man's condition.

She'd taken his pulse every couple of minutes and periodically checked his pupils. When she'd gently parted his thinning hair and assessed the gash, she'd gotten a groan out of him, which she'd seemed to take as a good sign, because she smiled faintly and patted his shoulder.

Rye had left her to her doctoring and stayed out of her way by propping himself against the far wall under a paint-by-numbers portrait of a snarling bear. From this observation point, Rye had

watched Brynn take off her coat and hang it alongside Brady's
on the rack just inside the door.

She was wearing a black sweater over skinny, dark-wash jeans
tucked into tall, flat-heeled black suede boots. They all looked
damn good on her. Rye couldn't help but notice and appreciate
the way the garments hugged this and molded to that.

Whenever she timed Brady's pulse by her wristwatch, an al-
luring vertical dent appeared between sleek eyebrows the same
dark color as her hair. By contrast, her eyes were light. Best he
could tell from a safe distance, they were more gray than blue.

Her hair hung past her shoulders, and there was a hell of a lot
of it. She had a habit of absently hooking strands of it behind her
ears, where they never stayed for long. Too heavy, he thought. He
doubted he could gather up all her hair even using both hands.
He'd like to try, though.

No sooner had that thought popped into his mind than he
questioned where it had come from. He shouldn't be looking at
her closely enough to notice the color of her eyes. Speculating on
the weight of her hair, and how double-handfuls of it would feel?
*Jesus.*

And all this time, while he'd stood silently by, assessing her at-
tributes, she'd ignored him as though he were invisible.

But she'd been aware of him, all right. Why else had she done
everything within her power to keep from looking in his direction? Was he so bad to look at? Irritated by that thought, he
decided to heckle her.

"Hey."

She looked at him.

"Did I say something to offend?"

She opened her mouth to speak, but just then they heard the
wail of approaching sirens. At the distant intersection, flashing
red, blue, and white lights split off from the two-lane highway
and started up the pockmarked road that he and she had walked
along earlier.

The lights created kaleidoscope patterns in the swirling fog. As they got closer, the vehicles took form: an ambulance and two police units, all running hot.

Suddenly, Brynn whipped her head back around to him. If he could have captioned her expression in his terminology, it would have been "Oh, shit."

His gut clenched with foreboding. He pushed away from the wall and took a step toward her. *"What?"* He emphasized the *t*, making the word a demand.

She wet her lips, which at any other time would have distracted him. Now, however, the nervous gesture served as a herald for something he sensed he didn't want to hear.

"Before they get here..." She'd stopped, swallowed. "I should clear up a misapprehension."

"What did I misapprehend?"

"You assumed that I was Dr. Lambert."

He shot a look toward the black box, then placed his hands on his hips and glared at her. "I fuckin' knew you weren't legit. You're not a doctor? Who the hell are you?"

She cast a quick look over her shoulder. The emergency vehicles were screeching up outside. "I am a doctor. Dr. Brynn O'Neal. I came in Dr. Lambert's place."

"Why?"

"I can't explain now."

His head nearly exploded with fury. "What the hell have you gotten me into, lady?"

*3:02 a.m.*

Rye had resumed his place with his back to the wall, grinding his teeth in agitation, taking in the scene, and thinking sourly that it must be a slow night in law enforcement.

From the look of things, every officer in the county had

heeded the 911 call. After the first two squad cars arrived, others showed up in rapid succession. You'd think on a foggy holiday eve, cops would be busy with fender benders, DUIs, and settling disputes at the reunions of dysfunctional families.

Instead, uniformed men and women—Rye had lost count after a dozen—had crowded into the compact office of the Howardville County Airfield. It was as though the crime of the century had been committed here tonight. Good thing it hadn't been, because they'd tromped all over the shoe prints on the floor.

In a jargon made up mostly of medical acronyms, Dr. O'Neal had given the EMTs a concise update on Brady's condition, then relinquished him into their care. Shortly thereafter, the ambulance had left with him, still unconscious.

Now Brynn was in conversation with two men in gray uniforms that designated them as sheriff's deputies. Because of the hubbub caused by the other people milling around but generally doing nothing constructive, Rye couldn't catch what she was saying to the pair, but, following a lengthy monologue, she flicked her hand toward him. As one, the three turned. Rye stayed as he was, with arms and ankles crossed, seemingly indifferent to their scrutiny. One of the deputies excused himself from Brynn and his fellow officer and strolled over, notepad in hand.

"Rye Mallett?"

"That's right."

"Spelling?"

Rye spelled his name, and, as the officer jotted it down, he introduced himself as Deputy Don Rawlins. "What happened here tonight, Mr. Mallett?"

"Dr. O'Neal and I got here, found the guy slumped over his desk, unconscious and bleeding."

"You a friend of his?"

"Never laid eyes on him. I'd only talked to him by radio."

"Tell me about that."

"I flew in from Columbus, Ohio, and was on final approach when—"

"Crummy night to be flying."

When Rye didn't respond, the deputy looked up at him from beneath the brim of his hat. Rye looked back and raised his eyebrows by way of asking if the deputy wanted to hear his story or not. The officer tipped his head for Rye to continue.

Disliking the deputy's attitude, he decided to stick with the lie he'd told Brynn at the crash site. "I was on final approach when my panel lights blinked out. Just like that." He snapped his fingers. "It was a flicker, but it came at the worst possible time. No instruments, no visual because of the fog. I was flying blind."

"You crashed."

In abbreviated, layman's terms, he described the crash. "I narrowly missed the doctor's car. It was a close call. We were both lucky. Wasn't as bad as it could've been. I walked away with nothing but a bump on the head to show for it." He pushed back his hair to show him the goose egg. The deputy looked at it with no detectable concern.

He said, "The doctor tells us your plane is banged up pretty good and not going anywhere for a while."

"It can't be buffed out, no."

"She gave us the general vicinity of where it is. We've got officers going out to take a look."

Rye grimaced. "I'm required to call the FAA and file an accident report. My phone was busted, and since discovering White, I haven't had time. I need to get some pictures of the craft, as is, so tell your guys not to disturb anything."

"I'll tell them," Rawlins said, but he didn't seem in a hurry to do it. "What caused your instruments to blink out?"

"A glitch. It's an old plane."

Rawlins looked doubtful. "I'm no pilot, but I know this is a tough place to fly in and out of. We had a guy fly in here last year. Sunday pilot. Came in too low, clipped the power lines as he—"

"I'm not that guy."

Rye's curt interruption seemed to rub the deputy the wrong way. "Oh, no?"

"No."

The lawman looked him over then gave a skeptical snort and wrote something on his pad. "What was so all-fired important that you had to fly here tonight?"

"I fly freight." Rye didn't think that would cut it, and it didn't.

"For who?"

"For whoever pays me."

"What kind of freight?"

"All kinds. Big, little, dead or alive. You name it."

"I'd like for you to name it. What were you flying tonight?"

"That." The deputy followed the direction of his pointing finger to the box where it still sat in the chair adjacent to the door.

"What is it?"

"Exactly what it looks like."

Impatience evident, the deputy shifted his weight. "What's in it, Mr. Mallett?"

"Don't know. Didn't ask."

The first statement was true, the second a lie, and gauging by the deputy's dubious expression, he knew it was. "The doctor didn't volunteer it?"

"No."

"Is that typical?"

"In my business, there's no such thing as typical."

"Who dispatched you?"

"The name of the company is Dash-It-All." Rye gave him the contact information, and he wrote it down. "If you don't mind," Rye said, "I'd like to call the owner myself and be the one to break the news about his plane."

"I do mind."

He gave Rye a smile that Rye would've enjoyed wreaking

havoc on. Instead, he gave an indifferent shrug and nodded down at the notepad. "You've got his number."

Rawlins called over another deputy, who was older but apparently lower in the department's pecking order. Rawlins ripped off the sheet of paper that had Dash's phone numbers on it and gave it to the other officer. He muttered instructions to him that Rye couldn't hear and pretended disinterest in.

Before the other deputy moved away, he said to Rawlins in an undertone, "Know who she is?" He bobbed his head toward Brynn.

Rawlins leaned back in order to see around the other deputy to where Brynn was being questioned. "Should I?"

"Wes O'Neal's daughter."

Rawlins's eyes narrowed on her. "You don't say."

"Wasn't sure at first, but then I heard her name. I'd see her around the department when she was just a kid. In and out of there a lot." The older deputy withdrew, presumably to phone Dash.

Rye's curiosity got the better of him. "Who's Wes O'Neal?"

Rawlins said, "You're not from around here, or you'd likely know. Where are you from, Mr. Mallett?"

"Not from around here." Rawlins gave him a baleful look, and Rye decided that annoying him further wasn't worth the time it would cost him. "Everywhere and nowhere. Air Force brat. We moved every couple of years, so I don't claim a home town or even a home state."

"Where do you live now?"

He rented an apartment in Oklahoma City only so he would have a mailing address. He had no personal attachment to the city. He'd chosen it for convenience. It was in the center of the country, making it easy to get into on his way back from somewhere and easy to get out of on his way to somewhere else.

He hadn't really lied to Brynn when she'd asked where he

lived. The rental was more a storage unit for his few belongings than it was a residence. As often as not, he was far from there, sleeping in a cheap motel or in the back room of an FBO until somebody needed a pilot on short notice.

Like tonight.

His eyes were drawn again to Brynn. She was talking, making small gestures. She reached up and looped a hank of hair behind her ear. As she listened to the deputy's next question, her teeth tugged at the corner of her lower lip, like she was nervous. Like she was lying.

"Address?"

Rawlins's question brought Rye back. He provided Rawlins with the address of his apartment. The deputy added it to his notepad. "After you crashed, what happened?"

Rye explained how he'd managed to get out of the airplane. "I was trying to figure out which way back to the road when Dr. O'Neal showed up." Leaving out how sneakily she'd acted when she found the plane, he related the rest.

"We got to her car, discovered the damage to the wheel, had no choice but to walk here. Found Brady White. That's it. Just like I told you at the start. That's everything I know. So can we wrap this up?"

But Rawlins wasn't finished with him. "You said you were on the radio with Brady. What was his last transmission?"

"He asked if I was nervous."

"About what?"

Rye smiled.

"What's funny?"

"That's what I came back to Brady with. My exact words. He was asking if I was nervous about the landing. I indicated I wasn't. He said I was due a couple of beers. That's the last I heard from him. I transmitted that I saw the runway lights, but he didn't respond."

"Why do you think?"

"I think because he'd been knocked cold. The radio wasn't on when Dr. O'Neal and I got here. I checked."

Rawlins said, "Okay," but not in a way that sounded like it was okay.

He then went through a series of routine questions: Had Rye seen any other persons or vehicles; had he touched or disturbed anything; did it appear to him that anything had been disturbed; had Brady White said anything? He answered no to all.

The older deputy came back and reported to Rawlins. "Mallett here checks out. That Dash character went nuts when I told him about his plane, but I calmed him down. He's emailing you the flight plan that Mallett filed, along with the paperwork on his cargo."

Rawlins pulled out his phone. As he accessed his email, he said to Rye, "Why didn't you give me all this?"

"You didn't ask for it."

Rawlins scrolled through the documents and stopped on the air bill. "Under client's name it says Dr. Lambert."

"I assumed that's who Dr. O'Neal was till she told me different."

"She came on Dr. Lambert's behalf?"

Brynn had said to him that she'd come in Dr. Lambert's place. There was a fine distinction between *in his place* and *on his behalf.* But Rye nodded in response to the deputy's question, because when you didn't have a freaking clue how to answer, a nonverbal reply was the safest.

"Black metal box," the deputy said, still reading from the shipping form attached to the email. "Doesn't say what's in it."

Rye gave another shrug. "Like I told you."

The deputy closed out the email and slid his phone back into the pocket of his puffy jacket. "You and Dr. O'Neal know each other before tonight?"

"No."

Rawlins tilted his chin down in apparent doubt.

"No," Rye repeated. "Never heard of her. Never saw her before she came walking out of the foggy woods. Didn't even know she was a woman. When I was told the client was a Dr. Lambert, I automatically figured a man."

"Feminists would jump all over that."

"I'm not proud of it. I'm just telling you that's how it was."

The deputy tried to stare a lie out of him, but ironically that answer was the unvarnished truth, so Rye stared back and didn't blink. Rawlins was first to back down. He used the toe of his boot to nudge the leather duffel at Rye's feet. "What's in the bag?"

"It's my flight bag."

"Not what I asked."

"Help yourself. But there's a nine-millimeter in there. I have a permit."

Rawlins extended his open palm. Rye pulled his wallet from his back pocket and produced the concealed carry license. The deputy inspected it as though Rye was on a terrorist watch list, several times comparing the photo on the license to Rye's face, then handed back the wallet, squatted down, and unzipped the bag.

He mumbled something about the contents looking like a hardware store wrapped in leather, but, right off, he located the zippered pocket with the Glock inside. He stood up with it in his hand and looked it over. "There's a bullet chambered."

Since he'd stated the obvious, Rye didn't say anything.

"How come?" the deputy asked.

"Bears."

"Bears?"

Rye hitched his thumb up toward the painting on the wall behind him. "Before I saw Dr. O'Neal's flashlight, I heard thrashing in the woods, something coming my way. I didn't want to come face-to-face with a bear or any other kind of predator. So I chambered a bullet just in case."

It was a logical explanation. Which wasn't to say that Rawlins believed a word of it. But before he could test its veracity with a follow-up question, the deputy who'd been questioning Brynn called, "Rawlins? Talk to you a sec?"

"Stay here," he said to Rye as he moved away to join his partner.

The crowd of personnel had thinned out. Apparently they'd come to the conclusion that the crime of the century hadn't been committed on their watch after all. Of those who remained, one was shuffling through White's paperwork as though to determine if any of it was relevant and would shed light on who had walked in and clouted him for no apparent reason.

Another was dusting the desk for fingerprints. When his interest moved to the collector's items on the shelf above it, and he was about to reach for the airplane model, Rye pushed away from the wall. "Hey! Don't mess with that."

Everyone stopped what they were doing and turned toward him. Rye looked at Rawlins, who'd been huddled with the other deputy, comparing notes. Rye said, "Whoever hit him didn't take time to handle his stuff. Leave it alone."

Rawlins took stock of the articles on the shelf, considered it, then shook his head at the fingerprinter. Everyone went back to what they'd been doing.

Rye resettled himself against the wall and looked toward Brynn. She, who like everyone else had turned when he admonished the man doing the fingerprinting, was regarding him curiously.

*3:21 a.m.*

Rye Mallett's stare was unmoving, unblinking, and unnerving.

She would give anything to know what he'd told the deputy. Their accounts of discovering Brady White would be similar, if not word for word. But she wondered about his version of their meeting at the crash site. How much had he told, how truthful had he been, what had he left out?

Working in her favor was the man's innate terseness and avoidance of conversation. He also had a self-proclaimed aversion to involvement. He would want this to be over and done with as soon as possible, the same as she, so she doubted he would elaborate or give the deputies anything except brief answers to direct questions.

For her part, she'd been guarded when answering the deputy's questions, but not so evasive as to arouse suspicion.

He had asked about the scratches on her hands. She had attributed them to stumbling into a thicket while making her way through the woods in search of the plane. "When I reached it, I was so relieved to discover the pilot alive and unharmed."

"You and Mallett know each other?"

"Not at all. He was stranded out there, and so was I. We walked here together."

The deputy—his name was Wilson something or something Wilson—had looked over at Rye where he was being questioned. Coming back around to her, he said, "Rough-looking character."

She'd had to agree. His stance was arrogant, his mannerisms insolent. He had a surly disposition, the reflexes of a rattlesnake, and an air of menace, which was a troublesome combination when being questioned at a crime scene by officers of the law. A more congenial attitude and friendlier aspect would've been beneficial to them both, but it was too late to advise him of that.

"As I said, I didn't meet him until tonight," she'd told Wilson. "But, honestly, I was glad to have him with me. The fog and all."

They'd gone back and forth like that without her revealing anything of substance. She'd been relieved when they moved from her initial encounter with Rye Mallett to their finding Brady White.

"The people who attacked him left shoe prints. Unfortunately..." She gestured at the floor.

The tips of Wilson's ears had turned red with embarrassment when he saw that any prints left were now smudged and useless as a means of helping to identify the perpetrators.

He'd asked a few more questions, then posed the one she'd most dreaded. "What was he delivering to you?"

"I can't tell you."

"Sorry?"

"To tell would be a violation of my patient's privacy."

Wilson had studied her for a moment, then said in a lower voice, "I know your daddy, Dr. O'Neal."

Her heart had bumped, but she'd kept her voice cool. "Do you?"

"Y'all going to spend Thanksgiving together?"

"No. I have to work tomorrow. In fact..." She'd made a grand gesture of checking her watch and, upon seeing the time, had made a small sound of distress. "I need to return to Atlanta as soon as possible, and since my car can't be driven, I need to be making other arrangements for getting back. How much longer will this take?"

Showing no sympathy for her time crunch, he'd stuck to the subject of her father. "When did you last see Wes?"

"We haven't had any contact in a long while. Years."

He'd poked his tongue into his cheek and continued to search her eyes for an uncomfortable length of time, then had turned away from her and summoned his crony. "Rawlins? Talk to you for a sec?"

And now, while the two deputies conferred in whispers, she and the pilot exchanged stares, and to her supreme consternation, it had been easier to withstand Wilson's incisive gaze than it was Rye Mallett's.

Seen in full light, he looked no more reputable than he had when he had her pinned to the forest floor. He had a rangy build, but, as she knew from experience, he was stronger than his leanness suggested.

His dark blond hair was thick and unruly and grazed the collar of his bomber jacket. No extra flesh softened his square and well-defined jaw, but it was dusted with a scruff only slightly darker than his hair. She couldn't tell the color of his eyes because the sockets were cast in shadow by the overhead light. But she felt the hostility they trained on her. Indeed, if looks could kill.

What bothered her most, he wore his ruggedness and hostility well.

Wilson's return came as a welcome relief from Rye's glower.

"I sent a deputy out to assess the damage to your car," the deputy said. "He confirmed that it can't be driven. I've called a tow truck, but they won't go out till daylight. You can ride to the department with me. Mr. Mallett can go with Deputy Rawlins. Okay?"

She got the sense that the question was asked out of politeness and not because her opinion of the plan made any difference. "Department?"

"Sheriff's office. We'll take your statements there. Get y'all some coffee. You'll be a lot more comfortable."

Having overheard the plan, Rye hissed an expletive. As coarse as it was, Brynn wanted to underscore it. "How long will that take?" she asked.

"Can't say," Wilson replied.

"There's nothing I can add to what I've already told you."

Wilson gave her a pleasant smile. "Maybe in the retelling, you'll think of something else."

"I won't."

"And anyway," he said, continuing as though she hadn't spoken, "we'd like to take a look inside that box."

# Chapter 7

*4:02 a.m.*

The two squad cars arrived at the sheriff's department at the same time, but Rye and Brynn were kept separated as Rawlins and Wilson escorted them toward the building. They didn't want them collaborating on their stories.

Police procedure. Rye got it. He just didn't like it. He was being treated more like a suspect than a material witness. The implication made him angry and apprehensive.

Just what the hell was going on? The answer lay with Brynn. She might not have aimed that laser at him herself, but were she and that damned box the reason someone had? Something was keeping her from being up-front, and not just with him. The deputies smelled a rat, too.

The four of them entered through a door marked "Official Personnel Only." No sooner were they inside than a gruff voice called out, "Brynn! Is that you, honey?"

The woman lumbering down the corridor toward them wore a deputy's uniform stretched to capacity over her full figure. With iron gray hair and lips so thin they were nonexistent, Rye placed her age as sixty-something. Her no-nonsense bearing was belied by her smile as she approached Brynn.

"I heard your name over dispatch and knew you were coming in. Couldn't wait to see you!"

Brynn smiled at her with genuine warmth. "Hello, Myra."

Myra wrapped her in a hug that looked bone-crushing, then set her back and held her at arm's length. "Look at you! I'm so proud of you, girl."

"Thank you."

"Still in Atlanta? And a doctor?"

"Yes to both."

"Mercy sakes," the woman said. "That's wonderful. Pretty as ever, too."

Brynn's smile became a bit more tentative, as though the woman's flattery made her uneasy. "I thought you would have retired by now, Myra."

"To do what? Sit and rock? Take up knitting or rose-growing? Just shoot me now. Besides, this department would fall apart if I wasn't here to hold it together."

Brynn laughed. "I don't doubt that."

Myra continued to beam, then seemed to remember that Brynn hadn't simply dropped by to say hello. "What happened out there at the airfield? Brady White's in the ER. What's going on?" She'd addressed the questions to Rawlins in a tone that was almost accusatory.

"We're trying to determine that," he replied. "Excuse us."

Under his and Wilson's prodding, Rye and Brynn were shepherded toward the staircase. Over her shoulder, Brynn said, "It was good to see you, Myra. Happy Thanksgiving."

As they started up the enclosed stairwell, Rye slid off his bomber jacket and folded it over his forearm. Rounding the landing, Brynn happened to bump elbows with him. When she turned her head to excuse herself, she caught a glimpse of the jacket's lining.

It stopped her where she stood on the tread above him. Her gaze snapped to his.

With exaggerated care, he refolded the jacket so that the well-endowed pinup girl, hand-painted on the silk lining, was no longer visible. "Sorry," he said, with all the sincerity of a snake oil salesman. "There's a world map on the inside."

"How convenient."

"It is, actually. Unfamiliar terrain can be tricky to navigate."

From behind them, Wilson said, "Move it along, please."

Brynn turned and continued up the stairs just ahead of Rye. He was tempted to grab a strand of wavy hair and yank her to a stop, then tell her she had her nerve being pissy with him, when it was he who had every right to be furious. He, who only ever wanted to be left alone to go about his business, now found himself embroiled in one hell of a mess of her making, and the nature of the mess was still a mystery to him.

The situation had gone tits up the instant that laser had skewered his eyeballs. Things hadn't improved. They continued to get worse.

A sheriff's office was never a good place to find oneself in the predawn. He had the uneasy feeling that he was entering the lions' den and realized he was bracing himself for whatever nasty shock came next.

Besides Wilson, Rawlins, and Myra, there were only a handful of personnel on duty, but as they reached the second floor, an older officer, who was on his way downstairs, hesitated when he saw Brynn and smiled in recognition.

"Well, I'll be," he said in the gravelly voice of a long-time smoker. After getting only a marginal smile and murmured hello from her, he held back whatever else he was about to say, doffed an imaginary hat, and continued on down the steps.

The staircase opened into a large squad room with a warren of desks, only one of them occupied by a sleepy-looking man in plainclothes who sat staring into a computer monitor.

"You and I will take room three," Wilson said to Brynn. Rye noticed that she headed toward an offshoot hallway without needing direction.

Rawlins followed them and said to Rye, "Down here." He passed the room Brynn and Wilson entered. Farther down the hall, he opened the door to a cramped office. He hung his coat and hat on a wall-mounted hook and motioned Rye in. "Have a seat. I'll be back."

"Can I please borrow a phone charger?" Rye asked.

"Sure." Rawlins pulled the door shut as he left.

Between Rawlins and Wilson, it was no contest as to which was the "bad cop." Rye wondered why he'd been unlucky enough to draw him.

He sat down in front of a desk that looked like it had sustained storm damage. The rest of the office was equally cluttered, the walls papered with outdated calendars, old wanted posters, and notices of one kind or another.

Several tacky golf trophies were jammed between books and files in the three-shelf bookcase. It also contained a bobblehead of a Clemson tiger next to a picture of a younger Rawlins wearing the full gear of the university's football team. A signed baseball was encased in a Plexiglas cube.

The things a man hoarded revealed a lot about the man and what he valued.

Rawlins was easy to peg. A former jock, clinging to glory days.

Brady White loved his family and aviation.

Rye Mallett?

He looked down at his brown bomber jacket where it lay across his lap.

It was vintage World War II. He'd discovered it in a trunk in a dusty antiques store that specialized in aviation memorabilia. It had been love at first sight. He'd asked the proprietor to please hold it for him until he could scrape up enough money to buy it. He left a ten-dollar down payment and paid on the layaway whenever he had some spare cash. On the day he'd gotten his pilot's license at age sixteen, he'd gone into the store, settled the balance, and worn the jacket out.

The store owner couldn't recall from where or whom he'd obtained the trunk, so Rye never learned the name or fate of the aviator who'd worn the jacket during the war. The patches on it designated his squadron and various air bases, but Rye never pursued those clues. He wasn't sure he wanted to know the pilot's fate, because odds were good that he hadn't survived. If he had, he never would have parted with his bomber jacket.

Rye ran his hand over the creased and scored leather, wishing he knew how each imperfection had come to be there. They were imbedded into the leather, representing chapters in the jacket's history. He'd added nicks and scratches of his own, making him an intrinsic part of it, yet he didn't consider himself its owner. He was merely its caretaker, the flyer to whom it had been temporarily entrusted until he passed it on to another.

Thinking back to Dr. O'Neal's prissy disapproval of the lining, he snickered. He stretched his legs out, tilted his head back, and closed his eyes. Except for the nap he'd taken on Dash's sofa, he hadn't slept in twenty-four hours. He was beat.

The next thing he knew, Rawlins was back. Rye sat up straight, dry-scrubbed his face, and glanced at his watch. He'd dozed for nearly fifteen minutes.

During that time, the deputy had been busy. His hands were so full, he had to push the door shut with his heel. He passed Rye a phone charger and pointed to the nearest wall outlet.

"Thanks." Rye took his spare phone from his flight bag and plugged into it.

Rawlins set a Styrofoam cup of coffee in front of him. "Cream's curdled and we've run out of powdered. I have sweetener." He scattered a variety of packets on the desk as he sat down.

"I'm good." Rye removed the plastic lid and sipped. The brew was scalding, strong, and bracing.

Rawlins set his cell phone within reach on his cluttered desk, drank from his cup of coffee, then worked an oversize paperclip off the sheaf of paper he'd carried in tucked under his arm. Rye saw that it was a stack of printouts of official-looking forms and documents.

*Fuck.*

Rawlins said, "You're a surprise, Mr. Mallett."

Rye kept his expression a blank. "How's that?"

"You look like a bum and act like a prick, but you graduated from the Air Force Academy with honors, flew dangerous missions in Afghanistan, returned from your second tour a decorated hero." Rawlins looked across the desk at him. "What happened?"

"I found God."

The deputy heaved a weary sigh and leaned back in his desk chair. "Your comic timing needs work."

"Speaking of timing, how soon can I get out of here?"

Rawlins reacted to that with a show of temper. "I don't want to be here, either, you know. The sun is about to come up on Thanksgiving, and my wife is mad as hell because a passel of kinfolk is descending at noon, and I forgot to pick up evaporated milk last night. Or maybe it was condensed milk. Whichever, she can't finish her pie-baking, and I'm catching the blame." He brought his chair upright like he was about to launch. "All because of you."

"I didn't do anything."

"No?"

"*No.* Well, except for keeping my plane aloft long enough to spare Dr. O'Neal's life, but good flying doesn't seem to go very far with you people."

"You ever been arrested?"

Rye hitched his chin toward the stack of paperwork. "What's it say?"

Rawlins thumbed through several sheets. "Says disturbing the peace."

"When and where, specifically?"

"That's rather the point," Rawlins returned dryly. "All over the place." He scanned more sheets. "Says drunkenness."

"Guilty. San Diego. Bad batch of tequila. Spent the night in the drunk tank, which was a lot more luxurious than the motel the skinflint client had agreed to cover. At least I knew whose pee it was on the floor."

"Reno, Nevada. Assault in a hotel room."

"You're reading it wrong. I filed the complaint. He assaulted me."

"He?"

"She failed to mention she had a husband."

Rawlins snuffled and shook his head. "Man. When you bottomed out, you bottomed out good, didn't you?"

"I'm an overachiever."

The deputy wasn't amused. "Who won? You or the husband?"

"I threatened to throw him out the tenth-floor window if he didn't back off."

"Were you bluffing?"

"We'll never know. He backed off before I was tested."

Rawlins studied him over his cup of coffee as he took another drink, then said, "You're lying."

"I'll swear under oath that it was the tenth floor."

"You're lying when you say you don't know what's in that box of Dr. O'Neal's."

"I don't."

"Or why Brady White was attacked."

"No idea."

"That's a crock of shit, Mr. Mallett."

Rye yawned widely.

Rawlins looked through more of the sheets. "You've spent a lot of time flying in Central and South America."

"I've logged thousands of hours."

"Any particular reason why?"

"Big continent. Lots of real estate to cover. Lots of out-of-the-way places that can only be reached by air. Peru alone has—"

"Have you ever flown weapons?"

"Only for the U.S. Air Force."

"Drugs?"

"Yes."

He could tell the swift admission took Rawlins aback.

"Once," Rye qualified, holding up his index finger. "Without my knowledge. The payload was knock-off designer handbags destined for a discount department store chain in south Texas. When I arrived and started unloading the freight, I discovered the damn purses were stuffed with heroin. I was pissed. Anonymously tipped both the DEA and Customs, but not before making the guy who set me up rue the day he was born."

"You're telling me that no one's ever tried to hire you—"

"I didn't tell you that. I'm approached all the time. Kingpins, penny-ante pushers, corrupt government officials. They've all offered me top dollar because they know I'll fly anywhere.

"But the thought of federal prison doesn't appeal to me, and, in any effing case, I'm *not a damn drug runner*." He stood up and pulled on his jacket. "You haven't thought this through, Rawlins."

"Sit down."

Rye remained standing and kept talking. "I'm up there, skirting mountains and power lines. Can't see a goddamn thing through the fog, relying on instruments and Brady White, who's doing all he can to help me make a safe landing. Now, why in hell, after walking away from what could easily have been a fatal crash, would I want to bash that man in the skull?" Rawlins didn't need to know that his initial intention had been to do just that.

"Easy," the deputy said. "You blamed him for missing the runway."

"No, I didn't."

"Your instruments blinked out? Come on, Mallett. Admit it. You screwed up big, and Brady was your scapegoat."

It was all he could do to keep quiet about the laser. He had not one iota of evidence that it had happened. It would look like whining, blaming the crash on something besides his own fallibility. Rawlins already had a trustworthiness issue with him. He would probably laugh out loud.

Rye also had nothing to back up an allegation that Brady White's attackers had been the ones who had shone the laser at him. But, being a conscientious cop, Rawlins would grudgingly look into it, and looking into it would take time, and Rye was long past ready to clear out. Let this going-to-fat ex-jock think what he wanted about the crash.

Rye told him the truth. "I didn't attack Brady, and I don't know who did." He picked up his flight bag. "You want to take that as my statement and have me sign it, fine. Type it up, and we're both outta here. You pick up canned milk on your way home to pacify the angry wife.

"Or. If you want to hold me for suspicion of a crime, I'll shut down all talk and lawyer up so fast your head will spin. Even if you put me in lockup, your passel of kinfolk will celebrate Thanksgiving without you, because you'll be here filling out forms, trying to make up for your misjudgment, and preventing your fine sheriff's department from being sued for keeping me in a holding cell when I didn't do anything."

The last word was still reverberating when Rawlins's cell phone rang. He picked it up and answered with his name. He listened, then reached for a notepad.

"How do you spell it? When did this take place?" For a couple of minutes, he scribbled notes as the caller imparted information. "You have an address for him? Okay, go see if he's at home. Find out where he was around two o'clock this morning. Let me know ASAP."

He clicked off, glanced across at Rye, then used speed dial to make a call. "Wilson, me. Shake anything out of Dr. O'Neal?"

Wilson must've replied in the negative.

"Me neither. Not much, anyway," Rawlins said. "Listen, Thatcher just called from the hospital. Seems Brady White had a heated argument day before yesterday with a local guy who keeps his plane in the hangar. He owed Brady for fuel and back rent. When Brady tried to collect, the man accused him of price gouging and refused to pay. Brady's holding the keys to the guy's plane until he receives payment." He coughed behind his fist. "Thatcher's going to check him out."

Wilson asked a few questions, which Rawlins answered in monotones.

Numerous sly and insulting remarks skittered through Rye's mind, but he figured that Rawlins was eating enough crow as it was. Besides, he was relieved to know that Brady White had regained consciousness. So when Rawlins clicked off, he said, "Brady came out of it okay?"

Rawlins shook his head. "He's still out. Our deputy got all this about the argument from his wife. She's standing vigil at the hospital. Has a lot of friends with her. The Whites are well thought of around here."

"I gathered." It was deflating news that Brady still hadn't come around. Rye waited a beat, then asked, "Can we get to that statement now so I can be on my way?"

"In a minute. Answer me this, why did you take issue over the fingerprinting?"

Rye shrugged. "I don't know. Impulse. Seemed a dumb and wasteful thing to do to artifacts."

"Huh." Rawlins studied him for a moment. "Why have you and Dr. O'Neal acted so squirrely about the contents of that box? What's in it?"

"I've told you a dozen times, I don't know. You'll have to get that from her."

"Good idea."

The deputy stood up and motioned Rye toward the door.

*4:42 a.m.*

Under duress, Brynn surrendered to Wilson the cell number of her colleague, Dr. Nathan Lambert.

She and Nate Lambert had worked together on various cases for the past several years. Both were specialists in their field, but Nate had ten more years' experience, and he flaunted it. He had a publicist who booked him for lectures and a publisher who was waiting for a book.

He'd made a name for himself, and his notoriety was such that he could now hand-select his patients, and he did. Many were among the rich and famous who checked into the hospital under aliases. Paradoxically, Nate had a penchant for name-dropping.

Wilson placed the call. Despite the hour, Nate answered immediately, as though he'd had the phone already at his ear. Wilson identified himself, and Nate's first words were, "Oh, God, no. Has something happened to Dr. O'Neal?"

"I'm here." She said it loudly enough for him to hear her through the speaker.

"Brynn, are you all right?"

"*I'm* fine. But my situation isn't. It's been an eventful night, and that's putting it mildly."

"Were you able to meet the plane?"

"Yes."

"Thank God." Brynn detected the vast relief in his voice and envisioned him running his hand over his marble-slick head, which he shaved with scrupulous timeliness. He said, "When I didn't hear from you, I got worried and checked with the contact in Columbus. Dash, I think it is? He assured me that the plane was on its way."

"You must have spoken with him before he was notified of the crash."

"The plane *crashed*?"

Wilson made a hand gesture that granted her permission to relate the consequential events that had taken place since she'd left Atlanta. Nate responded to each revelation with a shocked silence or sudden intake of breath, but he listened without interrupting her. She explained the circumstances concisely but comprehensively. When she finished the tale, she ended by reassuring him that the black box was in her possession and intact.

"Still sealed?" he asked.

"And padlocked."

"Wonderful." Then, after a brief pause, he asked with characteristic curtness, "So, what's the problem?"

Wilson jumped in ahead of her. "The problem, Dr. Lambert, is the juxtaposition of the two incidents. We're investigating the attack on Mr. White, and need to ascertain if it's connected in any way to the contents of this box."

"How could it be?"

"Precisely." Brynn gave Wilson a pointed look. "I haven't disclosed anything that would compromise our patient's privacy. But my stance on that has put me in a standoff with the investigators."

The door was pushed open, and Rawlins walked in. The limited space didn't allow for Rye Mallett to come all the way into the room, so he lingered on the threshold. During their brief face-off on the staircase, she'd seen that his eyes were green. They homed in on her now.

He looked perturbed and smug at the same time. She supposed he was annoyed over having been detained, smug over being vindicated when Brady White's altercation with a customer had come to light. When she'd overheard Wilson's phone conversation with Rawlins about it, she'd experienced a moment of smugness herself.

Until Wilson had remained insistent that she open the box.

"We have Dr. Lambert on the phone," Wilson told the newcomers.

For her colleague's benefit, she said, "Nate, we've been joined by Deputy Rawlins and the pilot of the plane, Mr. Mallett."

"Mr. Mallett," Nate said, "you have my deepest and most sincere gratitude for agreeing to fly tonight. I regret your accident and the damage done to your airplane. But I'm very glad you weren't injured or worse."

Rye replied with a laconic thanks.

Dr. Lambert then said, "Gentlemen, Brynn's detention is costing us valuable time which our patient cannot afford."

"I've tried to convey the urgency of the situation," she said, "but they have their own agenda."

"Agenda," Nate repeated, scoffing. He disdained anyone who tried to cramp his genius. "Am I to understand that the holdup is the matter of what's inside the box?"

"That's correct."

"Well then, Brynn, as long as our patient isn't named, and the container doesn't remain open for too long, accommodate them."


*4:53 a.m.*


For as long as Rye had been standing in the open doorway, he'd been gauging Brynn's reactions to what was going on. He'd noted each response, voluntary and subconscious. He'd marked each blink, muscle twitch, everything.

So when Dr. Lambert agreed to reveal what was inside the box, he saw the fractional widening of her eyes. He was aware of the hitch in her breath and her difficulty swallowing.

But those physical reactions probably went unnoticed by the deputies, because she recovered so quickly. "It's supposed to be kept airtight."

"Understood, Brynn." The doctor addressed her in a clipped

and condescending tone that made Rye dislike him for no other reason than that he sounded like an arrogant asshole. "But there appears to be no help for it. They've got their detective work; we've got our seriously ill patient. The sooner we appease them, the sooner we can resume trying to save a life."

She took a deep breath and let it out slowly. "All right. But I don't have the combination to the lock."

"Take me off speaker."

With a glance, she consulted Wilson, who nonverbally consulted Rawlins, who gave a brusque nod. He said, "I want to see what's inside."

Wilson took his phone off speaker and handed it to Brynn, then pushed the box across his desk to within her reach. She put the phone to her ear. "I'm ready."

The lock was a five-dial combination padlock. When the numbers were lined up according to her colleague's instructions, Brynn tugged open the metal ring. She looked at Wilson and Rawlins in turn. "Please reconsider. Exposure to air could contaminate—"

Rawlins didn't let her finish. He raised the lid himself.

Even from his vantage point, Rye could see inside the box. The interior was lined with black formed foam, even the lid. Four tightly sealed cylinders filled corresponding spaces cut into the foam. Vials of blood. All labeled.

"It's open," Brynn said into the phone. She listened for several seconds, then switched the phone back onto speaker and set it on the desk. "At Dr. Lambert's request," she told the deputies. "Go ahead, Nate."

"Dr. O'Neal and I specialize in hematologic malignancies. Blood cancers. We have a patient with an extremely rare form. The patient has undergone aggressive rounds of radiation and chemotherapy, to no avail. The only hope for survival is an allogeneic stem cell or cord blood transplant. But therein lies the problem. HLA matching. Human leukocyte antigens. These cell markers..."

Rye tuned him out and watched Brynn. While her pompous colleague waxed eloquent about CBUs and GVHDs, she stood with arms crossed over her middle, her lips rolled inside and compressed so tightly, they had gone colorless.

"What you're looking at, gentlemen, are blood samples taken from four different *possible* donors after a lengthy and extremely discouraging search. But we won't know if any is an acceptable match of our patient's HLA type until they're tested, and Dr. O'Neal and I want to do our own testing. Not that we mistrust the labs we use, but our patient is a high-profile public figure who insists on confidentiality, and, of course, we would like to get it right." On that droll note, he paused for breath.

"The samples are time-sensitive, and the testing is intricate because there's no margin for error. Meanwhile, the patient's time is running short. A donor must be found, and the necessary steps preceding a transplant begun. Soon.

"This should explain to you the immediacy of the situation, as well as Dr. O'Neal's efforts to preserve the integrity of the blood samples, and to protect the patient's identity, dignity, and privacy. Any more questions?"

Wilson dragged his hand down his tired-looking face, over his mouth and chin, then said, "Thank you, Dr. Lambert." He reached over and closed the lid on the box.

Lambert didn't acknowledge the thanks. He said, "Brynn, to prevent contamination or compromise—and let's hope to God none has occurred—please reseal the box and get it here with all due speed. Since your car is out of commission, how do you plan to get back to Atlanta?"

She picked up the phone, switched it off speaker, and said, "Finding transportation is the next order of business." For several moments, she held Rye's stare, then turned her head aside.

Rye's view of her was suddenly blocked by Rawlins's hard-boiled mug. "Come back to my office. Soon as you sign a statement, you'll be free to go."

# Chapter 8

*5:10 a.m.*

And they're still in there. Nobody's gone in or come out since the deputies took the two of them into the building."

Delores Hunt had listened with mounting impatience as Goliad updated her on the circumstances. "How long ago was that?"

"Little over an hour."

Delores lit a cigarette and blew the smoke toward the open French door to prevent Richard from catching a whiff, which he had a knack for doing even through walls. He hated it when she smoked. She only did so when she was extremely agitated. If he caught her at it now, puffing in frustration while she paced the width of the sitting room, he would know that something had gone terribly awry.

The last time she'd gone into the bedroom to see about him, he had begrudgingly agreed to change into pajamas and go to bed. The last series of radiation treatments had left him weakened and easy to tire, but neither he nor she had acknowledged that his former robustness was waning.

He had been quarrelsome and fretful because there had been

no further communication from Goliad, and they remained in the dark as to when they could expect Dr. O'Neal back in Atlanta.

His edginess would escalate to full-blown rage if he knew there had been another delay, the cause for which Delores couldn't explain to him because *she* didn't know it.

She had calmed him by admitting that there had been a glitch or two, but she'd attributed them to the ghastly weather and assured him that she, Dr. Lambert, and Goliad were on top of the situation.

She only wished that were the case.

Their lives had been turned upside down six months ago when Richard had been diagnosed with a cancer that neither of them had ever heard of. They had consulted Dr. Nate Lambert, a specialist of renown, but also a man known to them through social connections.

His god complex was barely tolerable, but it had its uses. With Nate's intercession, Richard's treatments had begun immediately and had been administered under a cloak of absolute secrecy. Not even their most trustworthy staff members knew that Richard was ill, Goliad being the single exception. No one else must know. It most certainly must be kept from the media.

Thousands of people were diagnosed with terminal cancer every day. They didn't make national news.

Senator Richard Hunt would.

"An hour, you say?"

"Yes, ma'am. Give or take," Goliad replied.

Fidgety with irritation, Delores assessed this new and disquieting information.

"I don't understand why so many officers converged on the airfield office. Were they investigating the crash? Why have Dr. O'Neal and the pilot been taken to the sheriff's office? In short, Goliad, what the hell is going on up there? What haven't you told me?"

After several portentous seconds, he said, "Timmy went a little overboard."

She picked up her lighter and clicked it a few times, watching the flame in a sort of self-induced hypnosis. "Explain that statement, please."

"He was fooling around with a laser."

"Excuse me?"

In his stolid manner that often made her want to scream with impatience, Goliad talked her through the sequence of events. "Once we got back to the airfield office—"

"Yes, yes. So you said, it was crawling with cops. Knowing that Dr. O'Neal and the pilot would find the man, why didn't you intercept them before they got there, *as I remember telling you to do*? Fog. That was your excuse."

"Fog was definitely a factor. I had to find a place to turn around. They couldn't have beat us by much."

"But they did. And now they're being questioned by police." She resumed pacing. "If this airfield man survives, can he identify you?"

"No. We came in behind him."

She wanted to ask why they hadn't just killed him. That would have left her with one less thing to worry about. She said, "I sent you up there on a simple errand. Keep your eye on Dr. O'Neal and make certain she delivers that box to us. All you've succeeded in doing so far is to invite the sheriff's office to our party."

Goliad was wise enough not to contradict her.

"Do you even know where the box is now?"

"One of the deputies was carrying it when they went into the sheriff's department."

"Christ." Delores lit another cigarette. "You're there now?"

"Right across the street, with a view of the door where they went in."

"Two men in a car surveilling the sheriff's office? Won't that arouse suspicion?"

"I don't think there's any danger of that. Looks like only a few officers are on duty. The streets are deserted."

"All right. Keep your eyes glued to that building. They can't detain Dr. O'Neal forever. She didn't assault anyone."

"I doubt they'll suspect it of her. They might the pilot, though. If he thought the guy at the airfield was the one with the laser, he'd have a motive for attacking him."

"All the better for us," she said. "If the police think he's the culprit, they'll hold him. If they release him, he'll have a plane crash to deal with. Either way, he's not our problem. Dr. O'Neal is. Stay on her tail, Goliad. If it looks like she's— Oh, Nate is calling in. Failure is not an option, Goliad."

Giving him no time to respond, she clicked off, then took several deep breaths before switching over to the incoming call. "Nate! I've been trying to reach you for hours. Where the hell is Dr. O'Neal? She should have been back well before now. Richard is frantic."

"Calm down, Delores. I just got off the phone with Brynn, who explained why she's been delayed. She was met with some difficulties."

"What kind of difficulties?"

She feigned ignorance about the happenings in Howardville. Nate Lambert was a brilliant physician. He was not a trusted confidant. Their inner circle consisted only of Richard and herself. They hadn't told Nate that Goliad had been sent to ensure Dr. O'Neal's timely return.

She listened as he naïvely described the hazards his colleague had encountered, beginning with the plane crash.

"You told us this company was reliable."

"I told you the company was the most reliable I could find that would agree to fly last night."

When Nate finished with his tale, Delores said, "I had a bad feeling that something untoward would happen if Dr. O'Neal went alone. Someone should have gone with her. Better yet, she shouldn't have been going at all. You should have. I'm on record as having told you so."

"Noted," Nate said. "But I didn't want to spoil my dinner plans and trek to the wilderness. You don't know Brynn as well as I do. She's capable and levelheaded. She's handled a mercurial situation with aplomb. She was remarkably unflustered when I spoke to her. Of course she was reluctant to open the box, but—"

"What?" This time Delores's astonishment was genuine. "She opened the box?"

"We really weren't given a choice. Those backwoods detectives were stiff-necked about it. Compliance was the only way to get Brynn out of there sooner rather than later."

"But—"

"It's fine, Delores. I had given explicit packing instructions, and it was done to my specifications."

"Richard's name—?"

"Brynn safeguarded it."

"Thank God."

"She has to sign off on her statement about the airfield incident. Once that's done, the unfortunate matter will be over."

"You're positive they're releasing her?"

"Forthwith. Fiasco averted," he said with annoying cheer. "We're back on track."

"What about the time this has cost us?"

"Only a few hours. Stop worrying."

"Easier said."

"How is Richard?"

"He's sleeping, but as soon as he wakes up, he'll want an explanation as to why she's not back and when we can expect her."

"Brynn is making arrangements to return as soon as possible. It's up to you how much of this to tell Richard."

"Don't leave me dangling, Nate. Keep me updated."

After disconnecting, Delores texted Goliad that Dr. O'Neal

had been cleared by the sheriff's department. *When she leaves there, stay on her!* He texted back a check mark.

*Fiasco averted.* Indeed. No matter how meticulously one planned, one still had to rely on others. The vagaries and failings of others drove Delores mad.

She took a deep drag on her cigarette and blew the plume of smoke toward the French door. Then, sensing movement in the room, she turned.

Richard stood on the threshold of the bedroom. Wearing only pajama bottoms, his appearance was incongruous with his combative stance. He didn't look weak and infirm now. His voice had lost none of its vibrato. "Stop shielding me, Delores. I'm not a child, and I'm not helpless. Yet. I demand to know—now: What has gone wrong?"

# Chapter 9

⟞⟝◈⟞⟝

*6:37 a.m.*

Are you family?"

"No."

"I'm sorry, sir. I can't give out patient information to anyone except a family member."

Rye looked away for a second or two before coming back to the woman at the ER's admission desk. In order to talk to him, she had slid open a panel of glass, but rules were a more substantial barrier than the partition.

He decided to appeal to her humanity. "Do you know Brady White personally?"

"I've known him forever. We were in the same class all through school. Marlene was a year behind us."

Rye assumed that Marlene was Mrs. White. "I'm not asking for details. I just want to know if he's going to be all right."

Her expression turned doleful, but she didn't waver. "It's hospital policy, sir. I can't give—"

She flinched when Rye rested his hands on the counter and leaned toward her. "If it wasn't for me, he wouldn't have been out there last night. I need to know he's going to pull through."

She adjusted her eyeglasses and looked him over, taking particular notice of his bomber jacket and flight bag. "You're the one who crashed his plane?"

"Yeah, I'm that one," he said, trying not to sound too wry. "I walked away from my ordeal. Brady didn't. Can you at least tell me if he's come around?"

She hesitated, looked over her shoulder as though fearing someone in authority might catch her violating policy, then winked at him and whispered, "Don't go anywhere. Let me check." She slid shut the panel of glass and disappeared through a doorway at the back of the office.

Rye was alone in the waiting room. The bright fluorescent lighting made it seem cold and inhospitable. The irony of that didn't escape him. He walked over to an eastern-facing window. Although Thanksgiving Day had dawned, there wasn't a pink sunrise to admire. The density of the fog obscured it.

At this hour, it would still be full dark in Austin. Too early to call.

Which actually made it the ideal time. It was doubtful anyone would answer, he wouldn't have to talk, but the call would be registered. He could honestly claim that he'd made an attempt.

He punched in the number. The call went through. He disconnected on the third ring. Done.

But then he realized that the number of his spare phone wouldn't be recognized. That call hadn't counted. He still had it to dread.

Dash would be up. Dash was always up. Rye called. Dash answered in his customary snarl, and when Rye identified himself, he said, "Well, it's about time. I've been—"

"My phone was busted, and before you light into me, let me fill you in on a few details that the deputy who called you last night didn't know."

For once in his life, Dash held his tongue for as long as Rye talked. He concluded by telling Dash how sorry he was about the Cessna. "I did my best. Wasn't good enough."

"Shit, Rye. The plane's insured. I'll collect the money and sell the undamaged parts, and come out ahead. It's worth more wrecked than it was intact. But if you'd've been killed—"

"You wouldn't have collected a thing. I'm not insured. My life isn't worth a dime."

"Don't joke."

"Wasn't."

After a short, tense silence, Dash asked, "You're sure about the laser?"

A tide of anger washed over Rye. "Don't insult me, Dash."

"Just asking a simple question. Don't read nothing into it."

Rye knew there was much more behind Dash's *simple* question, but he left it alone. "The beam hit me square in the eyes."

"All I needed to hear. I'd like to castrate the bastard."

"Get in line."

"Have the cops rounded up any suspects yet?"

This was going to be the dicey part. "I didn't tell them about it. I let them think I screwed the pooch." Rye figured Dash was too astonished to speak. He continued before he could. "Wouldn't have done any good to tell them, Dash. They'd only have my word for it, and I can see the eye rolls now. If I'd cried laser, it would've looked like I made up a far-fetched excuse for missing the runway."

"And that's worse than having them think it was your error?"

"This time, yeah."

"Want to tell me why?"

"It's complicated."

Dash snorted. "That much I know."

"It has to do with the client."

"Dr. Lambert, or the one who came to meet you?"

"Both, I think. This whole thing is off somehow. She protects that box like it's the Holy Grail."

*"She?"*

"Dr. O'Neal."

"The Dr. O'Neal you've been talking about is a she?"

"What? You've got something against female doctors?"

"Actually, I prefer 'em. What I've got an aversion to is a pilot who gets sabotaged and damn near killed in my plane, waits hours to call me with the *details*, and then when he does, takes me by the hand and leads me around the mulberry bush a few times and thinks—wrongly—that I'll be satisfied with that."

"I share your frustration, believe me. I don't know what's going on, either. I'd like to hang around till I find out who was at the other end of that laser and take a dull handsaw to his dick. But the best thing for me, and for you, too, is to soft-soap that in my accident report. Say it could have been a laser, not that it definitely was. I want to get away from here as soon as possible and write this off as a misadventure."

Dash thought it over. Then, "You saw inside the box?"

"Yes."

"Because I don't want Dash-It-All to get caught up in anything illegal."

"Hear you. I don't want to get caught up in anything, period. I've been cleared of any wrongdoing. Free to go." Without trying to sound desperate, he said, "Send me somewhere, Dash."

"Where are you now?"

"ER waiting room. I dropped by to see about the guy who got clobbered."

"That doesn't sound like 'writing it off.'"

"I owe him this much. Jesus."

"Okay, okay. And then you're ready to skip Dodge?"

"As soon as I've looked over the plane and talked to the FAA office in Atlanta. I doubt an agent will truck it up here before Monday, earliest. Probably he won't come at all. Keep checking your email. I'll send you pictures. You can forward them to your insurance adjuster."

"Never mind what I said a minute ago. Breaks my heart to think of that 182 being junked. It was a damn good plane."

"Breaks my heart for you. May be worth salvaging."

"We'll see."

"You got a flight for me?"

Dash blew out a gust of breath. "Rye, why don't you cut yourself some slack? You had a close call last night."

"All the more reason to get back up."

"I'm trying to do you a favor here."

"Do me a favor. Put me in the air."

Dash rumbled something that Rye didn't catch, then said, "Okay. First thing that comes up is yours. But it's Thanksgiving, and you're stuck in that burg. How will you get out?"

"I'll finagle a ride."

"To where? My first choice would be to have you in Atlanta."

"Mine, too."

"Let me know when you manage it. In the meantime, get some sleep."

"Okay."

"I mean it."

"I said okay. From Atlanta, you can send me anywhere. Doesn't matter where."

"As you've told me a thousand times."

"And thanks for being so decent about the plane."

"That's me, decent." Having said that, he clicked off.

Rye slid his phone into the pocket of his jacket. He adjusted his focus and looked at his reflection mirrored in the window glass. He made quite a sight. Warmed-over shit came to mind. His eyes were bloodshot from lack of sleep. His scruff was two days too long, and his hair looked like it had been groomed by a leaf blower. No wonder the lady at the admissions desk had regarded him with apprehension.

No wonder Brynn O'Neal had.

Last he'd seen of her, she'd been talking to her colleague

on the phone. Rawlins had led Rye back to his office and installed him there. Typical of military and police procedures, gears ground slowly. Getting the damn statement written up and signed had taken more than an hour. Once Rawlins cleared him, he had gotten out while the getting was good. Brynn had been nowhere in sight.

On the ground floor, he'd spotted Myra manning a desk in an otherwise vacant room. He'd stopped to ask her for directions to the hospital, and she'd provided them.

"How far is it?"

"Mile, mile and a half. I can drive you over."

"Thanks anyway. I'll hoof it."

He'd left by way of the employee door through which he'd been escorted in, officially ending his eventful but brief interaction with Dr. Brynn O'Neal.

*I can't wait to start never seeing you again.*

By now she would be on her way back to Atlanta, back to her Dr. Lambert, her terminally ill patient, her medical practice, her life, which he'd wanted to know nothing about. He'd seen the last of her. Connection severed. No further involvement. Not even a goodbye.

Just as well.

He told himself.

"Sir?"

The attendant was back, and she was smiling. He started toward her, but she pointed him toward the elevator. "Second floor. Marlene's watching for you."

At that point, he wanted to turn and run. He'd wanted to get matter-of-fact information passed along by a stranger. He hadn't bargained on having a one-on-one with Brady's wife, for godsake. But even he couldn't be heel enough to leave now.

He rode up and stepped off the elevator, immediately recognizing the woman from the vacation photo on Brady White's desk. She had a soft, matronly figure and a beautiful smile.

She reached for his right hand and clasped it between hers. "I know who you are, but, forgive me, I don't know your name."

"Rye Mallett."

"Mr. Mallett—"

"Rye."

"I'm Marlene. It means so much to me that you came to check on Brady. Thank you."

"Don't thank me. If it wasn't for me, he wouldn't have been at the airfield last night. How's he doing?"

"They're calling his condition 'guarded.' No skull fracture or depression. No bleeding has shown up on the brain scans. He's got a concussion, but I'll take that." She beamed a smile at him. "Your timing is perfect. They've given us only two minutes with him." She let go of his hand and started walking quickly down the hall.

Rye's long stride caught him up with her. "He's come to?"

"Only a few minutes ago."

"He's okay, then?"

"Groggy, disoriented, but he'll want to see you."

Rye panicked at the thought of a personal encounter. "You should be the one using the two minutes."

She smiled at him as they approached one of only three ICU beds. "He would never forgive me. But he doesn't know about the crash yet. I would appreciate it if you didn't mention it."

"No. Of course not. Has he said who attacked him?"

"He doesn't even remember it. The last thing he remembers is talking to you on the radio and hearing your engine. The doctor said it looked like he was struck from behind. Deputy Thatcher agreed."

Through the glass wall, Rye could see the man on the bed. He was hooked up to a variety of monitors that looked more complicated than a cockpit panel.

Brynn would know what they were for.

He hesitated on the threshold. Marlene went in ahead of him, then bent over her husband and said something to him. Rye saw his legs stir beneath the sheet. Marlene turned and motioned him in.

Rye walked to the bedside. Brady White wasn't recognizable as the man in the picture, but that was understandable. There was a bandage on his head. His eyes were open, but he seemed to have trouble focusing. However, he gave Rye a feeble smile and groped for his hand.

Rye took his and shook it, glad to feel its warmth. Going through his mind like a looped recording was, *Thank God you didn't die. Thank God you didn't die.* He couldn't have borne that.

"Thanks for coming out for me last night," he said. "I hate this happened to you. I want you to know how sorry I am."

Brady tried to shake his head but grimaced with the effort. In a scratchy voice, he said, "You made it in okay?"

Rye held his hands out to his sides to show that he was un-injured. "Whenever your number of safe landings equals your number of takeoffs . . ." He smiled, and it was returned.

Brady held up his first two fingers in a V. "Two beers."

"Don't think I've forgotten. We'll have them and talk flying."

Brady nodded. His eyelids flickered, then closed.

"Mrs. White." A nurse had come in, their signal to leave.

Marlene kissed her husband's forehead then rejoined Rye in the hall. As they walked back toward the elevator, she told him she would ride down with him.

While they waited for the elevator, Rye asked her if she thought the guy who rented space in Brady's hangar had been the one to attack him. "If so, that must've been some quarrel."

"I don't know the man except by name, and only through Brady. He described their argument as 'heated,' but that could have been an understatement to keep me from worrying. When Deputy Thatcher asked me if Brady had any enemies, I couldn't think of anyone else that he's been crosswise with."

Rye knew little of Brady White, but he seemed like a man who made more friends than enemies. Even if this dispute over the cost of fuel had cultivated him a violent enemy, how would that guy have known Brady was going to be out there last night when every other airport was shut down? Oh, and have a laser with him. And one angry lessee didn't compute with two sets of footprints.

Much more likely was that whoever had attacked Brady knew he would be on duty at the airfield, which meant they knew that Rye was scheduled to land there.

"Marlene, besides you, did Brady tell anybody about me coming in, give anyone my ETA?"

"Not to my knowledge. Why?"

"Just narrowing down the suspects."

"That's hardly your responsibility."

"I feel responsible."

She patted his arm. "The assault on Brady had nothing to do with you."

Maybe not directly. But did it have to do with Brynn O'Neal?

The elevator arrived. As they boarded, Rye switched subjects. "I take it that Brady is an aviation buff."

"Like you wouldn't believe."

"Does he fly?"

Her expression turned rueful. "No."

The elevator door opened on the lobby level. They stepped out, and Rye's heart kicked against his ribs when he saw Brynn alighting from a sheriff's unit parked in the porte cochere. Wilson was at the wheel. Brynn bent down and said something to him, then closed the door, and he drove away. She entered the lobby through the automatic doors. She was carrying that damn box.

Immediately spotting him and Marlene White, whom she must have recognized from the photograph on Brady's desk, she made her way over. She acknowledged him with a nod, then turned her attention to Brady's wife and introduced herself.

Mrs. White clasped Brynn's hand as she had Rye's. "Dr. O'Neal, thank you so much for seeing to Brady last night."

"Call me Brynn, please. And you're welcome. I only wish I could have done more. What's his condition?"

Marlene repeated what she'd told him. "He regained consciousness only a little while ago. Just in time for Rye to see him."

Brynn turned her gaze up to him. "You two talked?"

"We exchanged a few words. Not sure he'll remember any of it."

"Oh, he'll remember," Marlene said around a laugh. "He won't forget you telling him that you'll talk planes."

"I'm surprised he doesn't have his pilot's license," Rye said.

"He would if he could. All he ever wanted to do was fly. But he has a heart murmur caused by a faulty mitral valve. They discovered it when he was still in his teens, but he was probably born with it. He suffers mild symptoms that are controlled with medication. It doesn't prevent him from doing pretty much whatever he wants to."

"Except fly," Rye said.

"Except fly," she repeated sadly.

Brynn asked, "Doesn't it bother him to manage the airfield, watch other people do what he would love to be doing?"

"No, just the opposite. He's still plane crazy and enjoys the camaraderie with pilots." She looked over at Rye. "When he heard that you were thumbing your nose at the weather and flying in here last night, he was as excited as a kid. As he left the house, he said, 'I can't wait to meet this fellow.' Now he has. Your visit today will have meant the world to him."

"When he's recovered, I'll come back and take him flying."

Tears misted Marlene's eyes. She pressed her hand to her chest. "He would love that."

Rye could tell that his spontaneous offer had surprised Brynn. Hell, it had surprised him. He was aware of her searching his expression, but he didn't acknowledge her. Instead, he bent down, picked up his flight bag from off the floor. "Now that it's getting light, I need to go check on the plane."

"How are you getting out there?" Marlene asked. "You don't have a car, do you?"

"I'll figure out something."

"You'll take mine."

He chuffed and gave his head a hard shake. "I can't do that."

"Of course you can."

He searched for a reason to refuse. "Didn't a deputy drive you here last night?"

"He offered. I declined."

"Because you thought you would need your car."

"I thought I might. But I don't. I've got friends and relatives begging to know what they can do for me. If I need a ride before you get back, I'll have my choice. Let me go get the key."

"Mrs. White—Marlene, I can't take your car."

"Please. Brady would loan you his pickup if he could."

She was looking at him with such appeal, he could tell that it was important to her that he accept. He bobbed his head and gave her a gruff okay. "Thanks. I won't keep it for long."

"For as long as you need it, it's yours to use. I'll go get the key." She turned to Brynn. "Will you still be here when I come down?"

"I'm afraid not." She motioned toward the entrance. Wilson was just pulling his car to a stop. "My ride is back. I'm glad I caught you, though. I didn't want to leave town without checking on your husband's condition. Please tell him I wish him a speedy recovery. But not to rush it," she added with mock sternness.

"I'll tell him."

Brynn reached into her coat pocket. "I wrote down my cell number. I would appreciate knowing how he's coming along." Marlene took the slip of paper from Brynn, then clasped her hand as before. "Thank you again for what you did for Brady last night."

"It was precious little. I regret not having had the pleasure of meeting him when he was conscious."

"Maybe you could come back with Rye."

He and Brynn gave each other a fleeting look, but neither made a commitment.

Sensing the awkwardness she had unwittingly created, Marlene gave Brynn a quick goodbye hug, then told Rye she would soon be back with her car key. The elevator door opened as soon as she pushed the button.

Then he and Brynn were alone in the lobby. Even the woman at the sliding window had deserted her post.

Brynn looked up at him, but not directly. Somewhere in the general vicinity of his chin. She said, "I guess this is goodbye."

"I guess." He looked out at the sheriff's unit. "Wilson's chauffeuring you all the way to Atlanta?"

"No. The Ford dealership here in town leases cars. Of course it's closed today, but, under the circumstances, Wilson thinks the owner might open long enough for me to get a car. But I hated to call him so early on a holiday. I'm waiting until nine o'clock."

He nodded to all that but remarked on none of it.

After the short lapse, she asked, "You're going out to the crash site?"

"Yeah." He looked toward the entrance again. The vapor from Wilson's tailpipe was adding ghosts to the fog. "Maybe this stuff will burn off soon, and I can get some pictures on my phone."

"They won't be pretty pictures."

"'Fraid not."

"I'm really sorry about the plane."

"Me, too." He repositioned the strap of his flight bag on his shoulder and tried his damnedest not to notice the strand of hair that kept slipping from behind her ear and curving against her cheek like a black satin question mark. "You'd better not keep Johnny Law waiting any longer."

She looked outside and smiled. "I think he's a little ticked for having to babysit me."

Rye noted the time. "Less than two hours till nine."

"He's offered to take me to breakfast while we wait. Maybe a hot meal will improve his mood." Coming back to Rye, she said, "Well..." and stuck out her right hand.

He looked down at it, hesitated, then took it. "I hope your cancer patient makes it."

With that, her eyes met his head-on. "Thank you. Very much. So do I."

He sensed there was hidden meaning in her words, but he couldn't just stand there gazing into her rain-colored eyes in search of it, so he gave her hand a cursory shake and released it as though it had stung his palm.

She backed away several steps, then turned around and headed for the door. However, she hadn't covered but a few yards before she stopped and turned back. "There is one question I've been wanting to ask you."

He rolled his shoulders in a motion of assent.

"You said, 'They did what they came to do.'"

This time he rolled his shoulders to indicate puzzlement. Since it was entirely faked, he added a furrowed brow to help convey perplexity.

"When we discovered Brady, you said, 'They did what they came to do.' You were referring to his attackers, correct?"

"I don't remember saying that," he lied. "But, yeah, I was referring to whoever did it."

"You used the plural because there were two sets of footprints."

"Yeah."

"So if this man who quarreled with Brady was the culprit, he must've brought along an accomplice."

"Looks like."

"Did you mention that to Deputy Rawlins?"

"Slipped my mind. And, anyway, he's the detective. He should've thought of it himself."

"Hmm." She nodded agreement. "At the time you said that, it sounded as though you had an inkling of who *they* might be."

"I didn't. Still don't." That was true.

"Or that you had an idea of what their motive was."

"No clue." Also true.

Her doubtful gaze held steady on him and, becoming impatient with it, he said, "I don't remember saying that, and I don't remember what I was thinking. I was talking off the top of my head. Rambling."

She gave a skeptical laugh. "You have certain character traits which become immediately obvious to anyone who meets you. Rambling isn't among them."

She continued looking at him as though trying to will him to say more. When he didn't, she turned away and went through the automatic doors. They closed behind her.

His gut felt hollowed out.

He was hungry, was all.

The elevator arrived. Marlene White alighted, dangling a key fob. "It's parked in the lot across the drive," she told him. "Second row. Blue Honda. If you press this button—"

She broke off when she realized that his attention wasn't on her or the fob, but on Brynn. She climbed into the passenger seat of Wilson's car. As they drove away, Marlene said, "Such a sweet young woman."

"Yeah." The taillights disappeared into the fog. He came back to Marlene. "I mean, I don't know her. But she seems okay."

"It's a miracle how well she turned out, considering her daddy."

"I heard mention of him. Wes?"

"Quite a character."

"He's well known by everybody in the sheriff's office. Is he a cop?"

Marlene White looked at him, stunned. "*Cop?* Goodness no. He's a convict."

# Chapter 10

*7:29 a.m.*

Brynn and Deputy Wilson were among the handful of diners in the only café in town that was open that morning. A temporary sign taped to the door had notified potential customers that breakfast would be served from seven until ten-thirty and then the café would close for Thanksgiving.

A younger man was slumped in one of the booths and appeared to be nursing a hangover. Brynn linked the loner at the counter to the semi that was parked on the shoulder of the highway. She overheard a man in another booth ask the waitress what the special Thanksgiving breakfast consisted of. She told him that a slice of apple pie was added to the Going Whole Hog menu item. Both he and his companion placed their orders for that.

Except for the waitress, Brynn was the only woman in the place, making her feel conspicuous, and even more so for being seated with a uniformed sheriff's deputy. She was aware of speculative glances cast their way. Even the young man with the hangover roused himself long enough to look them over.

She toyed with a stack of pancakes and watched Wilson de-molish three sunny-side-up eggs and a half-pound slab of smoked ham.

Their meal took all of twelve minutes off the clock.

As the deputy pushed his plate aside, Brynn said, "You don't have to wait with me. I don't want to keep you from any plans you have for the day."

"My ex has the kids. They've gone to her mother's. Actually, I'm relieved to be missing that."

She smiled across at him, because that's what he seemed to expect.

But he did look down at his wristwatch and add, "It probably wouldn't hurt if you called him before nine o'clock. He's a nice guy, and I feel sure he'll be willing to help you out. But I'm bet-ting he would just as soon get the business over and done with before the ball games start."

Brynn figured that it was Wilson who would just as soon have the business concluded before the kickoffs. "I would like to get underway sooner rather than later."

"So you've said. And Dr. Lambert stressed how time-sensitive those blood samples are."

He eased back and looked under the table to where she'd sat the box on the floor when they'd claimed the booth. "You think one of them will match good enough to be a donor?"

Unlike his partner, Rawlins, Wilson had pleasant features and a benign smile. His interest in the samples seemed sincere. Brynn experienced a twinge of guilt over being less than completely straightforward with him.

In all truthfulness, she said, "We're hoping for the best possi-ble outcome."

"Must be tough, being a doctor, having a patient you can't cure."

"Tougher than you can imagine."

"I guess it's like me having an unsolved case. It gnaws at you."

"That's a fitting analogy."

He nodded. "Well, I don't want you to be held up any longer. Why don't I call this guy for you right now and give him the skinny?"

"The request might be better received coming from a law officer. It would seem more official."

That must've stroked his ego. He smiled at her as he reached for his phone. "I'll ask him to meet us at the dealership at eight o'clock. How's that sound?"

"Perfect."

He made the call. By the time he disconnected a few minutes later, a plan was in place. "He can leave right now. He'll drive a car over here and pick you up, if you don't mind dropping him back at the car lot on your way out of town."

"Of course not. Thank you."

"You're welcome. Should take him fifteen, twenty minutes to get here. Then you'll be on your way. You should let Dr. Lambert know. Relieve his mind."

"Good idea." She pulled out her phone and sent Nate a brief text.

After Wilson settled the bill, Brynn draped her coat over her arm and reached beneath the table for the box. "I need to use the ladies' room, so I'm going to excuse myself. By the time I come out, the man should be here with the car. You don't need to hang around any longer."

He put up token resistance as he slid out of the booth, but she was insistent. At the door, they shook hands.

"Good luck with your patient, Dr. O'Neal. If I'm ever terminal, I hope my doctor is as dedicated as you."

"That's very kind of you to say."

He put on his hat, brushed the brim of it with his index finger, and left.

Brynn followed a sign with a red arrow and the word "TOILET" stenciled on it. It led her down a long, barren hallway that ended with a right-angle turn. The restroom was on her left. She locked the door behind her.

After using the commode and washing her hands, she did what repair she could to her dishevelment by applying a lip gloss she'd stuck in a coat pocket before leaving Atlanta. The improvement was slight, but it was the best she could do. She picked up the box, lifted her coat off the hook on the back of the door, and flipped up the lock.

From the other side, the door was thrust open, and Rye Mallett barged in. He reached behind him, shut the door, and locked it.

Astonishment sent Brynn stumbling backward several steps. She dropped her coat but recovered immediately, and shock became outrage. "What the hell are you doing?"

"I want to talk to you." He bore down on her until he had her backed up against the sink. "I want to talk to you about your father."

"My father?"

"Dear ol' dad. That *Brynn! My, how you've grown* scene had led me to believe you were well known because your old man was the sheriff or something. Turns out Wes O'Neal—"

"I know his name."

"—is a thief! By trade."

She took a series of short, shallow breaths. "Who told you?"

"Doesn't matter. Point is, he's a crook, in and out of county jail so many times, they considered putting a revolving door on his cell. You were a regular at the sheriff's office. Staff there played dolls with you while waiting on CPS to send someone for you. You used to cry when they tore you away from people like Myra. You—"

"All right," she snapped. "You've made your point."

"Aw, no. I'm just getting started."

Although she didn't think he could possibly get any closer to her, he crowded in. To keep from touching, she had to arch over the sink. "Get *back*." She pushed against his chest with her left hand. "I don't know what you think—"

"What I think is that you're following in Daddy's footsteps, upholding the family tradition." He thumped the lid of the metal box tucked under her right arm. "What's in the box?"

"You saw what was in it!"

"What I saw, what Rawlins and Wilson saw, was a dog-and-pony show performed by you and your partner in crime, the *self*-esteemed Dr. Lambert."

"I don't know what you're talking about."

"Hell you don't. I was watching you. When Lambert said, 'accommodate them,' you looked like you'd swallowed a bug. You were as surprised as the three of us when Rawlins raised the lid and all we saw were tubes of blood. If that's what they are."

"That's exactly what they are, and I wasn't at all surprised."

"Right, more like disbelieving, holding yourself together while Lambert dazzled us with bullshit."

"Everything he said was scientifically sound."

"Deliberately scientific. Intentionally over our heads. Meant to distract."

"You're delusional. How do you know what I was feeling, thinking? Are you a mind reader?"

"Lip reader."

"What?"

"Cockpits can be noisy. I learned to read a copilot's lips. Nine, four, three, two." He placed his hands on his hips, thrust his face to within inches of hers, and repeated the numbers in a taunting whisper. "Nine, four, three, two."

She braced her hands on the ledge of the sink behind her in order to keep her balance. "The lock."

"The lock. I read your lips as you rolled each number into place. Missed the last one. What is it?"

He'd read her lips? That was almost as unsettling as him

being only one digit short of knowing the combination to the padlock. His eyes were like magnets now, holding her in thrall.

But she looked away, turned her head aside, and tried to regain her equilibrium. "Would you give me some space, please?"

He eased away from her and took a half step back.

She took a few short breaths. "How did you bump your head?"

"What?"

"You've got a bump at your hairline." She reached up to touch it, but he yanked his head back.

"Banged it on impact. It's fine. Did you get a car?"

She was still dazed by his sudden reappearance and confounded as to how she was going to deal with his fresh knowledge of the box and its contents. Her thoughts were darting helter-skelter, overwhelming her with calamitous implications. She willed them to slow down and concentrate on what he had asked her. In stops and starts, she explained the arrangements that had been made.

"Wilson's not coming back?"

"No. He was as relieved to ditch me as I was to be ditched." Her mind was beginning to clear, and with clarity came questions. "How did you know we were here?"

"You mentioned that Wilson was taking you to breakfast, and the lady running the admissions desk at the ER told me this is the only place open today. I drove over in Marlene White's car, saw you through the window, parked, and waited to see what would happen. When Wilson left without you, and you didn't return to the table, I hurried around back. Found the delivery door unlocked."

"Very resourceful."

"Determined."

"Determined to chase me down? Why?"

"Why do you think? I want that number. I want to take another look, see what contraband I flew in here last night."

"It's not contraband. It's blood samples."

"Then what's the harm in giving me the number?"

"It's supposed to be kept airtight."

"Good argument, just the right amount of logic, but I don't believe you."

She glared at him and remained silent.

"Okay, have it your way," he said. "How long before the car man gets here?"

"Wilson estimated fifteen to twenty minutes, half of which have elapsed."

He glanced behind him at the locked door. "Not long then before you'll be missed," he said, musing aloud.

"Missed? I won't be missed at all, Mr. Mallett."

"From here on, why don't you call me Rye?"

"I'm happy to. Go to hell, *Rye*. But first get out of my way. I'm leaving. If you don't allow me to leave, I'll—"

She didn't even have to finish before he raised his hands in surrender, stepped aside, and tilted his head toward the door. "You want to go, go."

She looked toward the locked door, then back at him. "What's the hitch?"

"No hitch. Bye-bye. Been nice knowing you."

She stayed where she was. "Why the foreboding undertone?"

"Did it sound foreboding?"

"You know it did."

He shrugged. "It's just that if you leave with only a Ford dealer to protect you, who knows what they might do."

"They? Who?"

"The two guys in the corner booth. Both dressed in black suits. One tall, Hispanic, hard body, handsome devil. The other smaller, hyper, pointy nose, and ears like a fox. Did you notice them?"

"They ordered apple pie with their Whole Hog breakfast. What have they got to do with me?"

"You tell me, Dr. O'Neal."

"I've never seen them before in my life."

"No? Well, I have. Know when? As I was leaving the sheriff's office. Know where? They were sitting in a black, late-model Mercedes, parked across the street and almost out of sight behind a hardware store, like they were keeping an eye on the place, like they were waiting for somebody besides me to come out."

His eyes scaled down from her face to the toes of her boots and up again. "As nice a prize as you would make, I don't think they're after your sweet self, so much as that box you're welded to. More to the point, they're after what's in it."

Of their own volition, her lips parted with alarm.

"Riiiight," he said. "That weird pair were waiting for *you*, and *you* are going to tell me why, and *you* are going to tell me *now*."

She raised her chin in defiance. "Or what?"


*8:32 a.m.*


Rye gave the small of Brynn's back a nudge to get her across the threshold, followed her into the room, and closed the door with a solid thunk. He pressed the button on the doorknob and slid the chain lock into place. The curtains were drawn, but there was an inch-wide separation in the middle of the window. He overlapped the edges to close it.

The decor was standard mountain-cabin-in-the-woods à la the sixties. The artwork on the knotty pine–paneled walls was reminiscent of the bear in Brady White's office, the bedspread striped in earth tones, the lampshades made of burlap. In the bathroom, everything was tan and basic motel issue.

While he conducted his brief inspection of the layout, Brynn didn't move from the spot where she'd taken root just inside the door. She said, "After a drive long enough to make me car sick—"

"Mountain roads. It's not my fault they're winding."

"But I thought you were going to the airplane."

"I thought so, too. Change of plan. Besides, it's still too foggy to take pictures."

"What are we doing here?"

He set his flight bag on the seat of a chair, then removed his bomber jacket and tossed it onto the bed. It landed with the lining side up. Brynn frowned with distaste.

"Don't be so hard on her," he said. "She's kept me warm many a night." He waited a beat, then added, "But since you're here . . ." He left the suggestion hanging.

"Dream on. I'm not a pinup girl."

His gaze lowered to her mouth, and then to her breasts, and when it reconnected with hers, he said, "You'd do."

Suddenly they were no longer sparring. Those two words, and the raspiness with which he'd spoken them, had caused a seismic mood shift. Worse, both of them were aware of it.

To set things right again, he turned away from her and forced a light laugh. "Relax, Dr. O'Neal. I don't have designs like that on you."

"Answer my question."

"I forgot what it was." He sat down on the bed, pulled off one boot and let it drop, then the other.

"What are we doing here?"

"Oh, that. I'm waiting you out."

"Waiting me out?"

"Until you give me the last number of the combination."

"You don't need it. You've seen inside." She hefted the box by the handle.

He got up, wrested it from her, and set it on top of the dresser. "When I asked the first time what was in it, why didn't you just say, 'It's four vitally important and time-sensitive blood samples that must be kept airtight'?"

He shook his head. "Instead, you acted squirrely. That's Rawlins's word, and, as bad as I hate to agree with him, it's a perfect description. From the time you came sneaking out of the woods toward the plane, you've been disingenuous."

"That's a step up from dodgy and squirrely."

He fixed a stare on her. "I'm not playing, Brynn. My reputation is on the line and so is Dash's. Trust me on this, I'm not screwing around."

"Neither am I."

"Fair enough." He pointed to the box. "Something's inside the lining. Just like there's a world map on the other side of that beauty." He nodded down at his jacket. "If there's nothing else in there, why didn't you scream bloody murder when I hustled you out of that café?"

She opened her mouth, but nothing came out before she quickly closed it.

"See, that's what I thought," he said. "You wanted to avoid those two guys because they worry you. You're up to something, and I want to know what it is. I wish you'd tell me now and save us both time and hassle. And money. I'm out forty-five bucks for these charming accommodations. I don't want to be here any more than you do."

"Nobody asked you to poke your nose in."

"No, I wasn't asked. I was *obligated*."

"How so?"

"Whatever is in your precious box cost Dash an airplane and could have cost Brady White his life. So you had just as well take off your coat and get comfortable, because you're not leaving this room until I know what's so goddamn valuable."

"My coat stays on."

He made a suit-yourself gesture, then looked down at the box. "Who'd you steal it from?"

"I didn't."

"Says the career thief's daughter. Is your old man in on it?"

"I haven't seen him in years."

"Marlene White heard he'd made parole."

"I heard that, too."

"You haven't seen him since his release?"

"No." He looked at her with skepticism. She repeated her no with emphasis and added, "He's got nothing to do with this."

"What is *this*? What's the contraband? An explosive devise of some kind? It's set to blow at a given time, and you don't want to be around when it does. Is that why you're in such a big hairy hurry to hand it off?"

"Are you insane?"

"Are *you?*"

"No."

"What about your cohort Dr. Lambert?"

"He's a genius."

"A genius who adheres to some radical credo—"

"No!"

"You're right. A bomb doesn't sound like him. Too militant. Too ballsy. Not scientific enough." He stroked his chin as though considering. "You two are going to poison Atlanta's water supply? Contaminate the CDC with a smart virus? Inject one into the hot dogs at Turner Field?"

She bent her head down and rubbed the space between her eyebrows.

"Am I warm?" he asked.

"Nowhere near."

"Then open the box and show me what's under the foam lining."

"There's nothing under there."

"Then prove it. Let me see."

"No."

"Brynn—"

"No!"

He held her stare while seconds ticked off, then he squared up the box with the edge of the dresser and dialed in the four numbers he knew. She placed her hand on his wrist. "Wait. Don't.

Please. The contents could be compromised. I swear that's the truth."

"Okay. I'll believe that much. But we're not talking about blood samples, are we?"

"They did come from possible donors."

"I'll even buy that. Keep going."

She looked at him with appeal. "Can't you be satisfied with knowing that it's vital I get this to Atlanta with all due haste?"

"Tell me why it's vital."

"I can't."

"Because you're involved in something illegal."

She didn't say anything.

"Silence means yes."

She came back with asperity. "Silence means it's impossible to give you a simple yes or no. But I swear that it's not illegal in the sense you mean."

"Then tell me in what sense it's illegal."

"I can't!"

"Why?"

"Because it's delicate and complicated, and I don't trust you."

She could have answered him in any number of ways that wouldn't have surprised him, but this did, probably because it sounded truthful and unmitigated. "How come?"

"I don't even know you."

That sparked a reaction from him as automatic as an alarm from a cockpit instrument. "Well, we can fix that."

He cupped the back of her head in his palm and drew her up to meet his mouth.

# Chapter 11

*8:44 a.m.*

The instant Rye slid his tongue between her lips, he acknowledged that he'd been waiting for any excuse to kiss her.

He heard a little catch in her breath, felt a small puff of it against his lips. Both were sexy as hell and encouraging. He angled his head. The deeper he explored, the better she tasted, the more carnally his intent was channeled. Somehow he'd known her mouth was made for this.

Reaching inside her coat, he curved his arm around her waist and pulled her to him. He felt the giving fullness of her breasts when matched to his chest. A slight shift of his left thigh, and the alignment of their bodies below their waists improved. God, did it ever.

Every sexual impulse he had kicked into overdrive, making him so damn hard, and, for a few mind-blowing seconds, he felt a corresponding softening, an invitational tilt, a momentary fitting of hardness into hollow.

Then she tensed up and broke the kiss, lowering her head, catching a few strands of her hair in his scruff.

He released her gradually. When his arms fell away, she

stepped around him, careful not to touch him, careful not even to brush against his clothing. As she moved past, he pivoted in order to keep his eyes on her.

She stopped a short distance away and raised her hand to her mouth. Her back was to him, so he had no way of knowing if she was covering her mouth in mortification, testing her lips for moisture, dabbing at a whisker burn, or wiping away the taste of him.

"You can't seduce the combination out of me."

That remark pissed him off. But when she turned around to face him, he had a smirk already in place. "Wasn't trying to. It's just that you know me now. Better, at least. Pretty damn good, in fact."

She gave him a murderous look, which only caused him to grin.

"Surely you can trust me enough to tell me about the two guys trailing you."

"I don't know anything about them." She began to roam the room, seemingly without any purpose except to evade his questions.

"No idea who sent them?"

"You're assuming they were sent, that they weren't just two men having breakfast."

"I would guess that they're undercover FBI."

She stopped her aimless roaming and looked at him.

"Narcs maybe?"

She turned away and resumed the agitated prowling.

"The big guy might pass for an agent, except that feds don't drive Mercedes. The little guy, no way. He's a punk."

She was fiddling with the card on the nightstand that listed TV channels. "How do you know what he is?"

"I recognize the type. They're all over the world. Different languages, different colors, religions, causes. But they're always looking for a fight, and they thrive on bloodshed." He gave her a meaningful look. "Which is why I think you're in over your head, Brynn, and you don't even realize it."

She laid the card back on the nightstand. "Why do you care?"

He placed his hand over his heart. "Because I'm such a nice guy."

For that he got another dirty look. "Why are you sticking around?" she asked. "Why aren't you long gone?"

"I wish I was."

"So?"

"Think of the shoe prints, Brynn. One set large, one small. I'm damn near certain those two men in the café were Brady's assailants." He walked toward her, wanting to gauge her reaction to what was coming. "I also think it was them who zapped me with a laser just as I was about to land."

She recoiled. Her lips parted. He didn't believe she could have faked how astounded she appeared. "A *laser*?"

"Not the kind you buy to bamboozle your neighbor or drive your cat crazy. High grade. Industrial strength. Powerful enough to penetrate that fog and damn near my skull."

"I've heard of that happening to pilots. A lot, lately."

"Well, it happened to me last night. I would have made that landing if I hadn't been blinded seconds before touching down."

"You could have been killed."

"That's crossed my mind a few dozen times."

"Did you tell Rawlins this?"

"No, and I have my reasons."

"Why didn't you tell me last night?"

"Because I didn't know you, either." He let that reverberate for a few seconds before continuing. "For all I knew, you were the culprit. The way you crept up on the plane made me suspicious. But once I saw how protective you were of that box, it didn't make sense. Why would you want to sabotage the airplane carrying the treasure chest?"

"I see. You don't think I'm an attempted murderer, but only because it doesn't make sense."

"Oh, did that hurt your feelings?" He scoffed. "Don't cop that self-righteous attitude with me, Brynn. I'm not the one keeping secrets." He gave her a hard look. "I don't really think you're a terrorist bent on killing a lot of people, but I do think you're in possession of something that belongs to somebody else. Or at least to somebody who claims rights to it.

"Diamonds, the key to a safe deposit box, a human finger bone excavated on Mars. The booty doesn't matter to me. It's yours to keep. Split it with your daddy. I don't care, except for the role I unknowingly played in transporting it. If it's illegal, I could do jail time and lose my pilot's license."

"If you're so worried about it, then take me back to town, to the Ford dealer, and let me leave."

"No. That's not the only reason I'm staying. I want payback for the damage done to Dash's plane, and the attack on an innocent man."

"That's the obligation you feel."

"Yeah, that's the obligation I feel."

"Your worst nightmare."

His focus sharpened on her.

Softly, she said, "Involvement."

He didn't realize she'd heard him say that or that she would have tucked it away in her memory bank to take out and air now. All the emotions that invoked coalesced into anger.

"I'm tired of this dance." He went over to the dresser. The first four dials on the padlock were as he'd left them minutes earlier. Only the last one remained. It was on the four. That didn't unlock it. He rolled it to the numeral one. That was no good, either. "I've got a maximum of eight more tries."

He went through them, taunting her as he counted them down, but her expression remained impassive. After the nine failed, she said, "You've only got one more chance, and it's futile to try it."

"We'll see."

He dialed the zero. The lock stayed locked. Cursing, he turned to her.

"Told you."

He fumed in silence, then said, "Fine. Play your game, but you'll do it without your toy."

He picked up the box and clamped it against him with his arm. "Until I know what's in it, and have my reckoning with the people who tried to crash me, it stays with me."

"Put it down."

"Nope." With his free hand, he grabbed his flight bag and headed for the bathroom.

"What are you doing?"

"I'm going to shower and then get some sleep."

"*Sleep?*" Brynn placed herself in his path. "We don't have time for that. If you don't believe anything else, believe me when I say that it's imperative I get that box to its destination."

"Which is?"

He gave her a ten count, and when she didn't reply, he bumped her aside with his hip, continued on into the bathroom, and slammed the door behind him.

*9:01 a.m.*

"We lost her."

Goliad's update wasn't what Delores and Richard Hunt had expected to hear, and the news certainly didn't go over well with either.

Following their bodyguard's last call, Richard had demanded to know everything Delores had been withholding from him about the situation in Howardville. She had laid out the facts the way a blackjack dealer dealt cards, methodically, one at a time. After each, Richard had calculated his odds of winning the hand or losing huge.

He'd been dismayed over how badly the job had been botched, and angry at Delores for glossing over the worst of it. "All I got was a weather report!" he'd shouted.

Her only defense had been that she'd wanted to prevent him from worrying.

"I appreciate that consideration," he'd told her in an effort to suppress the full ferocity of his anger. "By the same token, I resent being kept in the dark. Don't do it again. Ever."

He had accepted her tearful apology along with her promise not to hold back anything from now on, no matter how dire circumstances became. She'd sealed her promise with a kiss and reminded him that the situation wasn't all that bleak.

No one knew of his connection to any of last night's events. No one knew of his illness. The media had believed the statement his office had released about their plans for the holiday: They were spending a quiet Thanksgiving alone at their beloved estate in Georgia. They welcomed a respite from the Washington social scene. They valued their time together at home. Blah blah blah.

With confidence, she had said, "We encountered some speed bumps, but they're behind us now. I have Nate's assurance that all is well."

Her confidence had been premature.

Dr. Brynn O'Neal's whereabouts were unknown. Goliad and his nitwit partner had lost track of her.

Propped up in bed with pillows behind his back, Delores at his side, Richard had assumed the facial expression that opposition senators hated to see at the podium during a debate.

There was no gentleness in it, no suggestion that he might reconsider his position and compromise. His visage was as indomitable as the faces carved into Rushmore. It could intimidate even Delores.

She covered his hand with hers, but he shook off the comforting gesture and barked, "What happened, Goliad?"

Talking to them through the speakerphone, he gave them bullet points, as was Richard's preference when receiving bad news. He wanted to know the worst aspects of a crisis first. The fine print could be added later.

"She left the sheriff's department with the same deputy she'd ridden with before. He dropped her at the hospital."

"The hospital?"

"The ER, sir. My guess is that she went to see about White, the airfield guy. The deputy returned for her a few minutes later. They went to a café. Timmy and me went in, sat fairly close, but not so close that they'd notice. They talked a little, ate breakfast."

"Talked about what?"

"We weren't close enough to hear. But they were smiling, friendly."

He described how the two had parted company. "She went down the hall to the restroom. She didn't return in a timely fashion. I went to check. Restroom door was open, nobody in there. An exit opened into an alley. I ran to both ends of it. She was nowhere in sight.

"When I rejoined Timmy in the dining room, there was a man asking the waitress had she seen the doctor, said that he was to meet her there with a car. The waitress pointed him toward the back. He was out of sight less than a minute, returned looking steamed. He left in the car he came in."

"Did you go in search of her?" Delores asked.

"Yes, ma'am. Wasted no time. There's not much to downtown. We covered every bit of it. Twice. All the businesses are closed. No place for her to go. She was just...gone."

"How could she have disappeared, in that short span of time, on foot?"

"I can't explain it, sir."

No one said anything for a time, then Richard said, "Well? That's it? 'We lost her.'"

"I had an idea," Goliad said.

"Praise be," Delores said.

Goliad continued. "The last place she was before going to the café was the ER. We went back to check it out. I left Timmy in the car and went inside. Nobody was there except a woman with a bleeding finger wrapped in a dish towel, and the admitting nurse. I told her I was looking for Dr. O'Neal and described her. She said she'd seen her talking to White's wife. And the pilot."

Delores and Richard looked at each other. She raised a brow. "That sounds cozy."

"That's what I thought," Goliad said. "So I chatted up this lady some more. Turns out Mrs. White lent the pilot her car so he could drive out to the crash site."

"Do you think he and Dr. O'Neal rendezvoused outside the café?"

"Didn't see him. This might be nothing."

"But it *could* be something," Delores insisted.

"Could be. The pilot left the sheriff's office on foot, but he's got wheels now. The doctor doesn't. Only thing is, all we have to go on is that the car he borrowed is 'blue.'"

"What's the airfield guy's first name?" Delores reached for a pad and paper.

"Brady. Brady White."

She wrote it down. "I'll get people checking on cars registered to that name. What county?"

Goliad told her.

"It shouldn't take long," Delores said. "I'll text you the license plate as soon as I have it."

"We'll start by going to the crash site," Goliad said. "But, like I said, this might be nothing."

Richard warned, "I don't want to hear any more *buts*, Goliad. Or any other kind of excuse."

"No, sir."

"And keep a leash on that Timmy. What the fuck was he doing with a laser?"

"He won't be using it again, sir. A creek runs through town. The laser's at the bottom of it."

"Call us with better news next time." Delores disconnected, then scooted off the bed, taking the phone with her. "We need that license plate number ASAP. I'll rouse someone on staff, make up a reason that'll convey urgency, but not panic." She was already rapidly punching in a phone number.

Despite the gravity of the situation, Richard chuckled. "I love to see a take-charge woman in action."

She blew him a kiss. "You ain't seen nothing yet." Then, into the phone, "This is Mrs. Hunt. The senator requires some information. Immediately."

She gave the order with the confidence of someone who knew it would be acted on without delay. She disconnected and instantly began tapping in another number.

"I hope you're calling Nate Lambert," Richard said.

"He was awfully cavalier an hour ago," Delores said. "I have some hard questions for him. Starting with if he knows where the hell his colleague is."

# Chapter 12

———◦◦———

*9:39 a.m.*

Brynn had survived her childhood, which in itself was a miracle. Even more miraculous was that she hadn't been too badly scarred by it. While other people encountered stumbling blocks in the course of their lives, her impediments had been comparable to mountain ranges.

The first had been the loss of her mother, who succumbed to pancreatic cancer when Brynn was only five years old. Her upbringing then had fallen to her father.

Anyone who had ever met Wes O'Neal liked him. He was described as a "real character," radiating bonhomie and always ready with a joke. He was good-natured, gregarious, and, in an odd twist, generous. Odd, because he also had a larcenous streak.

During his repeated incarcerations, Brynn was placed in foster homes. Sympathetic teachers and townsfolk also took her under their wings, making certain she had Christmas and birthday gifts, providing clothing when needed, seeing to it that she didn't miss out on extracurricular activities, simulating as normal a life as possible.

But for all the many kindnesses they extended her, they feared that her personality would be warped. Who could possibly withstand that level of instability without suffering permanent psychological damage? Wes O'Neal's girl wasn't expected to amount to much.

Brynn had resolved early on that she would.

The day after graduating high school, she'd left Howardville. Wes had been serving three-to-five in state prison, so he hadn't been there to see her off. His absence was noted by her but not bemoaned. Long before then, she had accepted that in order to get anywhere, she must go it alone.

She hadn't enjoyed the typical college experience. From freshman year through med school, she'd been awarded most of the various scholarships and grants for which she had applied, but she'd had to supplement them with part-time jobs. Between studies and work, there hadn't been much time for a social life.

Occasionally, she would fall into a romantic relationship, but none of the men had meant as much to her as her quest for success. Only one had broken her heart with his repeated infidelities, but one day she came to the realization that he wasn't worth the anger and anguish she'd spent on him. She'd excised him without regret.

All the sacrifices had paid off. She was now affiliated with a hospital that was renowned for its research. She was financially secure and self-sufficient in every area of her life. She'd earned the respect of her colleagues. Her patients trusted and relied on her.

Most important, Brynn O'Neal relied on no one.

But as Rye Mallett shut the bathroom door in her face, she acknowledged that she was out of her element and at a total loss as to what she should do next.

Having squeaked past the authorities, she wasn't going to draw them back in by reporting herself stranded with—she wouldn't go so far as to say kidnapped by—Rye Mallett. Bringing the attention of law officers to herself was the last thing she wanted, and she reasoned that Rye had counted on that reluctance.

And the two men in the café? Had they been responsible for the events of last night, as Rye suspected? If so, and if it was the box they were after, she could be in danger from them.

If she were physically able to wrangle the box from Rye, or if she demanded he give it back, and he did so without contest, what would she do then? Strike out on foot? She'd seen Rye slip Marlene's key fob into the front pocket of his jeans, so there was no retrieving it, and, even if she could, she wouldn't steal the lady's car.

It seemed that she was stuck. But she couldn't remain in this limbo state. She had to come up with a solution, and fast. At Deputy Wilson's suggestion, she had texted Nate from the café, but she'd been ambiguous about her departure time. She'd told him "soonish." He hadn't texted a reply, but that wasn't unusual. He often couldn't be bothered.

Even so, he and the Hunts would expect her to be halfway to Atlanta by now.

Whatever fallout she faced when she got there, she had to get there, and her options had dwindled down to one.

Rye came out of the bathroom.

He was fully dressed except for his boots. He'd swapped his wrinkled shirt for another that was just as wrinkled, but smelled of fresh laundry. It was buttoned only halfway up. His hair appeared to have been roughly towel-dried and left at that. But he had trimmed his scruff. Through the door, she'd heard the whirr of an electric razor.

"I left you a towel," he said as he slid his leather bag off his shoulder and returned it to the chair. He then moved to the opposite side of the bed from where she sat and flung back the bedspread. He snapped off the lamp on the nightstand and lay down on his side, facing away from her, hugging the black box against his chest like a teddy bear.

As though standing on the end of a high diving platform and about to take a plunge into icy waters far below, she drew a deep breath and let it out slowly. "GX-42."

He rolled onto his back and turned his head toward her. "What?"

"That's the formula name the pharmacologist gave the drug he's been developing."

"Pharmacologist."

"I'm not trying to take lives, Rye. I'm trying to save them. Or at least extend them."

He looked deeply into her eyes as though searching for duplicity.

"You don't believe me."

"I don't know yet," he said. "Why all the secrecy?"

"GX-42 is an experimental drug that hasn't yet been FDA-approved for clinical trials."

"You mean on people."

"Yes. How much do you know about drug development?"

"Give me the version for dummies."

"By the time a new drug is marketed, it's been put through rigorous and endless testing. It must pass through three stages. That doesn't sound like many, but each stage of testing stretches out for months, more often years."

"Okay."

"That applies to your everyday big money-makers with a large market, like a new beta blocker or anti-inflammatory. It's an even longer process for an orphan drug."

"What's that?"

"A drug being developed to treat a rare disorder. It would benefit a comparably small number of people."

"So those drugs get low priority."

"Not as low as they got before the Orphan Drug Act was passed several years ago. But research funding relies almost solely on grants. GX-42 is an orphan drug. But this company has devoted personnel, money, and years to developing it. It's passed the first two stages. Clinical trials are the final. GX-42 has been submitted, but as yet hasn't been approved."

"And your patient can't wait around for it to get the green light. There's nothing you can do to hurry the agency along?"

"There is what's called expanded access. Compassionate use. It's an exemption made for a patient when all other treatment options have been exhausted."

"Last-ditch effort."

"Yes. The FDA is open to granting these exemptions, but certain criteria must be met. The requirements are stringent. The request must be filed by a physician for a particular patient. Nate and I have applied for one. The review board is still considering our application."

Rye assimilated all that. "So, the box. You had the drug smuggled in from another country where it's already in use?"

She had no reason whatsoever to trust this man. If what he'd told her was true, he lived the life of a vagabond. He was rude and came across as being self-interested, indifferent to anyone's welfare except his own.

Yet he felt obligated to his friend Dash for the loss of his airplane, and to Brady White. He'd intervened when the aviation memorabilia was about to be dusted with black powder. Marlene White had seen some honor in him, or she wouldn't have trusted him with her car.

What Brynn had to tell him was a thousand times more consequential than the loan of a car, but she was convinced that he wasn't going to end this standoff until she enlightened him, and she had little time to spare.

"No," she said. "There's a similar drug being tested on a small group of patients in Europe. GX-42's capabilities exceed that one." She looked across at the box. "Last night, a single dose was smuggled out of the lab."

"Something Corp. I saw the name on the air bill."

She nodded. "Researchers there have seen amazing results in test animals. They trust the drug's safety and effectiveness. Nate and I trust them."

"You believe it will work."

"I believe it's worth trying on patients who have no other hope, and who are being denied even that hope because of a rubber stamp."

"These patients have nothing to lose."

"Except their lives."

"What about negative side effects? Could it make the patient worse off, not better?"

"That's one of the beauties of it. During the past year of testing, the lab animals that died did so of the cancer, but didn't suffer any harmful effects of the drug."

"How's it given?"

"An IV infusion."

"Okay. Just so I'm clear. You and Lambert conspired with a pharmacologist at this drug-manufacturing outfit to make up a batch and send it to you, so you could give it to a patient who has blood cancer."

"With anomalies that make this malignancy particularly rare."

"Did money change hands?"

She lowered her gaze. "How very perceptive of you."

"Not really. Everything is about money. Let me guess, Lambert is willing to spend some coin to buy himself a Nobel Prize."

She shook her head. "The patient is spending the coin."

"Ah. I remember Lambert saying the patient was high-profile."

"Powerful. Wealthy. A household name to many."

"Give me a hint."

"No."

"Male or female?"

"No."

"You can trust me, Brynn."

"I've trusted you enough to confess to something that could land me in prison."

"Maybe they'll put you in a cell near your old man."

She didn't return his teasing grin.

"Sorry," he said, looking it. "Bad joke."

"Doesn't matter."

He stared thoughtfully into her eyes and said in a soft voice, "I think it does."

That also was perceptive of him. Too perceptive for comfort. She struck back with impatience. "What matters most is *time*."

"The patient is that critical?"

"No. Yes. But that's not the reason for the haste. Once the compound is mixed, it has a short shelf life of forty-eight hours. That's been one of the more practical reasons its approval has been withheld."

"But also why it had to be flown in last night."

"Exactly. And why I must return with it today. Now. But instead of speeding back…" She spread her arms in a gesture that encompassed the room and the situation.

"Who are the two heavies, Brynn?"

"I have no idea."

"Come on."

"I swear!"

"Well, I would swear that they were also at the airfield last night to meet the plane."

"Why would they attack Brady?"

"So he wouldn't call in a 911 when I crashed. They needed time to intercept you."

"You're guessing."

"You think I'm wrong?"

"Not exactly *wrong*. I just don't know that you're right. In my work, I have to deal in absolutes."

"In my work, too. But don't tell me that you never go with

your gut when it comes to a diagnosis." He assessed her expression and said, "Thought so. My gut's telling me that Jekyll and Hyde's plan was to waylay you. They flubbed it, so they've been following you, waiting for the next opportunity. But you were surrounded by sheriff's deputies up until the time I moved in."

His theory was sheer speculation, but feasible. "But if they were after the GX-42, why would they have shone that laser at you and risked your crashing?"

"I can't figure that, either. But at best, their intentions were unfriendly. At worst, I was considered disposable and so was Brady White. Now, if I were you, I'd take that as a bad sign as to my own future."

She pulled her lower lip through her teeth but stopped when she realized he was watching her do it.

He said, "You're scared, Brynn. You were scared before I outlined why you should be. You've been scared ever since you came creeping out of the fog toward my plane. Why?"

"Oh, I don't know. Let's see. Could it be because my misconduct could cost me my license to practice medicine? If the patient has a negative reaction to the experimental drug and dies as a result, I'll have committed murder. Don't you think that's enough to make one scared?"

"I don't know. I don't get scared."

He didn't say it in jest. He was dead earnest. But under her intent scrutiny, he shook off whatever it was that had turned his expression so serious and chinned toward the bathroom. "The water's hot. I used the bar soap, but there's some flowery smelling gel."

"I'm not going to shower."

"Afraid to get nekkid? I already told you, your virtue's safe with me."

"It's safe with me, too, Mr. Mallett. My concern is time." She tapped the face of her watch.

"You've laid a lot on me, including the fact that I flew an illegal drug across state lines. I could enter a plea of ignorance, and maybe they'd let me off, but it could still put Dash out of business and cost me my pilot's license."

She hesitated, then said quietly. "You could avoid those risks by turning me in."

He studied her as though considering it, then grumbled, "I don't want the hassle. Another go-round with Rawlins? No thanks. I'm already ensnared more than I want to be."

"You wish I hadn't told you, don't you?"

He didn't reply to that, but said crossly, "I deserve at least a few minutes to ruminate, don't you think? While I'm at it, you had just as well avail yourself of soap and water."

She had to admit that a hot shower was an appealing prospect. She looked with longing toward the open bathroom door, then stood up and shrugged off her coat. She laid it at the foot of the bed and walked toward the bathroom. Over her shoulder, she said, "I've probably burned my bridges with the car dealer. While you're ruminating, try to devise a way for me to get back to Atlanta."

He may have declared her virtue safe, but she locked the bathroom door anyway.

The water was hot. She used the shower gel, which didn't smell all that flowery. When she rinsed her hair of shampoo, she was chagrined to see twigs and dead leaves in the water swirling toward the drain, leftover debris from when Rye had kept her pinned to the forest floor.

Best not to think about those few minutes and the pressure of his thighs against hers. Or of the light brown chest hair she'd glimpsed, compliments of his open shirt. Or speculate on the yummy trail that was beneath those few done-up buttons. Or remember the erotic heat that had blossomed in her center when he so perfectly paired their bodies during that kiss. She had let it continue for far too long. And for not nearly long enough.

He wasn't a pretty boy, not dashingly handsome. But there was an essence of danger about him, a latent volatility, a raw sexuality to which women inevitably responded, unwisely and ultimately with remorse. He was the type of man who wouldn't remain romantically attached for longer than twenty minutes at a time. But those twenty minutes—

Brynn yanked her thoughts away from him. From that. She couldn't let anything distract her from getting back to Atlanta with the vial of GX-42 in time.

When she emerged from the bathroom, clean but wearing the same clothes, Rye was still lying on his back on the bed, staring at the ceiling in deep thought. His right arm rested atop the black box. Without prompting, he said, "I told Dash I would try to get to Atlanta later today."

"How are you going to get there?"

He turned his head on the pillow in order to look at her. "It's possible that we could persuade Marlene to let us take her car. You could get your juice to your patient. I could fly anywhere in the world from Atlanta."

"What about the airplane here?"

"It's still too foggy to take pictures today, and the plane can't go anywhere until an insurance adjuster sees it. Dash is handling that."

She sat down on the edge of the bed. "How would we get Marlene's car back to her?"

He gave a soft laugh. "You're worried about the logistics of returning a car when you're smuggling a bootleg drug?"

She gave him an abashed smile, stood up, and reached for her coat. "It's a good suggestion. We'll probably find her at Brady's bedside."

"We probably will. When we get there."

The add-on arrested her in motion. She noticed that he didn't look like he was going anywhere any time soon. His shirt was still buttoned only halfway, his boots lay on the floor, his bomber jacket was draped over the back of the chair where his flight bag occupied the seat.

He said, "I can't fly until I get some sleep."

"You can't go to sleep now."

"I'm practically there already. I've been up for"—he checked his wristwatch—"going on thirty hours."

"That's not my problem."

"It is if you want my help getting back to Atlanta. And forgive me for saying so, but you don't look all that perky yourself. Lie down. We'll sleep—"

"I don't require your help, you know. I can manage this alone."

"Great. Glad to hear it. Good luck. Shut the door gently on your way out." He rolled onto his side and tucked the box against him.

"Give me the box."

"The box stays with me," he mumbled, adjusting his head more comfortably on the pillow.

"It's not yours!"

In a sudden move, he left the box where it was, rolled to his opposite side, came up onto his knees on the edge of the bed, and took her by the shoulders where she stood. "It's not yours, either, is it?"

She refused to answer.

"How do I know? Two things. You haven't explained the men tracking you."

"How many times do I have to tell you? I don't know who they are, what they want, and it's probably a mere coincidence that you saw them parked across from the sheriff's department."

"Better odds of winning the Powerball. But, for argument's sake, let's say it's a mere coincidence. Reason number two, why haven't you called Dr. Lambert to report this latest snag? Why haven't you asked for *his* help returning to Atlanta?"

She expelled a huff. "Because I didn't want to alarm him,

much less the critically ill patient, by telling them that I'd been further delayed. Besides that, I haven't had cell service since you whisked me out of that café."

He glanced beyond her shoulder. "There's a telephone on the bedside table."

"With a lock on it! I'd hate for you to be out more than your forty-five bucks."

She struggled against his hold. He let go of her, but his incisive gaze didn't. She stared back, refusing to be the first to look away.

Abruptly he asked, "Who thought of the blood sample ruse?"

"Nate. Just in case the box were opened for any reason. But I wasn't sure the pharmacologist had done it correctly."

"I was right, then. You were nervous when Rawlins opened the box."

"Very. The drug is packed inside the foam lining, as you guessed."

He thought on that. "What's the deadline before the stuff goes bad?"

"The vial was capped at nine last night. It will take an hour to infuse. Therefore the drip needs to be started no later than eight o'clock tomorrow night."

"*Tomorrow* night? Then what's the rush? You've got plenty of time."

"Eight o'clock tomorrow is the absolute deadline. I, we, want to make sure it makes it there with time to spare. We want everyone to be relaxed, not stressed. Anxiety wouldn't be good for the patient."

"Or for you either, I think."

She didn't speak to that.

He looked at her for a moment longer, then said, "I never sleep for very long at a stretch. I'll set an alarm for five hours." He began setting his watch.

"Three hours," she said.

"Four."

He fiddled with his watch, then held his wrist out to where she could read the time he'd set. "See? I didn't cheat you a single minute." He lay down, turned onto his side facing out, and cradled the box.

"You're a bastard," she said.

"I think I like freight dog better."

After that, she heard nothing but deep breathing. She leaned forward and across the bed so she could see his face. He'd already fallen asleep.

*10:07 a.m.*

Rye was playing possum. He wasn't about to fall asleep until Brynn did.

But she was restless and frustrated. She paced the length of the bed several times. She went over to the window and parted the curtains just wide enough to peek through the crack, then impatiently overlapped them again after cursing the persistent fog.

She returned to the bed and sat down on the other side of it. Sighing with resignation, she removed her boots, then lay down and pulled the bedspread up over her. She didn't move again.

He knew the instant she fell asleep because the cadence of her breathing changed, and he found himself charting its lulling tempo. He was tempted to turn and check out the rise and fall of her chest but didn't. He recalled how good her breasts had felt against his chest and knew they'd feel even better in his hands.

And he had to keep his hands off her.

His hands he had control of. His head was another matter. He clearly remembered how well their bodies had conformed to each other at the notch of her thighs. And that wet, seductive kiss. Her mouth.

He squeezed his eyes shut against the images that flickered

through his mind like a silent movie. A silent X-rated movie. His cock swelled. But he willed it down. Because, for all her appeal, getting tangled up with Brynn O'Neal would be a bad idea.

More likely than not, she was a thief. He knew for certain that she was a liar.

While she'd been showering, he'd called the FAA office in Atlanta. He'd reported a no-casualty crash and promised to send a full report as soon as the fog cleared and he could get photos. The agent he spoke to was fine with that. No one wanted to work over the holiday weekend. All together the conversation had lasted three minutes.

The cell phone service had been perfect.

# Chapter 13

———◈———

*1:28 p.m.*

Brynn, wake up."

"Hmm?"

Her shoulder was shaken. "Wake up."

Feeling as though she were being roused from a coma, she opened her eyes and blinked Rye into focus. "It's already been four hours?"

"No, but we have company."

He left her, skirted the foot of the bed, and went over to the window, where he peered through the split in the curtains. "I heard their car. They're just pulling up."

"Who?"

"Your mere coincidence duo."

That brought her wide awake. She kicked back the bedspread, came off the bed, and watched in alarm as Rye took his pistol from his flight bag. "What are you doing with that?"

"If we're lucky, nothing." He slid it into his back jeans pocket and covered it with his shirttail. Giving her a fulminating look, he said, "You've got one more chance to tell me who these guys are."

"I don't know."

"Yeah, and there's no cell phone service, either."

Having caught her in that lie, he had a right to be angry, she supposed.

Still seething, he said, "Take off your jeans."

"What?"

"Take off your jeans," he repeated, enunciating each word. "Or at least make it look like you're pulling them back on." He glanced through the curtain. "You've got ten seconds."

While instructing her, he'd been unbuttoning his fly and had got it undone just as two hard knocks landed on the door. He grabbed the pillow he'd been sleeping on and pitched it over next to hers.

A harder, louder knock.

In a grumpy and scratchy voice, Rye said, "Who is it?"

"We're looking for Dr. O'Neal."

"What do you want with her?"

"Is she in there?"

"Are you sick?"

The person on the other side of the door called out, "Dr. O'Neal?"

With a curt nod, Rye signaled for her to answer. Her heart was in her throat. She didn't need to pretend to stutter. "J-Just a second."

"Hurry up," said the voice through the door.

She undid her jeans and lowered them a few inches. Rye opened the door as wide as the chain lock would allow and said through the crack, "Somebody had better be dying."

Through the sliver, Brynn could see the tall, handsome man from the café. He said, "Let us in."

"Like hell I will," Rye said. "Who are you?"

"Makes no difference to you. Unlock the door."

"Give me one good reason why."

"Dr. O'Neal's patient."

Rye looked back at Brynn, his expression an unspoken question.

Her mind was in turmoil, but she wanted to know who had sent these men and why. She gave Rye a go-ahead nod to let them in.

His eyes boring into hers, he shut the door and was intentionally clumsy sliding the chain from the slot, rattling it noisily as he whispered to her, "Whatever I say, go along, or I swear to God I'll leave you to them."

Only then did Brynn realize that the box was no longer on the bed. It was nowhere in sight.

But she didn't have time to ask Rye what he'd done with it. The chain fell loose against the jamb. He flipped the lock on the doorknob. The large Hispanic man caught her doing up her jeans when he came in, shouldering Rye out of his way. The punk—Rye's description fit him to a tee—followed his partner inside and snickered as he took in the scene Rye had staged.

For effect, Rye was buttoning his fly with his left hand, unhurried, looking not in the least embarrassed, but extremely put out with her. "'No strings,' you said. I should've known better."

She ignored that and addressed the tall man. "All right, you're in. Who are you, and what do you want with me?"

"We were sent to check on you."

"I need checking on?"

His dark gaze took in the room, Rye, then came back to her. "Apparently."

"I explained to Dr. Lambert—"

"Wasn't him who sent us," he said, interrupting her. "Your *patient* has been fretting over you getting back in time."

"There was no cause to fret. I'm well aware of the deadline, Mr. . . . ?"

"Goliad." He tipped his head in the other's direction. "That's Timmy."

"And how do I know you work for...my patient?"

"You want to verify it, fine. Call him. He and his missus will be glad to know we finally tracked you down." He gave the room another survey, stopping on the bed. "Can't say they'll be happy to learn the reason for your delay."

"How did you know where I was?"

"We started looking for the blue Honda, but that was taking too long. So we tracked your cell phone. Signal brought us right to you."

"You went to a lot of trouble to find me."

"That's what I get paid for."

"But I saw you in the café. If you were looking for me, why didn't you come over and make yourselves known to me then?"

He gave her a meaningful look. "While you were in the company of a deputy sheriff?"

"Oh. Well, the reason for that had nothing to do with my medical errand. Soon after I got here last night—"

Goliad interrupted her. "We know all about it."

"Oh? How?"

"Dr. Lambert," he replied smoothly. "He explained everything to my boss. First, the plane crashed."

She gestured to Rye. "He was the pilot."

Rye was leaning against the wall, ankles crossed, which Brynn was beginning to recognize as a pose typical of him. He looked annoyed, but not especially interested in what was being discussed. However, she noticed that his hands were stacked between his butt and the wall, within easy reach of the pistol in his back pocket.

His eyes were at half mast as he said to Goliad, "What do you know about the crash?"

Ignoring Rye's question, he asked, "What's your name?"

"Something better than Go-lee-ad."

Goliad continued to stare at him. Rye shrugged and told him his name.

Goliad stared a few seconds longer, as though committing Rye's face to memory, then returned his attention to Brynn. "Bottom line, you walked into a crime scene and were taken to the sheriff's office to give your statement."

"Which took much longer than I anticipated," Brynn said, feigning asperity when what she actually felt was apprehension. There was no question now that Rye had been right. These men had been keeping track of her on behalf of the Hunts.

Trying not to appear unnerved, she continued. "Thanks to Dr. Lambert's intervention, the matter was settled. Did he tell you about my car?"

The man nodded.

"Since it can't be driven, Deputy Wilson was kind enough to arrange a car rental for me. When you saw us in the café, we were waiting for the man to deliver it."

"Except you snuck out the back with the flying ace." That from the fox-faced Timmy, who gave Rye a wicked grin. Rye didn't grin back.

Brynn said to Goliad, "It seemed to be taking a long time. I feared there had been a breakdown in communication. In the meantime, Mr. Mallett had borrowed a car, the Honda you mentioned." She tilted her head, asking Goliad, "By the way, how did you know about that?"

"Go on with your story."

"There is no *story*. Mr. Mallett offered to give me a ride to Atlanta."

The punk made a nasal sound. "In exchange for nooky."

Rye moved nothing except his eyes, which cut to Timmy. "Bet your mouth wouldn't be so clever if you didn't have that blade up your sleeve."

Timmy's smug grin vanished. He took a step toward Rye. "You wanna—"

"Timmy. Drop it."

Goliad's voice snapped like a whip, effectively halting Timmy and whatever form of attack he had planned. He backed down but continued to glare at Rye with malevolence.

Goliad said to Brynn, "Dr. Lambert assured my employers that you would be rushing back. But you're not. What are you doing here with him?"

"None of your damn business," Rye said.

"But it is, Mr. Mallett."

"I don't see how. The doctor here is a grownup. She isn't married." He looked over at Brynn. "Are you?"

Before she could respond, Goliad asked, "Where's the box?"

Rye muttered, "That damn thing."

The big guy turned to him. "What's it to you?"

"I hauled it from Columbus, having no idea what was in it. If I'd've known, I would have put it in the back of the plane, the *far* back, not in the seat right next to me. Feel like Dracula. I've flown lots of weird cargo, but never a box of blood. Or if I did, I didn't know it."

Brynn jumped in. "He saw what was inside when the deputies made me open the box."

Goliad's obsidian gaze gave the room another sweep before returning to her. "I ask again, where is it?"

Before she could answer, Rye said, "It was kinda killing the mood for me. I shoved it under the bed."

At a gesture from Goliad, Timmy went down on one knee, raised the hem of the bedspread, and looked beneath the bed. He stood up with the box held between his hands.

"Thanks, shorty." Before anyone was prepared for it, Rye snatched the box from Timmy.

Goliad took two steps toward him, but he was drawn up short by the pistol in Rye's right hand, aimed at his chest. "Timmy, you try sticking me, and I'll blow a hole through your elbow."

Brynn gasped, "Rye, what are you doing?"

Goliad patted the air. "Last thing my boss wants is trouble."

"Well, I've already got trouble with your boss for sending you to bang on my door and demand to be let in."

"Put the gun down," Goliad said. "Timmy, back off. Everybody take a deep breath."

"My breathing's fine, thank you," Rye said.

"Give me the box, and we'll be on our way."

"No can do."

"It doesn't belong to you."

Rye glanced at Brynn. "Are you going to explain, or want me to?"

Goliad shifted his sizable body to better see her while remaining watchful of Rye. "Explain what?"

Brynn tried to appear as though she knew exactly what Rye's explanation consisted of. "Perhaps you had better."

Rye addressed Goliad. "Until the box is delivered, I'm responsible for it."

"You delivered it last night."

"Not technically." His hand made a jerky movement that shifted the gun's aim from Goliad's chest to the ceiling.

Timmy lurched forward.

Goliad barked, "Calm the fuck down, Timmy."

"Yeah, Timmy, calm the fuck down," Rye said. "While you're at it, take two steps back."

At a brusque nod from Goliad, Timmy complied. "You'll get yours," he snarled.

Rye ignored him and said to Goliad, "Are we cool? I'm going to put the gun away and reach into my back pocket for the receipt."

"Receipt?"

Moving slowly now, Rye slid the gun back into his pocket and took from it a folded sheet of paper. "A receipt with the name Dr. Lambert printed above the signature line." He shook out the folded receipt and held it up so Goliad could read the name. "I've learned that Lambert's first name is Nathan. Even without checking her driver's license, I know that she ain't him," he said, tilting his head toward Brynn.

"I'm supposed to deliver the payload to the person on the receipt unless a courier"—again he indicated Brynn—"has written permission to take delivery. She doesn't."

That was the first that Brynn had heard of this, and she seriously doubted its veracity. Even if it were an FAA regulation etched in stone, Rye wouldn't rigidly adhere to a technicality that inconvenienced him to that extent, or at all.

But she didn't have to believe it, as long as the two other men did. If Rye's speculations about them were correct, they had tried to crash him and had assaulted Brady White. It didn't surprise her that Richard and Delores Hunt would occasionally require bodyguards, but these two seemed more suited to protecting a crime boss than a U.S. senator and his wife. They frightened her.

Rye had threatened to leave her to them if she didn't play along with him. In the past couple of minutes, he seemed as dangerous as they, but at least he was the devil she knew.

She continued to play along. "When I volunteered to come up here and get the package, I didn't realize that written authorization was necessary, nor did Dr. Lambert. I've told him it doesn't matter," she said, casting a sour look in Rye's direction. "He's been mule-headed about it."

Goliad's eyes narrowed with suspicion and said to Brynn, "You had the box with you in the café."

"Which is why I got my ass chewed good by the guy I was flying for," Rye said. "He caught my boo-boo, reminded me that if this box isn't delivered to Lambert, he can get into all kinds of dutch with the FAA, and I'd get fined or my pilot's license suspended, neither of which I want to happen.

"So, I started trying to chase down Dr. O'Neal. This lady at the hospital told me where she and the deputy had likely gone for breakfast. I beat it over to the café, went in through the back, bumped into the doctor outside the restroom. We got to talking and..." He raised his brows suggestively. "Wound up here. Bad call, as it turns out," he added, looking over at Brynn with irritation.

"Would you accept an e-signature?" Goliad asked.

"I would," Rye said. "But the codger who sent me has probably never even heard of an e-signature, and wouldn't trust it. He's leery of technology, and he's even more leery of people showing up in the wee hours to claim cargo not addressed to them.

"He said get Lambert's John Hancock, and that's what I'm going to do. I'll hand-deliver the box. After Lambert signs off, what happens to it, or to any of you, is none of my concern. I'll be out of it, free and clear, and so will the charter company."

"We'll deliver it to Dr. Lambert," Goliad said. "Get his signature and email you a copy."

Rye scoffed. "Cross your heart?"

Unfazed by the taunt, Goliad said, "Dr. O'Neal and I will take full responsibility. This won't come back on you or the charter company. She and I will see that Dr. Lambert gets the box."

Rye hugged it more closely. "I'm supposed to trust that? Sorry, but I have no confidence at all in your truth-telling. Doll face here has been lying to me from the get-go. Now you two show up, looking like B-movie muscle, claiming to work for somebody who tracks other people's cell phones. I don't know who that person is, don't know you one-named wonders, don't know her, and, if Dr. Lambert doesn't produce a photo ID when we meet, he's not getting this box, either."

Timmy was restless, bobbing up and down on the balls of his feet. "Why don't we just kill him and take it?"

"Tell him why that's a bad idea, Goliad," Rye said. "No? Okay, I will." He looked at Timmy. "Because it would create a lot of time-consuming problems to deal with. My corpse. Trace evidence. A mess to clean up. According to Goliad your boss doesn't want any trouble, and, besides that, he's obsessed with the ticking clock." Going back to Goliad, he added, "Am I right? If not, I would already be dead."

Brynn's heart was in her throat. He was all but daring them. Goliad, however, didn't respond, leading her to believe that Rye had tapped into the heart of it.

He continued, "Look, I don't know what your racket is, nor *do I care*. It can be innocent or criminal in nature, makes no difference to me, except that if it's criminal, I want to be clear of it so my license isn't jeopardized.

"So I'm sticking to the rules. I'm going to deliver the box to the name on my sheet. Once it's in Lambert's hands, I'm gone, and it can't be soon enough to suit me. We can wrap this up real easy, real quick by loading up and getting on the road to Atlanta." He looked at each of them in turn. "Sound like a plan?"

Brynn was trying to read Rye's mind and discern what his actual plan was. But how it would play out wasn't left to either of them.

Goliad made the choice. "It's an excellent plan, Mr. Mallett. We'll all ride together."

# Chapter 14

*2:02 p.m.*

When Deputy Rawlins answered his cell phone, Wilson asked, "What are you doing?"

"Trying to watch a football game, but one of the nephews vomited crab dip all over the rug, so I had to pause the game while they're cleaning it up."

"I've got the game on. Want to come over here?"

"The wife would kill me."

"Tell her we're working a case."

"Are we?"

"The guy who quarreled with Brady White? His alibi is solid. He's skiing in Colorado."

"I wasn't sold on him anyhow."

"Then you're gonna love this. Dr. O'Neal didn't take delivery on the car I arranged for her. She skipped."

"Be right there."

"Bring a bag of chips. Never mind the crab dip."

They lived no more than a five-minute drive from each other, but by the time Rawlins got to Wilson's apartment, Wilson had a six-pack iced down in his Igloo. He uncapped two bottles and, as

145

he sank into his recliner, passed one to Rawlins. "Happy Thanks-giving."

They clinked bottles and drank.

Rawlins took a seat on the sofa, opened the bag of chips and munched a couple, then got down to business. "Where'd she go?"

"To the restroom."

Rawlins stopped chewing and looked quizzically at Wilson.

Wilson explained what he'd gleaned from the car dealer and the waitress at the café. "Nobody's seen her since."

"Wanna bet?" Rawlins drawled and took another sip of beer. "Mallett?"

Rawlins shrugged. "He's the type."

Wilson nodded in grudging agreement. "Damn his hide."

"His hide and hair."

Wilson, who'd lost more than half of his, gave his partner a wounded look.

"That hurt."

Rawlins chuckled.

After taking another drink of his beer, Wilson began absently scraping the bottle label with his thumbnail. "I've got an ear worm."

"What song?"

"Not a song. Something I overheard, at the department, as we were walking upstairs with them. The doctor and Mallet had an exchange there on the landing."

"I remember you telling them to move along."

"Right, but it's what he said I keep going back to."

"Relative to—"

"Nothing at the time," Wilson admitted. "Not till later."

"Okay."

"His jacket. He'd folded it over his arm to where the lining showed. White silk, but old-looking, yellowed. It's got a pinup girl painted on it."

"Like they used to paint on the noses of bombers?"

"Before political correctness," Wilson said. "It wasn't lewd. The girl's got clothes on. More teasing than anything. But when the doctor saw it, she took exception, and let him know it."

"What did she say?"

"Nothing right away. But you know that look they give you. Like, 'Will you grow up?'"

Rawlins said, "I know the look."

"So Mallett refolded the jacket, gave this mock apology, and told her that there was a world map on the inside."

Rawlins listened, crunched, drank from his beer. "Okay."

"Well..." Wilson glanced at the muted TV. A receiver had just dropped a perfect pass, but neither was interested in the game any longer. "It got me to thinking that maybe we were shown blood samples to keep us from looking at something underneath them."

Rawlins set his beer on the coffee table. "Like inside the foam lining."

"Like that."

They held each other's gaze, then Wilson took the bag of chips from Rawlins and dug in. Rawlins stared blankly at the TV as he thought it over. "Brady's head wound looks like the kind made with the butt of a gun, and Mallett has that pocket pistol. But it's small, and there wasn't any blood on it when I took it from his bag."

Wilson noshed. "And why would he want to clobber Brady?"

Rawlins admitted that Rye Mallett had put that same question to him.

"Did you come up with a motive?" Wilson asked.

"None that held water."

"Dr. O'Neal insisted that I take her to the hospital so she could personally check on Brady's condition before leaving town. Either her worry was genuine, or she's one hell of a good actress. I was surprised to see Mallett there."

"He was?"

"There when I dropped her off and there when I picked her up."

"He was lurking at the hospital? Why? Worried that Brady would wake up and point the finger at him?"

"According to Thatcher, Brady doesn't know who hit him. He was struck from behind."

"If Brady had died, whoever hit him would be facing a much more serious charge. Manslaughter, if not murder. That would make a suspect nervous."

"Nervous enough to make a visit to the hospital?" Wilson set aside the chips and dusted salt off his hands. "Hell, I don't know. But if he's that cold and calculating, I don't see how he could look Marlene in the eye."

"Mallett talked to her?"

"Dr. O'Neal did, too."

"Huh." Rawlins frowned in thought, then stood up and reached for his coat. "Then I think we should talk to Marlene."

Although they were officially off duty, they chewed mints on the way to the hospital so no one would smell the beer on their breath. The admissions nurse knew them by sight, even in plainclothes.

"Marlene White still here?" Rawlins asked as they approached the window.

"Some of the relatives have trickled out, but they told me that she won't leave."

The two deputies took the elevator up. In the waiting room, Brady's wife was surrounded by well-meaning people. Rawlins asked if they could speak with her alone. They stepped out into the corridor.

Weary as she looked, her concern was for them. "I'm sorry you're having to work on a holiday."

"We're sorry you're spending it here," Wilson said. He inquired after Brady.

"Holding his own," she said. "Deputy Thatcher told me that

the man Brady quarreled with has been cleared. I don't know anyone else who could have done this."

Wilson waited a beat, then said, "Dr. O'Neal was set on stopping here before she left for Atlanta."

"It was so kind of her to come by. Her and Rye both. I think his visit was a tonic for Brady."

"He visited Brady?"

"For only a minute."

"They talked?"

"Oh, yes. Rye felt responsible for what happened. He promised to take Brady flying when he's well. Brynn was equally sweet. I hoped to say goodbye to her, but she was already leaving when I returned with the key. Rye was watching her through—"

"Excuse me," Rawlins said. "What key?"

"The key to my car. I loaned it to him."

The two deputies looked at each other before going back to her. Rawlins said, "You loaned your car to him?"

She explained how that had come about. "He was reluctant to take it, but I insisted. He was going out to the crash site. I told him to keep the car for as long as he needed it."

"Has he brought it back yet?" Wilson asked.

"No, and he was very apologetic over having to leave it."

Wilson held up a hand. "Leave it?"

"He called…oh, maybe a half hour ago. I've lost track of time."

"What about the car?" Rawlins said, prodding.

"He said he had to get to Atlanta. A spur-of-the-moment thing. He wouldn't be coming back through town."

With a renewed sense of urgency, Wilson asked, "He left your car near the crash site?"

"No."

She gave them the name of a seedy motor court about five miles outside of town on a two-lane state road that wasn't heavily traveled.

"I told him that it was no problem at all for me to send someone out there to pick it up. My brother and nephew have already volunteered to go. I suggested Rye leave the key with the desk clerk, but he said he didn't trust him. He told me where he'd left it hidden."

*2:41 p.m.*

When Wilson and Rawlins walked into the cabin rental office, they understood why Mallett might be mistrustful of the attendant. He was stoned. His lazy grin was comprised of crooked and rotting teeth. "Which one of you is her old man?"

"Neither."

The deputies produced their badges.

"Awww, ssssshit." The clerk threw a nervous glance over his shoulder toward an open door, through which could be seen a messy office.

Rawlins said, "We'll forget that it reeks of weed in here if you tell us whose old man you thought we might be."

"I don't know."

"Try again."

"I never saw her. Only the dude came in."

"What did the dude look like?" Rawlins asked.

"Tall, blond hair, leather jacket. Sunglasses." He looked out the window at the fog. "Can't figure why."

"What time did he check in?"

"What time?" In thought, he scratched his pimply cheek. "Before nine?" He put it in the form of a question, as though it were the guessed-at answer on a pop quiz.

"What name did he register under?" Wilson asked.

"Didn't. Paid cash and asked we keep it just between us."

"Hmm," Wilson said. "Smoking dope and cheating your employer out of a cabin rental. You've had a busy day."

The allegations made the clerk considerably more helpful. "He said they ran out on the Thanksgiving get-together to have a shagfest, and that if anybody came in asking had somebody rented a cabin in the last hour or so, I was to play dumb."

"That would be a stretch," Rawlins deadpanned.

The clerk divided an avid look between the two deputies. He licked his crooked front teeth. "He looked like a dude that's been around. What did they do?"

"We can't disclose that."

"Well, whatever, wasn't much of a shagfest. They've already vacated."

"Their car is still here."

When pulling into the compound, they'd spotted the blue Honda parked outside the cabin farthest from the office and the road.

"So how'd they leave?" Rawlins asked.

"With the two guys."

Rawlins and Wilson shared another look of misapprehension. "What two guys?" Wilson asked.

The clerk began to look uneasy. He raised both skinny arms in surrender. "This ain't none of my doin', and I want no part of it. I'll give the owner the money for the cabin. Swear."

"What two guys?" Wilson repeated.

"All's I know, they drove in here in a black car. Didn't stop at the office. Went directly to the cabin. A few minutes later, they drove out again. The dude was in the back seat on the driver's side. Woman with long hair was on the other side of the back seat. Never saw her face. Just the back of her head through the rear window."

"Which direction did they go?"

"To the right."

"South."

He blinked. "I guess."

Rawlins persisted. "What kind of black car?"

"Didn't notice the make, but it was new. Wheels were shiny chrome. Flashy."

"Mercedes sedan," Wilson announced, surprising Rawlins, who turned to him for elaboration.

"They were at the café," Wilson said. "Got there shortly after the doctor and me. They parked across the street, but I noticed the car." He gave Rawlins a description of the two men. "I remember thinking the car had to belong to the big guy. Clothes were wrinkled, but quality."

"What about the other one?"

"He was dressed in a dark suit, too, but he'd have looked more at home in a gangsta hoodie."

"What did they do when they came in?"

"Took a booth. Ate breakfast. Didn't talk much or show any interest in her or me."

"What about her? Did she react when she saw them?"

"No. In fact, her back was to them till we went to the door and said goodbye."

"But that's where and when she brushed you off," Rawlins said.

Wilson extended his hand to the desk clerk. "Give me the key to that cabin."

The attendant fished around in a cluttered drawer and produced a key with a cardboard tag that had the number ten on it. Wilson took it from him. He and Rawlins headed for the door.

"Can I come?"

"No," the deputies chorused.

The towels in the bathroom were still damp. The bed and pillows had been lain on. Other than that, there was nothing in the cabin cluing them to where Brynn O'Neal and Rye Mallett had gone, nothing identifying the two men they'd left with.

"I don't suppose you got that Mercedes's license plate number."

Wilson shook his head with chagrin. "Not even a partial."

Rawlins headed for the open cabin door. "Well, lucky for us the café got burglarized last spring."

Wilson caught his chain of thought and hurried to catch up. "The café has a security camera."

"Installed the week after the break-in." Rawlins walked toward his SUV.

Wilson slowed down only long enough to retrieve Marlene White's key fob from under the rock where Mallett had told her it would be. Wilson had offered to drive the car back for her and park it in the hospital lot. "I'll leave the key for her at the admissions desk," he told Rawlins. "Pick me up out front."

"On the way, I'll call the owner of the café and tell him to meet us there. I want to see his security camera video."

"He won't like it. It's Thanksgiving."

"I don't care if it's the Second Coming. Brady is still in ICU, condition guarded. Rye Mallett and Dr. O'Neal might have made nice with Marlene, but they still have a lot to answer for."

*3:03 p.m.*

"I knew we shouldn't have trusted her to go alone," Delores said. "I told Nate as much. This proves my instinct was right." She reached for the crystal stem at her place setting and raised the glass of wine to Richard.

They toasted and drank.

The traditional Thanksgiving meal was being served to them in their formal dining room. They were having it midday in anticipation of the eventful evening. The senator sat at the head of the long table, Delores adjacent to him on his right. They had dressed for the occasion to keep up appearances of normalcy, if only for their housekeeper-cook.

Minutes before they were due in the dining room, they had received the call from Goliad that they had been nervously awaiting. For the most part, the news had been good. Dr. O'Neal had been located.

However, the circumstances in which she'd been found had sent Delores into orbit. She was still circling.

"What could *possibly* have induced her to have a *rendezvous* while the *clock* is ticking down?" She punctuated the words by stabbing her fork into a slice of turkey breast meat.

"Animal magnetism?"

Her fork clattered against the china plate. "How can you joke about it, Richard? Although the way Goliad has described this pilot, it does sound as though he's still evolving."

He smiled. "I doubt he's that low, or Dr. O'Neal wouldn't have found him attractive."

"I don't care if he's been named Sexiest Man Alive, what could have possessed her?" She ignored her plate of food and followed the progress of her fingertip around the embossed pattern on the tablecloth. "I hope it was only sex that kept her away for so long. It all sounds very fishy, like she and this pilot have teamed up.

"That business about the receipt sounds like utter nonsense. You're a senator. Have you ever heard of an FAA regulation to that effect?" Without waiting for Richard's answer, she threw her linen napkin onto the table and stood up. "I'll have someone in your office look it up."

"Delores, sit down."

His imperative tone halted her. She looked at him with surprised affront.

"Dr. O'Neal is a young, healthy, and independent woman. She wanted to go to bed with the man. Stop making something monumental of it." He spoke in a measured and reasonable voice, which had much more impact than a rant. It suggested anger barely contained, a fragile control over his temper.

Delores slapped her hand over the center of her chest. "Well, forgive me if saving your life is monumentally important to me."

He took a deep, steadying breath. "I apologize for using such a strident tone with you. We're both on edge." He stood and held her chair. "Please, Del. Let's finish our meal."

She sat and resumed eating, but her passivity didn't last for long. "And Nate," she said his name with disdain. "He hadn't even noticed that his colleague was hours overdue."

He had failed to return their repeated calls, and when he finally had, it was to tell them that he'd received a text from Brynn just before eight o'clock, saying that she would be leaving Howardville soon. He reminded them that he'd been up all night. Thinking all was well, he'd turned off his phone and had gone to bed to nap.

He apologized profusely for his lack of vigilance and was greatly relieved to hear that Brynn was being escorted back by men in their employ. He was waiting for her at his office.

Delores said, "Nate was appalled to learn what she'd been doing during those lost hours and promised to take up the matter with her."

"Will he revoke privileges, do you think? Or ground her?" Richard asked, keeping a straight face.

"More joking?"

"I just don't see this as the end of the world. Goliad has the situation in hand."

She murmured in agreement.

Richard eyed her keenly. "But?"

She stared into the near distance, then set her cutlery on her plate, her food barely touched. "I don't want to leave anything to chance, or to anyone unreliable, as Dr. O'Neal has proven herself to be. It's up to us, you and me, to make this work."

Realizing there was more to what she had to say, Richard leaned back in his chair and patted his lap. She came around and sat in it. In a wifely manner, she adjusted the Windsor knot of his necktie.

"I've had an idea," she said. "It's rather audacious. Don't say no until you've heard me out."

"I'm intrigued. What do you have in mind, darling?"

# Chapter 15

*4:12 p.m.*

When they left the cabin, Goliad offered to place the black box in the trunk of the Mercedes, but Rye had insisted on it riding in the back seat with him. It was on the floorboard between his feet. His flight bag was in his lap. Snug in the pocket of his jacket was his nine-millimeter. Sans clip. At Goliad's insistence.

As Rye reluctantly surrendered the clip, Goliad had told him that as soon as Dr. Lambert signed off on the delivery of the box, Rye would get his bullets back.

He hadn't specified *how*.

Rye hadn't been fooled into thinking that Goliad believed the tale he'd spun about needing Lambert's signature on the receipt. Goliad had brought him along only because he hadn't known what else to do with him. But after the drug was delivered to Lambert, Rye would be expendable. Possibly, so would Brynn. He tried not to let on that he was aware of that.

Riding with his head resting on the back of the seat, eyes closed, he pretended to be dozing, but he was wide awake and acutely aware of every movement made by the others in the car.

In the passenger seat, Timmy fidgeted as though bugs under his skin were trying to work their way out.

Goliad maintained a speed just below the limit, kept both hands on the wheel, eyes on the road, except occasionally when he looked at Rye in the rearview mirror.

He was a seasoned pro. Too intelligent to let his temper dictate his actions. There was a quiet dignity about him. He would kill Rye if need be, but he wouldn't do it with gusto as Timmy would.

Different styles, equally lethal, accountable to their employers, the unnamed mister and missus, one of whom was the patient. Rye wondered who they were to be able to trace cell phones and have people, like this pair, doing their dirty work.

Was Nathan Lambert another of their puppets? Or was Lambert pulling the strings? Brynn had described him as a genius, but that wasn't necessarily an endorsement. A lot of geniuses were madmen who used their brilliance as justification for committing atrocities.

But whether Nate Lambert was a saint or sinner, immediately after handing the box over to him, Rye needed to get the hell out of there.

His dilemma was achieving that, while at the same time getting payback for Dash and Brady White, whom he had intentionally avoided mentioning in the cabin standoff. If he'd tipped his hand about the revenge he sought, bloodshed probably couldn't have been avoided.

He needed a plan of action. But how could he formulate one when he wouldn't know what kind of situation he was walking into until he was already in it? He didn't even know the specifics of their destination. They could be on their way to a penthouse or a dump ground. He had to be prepared for anything.

And what about Brynn?

He still didn't know what role she was playing in this fucked-up drama.

Being apprehensive of Goliad and Timmy, she had gone along with his rigmarole about the receipt, sounding just hacked enough to be convincing. But that didn't mean there was blind trust between the two of them. Was what she'd told him about GX-42 just another in a series of lies and half-truths?

*A miracle drug with a short shelf life? Really, Brynn?*

If that was true, and said drug was destined for a patient whose days were numbered without it, and Brynn was delivering it with more than twenty-four hours padding, which was exactly what she'd been desperate to do, then why wasn't she chatty and bubbly with anticipation of soon achieving her goal?

Instead, she'd been silent and forlorn ever since their departure from the cabin.

They hadn't been given an opportunity to speak alone, and, dammit, he needed to know what was going on with her. He stopped pretending to doze and looked over at her. She was looking out the car window at Atlanta's skyline, which had appeared on the horizon, visible but blurred by fog.

She seemed about as excited to see it as a lifer approaching Alcatraz.

Her posture was rigid with tension. Her hands were in her lap, clasped in a death grip. He reached across the seat and cupped his hand over them. Jumping like she'd been shot, she turned to him. Their eyes locked. They didn't say anything. Couldn't.

Nor could he account for her expression of stark desperation.

She knew something that he didn't. Frustrated by his inability to crack her reticence, he pressed his fingers around her clasped hands as though to squeeze truthful information from her.

Then, startling everyone, his cell phone rang.

Timmy turned his head, his vulpine face appearing in the space between the two front seats. Goliad's unblinking eyes met Rye's in the rearview mirror. "Answer it," he said.

Rye took the phone from his jacket pocket and saw that the caller was Dash. He clicked on. "Here."

"Where's here?"

"Coming into Atlanta."

"That's good. You finagled a ride?"

"In a manner of speaking."

"Did you talk to the FAA?"

"Monday at the earliest."

"Figured."

"I may have to go back up there to get pictures. Couldn't to-day."

"We'll work around it. You had any sleep?"

"Not much."

"Get some more. You fly tomorrow night. I took the liberty of booking you a room. I'll text you where."

"Okay."

"Don't be in a rush to thank me or anything."

Dash paused as though waiting for him to respond, but he had a listening audience that Dash didn't know about, so he didn't say anything.

After heaving a long-suffering sigh, Dash continued, "I also got you a seat on a cheapo commercial carrier that'll get you back here."

"What time?"

"Little after nine. Unless you're delayed."

"There's still fog."

"Yeah, but not like what it was. It's clearing from the west. ATL is scheduled to reopen within the hour, but the airlines will be playing catch-up, and until they do, it'll be the end of civilization as we know it, which is why the room wasn't easy to come by. Had to use my platinum card."

"If flights are that backed up, why don't I just charter and fly myself?"

"No budget for that. You don't make it, Rye, I'll have to send somebody else."

Rye looked over at Brynn, who was staring at the back of

Timmy's seat, unmoving and unmoved, seemingly uninterested. "I'll make it," he told Dash.

"Assuming you do, get over here as soon as you land. I'll have one of the nineties on the step."

"Copilot?"

"Do you want one?"

"No."

"I knew that without asking."

"What's the cargo?"

"Pallets of leather. A furniture manufacturer is out of Roman Red, and they want it yesterday."

"Where?"

"Portland."

"Maine may still be socked in tomorrow."

"Not Maine. Oregon. Clear as a bell out there. Well, except for the rain, but what are you going to do? It's Oregon."

"Right."

"What's the matter with you?"

"Nothing."

"I thought you'd be happy. You sound like your puppy just died."

"I'm beat, that's all. Ready to get horizontal."

"I'll text you the hotel info."

"Thanks for rustling up the job. I'll get back to you in the a.m." He clicked off and dropped the phone into his pocket. "How much farther?" he asked, addressing the question to the pair of eyes in the rearview mirror.

"Not much."

"You're a fountain of information."

Rye had flown through Atlanta more times than he could count. He knew it from the air, was well acquainted with the main airport and all the FBOs in the area, but he wasn't that familiar with the freeway system.

He tried to keep track of the route Goliad took, but when he steered the Mercedes into the unattended parking garage of a multistory office building, Rye knew that he would have trouble finding his way back to a major thoroughfare. Even if he had a car, which he didn't.

And even if he got out of here alive, which was questionable. Not that he feared death. In fact, he flirted with it, courted it, dared it on a daily basis. He just didn't want his death to be at the hands of a lowlife like Timmy.

He wasn't afraid of dying. He was only afraid of dying ignobly.

Goliad drove up two ramps of the garage and pulled into a space on the third level, which was the top one. He cut the engine and turned to address Brynn. "Text him. Tell him we're here."

She did as instructed. Without waiting for a reply to the text, Goliad opened the driver's door and got out. Timmy did likewise on the passenger side. Brynn got out. Rye was the last to alight, his bag shouldered, the box secured between his other arm and his torso.

"I've never been here before," Goliad said to Brynn. "Lead the way."

She made brief eye contact with Rye as she walked past him and toward a single elevator. It took forever to arrive. While they waited, no one said anything, although Timmy was cracking his knuckles and whistling softly through his teeth.

They crowded into the small enclosure. Brynn punched the button for the fifth floor. They rode up; the door slid open. As they stepped from the cubicle, Brynn motioned them to the left. A man was standing in an open doorway where the lushly carpeted and richly paneled hallway came to a dead end.

At his first glimpse of Nate Lambert, Rye decided he didn't like his looks any better than he'd liked his phone voice. Men that skinny and pale shouldn't shave their heads or wear trousers that narrow in the leg and cropped at the ankle. Even someone as untutored in fashion as Rye could've told him that.

The four of them filed down the hall, Brynn in the lead, Rye behind her, Goliad and Timmy bringing up the rear. Lambert acknowledged the two heavies with a nod. He spotted the box under Rye's arm, and it held his attention for several seconds. Then, as they got closer to him, he focused on Brynn.

"So glad you could make it, Dr. O'Neal."

She fired a volley back. "It hasn't been a fun day for me either, Nate."

"That's not what I heard." He looked Rye over, his distaste apparent. "*This* is the dashing bush pilot you found irresistible?"

Brynn drew herself up to her full height but didn't honor the insult with a comeback, demonstrating a hell of a lot more class than Lambert. For all his nattiness, he was an asshole.

Rye stepped forward, coming even with Brynn. "You want this box, or what?" He whipped the receipt from his back jeans pocket and extended it, still folded, to Lambert.

The doctor pulled a pair of reading glasses from the breast pocket of his shirt and put them on. He took the sheet of paper by one corner as though it were germy and made a production of shaking it out. He scanned it, then snapped his fingers repeatedly and impatiently. "Pen?"

"Photo ID?"

Lambert glared at him over the top of his silly glasses. "Excuse me?"

"Photo ID," Rye repeated.

Steam could have been coming out of his ears, but he took a wallet from his pants pocket and showed Rye his driver's license. "Is one sufficient? I also have several that are professionally related."

"One's fine. Anybody got a pen?"

Brynn didn't act on the request. She stood with her arms crossed over her middle and stared at the floor. Goliad produced a ballpoint pen. Lambert snatched it from him, flattened the paper against the wall, and scrawled his name across the bottom.

He gave the sheet to Rye, who refolded it and stuck it in his pocket, then passed the box to Lambert. "You want to open it, check the contents?"

"The samples have already been exposed to air unnecessarily."

"Then that's a no?" Rye said. "Good. Sight of blood makes me queasy."

Lambert tucked the box under his arm and asked with impatience, "Is that it, then?"

"Delivered. Everybody's happy. I'm gone."

As he turned away, Brynn caught the sleeve of his jacket. "Thank you."

Her touch, the husky intimacy with which she'd spoken the two words, elicited heat, low and central and deep. He looked down at her hand, then into her eyes, and all too aware of the onlookers, said, "Just doing my job."

After the slightest of hesitations, she said, "Fly safely." Then, withdrawing her hand, she stepped around Lambert and went into the office.

Rye turned. Right behind him were Goliad and Timmy, standing side by side. He pushed his way between them and continued on toward the elevator. He overheard Lambert say, "Thanks for your intervention, gentlemen. If you can see yourselves out? The Hunts are waiting to hear from me." Then the office door was soundly shut.

At the elevator, Rye punched the down button. When Goliad and Timmy joined him, he held out his hand, palm up. "I'll take my clip now."

"I think I'll keep it," Goliad said.

"Oh, now that's a shocker." Rye muttered an obscenity, then, turning away from them, said, "I'm over the two of you. I'll take the stairs."

"Hey, slick, before you go..."

Rye shoved open the door to the stairwell and looked over his shoulder at Timmy.

He tipped his head toward the end of the hall. "On her back or hands and knees?"

Rye left him cackling over his own wit.


*4:57 p.m.*


When the elevator door opened on the third level of the parking garage, Rye was ready with the fire extinguisher. He sprayed them with the foam, most of it aimed at their faces. "It's not a laser, but you get the idea."

He threw the fire extinguisher at Timmy's head. It connected. He howled and bent double. Rye knew he would come up with a knife in his hand.

"Goliad, was he the laser man?"

Goliad, clawing foam out of his eyes, nodded, spat, "Stupid little shit."

Rye danced backward as Timmy came stumbling blindly toward him, yelling foul epithets as he made wild arcs with a switchblade.

"And Brady White?" Rye asked.

Shaking foam off his hand, Goliad said, "I hit him."

"Then you're next."

"I kept White alive. Timmy wanted to slit his throat."

Rye growled as he caught Timmy's arm in mid-swing and, with momentum in his favor, propelled him backward until he came up hard against a concrete pillar. Rye hammered Timmy's hand against it until he let go of the knife; then he delivered an uppercut to Timmy's chin. The back of his head smacked against the unforgiving column.

"That's for Brady. This is for the laser and the man whose

plane you wrecked." He rammed his fist in the man's shallow belly and swore he reached his spine. "This is for insulting Dr. O'Neal." He backed up and put all he had into the kick to Timmy's genitals.

Timmy screamed, grabbed his crotch, and pitched forward onto the floor.

By now, Goliad had drawn his weapon but held it at his side as he faced off with Rye.

Rye motioned to the handgun. "Are you going to shoot me?"

Goliad shook his head. "He had it coming."

"Thanks for not killing me in the cabin. You could have."

"Wasn't the time."

"Should I be looking over my shoulder for you?"

"I don't have any orders regarding you now. Can't promise I won't."

"And Brynn?"

He hesitated, then repeated, "Can't promise I won't."

Understanding passed between them. "Fair enough." Rye backed away a few more steps then turned and walked quickly away.

He didn't start running until he reached the ramp; then he bolted and didn't stop, not even when he reached the street. He ran full out for two blocks before realizing he was leaving a trail of blood.

# Chapter 16

———◦◉◦———

They're *out*?"

Nate, speaking into his cell phone, ran his hand over his head, a gesture of frustration and impatience that Brynn had seen him do hundreds of times. She now had the inane thought that perhaps he was checking it for bristle.

He had placed the black box on his desk, within a foot of where she sat. She stared at it while Nate continued his harangue with whoever had answered the Hunts' land line after calls to the senator's cell phone and that of Mrs. Hunt had gone to voice mail.

"How can they be 'out'? They had dinner at home, correct?" The reply caused him to check his gaudy wristwatch. "Then where would they have gone? Fine, fine. Look, if they instructed you to tell anyone who called that they were not at home, I assure you they were not including me."

That went on for another minute or so. Brynn thought she might scream before he finally disconnected. "She swears they're not there."

"Maybe they aren't."

166

"They wouldn't choose now to go for a Sunday drive, Brynn. Or were you thinking that maybe they went to the movies?"

"Don't talk down to me like that, Nate."

He didn't apologize for his condescension. She doubted he'd even heard her. He was stroking his head and pacing. "I don't understand this at all. Delores has been hounding me since that catastrophe last night. Hounding me! Calling every half hour, asking what your status was, when you would be back."

He paused and looked at her with contempt. "While I'm trying to keep her and Richard calm, you're off gallivanting with that...whatever. Jesus!" He threw back his head and looked up at the ceiling as though searching for an answer to his incomprehension. "I can't believe he can read, much less fly an airplane."

"He's an Air Force Academy graduate. He flew rescue missions in Afghanistan."

He scoffed. "Is he also a spy for the CIA?"

Actually, it was Wilson who'd shared with her what had shown up when they checked Rye Mallett's background. His character profile had changed dramatically after his second tour of duty. He must have experienced something deeply affecting during his service, but she would never know what it was.

*Just doing my job.*

He'd seen it through, washed his hands of the whole ordeal, and walked away from it, as he'd said he would. One day, when a medical breakthrough was announced, he might wonder if it was connected to the pharmaceutical he'd unwittingly smuggled. More than likely he wouldn't recall her name, but he might remember her as that woman who had complicated his life and temporarily kept him tethered to the ground when he would rather be airborne.

Her wish never to see him again was no longer as desirous, but it was too late to recall it. Anyway, he was gone, and a clean break was best under the circumstances. Her focus, her sole focus, must be on the GX-42.

Her eyes on the box, she said, "Nate? Are we doing the right thing, giving this to Richard Hunt?"

Hearing the misgiving in her voice, he stopped pacing. "Absolutely." Her uncertainty must have been apparent, because he rapped the top of the box with his knuckles and repeated, "Absolutely. We made our decision, Brynn."

"I know, but—"

"We can't backtrack now. It's out of the question."

Still, she wondered if her colleague had ever harbored a grain of doubt; but even if he had, he would never admit it. In any case, the die was now cast. "Did you get any indication of when the Hunts would return home?"

"The housekeeper claimed not to know. I'm to stand by, and she'll notify me. That's what she said. 'Stand by.' Can you believe it? A *maid*."

"I hope it's not long. I'm exhausted. Is there a possibility of waiting until tomorrow?"

"No, they've been emphatic. No more delays, during which shit seems to happen." He checked his watch again.

He was eager to do it, and not only for the Hunts' sake. He didn't want to postpone getting on the road to acclaim and medical superstardom. Brynn just wanted it to be done so she could stop second-guessing, vacillating, lying, and half-lying.

Inside her coat pocket her cell phone vibrated. She took it out and saw that she had a text. The sender was identified only by a number, no name.

*The HUNTS & I want to know what your game is. Your parking space. Now.*

Her heart nearly leaped from her chest. She took a swift breath. Hearing it, Nate came around. "What's the matter?"

"Nothing. It's…my car. It's been repaired. Someone from Howardville drove it here."

He looked at his watch. "Now?"

"I know, right? I predicted it would take several days to fix."

"Have them park it and leave the keys under the mat."

"There's paperwork. You know what that's like," she said and gave a light laugh. "I'll run down and see to it."

"Come right back. We'll be leaving on a moment's notice."

She acknowledged that. As soon as she pulled the door shut behind her, she sprinted down the hall and, knowing how slow the elevator was, took the stairs to the first level of the parking garage, where she had a reserved space with her name stenciled on the wall above it.

The space was empty except for Rye, who was looking mean and mad and *bloody*.


*5:22 p.m.*


As Brynn rushed toward him, she exclaimed, "What happened to your hand?"

"That fucking punk."

"Timmy?"

"He got the worst of it."

"You fought with him? I thought you'd left."

"Well, I didn't."

Rye had watched from several blocks away as the black Mercedes left the parking garage. When it passed his observation point, he saw that Goliad was driving and Timmy was slumped against the passenger door.

By all appearances, they were done for the night. But Rye wouldn't have put it past Goliad to circle back. Following the fight, he might have gotten orders regarding Rye.

He'd given them five minutes, which had seemed interminable. They didn't return. On his walk back to the garage, he booked an Uber car. When it arrived, he gave the driver an extra twenty to wait and texted Brynn. He'd taken a risk by hanging around, but he figured that she would rush right down when he dropped her mystery patient's name, and she had.

"Does it hurt?"

She would have taken his hand, but he kept it out of her reach. "No." Then, "A little."

Timmy's knife had made a neat slice across each of the first knuckles of his left hand. The blood wasn't coagulating as rapidly as it should because he'd been repeatedly flexing his fingers, then contracting them into a fist. "To keep them from getting stiff," he said to Brynn, who was watching him do it. "I've got to be able to grip the yoke. I'm flying tomorrow."

"I heard. You should put something on them. My office is on the fourth floor. We could go up—"

"Forget it." He secured her biceps and steered her toward the exit. "Who are the Hunts?"

She dug her heels in and jerked her arm free. "Where did you hear their name?"

"Your dickhead colleague let it slip. Hunt. That's the deep pockets behind this drug smuggling operation?"

She held her tongue.

"Nothing? No? Okay, I gave you one last chance. From here out, you're on your own. Remember, I gave you fair warning."

He left her standing there and walked away. He was almost to the exit, and beginning to think she'd called his bluff, when she ran after him.

Short of breath, she asked, "Warned me of what? Where are you going?"

He kept walking. "The nearest police precinct. I don't want my ass hauled to jail when the rest of you go."

"Wait!"

He stopped and turned, looming over her. "You were going to steal that box for yourself up there in Howardville. Then everything that could go wrong did. You played me, you played the deputies, but ultimately, you were given no choice except to go along with the goons Hunt sent and deliver the box to Lambert."

She didn't respond, but he took her silence as affirmation of all he'd said.

"Is it even a drug, Brynn?" he asked.

"Yes."

"GX—"

"Yes. Yes! Everything I told you about it."

"Okay. Is the patient Mr. Hunt or Mrs.?"

"Mister."

"And he's—"

"Desperate."

"He'll die without it."

"One can hope that with treatment—"

"Skip the bedside manner. Will he die?"

She gave curt nod.

"So why didn't you want Lambert to have the medicine?"

She said nothing.

"Brynn? Why? Why were you planning to steal it?"

She made a small, defeated sound and pushed back her hair. "What difference does it make now? Nate's got it. As you said, everybody's happy."

"Everybody but *you*." He stayed as he was, holding her stare, then took her arm and propelled her toward the street.

Again, she put on the brakes. "I told Nate I would be right back."

"You won't be."

He continued nudging her out the exit. On the street, the fog was noticeably thinner, but the temperature was much colder. It had started to rain. He hurried her toward the Uber car idling at the curb, opened the rear door, and motioned her in.

"I can't walk out on him now, Rye. We're doing the procedure tonight."

"The stuff doesn't go bad till tomorrow night."

"They don't want to wait. If I disappear again, they'll panic."

"Oh, we wouldn't want to start a panic, would we? I can prevent that right now by going back up to the fifth floor and spilling my guts to Lambert. He'll probably be as curious as I am to hear why you were trying to keep that life-sustaining drug out of his soft, pasty hands."

"What's it to you, mister no involvement?"

"Because without my knowledge, you made me an accomplice in your scheme. Whatever the hell it is. God only knows. I sure as hell don't. But I'm going to find out. From you.

"So either you and I go have a private little talk about your mountain escapade, or we go up and have a three-way with the colleague that you wanted to cheat out of his miracle cure. You decide, Brynn. You've got one second."


*5:34 p.m.*


Delores shrugged the mink jacket off her shoulders and asked the chauffeur to turn down the heater. "It feels like the tropics in here."

The driver apologized and made an adjustment on the limo's thermostat. Delores thanked him and raised the partition. Privacy now secured, she smiled over at Richard. "Well?"

"It was brilliant, Del."

"I thought so."

She deserved to gloat over the success of their afternoon project. Richard reached across the car seat and stroked her cheek. "It was an inspired idea. One I wish I could take credit for."

She kissed the back of his hand. "I hope it didn't exhaust you."

"I'm tired. But it was worth the effort." He took his phone from his breast pocket and turned it on. "Nate has called me four times."

She reactivated her own phone. "And me three. That must mean he has it."

"He does." Richard gave her a campaign poster smile. "Goliad texted that Dr. O'Neal and the goods were delivered into Nate's hands about an hour ago."

"Thank God."

"Call Nate. He's probably apoplectic."

She made the call and put the phone on speaker. Nate answered immediately. "Delores, where in God's name—"

"Before lecturing me, wait until you hear why we were temporarily out of touch."

She gave him the lowdown. "It was a spur-of-the-moment thing. The only person we notified beforehand was Richard's assistant. She'd been a little miffed at us for not doing something publicly in observance of Thanksgiving, so she jumped on the idea, scrambled, and got media there. We were seen, photographed, recorded. Richard gave a sound bite. It will be on tonight's news."

"Good play!" Nate said.

"We thought so." She cast Richard a smug smile. "Meanwhile, you took delivery on a package for us?"

"It's right here. Where are you now?"

"In the car on the way home."

"I'll meet you there."

"Nate?" Richard said. "Is there any special preparation I should make?"

"Yes, pour Delores a stiff drink."

They all laughed.

Nate continued. "Really nothing. Get comfy. Brynn and I will put in an IV. Basically that's all there is to it."

Delores said, "We don't know how to thank you for this, Nate."

"Oh, I have lots of ideas for that. Maybe you could arrange for a wing of the hospital to be named after me."

"You think large, Nate," Richard said.

"If I didn't, Delores would soon be a widow. See you in a bit."

Delores clicked off. Richard frowned. "With what we've paid him, he could buy his own hospital wing. Cocky bastard."

She unbuckled her seat belt and scooted across the back seat to snuggle against him. "He is. But he's *our* cocky bastard, and it's always beneficial to have one indebted."

# Chapter 17

After ending his conversation with the Hunts, Nate went into the bathroom in his office. He took the box with him. He was not letting it out of his sight again.

He washed his hands and brushed his teeth. He checked his head and reasoned he had time to shave it. He took off his tie and shirt and went about the ritual proficiently.

He was buffing his sleek head with a towel when he realized that Brynn was taking an awfully long time in the garage. He called her to alert her that they would be leaving promptly for the Hunts' estate.

She didn't answer. She was probably in the elevator.

He selected a fresh shirt and tie that were understated but should show up well on camera. With the stipulation that it would be for private viewing only, the Hunts had granted him permission to make a video, with his narration, as Richard was getting the infusion.

Although after Richard became a first in medical history, they might change their minds about keeping it from the public. Nate surmised that they would want to milk it for all it was worth. In which case, he would have documentation.

After checking his reflection in the mirror one last time, he went back into his office. He set the black box on his desk and was pulling on his suit jacket when he heard carpet-muffled footsteps approaching the door.

Brynn. He pulled open the door and was about to say, *It's about time*, but the words died on his lips. He blinked several times in bafflement.

One of the two uniformed men said, "Dr. Nathan Lambert?"

"Yes. Who are you? What do you want?"

"I'm Deputy Wilson. Rawlins," he said of his companion. "We spoke to you on the phone in the wee hours this morning." He then aimed his finger beyond Nate's shoulder toward the desk. "What we want is to take a second look inside that box."

Nate's knees turned to jelly. "I was just on my way out. Can this keep?"

"I'm afraid not," Wilson said. "We've come all the way from Howardville to see you."

Nate crossed his arms. "Which brings me to my second question. Aren't you out of your jurisdiction?"

"We called ahead to the DeKalb County Sheriff's Office. They're aware of why we're here."

"Well then, the sheriff's office is one up on me," Nate said. "I thought we had cleared up this issue over the phone."

"We did, too." Those were the first words out of Rawlins's mouth, but Nate had been uncomfortably aware of the deputy's suspicious scrutiny. "The situation has grown more serious."

"How so?"

"To start with, Brady White has—"

"Who is Brady White?"

"The man who was assaulted at the airfield."

"Ah, I don't recall ever having been given his name. Proceed."

Rawlins waited a beat or two. "Mr. White's condition hasn't improved all that much."

"I'm terribly sorry to hear that," Nate said. "But it still doesn't explain why you've come to me."

"Reason we've come to you is because if Mr. White doesn't make it, then Rye Mallett and your colleague Dr. O'Neal are upped to material witnesses in a homicide investigation. And, by extension, you."

"*Me?*"

Wilson used the hat he held in his hand to point toward Nate's desk. "That's your box, and we think it contributed to the motive of whoever assaulted Mr. White."

Nate's palms began to sweat, but he maintained his imperious expression. "I can accept that this Mallett character might very well be involved in criminal activity. But Brynn O'Neal? Never."

Rawlins said, "Even though it runs in her family?"

"Criminal activity?"

"Her father. He has a record as long as your arm."

Nate's ears began to buzz. "I wouldn't know that, because I know nothing of Brynn's personal history. She and I are nothing more than colleagues. Not family, not really friends. Our patients occasionally overlap, requiring us to consult on their diagnoses and treatments. That's the extent of our relationship."

The two deputies exchanged a look. Even to Nate, that had sounded like cover-your-ass backpedaling.

Rawlins asked, "When's the last time you saw her?"

Nate looked at his watch and only then realized how much time had passed since Brynn had gone down to the garage. "She returned from Howardville around four-thirty. She and I are due to begin testing the blood samples right away. That's where I'm off to."

"So...?" Wilson looked past him. "She here?"

"In the building, yes. But she was summoned down to the parking garage to deal with the return of her car."

The officers exchanged another look, a convention he found annoying. *"What?"*

"Dr. O'Neal's car is still hooked up to the tow truck, waiting for the body shop in Howardville to reopen after the holiday weekend. Monday, seven a.m."

Blood rushed to Nate's head. He would kill her. He would absolutely eviscerate her and hang her carcass out to dry.

"Then she lied to me," he said. "She received a text and dashed out. All I know about it is that she arrived here at—"

"How?"

"How what?"

"How did she arrive?"

"An interested party had sent a car and driver to bring her back to Atlanta."

"Did this driver drive a black Mercedes?"

"I don't know."

"License plate number—"

"I don't know. I didn't make the arrangements."

"Who's the interested party?"

"My patient. Whose life is hanging in the balance while you're asking irrelevant questions about motor vehicles."

"Did you see the driver?"

"He escorted Brynn to this door."

"Big Hispanic guy? Little fellow with him?"

"That's them. The pilot was also tagging along." Nate didn't conceal his low regard for Rye Mallett as he told them about the FAA-required signature. "To be frank, I think he made it up."

"What for?"

"First off, to be ornery. And possibly because he was hounding Brynn. He and she had a tryst."

"In a cabin," Wilson said. "We know about it."

Nate sniffed. "It demonstrated a disturbing lack of discrimination and judgment on her part. Which is why someone was sent to retrieve her."

"Her, or the box?"

"Both. You know about its importance."

"I'm not sure we do."

"I explained it to you this morning."

Rawlins said, "Yeah, but we'd like to take another look inside."

"I can't risk exposing the contents to light and air again until I'm in a sterile environment."

"Fine. We're free now." Rawlins motioned down the hallway toward the elevator. "Is your car in the garage here? I'll ride with you. Wilson can follow us."

Nate tried to conceal his alarm. Meanwhile his mind was darting about in search of an excuse. He took a deep breath and drew himself up. "Gentlemen, Brynn's conduct this morning is uncharacteristic of the professional I know. But I don't believe for a moment that she was involved in any law-breaking activity last night, or today, or at any time, although I don't have the same confidence in the integrity of the man with whom she shared several hours in a cabin.

"I'm certain that Brynn will soon come to her senses and resume her responsibilities to our patient. If she doesn't, she'll suffer consequences which could impact her professional future. I have a substantial amount of influence at the medical facility with which we're both affiliated."

He looked at his watch, then shot his cuffs.

"Now, I appreciate your commitment to your duty. I admire you for conducting such a thorough investigation into the assault on Mr. White. But, presently, you really must excuse me. I have an appointment."

"And we have a search warrant," Rawlins said.

Nate's sphincter clenched. "You have a search warrant?"

"For the box."

"Wh...why did you feel it necessary to obtain a search warrant on Thanksgiving night?"

"Because we thought you might balk."

"I beg your pardon. I do not *balk*."

"Sheriff's office here cooperated," Wilson said. "We stopped at the judge's house to get the warrant signed."

Rawlins produced it from an inside breast pocket of his puffer jacket, unfolded it, and held it out for Nate to read. "Open the box, Dr. Lambert."

The more he protested, the worse it would look for him. Recognizing that, he backed into the office and motioned them toward the desk. Trying to keep his hands steady, he scrolled the dials on the padlock and opened it. He raised the metal lid.

Rawlins pulled on a pair of latex gloves and methodically removed the sealed test tubes, examining each one before placing it on the desk, leaving four circular cutouts in the foam.

"There," Nate said. "What did you expect to find?"

Ignoring him, Rawlins dug his fingers into the edge of the foam and began working it up and away from the metal. "Let's see what's under here." He pulled the lining up and out.

Nate's slick, shiny head broke a sweat.

*6:02 p.m.*

The room had been booked in Dash's name, his real name, the one on his platinum card. That could be advantageous if anyone were to canvass local hotels in search of a Rye Mallett or Brynn O'Neal.

It was a chain hotel near the airport. Rye had to show the check-in clerk his photo ID, but the harried young man gave it only a cursory glance, which he wasn't likely to remember. He was overrun with demanding complainers who had set up camp in his lobby while waiting for either a room to become available or for the airlines to put them on a flight, whichever came first.

Rye wouldn't have been all that surprised if Brynn had pulled a vanishing act while he was checking in, but she was waiting for him at the elevator bank as agreed. They rode up in silence and got out on the seventh floor, which was blessedly quiet compared to the mob scene in the lobby.

They went into the room. Rye flipped the bolt. She switched on a lamp on the nightstand, then faced him, bristling. "Was it really necessary to throw my phone away?"

On the drive from downtown, he had asked to see her phone. Without asking why, she'd handed it over. Then before she could stop him, he removed the SIM card and tossed the phone out the car window.

"You want Goliad and Timmy coming after you again?"

"Their company might be preferable."

He tapped his chest. "I'm the one who has the right to be angry. You don't get to be mad till I'm finished."

"Then get on with it."

He tossed his coat onto the bed. "Your SIM card is intact. You've got all your data. You can buy a new phone tomorrow."

"In the meantime a patient could have an emergency."

"So check in with your answering service periodically. I'll lend you my phone to call them."

She simmered, and he let her. Then she asked, "How did you get my number to text me?"

"I asked Marlene for it. Told her I would let you know when I'd be going back up there to take Brady flying."

"Have you gotten an update on him from her?"

"No. You?"

She shook her head. "I suppose it was she who told you about my dad?"

"I had assumed he was a cop. Ha!"

"You heard he was a thief, and thought 'like father, like daughter.'"

"Prove me wrong, Brynn."

"I don't have to prove a damn thing to you."

In angry strides, he walked toward her. "Aren't I entitled to know what you dragged me into?"

"It's irrelevant now."

"Is it?"

"Nate has the box, doesn't he?"

"What excuse did you give him for cutting out? Did you tell him you were meeting me?"

"No. I lied."

"You're good at that."

Rather than taking offense as he expected, she looked chagrined and actually backed up to sit on the foot of the bed, shoulders slumped, head drooping. "Obviously not all that good," she said ruefully. "You saw through me from the start."

"Well, I was looking close."

Her head came up. Their eyes met. Though neither moved, the space between them seemed to shrink. The atmosphere became weighty, teeming with the memory of one kiss.

"You had signed off," she said, her voice barely audible. "Free to go. Why did you come back?"

He approached her slowly and, when he reached her, pushed the fingers of his right hand up through her hair and tilted her head back. "You know one reason." He looked into her eyes in a way she couldn't possibly mistake.

"You haven't acted on it," she whispered.

His body was demanding that he do. He wanted to immerse himself in the passion promised by her uninhibited kiss, longed to lose himself in her, seek and find a few minutes of oblivion and peace. It took every ounce of willpower he possessed to resist the temptation.

"And I won't." He let go of her hair and withdrew his hand. "If somebody fucks with my freedom to fly airplanes, they're fucking with my *life*, because flying is all I've got. You put it in jeopardy, Brynn."

"Not intentionally."

"Not at first, maybe. But you haven't told me the whole of it."

"I have," she protested, her voice wavering. "You know what's in the box, and why I went to extremes to safeguard it."

"The drug."

"Yes."

"Meant for Hunt."

"Yes."

"But you tried to steal it. Why?" He planted his fists on either side of her hips and leaned over her. "Black market?"

"I'm not a criminal!"

"You and your old man—"

"No!"

"Then tell me, dammit. Why were you trying to keep it from Lambert? Professional jealousy? To prevent him from getting the glory?"

"No."

"To prevent Hunt from getting the drug?"

Her lips parted, but nothing came out.

He reacted with a start, and said again, "To prevent Hunt from getting the drug?"

Her eyes misted.

"Brynn? Why didn't you want him to get it?"

On a sob, she said, "Because I wanted it for someone else."

# Violet

———◦◉◦———

"My name is Violet Griffin, and I have cancer."

I practiced saying it a lot of times before I stood in front of my kindergarten class and told all the kids at one time.

The reason was because I had come back to school after getting chemo and my hair had come out. My doctor—not Dr. O'Neal, because I didn't know her yet. My first doctor told me I would lose my hair, so it wasn't a surprise. But I cried anyway. So did Mom. Not when she was brushing my hair and big wads of it got stuck in my brush. But after, when she and my dad went to bed, I heard her crying. She had told me over and over that I was beautiful and that hair doesn't matter.

But it sorta does. Especially when it's all gone and you have to go back to school and make a speech about it in front of the class.

Miss Wheeler, my teacher, patted my arm and told me, "Embrace it, Violet." I wasn't sure what embrace meant, but when she said, "Own it," I knew she meant that none of the kids at school would make fun of my bald head if they knew I was sick.

I didn't want to be the only kid in my school with cancer, but I was.

When you've got cancer, people talk to you different. Sometimes they whisper. I want to tell them that cancer doesn't hurt my ears, and that it's okay for them to talk normal.

Since I got cancer, my brothers have turned all weird, too. I think Daddy had a talk with them. They used to hide my dolls, and throw the ball too high for me to catch, and laugh when I did a ballet twirl and fell down, but now they don't do any of that stuff. I wish they still did. I don't want them to be nice to me just because they think I'll die before them.

That day I had to tell the kids at school that I had cancer was two years ago. I'm in second grade now. Only I can't go to school these days. If I get well, I'll have a lot to catch up on.

I was thinking about that day in kindergarten because today is Thanksgiving, and Mom said we should count our blessings, and the main one, she said, is that we're here in Atlanta so I can get well. We missed having turkey with my brothers and Daddy, though. They're at home. Mom and I FaceTimed with them, then she went out in the hall with the phone and talked to Daddy by herself, and when she came back in, she smiled the way she does when she's sad and doesn't want me to know it. But I know it anyway.

She laid down with me, and pulled me close to her, and we watched the parade on TV. I wish I could go to that parade and see the Rockettes. Mom said we will next Thanksgiving. But I don't think we will because Dr. O'Neal would have to kill my cancer first.

She's a special doctor for my kind of cancer. There are all different kinds, you know. Mine is in my bones and blood, and it's a bad kind to have.

But Dr. O'Neal can kick its butt. That's what Daddy told me when I left to come to the hospital here. He winked at me. Probably because he said "butt."

When Dr. O'Neal and Mom talk about my cancer, they go

outside my room in the hall. Sometimes Dr. O'Neal puts her hand on Mom's back and rubs it and looks sad. That's when I know the news isn't good. *Not as successful as we'd hoped.* That's how the doctors say that the cancer is getting worse.

My treatments cost a lot of money. One day, I heard Dr. O'Neal tell Mom not to worry about that right now. She really wants to kill this cancer.

Dr. O'Neal is my best friend even if she is old. She likes me. Sometimes she tells Mom to take a break, and even if Mom says no, Dr. O'Neal shoos her out and stays with me for a while. We talk about a lot of stuff. Everything but my cancer. I think she doesn't want me to know how bad it is, but if it wasn't bad, I wouldn't be here, would I?

We talk about how being a ballerina must be the best thing in the world to be.

She brought me a coloring book with just ballerinas in it. We've colored nearly all the pages, but she said that when that book is full, she'll get me another one. She painted my toenails pink, the color of ballet slippers. She says someday I'll be a famous ballerina, and she'll come to see my show and wave to me from the audience.

But I might be a Rockette instead. She could still wave to me.

Dr. Lambert would probably never come to see me in a show. He's very busy and always in a hurry.

Yesterday, Dr. O'Neal brought me a Thanksgiving card. On the front was a silly turkey wearing a Pilgrim hat. I put the card on the table next to my bed. Dr. O'Neal wished me a happy Thanksgiving and told me she had something very important to do, but that she would be back soon.

She hasn't come today, though. But maybe she will. I hope so. I need to tell her that I don't feel good. I hate to tell her that. But she needs to know if she's going to kick the cancer's butt.

But I don't want Mom to know that I don't feel good. She's already scared I'm going to die.

# Chapter 18

*6:27 p.m.*

Rye left Brynn sitting on the bed and went into the bathroom to wash his hands. He wrapped a cloth around the leaky cuts. When he came back, he opened the minibar fridge. "Name your poison."

"Water, please."

"It's on Dash."

"Just water."

He passed Brynn a bottle of water and opened a can of Coke for himself, then dragged the desk chair over and straddled it, facing her.

"Who's your patient, Brynn?"

"A seven-year-old girl named Violet."

"She's dying?"

"Probably before she turns eight. Unless I'm granted a compassionate use exemption for her."

"She's the patient you applied for?"

"To no avail."

"What's the hiccup?"

"Largely funding. For an exemption trial, the product

187

company must be willing to provide the drug, and GX-42 doesn't come cheaply. For one patient, it wouldn't be cost effective."

Rye propped his elbow on the back of the chair and rubbed his thumb across his lips. "Does Violet live here in Atlanta?"

"Outside Knoxville. Working middle class family, and it takes the incomes of both parents to support it. Her mother is on leave from her job. Violet has two older brothers. Coming here has imposed a tremendous hardship on all of them. Financially, emotionally. Every way. But all were willing to make sacrifices in order to send Violet here."

"To be treated by you."

She gave a modest shrug. "The research I've done has been documented in medical journals. Violet's oncologist in Tennessee recommended me."

"You're famous?"

She smiled at that. "My name is familiar to a few who specialize in hematologic cancers."

"Lambert?"

"Much better known."

"He sees to it."

"Nate has an inflated ego, yes."

"Who is Hunt?"

She gave a significant pause, then said, "Senator Richard Hunt of Georgia."

Rye stared at her, almost expecting a punch line, but Brynn was as somber as a death knell. Losing taste for the cold drink, he turned in his chair and set the can on the dresser. Coming back to Brynn, he said, "Well, shit."

"You know of him?"

"I've heard of Senator Hunt a lot, but till now I couldn't have told you what state he's from."

"He's serving his second term in office. You've heard of him because he places himself in the middle of things and seems to thrive on keeping the congressional waters churned. He can be a charmer, an arm-twister, or a gladiator, depending on the issue under debate and the strength of his opposition. He's handsome and knows it. He plays the media like a maestro."

"How'd he make his money?"

"Sole heir of his family's company." She named it, but Rye wasn't familiar with it. "Manufacturer of portable buildings. Construction site offices. Temporary housing units."

"Like FEMA uses?"

"Yes."

Rye cocked an eyebrow.

Brynn said, "He sold out before running for office to avoid a conflict of interest."

"Oh, of course," he said with only a trace of conviction. If Richard Hunt would pay for a pharmaceutical not yet available to anyone else, he'd cheat at other things, too. "Family?"

"Happily married to second wife, Delores. No children from either marriage."

"How old is he?"

Again, she paused before saying quietly, "Sixty-eight."

They exchanged a meaningful look.

Brynn added, "He's a very young sixty-eight. Except for the cancer, he's physically fit. Robust. His wife is considerably younger."

"He and Violet have the same cancer?"

"They are two of less than sixty thousand in the U.S. But if GX-42 works on their cancer, its use could become much more widespread for patients with similar blood cancers."

"What does it do exactly? Layman's terms."

"In England, there's a drug currently being used in clinical trials on patients awaiting a stem cell transplant. That drug assists the patient's marrow—damaged either by cancer or its harsh treatments—to produce healthy blood cells that their own immune system won't attack. It retards the progression of the cancer and helps prevent metastasis. It tides them over, so to speak, until a match is found for transplant.

"Which is wonderful. But GX-42 goes beyond. When tested on animals, it has been longer acting and has had a more permanent effect. Periodic infusions, often months apart, have maintained the production of healthy blood cells in the animals.

"Nate and I believe it will do the same in humans. It will serve the purpose of a stem cell or cord blood transplant, but it would be like having a shelf-ready, universal donor. No match necessary. Far less chance of patient rejection and susceptibility to inflection. Even if it doesn't sustain the patient indefinitely, we know it will provide more time to find a matching donor for transplant."

Rye absorbed all that, then pushed himself out of the chair and walked over to the window, slowly unwinding the washcloth from around his hand as he went. The cuts looked angry, but they'd stopped bleeding.

Brynn said, "You should put an antiseptic on them."

"Maybe later."

"Where did Timmy attack you?"

"He didn't. I attacked him." He described the altercation.

"You got payback for Brady and Dash."

"Some. Not enough."

"Was Timmy badly hurt?"

"Nothing permanent."

"Goliad?"

"He and I came to a meeting of the minds. But it might be temporary."

"What does that mean?"

"First things first, Brynn. I'm trying to wrap my mind around all this."

He flipped back a panel of the drapery. Hartsfield-Jackson was several miles away, but Rye saw that it had reopened. A passenger carrier on final approach materialized out of the low cloud cover and sailed over the hotel parking lot.

"MD-80."

Brynn asked, "You can tell that?"

"I can tell."

He let the drape fall back into place and turned around. "You have two patients. Why weren't two batches mixed?"

"The pharmacologist didn't dare. He was terrified he would get caught mixing one and smuggling it out."

Rye walked back toward the bed, and when he came even with Brynn said, "Hunt has had sixty years Violet will never get."

"We can't play God, Rye."

"Somebody did. Who picked the senator over the little girl?"

"Nate and I reached a mutual decision, based on numerous factors."

"Such as?"

"The patient's general health, the patient's autoimmune—"

"Bullshit. It was decided by the patient's pocketbook. How much?"

"I wasn't privy to that conversation."

"You mean negotiation."

Not quite meeting his eye, she said, "I'm told the Hunts committed a sizable amount toward future research, but on the condition—"

"That he got it. You think God gave a thumbs-up on that deal?"

"He must have." Looking angry, she stood up, went around him, and thumped her water bottle onto the dresser. "Because last night when I took matters into my own hands, look what happened. You crashed. Brady is in ICU. I'll pay dearly for skipping out on Nate and the Hunts tonight. Character assassination will only be the beginning."

"They can't shred you without admitting to wrongdoing themselves."

She dismissed that argument with a chuff. "They're capable, believe me. They'll probably figure out a way to have my medical license revoked. Which I was risking anyway. But the worst of it..." Her voice cracked. She tried again. "The worst of it is that I can't save Violet."

"You can save Richard Hunt."

"After leaving Nate's office? No. They wouldn't let me near him. I campaigned hard for Violet. In the end, Nate won out, I conceded. But I guess neither he nor the Hunts were convinced of my commitment."

"So Goliad and Timmy were sent up to Howardville last night to keep tabs on you, make sure you didn't abscond with that box."

"Which is precisely what I had planned to do, and was willing to suffer the consequences." She raised her hands in a helpless gesture. "You know what happened to that plan. So, on the long drive back to Atlanta, I looked at it from a purely objective standpoint.

"The GX-42 wouldn't be wasted. A life would be spared, and, as you reminded me last night, I swore under oath to save lives. Any life. I had geared myself up to assist Nate tonight, and to be glad about it." She paused for breath. "But then you sent me that text."

"Which you could have ignored. Why didn't you?"

"Honestly? It provided me a good excuse to abandon Nate, the Hunts, all of it. Turns out that my objectivity wasn't so strong after all. Knowing Violet was lost, I lost heart.

"Now they'll know without doubt that I'm a traitor to the cause. Nate will be livid with me for making him look bad with the rich and powerful Hunts. On the other hand, if the drug works as we fully expect it to, he'll be delighted not to have to share the praise."

"You'll miss out on getting the credit."

"Violet will miss out on much more." She swiped a tear off

her cheek, turned quickly away, and headed for the bathroom. "Excuse me. When I come out, I'll call for a car."

"Brynn—"

"I never cry in front of anyone." She went into the bathroom and closed the door behind her. The lock clicked.

Rye went to the door and knocked. "Brynn."

"Give me a few minutes. Please."

Cursing under his breath, he backed away. He supposed she had earned a crying jag.

He lifted his bomber jacket off the bed and took his cell phone from the pocket. He sat down on the end of the bed where Brynn had been, holding the phone in his palm, bouncing it a couple of times in indecision, then, before he chickened out, tapped in a number.

"Hello?"

"Hey, Mom."

She gushed a breath around his name. "Oh, it's so good to hear your voice."

"I called this morning."

"It said unknown caller."

"Yeah, I'm using a spare. Anyhow, the day got away. I'm not interrupting Thanksgiving dinner, am I?"

"No, we ate early. Enough food to feed an army. We've got leftovers that can easily be warmed up if you're calling to tell me you're on your way."

The hopefulness in her voice made him squeeze his eyes shut. "I'm a long way from Austin. In Atlanta. Grounded by fog."

"It's been on the news. You're not flying—"

"Not tonight. Tomorrow."

"Where are you off to?"

Did it matter? No. But he told her anyway. Then, "Do I hear a baby crying?"

"That's Cameron. He's been fussy all day. He's teething."

Cameron, his youngest nephew. He'd seen him only in pictures his proud brother had texted, along with subtle admonitions that if he could fly from coast to coast on a daily basis, surely he could make a stop in Texas to see his family.

He cleared his throat. "So, uh, the whole brood is there today?"

"Except for you. You're missed."

"I miss everybody, too. But, you know, work. It's crazy." Of course work wasn't the reason he didn't go home, and she knew that.

"Your dad's out on the porch. He'll want to—"

"No, don't bother him. I'll try to call again in a day or so, talk to him then."

"Rye—"

"I'd better go and let you get back to the party."

"Rye. We want to see you. We don't have to talk about...about anything you don't want to. Please. Can't you come home for a couple of days, at least?"

"I'll try to do that."

"When?"

He plowed his fingers through his hair and held his forehead in his palm. "When I can, Mom."

She didn't ask when that might be. She had asked before and had never received a definitive answer. He didn't have one to give her.

Her voice husky with restrained emotion, she said, "Be careful, sweetheart."

"I will."

"Promise me."

"I promise."

"I love you, Rye."

"Love you, too."

He disconnected, held the phone against his lips, then, fed up with himself and life in general, tossed it onto the dresser. It landed just as Brynn opened the bathroom door.

She glanced at the discarded phone, then looked at him. "Who was that?"

He stayed as he was, just looking at her where she stood poised on the threshold between the two rooms, hair a mass of dark swirls backlit by the bathroom vanity lights. Those damn gray eyes, lined with the blackest of black eyelashes, now wet and spiky from recent tears, were regarding him with concern.

He said, "Come here."

Her footsteps were hesitant, but she came to stand directly in front of him. He placed his hands on the sides of her waist, pulled her between his legs, and pressed his face into the hollow where her ribs separated.

She settled her hands on his head, so tentatively that at first he thought he'd imagined it. "Rye? What are we doing?"

Running his hands up and down the backs of her thighs, he nuzzled her middle, then tilted his head back and looked into her face. "Nothing." He reached for his jacket again and spread it open across his thighs. "It's a shame you don't like her."

Brynn looked down at the painting and gave a faint smile. "She's growing on me."

"Yeah? That's good. Because she definitely has her uses."

Brynn looked again at the pinup girl, then regarded him warily. "I'm not sure I want to hear what they are."

He grinned. "I'd enjoy detailing some of them, but I can't make you late."

"Late?"

He worked his fingers into a small tear in the seam where the silk lining was stitched to the leather, then reached for Brynn's hand and turned it palm up.

"Before Lambert and the Hunts get to you, you've got to get this to Violet."

In her palm lay the bubble-wrapped vial of GX-42.

# Chapter 19

———◆———

Deputies Wilson and Rawlins watched Nate Lambert back his Jag from his reserved parking space and drive out of the garage.

Replacing the formed foam inside the box hadn't been as easy as removing it. Once that was done, apologizing for their mistrust and for wasting more than half an hour of the doctor's valuable time, they had insisted on seeing him out of the deserted office building and safely on his way.

Rawlins waited until Lambert's taillights were no longer in sight, then remarked to his partner, "This may go down as being the worst Thanksgiving ever."

"You'd rather be at home with a wife on the warpath and puking kids?"

"Maybe. Because this sucks."

Wilson snorted a mirthless laugh. "Not often do I have this much egg on my face. I would have sworn we'd find some kind of contraband."

"Me, too. And you know what? I think our friend Dr. Lambert thought we would, too."

"Yeah?"

"Yeah. It looked to me like he was as shocked as we were to come up empty."

"I know he wasn't glad to see us on his doorstep," Wilson said. "But was he afraid of being caught red-handed at something illicit? Or was he just being an asshole?"

"He's definitely an asshole. But when I produced that search warrant, he looked exactly like my nephew did right before yakking the crab dip."

Wilson thought on it. "It was the same expression Brynn O'Neal had when we made her unlock the box."

"That's another thing. What's up with her? Why did she lie to Lambert about her car?"

"To make a clean getaway."

"Yes, but why?" Rawlins persisted. "This morning she was itching to get back here to him and their patient."

"That's what she *said*, but that's not what she *did*. She ran off with Mallett. I'm telling you, this whole thing—" Wilson broke off, walked a few feet forward, then knelt on one knee in the parking space next to Lambert's and looked more closely at the spots on the concrete floor that had drawn his attention. "Blood."

Rawlins joined him to take a look. "Relatively fresh."

Wilson called attention to the name on the wall. "In Dr. O'Neal's parking space."

It wasn't a copious amount of blood, but the quantity didn't signify as much as its being there at all. The two deputies tracked the intermittent drops as far as the exit, but once beyond the cover of the building, the trail had been washed away by rain.

"Whoever was bleeding walked out of here," Wilson said.

"Then what?"

"Hell if I know. Maybe somebody just got a nosebleed."

Rawlins turned to Wilson, looking skeptical. "Is that what you really think?"

"No."

"Me neither. Based on everything else that has happened, I think we ought to bring in Atlanta PD." He glanced around, spotting the security cameras mounted at strategic points in the ceiling. "We should have a video of what went down here. I'll call it in. You get a home address for Brynn O'Neal. We'll start looking for her there."

They were walking quickly toward the SUV when Rawlins's cell phone rang. "Probably the wife demanding a divorce."

But it was Myra. Rawlins put her on speaker. She cut to the chase. "Two things. Thatcher went off duty, so Braxton took over for him at the hospital. He just called. Brady's bum heart—"

"He has a bum heart?"

"Everybody knows that," she said with exasperation. "It's giving them some concern. Vitals-wise, he's lost a lot of ground. His cardiologist is on his way to the hospital as we speak. Marlene's fit to be tied."

"Hell," Rawlins said, exchanging a worried frown with Wilson. "What's the second thing?"

"The license plate number on that black Mercedes."

"The café's camera angle was wrong. We didn't get it."

"That camera didn't, but the one at the hardware store did."

"Across from our department?"

"Slow day, so I drummed up a project. I had all the cameras downtown checked for pictures of a black Mercedes. It was parked around back of the hardware store for over an hour just before dawn."

"While we were questioning Dr. O'Neal and Mallett."

"Um-huh. I don't think that's a coincidence." She paused, then, "Is Brynn in trouble?"

"We're trying to ascertain—"

"Don't feed me that cop crap, Rawlins. Talk to me like a person. I've known that girl since before her mama died. I don't want anything bad to happen to her, now she's made something of herself."

"Neither do I, Myra. But did you ever know her to follow her daddy's example?"

"You mean steal?"

"That's what I mean." When she hesitated to answer, Rawlins said, "Tell us straight."

"She was a scrawny thing. All knees and elbows. Twelve, thirteen. Thereabouts. She took a coat from the girls' locker room. Claimed it had been hanging there for several days, nobody missing it. It was cold wintertime."

"And she needed a coat," Rawlins said.

"She didn't take it for herself. She gave it to a country kid who came in on the school bus every morning near frozen."

Rawlins looked over at Wilson, who rubbed his fingers across his forehead as though it had begun to ache.

"Okay, Myra. We get your point," Rawlins said. "Text me that tag number, please."

"Will do. But I already got who the car is registered to."

"Listening."

"Delores Parker."

"Doesn't ring any bells."

"I'm not finished yet," she snapped. "That was her maiden name. Married name is *Hunt*. Delores Parker Hunt."

"Holy shit."

Myra snorted. "That's what I said."

*6:44 p.m.*

Brynn stared at the vial in her hand with stupefaction, then looked into Rye's face. "How did you get this? When?"

"When I was in the cabin bathroom showering."

"You've had it all this time?"

He shrugged.

"How did you get the lock open?"

"I knew I had those four numbers correct and in sequence, or you wouldn't have looked sunk when I read them out to you. It occurred to me that I'd missed the first number, not the last. I tried that, and, on the numeral three, the lock opened. Then I found the vial under the lining. It was in my jeans pocket when I came out of the bathroom."

"All the time we were asleep and you were clutching the box?"

"I didn't make the transfer till I saw Goliad's car coming up the drive toward our cabin. I ripped open the seam in my jacket and slipped the vial inside before waking you up."

During this exchange, he had pulled on his jacket and was herding her toward the hotel room door. She was resistant. "Hold on. I'm trying to think this through," she said. "You knew it was a drug even before I told you."

"No I didn't. I had the vial, but it's all wrapped up. I didn't know what was in it, or what you planned to do with it. It actually could have been poison for the hot dog meat."

"Okay, but then *after* I explained what it was, why didn't you tell me you had it? That whole long ride to Atlanta, I was miserable."

"And I couldn't figure out why. Why were you unhappy about handing it over to Lambert? For all I knew, you and your daddy had intended to blackmail him with it, or you had a higher bidder. Something. If whatever you were up to was illegal, you'd made me culpable. I couldn't leave with that hanging over my head."

"So you texted me in the hope of beating a confession out of me."

"Which I did. Now I know you're only a little crooked."

"And that's okay with you?"

"The difference being motive." He looked at his watch. "You know it's going to hit the fan when Lambert discovers his wonder drug has been heisted. He might have already. We shouldn't have trouble getting a taxi or Uber outside the hotel."

"You're coming with me?"

"Assuming Lambert realizes by now that he's been had, Goliad will be only a phone call away. I'll see you safely to Violet, then there won't be anything Lambert or the senator can do without blowing the whistle on themselves."

He pulled her coat off the hanger in the closet and held it for her. She zipped the vial into an inside pocket.

"Where is Violet?" he asked.

"While she's been undergoing radiation, she and her mother have been staying in an outpatient facility on the hospital campus."

"Does Lambert know where she is?"

"Of course. He examines her routinely."

"That'll be the first place he looks for you. We've got to beat him there."

He opened the door and pushed her through.


*7:15 p.m.*


In the distant vaulted entry hall, a grandfather clock chimed the quarter hour. Other than that, the silence following Nate Lambert's declaration was so profound, Delores actually felt the pressure of it against her eardrums.

She and Richard sat side by side on the sitting room sofa. Nate was standing before them, the luckless messenger imparting the news that the castle had been breached.

Delores said, "What do you mean, it wasn't there?"

For all Nate's apparent uneasiness, his voice remained waspish. "I put it in words that couldn't possibly cause confusion, Delores." Spacing the words out, he enunciated, "The vial wasn't there."

"How did that happen? Did it ever leave the lab?"

"On the way over, I called the pharmacologist. He swears he did exactly as I instructed."

"Only he, you, and Dr. O'Neal had the combination to the lock?"

"I gave it to her over the phone last night, but not within hearing of—"

"Oh, for Christ's sake, Nate. We can stop dancing around it, can't we? She fucking stole it!"

Delores stood up, went over to the bar, and splashed whiskey from a decanter into a glass. She shot it, then poured another, and carried it over to Richard.

"He probably shouldn't be—"

"Shut up, Nate."

With a nod of thanks, Richard took the glass from her and drank the scotch with only slightly more temperance than she had, then set the empty glass on the coffee table.

"We all know what happened," he said. "The question is, what are we going to do about it?" He looked first to Delores and caught her lighting a cigarette. In view of the crisis, he didn't rebuke her. "Where is Goliad?" he asked.

"Once the box was delivered, I dismissed him for the night." She gave Nate a scathing look. "Little knowing that his services would be required again so soon."

Nate leaped to his own defense. "You two can't blame me for this."

Delores arched a penciled brow. "Blame you? I want to draw and quarter you."

"The blame lies entirely with Brynn."

"Like hell it does. I told you not to trust her. You didn't listen."

"I wouldn't have sent her up there last night, had I known then what I've learned since."

She propped a hand on her hip and tilted her head. "Well?"

"Criminality runs in her family. Her father has a long record."

Richard looked at him through narrowed eyes. "This woman worked with you, she treated your patients alongside you."

"Yes, but——"

"She treated *me!*" Richard's voice vibrated with restrained wrath. "And you allowed that, knowing nothing of her background?"

"Her credentials were impeccable. It never occurred to me to check her family tree. Clearly a mistake."

"Clearly a catastrophe," Delores said.

Richard stood up and rounded the sofa. He braced his hands on the back of it as he would a podium and lowered his head. Delores remained quiet, not wanting to break his concentration. When Nate seemed about to, she shot him a look that muted him.

Eventually Richard raised his head. "It's not catastrophic until the life span of the drug expires. We've got a bit over twenty-four hours to find Dr. O'Neal and retrieve it."

Delores flew into action. "I'll call Goliad. *You,*" she said, pointing her cigarette at Nate, "start writing down any places Dr. O'Neal might have gone when she left you. Is she in contact with her outlaw father?"

"I wouldn't imagine that——"

"Don't imagine, Nate. Find out. In the meantime, call that pharmacologist and tell him to mix another dose. The weather has cleared. We'll send our jet for it."

"He won't do it, Delores."

"Offer him more money."

"It's not a matter of money."

"Oh, that's funny," she said. "Tell me another."

Nate gave a stubborn shake of his head. "He's a scientist. He's motivated by positive lab results, and actually feels corrupted for taking money to mix the one dose. What money he did accept will go toward covering the cost of the components. The only way he would agree to make more would be with the company's authorization for an FDA compassion exemption. We would have to go through the proper channels and apply."

"Do it."

"I would have already, Delores, except that you were adamant about anonymity. These clinical tests are meticulously documented. There's no way I can keep Richard's name out of it."

"No," Richard said without taking even a moment to consider it. "If it gets out that I'm terminally ill, it would empower every enemy I have in Washington."

"Perhaps enough hush money would buy confidentiality," Nate ventured.

Richard scoffed at that. "What planet are you on? I'm in public life. Fodder for the media. Anybody along the chain would leak this tidbit in a heartbeat. You would probably sell the story to the tabloids yourself."

Nate drew himself up to his full height and gave the hem of his European suit jacket a tug. "I'll overlook that insult because you're my patient, you've suffered a disappointment, and you're overwrought."

He paused as though waiting for Richard to apologize. When he didn't, he continued. "I advise you not to dismiss the suggestion out of hand. Your name on the application would add considerable cachet."

"No."

Delores said, "Richard—"

"*No*, Del."

She turned to Nate. "Richard has spoken. Sweeten the pot. Your laboratory friend might not be quite as high-minded as you believe. You can use the desk there."

Nate did as told and got on his phone.

Richard retreated into the bedroom. Delores ground out her cigarette and followed him. He said, "Close the door."

He took one of the matching overstuffed chairs in front of the window overlooking their private terrace and the landscaped grounds beyond. She took the other. Seeming to be deep in thought, he drummed his fingers on the padded armrest.

Delores was itching to spin into action, but she gave him time to contemplate. Eventually he asked if she had called Goliad.

"I was about to. I wanted to hear your thoughts first."

Still thoughtful, he nodded. "This started out as a last-gasp effort to save my life. Nevertheless, I've had occasional twinges of guilt, some reservations regarding the morality of this...undertaking."

"I've tried to assuage those twinges and reservations."

"For the most part, you have, though some lingered. As recently as last night. But these complications, one piled on top of the other, have given this a different slant. It's become a challenge. It's taken on the properties of a campaign."

"You've never backed down from a challenge or—heaven forbid—lost a campaign."

"No, and I don't intend to." He reached for her hand. "You know what's required to win?"

"A cutthroat attitude."

He smiled. "You've been listening."

"For the past sixteen years. Listening and learning. Take no prisoners. Win at all costs. To you, it's more than a motto with a nice ring to it."

"It's a credo."

"I'm the most faithful of disciples."

"I want to win this one, Del."

"You will. It's a certainty."

"But not enough. I need to win...and leave the slate wiped clean."

They exchanged a look of mutual understanding, and she sealed it by squeezing his hand.

"I'll recall Goliad to duty, and alert him that we will be requiring his special services."

The senator nodded.

Delores reached across and patted his knee. "You rest, darling. Leave everything to me." She slid off her shoes, curled her legs up under her, and relaxed into the chair as she placed the call to Goliad. He answered right away. She explained the situation.

"Dr. O'Neal has proved herself adept at disappearing. We need you to find her again."

"Understood, ma'am."

"You know where to start, and there's no time to waste. Go now. Take your sidekick with you."

"Timmy is indisposed."

Delores's voice turned as brittle as an icicle. "Indisposed?"

Richard was instantly alert to the change in her tone. He gave her an inquiring look, but she raised her index finger, indicating that she would fill him in after the call.

Goliad said, "Timmy provoked Mallett. Mallett didn't take it lying down."

The details were sketchy, but he went on to describe a fight in a parking garage.

"Timmy cut the guy. His hand was bleeding. But in the end, he was upright and okay enough to leave in a run."

"And you let him?"

"Yes, ma'am. There were security cameras everywhere."

"I see."

"Anyway, Timmy's peeing blood."

"I don't care if it's gushing from every orifice. Get him up and out, and find that doctor. Get the vial, then deal with her. I could do without any more bother from the pilot, too. Do you understand what I'm saying, Goliad?"

"Yes, ma'am. I'll take care of it. Of both."

"See to it immediately. And don't keep us in suspense, either."

"No, ma'am. I'll let you know."

Delores clicked off and recounted the conversation for Richard. "I fear you were right about this Timmy," she said. "If he's going to be violent, he should at least be effective. Mallett should be dead."

Richard laughed softly. "Goliad will take care of it."

"Of course he will."

He would. Goliad would do whatever she asked of him. He was madly in love with her.

# Chapter 20

*7:38 p.m.*

In order to avoid the bedlam in the hotel lobby, Brynn and Rye had used a side exit. They'd had to wait only a few minutes until the car he'd called for arrived, but they were prevented from moving as fast as they wished because of heavy traffic on the freeway. At times their speed was reduced to a crawl.

Rye had been right: It was mandatory that Brynn get to Violet before either Nate or the Hunts stopped her. The snail's pace contributed to her stress.

After a lengthy silence, Rye startled her by asking, "What about nurses? Staff? You show up on Thanksgiving night, won't that arouse suspicion?" Apparently, he'd been thinking about possible obstacles she might face.

"This facility is like a hotel. There's an attendant on each floor with basic nursing training. They can replace IV bags, take and record vitals, but they're there largely to notify the patient's doctor or emergency staff of any drastic change in a patient's condition."

"You have her parents' permission to use the drug on her, even though she'll be the first patient it's been tried on? You've discussed it with them?"

"You ask that *now?*"

"Well?"

"Of course I've discussed it with them. None of the stem cell donor registries have found a suitable match for her. Not even her family members came close enough. Her parents see this drug as a lifesaver. They were involved in the application process for the exemption."

"So they'll be open to you giving it to her tonight?"

"Without hesitation. This last round of radiation was meant to prolong Violet's life, not save it. It's been grueling. It's weakened her. Her mother and father wouldn't have subjected her to it, except for the hope of her living long enough for the exemption to be approved. Believe me, Rye, this is the answer to their prayers."

He said, "What about Lambert? You said he sees Violet routinely. Won't her mother wonder why he's not in on it?"

"She'll probably ask. I'll tell her that he's seeing another patient. Which I'm sure is the case. As precarious as my situation is, I wouldn't want to be in Nate's shoes right now."

"Lambert," he said with scorn. "Between the senator and the girl, there was never a question of who he would give the drug to, was there?"

Rye's question may have been asked rhetorically, but it caused Brynn to think back on her frequent debates with Nate. From the outset, he had argued in favor of Richard Hunt, citing the contributions an influential congressman could make to society and the nation, whereas Violet had a long way to go simply to catch up to her grade level in school.

He also padded his arguments by comparing their physical preparedness to get the drug. Senator Hunt's illness had only recently been diagnosed and was in the primary stages. Since his system hadn't yet been weakened by other treatments, he had more stamina. He suffered no other health issues. Overall, the drug had a far better chance of succeeding with him than with Violet, whose system had been ravaged.

Brynn had argued that because of Hunt's superior condition, he had more time to wait out the FDA's approval. Violet didn't.

"It's an unwritten law not to criticize a colleague," she said. "And, regardless of Nate's abrasive and unlikable personality, he is brilliant. But, yes, I believe his decision was influenced by Richard Hunt's status. And money."

"He used a sick little girl as his bargaining chip to drive up the price." Rye mumbled a foul deprecation. "Do the girl's parents know about the competition?"

"No. They don't even know there is another patient similarly afflicted, or about this smuggled dose. I didn't want their hopes raised in case I failed to intercept it."

"They may have qualms about it being ill-gotten."

"They won't."

"You're sure?"

Softly she asked, "What if it were your child?"

"I'd have busted down the door of the lab and stolen it myself."

She smiled at his vehemence.

"You think I'm kidding."

"Not at all. I know you're deadly serious."

"What about Violet? Will she be afraid to get it?"

Brynn shook her head. "Her parents and I agreed never to mention the GX-42 to her."

"In case it doesn't work."

"To hold out the hope of a miracle cure and then have her hopes dashed? That would be too cruel."

"She knows she's terminal?"

"The word hasn't been used around her, but she's clever enough to realize that she's very sick. All the treatments she's undergone, the grueling testing. And she's made friends, known other children who succumbed."

"Jesus."

"Yet, miraculously, she retains a child's sunny outlook. She loves Disney princesses and talks of becoming a ballerina. When she's teased, she giggles. She squabbles with her brothers. Except for having a rare blood cancer, she's an ordinary little girl."

Rye rubbed his fingers across his brows, and, for several minutes he looked out the rain-streaked car window without saying anything.

She said, "You're mulling over all the moral and ethical implications, aren't you?"

He turned back to her. "Fair to say they're ambiguous?"

"Fair to say. You've had only an hour to contemplate them. I've had months, Rye, and don't believe for a moment that the conclusion is clear cut. It *is* playing God. Who gets the kidney, the lung, the heart? The choice is never easy.

"True, I favored Violet. But not because she is an adorable little girl, and Hunt is, well, Richard Hunt. I didn't base my decision on who I liked best. For me, the decision came down to one thing. *Time.* He has it, Violet doesn't."

"Okay. I believe you, and I agree."

"Then why are you gnashing your teeth?"

"What if you're caught?"

"I will be. Because I must document every single aspect of her progression."

"Or digression."

"Or digression. The records will help determine the future of the drug, so they can't be fudged. But I've looked at it from every angle and—"

"Every angle you know about. There are probably dozens of *angles* you don't foresee, any one of which could ruin you."

"I've weighed the risks, Rye. To my reputation. My career."

"As of last night, your life was put at risk."

"Yes! By a crashing airplane!"

He moved his face closer to hers so he could make himself heard without the driver listening in. "By two men in dark suits,

Brynn. Their marching orders came from Hunt. If I hadn't been there, what lengths would they have gone to to get that box from you? How far had they been instructed to go?"

"I grant you that their arrival on the scene was disquieting. But after Violet has the drug in her bloodstream, the contest will be over."

"Don't bet on it. What little I know about Hunt is that he doesn't like to lose. He sure as hell doesn't lose graciously. Neither does your pal Nate."

"I expect repercussions, but I'm not letting them stop me. Because after wading through all my misgivings, juggling the pros and cons, one overriding fact remains." She raised her index finger. "This is Violet's last and only chance for a longer life. So I'm doing it, damn the consequences."

"If it goes well, Lambert will come after you for claiming his crown. He'll cry foul, parade out a long line of ethical violations. You'll be made to answer for giving a seven-year-old a drug that hadn't been approved."

"Let him bring it on. Violet's improvement would vindicate me, especially with other doctors who have patients in similar circumstances. They would rally to me."

"Okay. If everything's well and good, you may get a slap on the hand by some AMA review board and warned not to try a trick like that again." He paused for emphasis. "What happens if it all goes wrong? In addition to potential legal ramifications, think worst-case scenario, Brynn."

"Worst-case scenario would be that I had the means and opportunity to try to save Violet, and didn't."

"This little girl may be the last patient you're ever allowed to treat."

"Then she's the one I took the Hippocratic oath for."

Her comeback had more heat behind it than she'd intended, but she realized just how angry his third degree was making her. "Why are you so hung up on the potential consequences to me?

Less than twenty-four hours ago, you wanted to know nothing about my life."

"You're right," he said tightly. "Why should I give a damn about your future in medicine?"

"I just don't understand why you shuttled me from the hotel in a mad rush to get the GX-42 to Violet, and now you're trying to talk me out of giving it to her."

"No I'm not."

"Then what?"

In a thrumming voice, he said, "Because I'd like you to admit, if only to yourself, that you're not doing this strictly for Violet. You're also doing it for *you*."

Her cheeks flamed. Furious, she tried to turn her head aside, but he captured her chin between his thumb and finger and forced her to face him. "Why, Brynn? What are you trying to prove?"

"What are you?" she fired back, lifting her chin free. "Why did you take to the sky last night, knowing the danger? Why is it you live only to be airborne? You don't light anywhere for longer than you absolutely must. 'I'm outta here.' That's your refrain. Just what is it on the ground that you're trying to outfly?"

Still breathing hard with pent-up anger, he continued holding her stare, then said abruptly, "We're here."

"Oh." Shaking off her anger, she told the driver at which entrance to let her out.

Rye said, "I'll walk you inside."

"There's no need."

"Hell there's not," he said. "I don't want you winding up on the tip of one of Timmy's knives."

"How thoughtful."

"I'm thinking of myself. I don't want to live with it on my conscience."

They got out, and he dismissed the driver. Looking around,

taking in the surrounding area, he asked if the building had security.

"A guard at the public entrance, twenty-four-seven."

They went through an open iron gate into an unsheltered courtyard where paved walkways wound around flower beds and grassy areas dotted with park benches. Brynn raised her hood to protect herself from the rain. Rye remained bareheaded.

As they entered the multistory building, Brynn spoke to the guard on duty, addressing him by name. Seated at a table, he acknowledged the greeting with a lazy wave, but never took his eyes off the small TV tuned to a crime drama.

Speaking out of the corner of his mouth, Rye said, "If he's security, I don't feel all that safe."

"You're the most disreputable-looking person I've ever seen in here."

"That's what bothers me. He didn't give me a second glance."

They walked along the deserted corridor to the bank of elevators. She punched the up button.

He said, "You still have the stuff?"

She patted her coat pocket. "I'm glad the pharmacologist had the foresight to seal it in bubble wrap."

"Yeah, it's seen some miles since it left the lab."

Although there was no one in sight except the guard, Rye remained watchful and edgy, aware of every motion and sound. Noticing that he was flexing and contracting his fingers again, she said, "You really should put something on those cuts."

"When I can get around to it." He glanced up toward the ceiling. "What floor is she on?"

"Three."

He nodded as though that was of major importance. She supposed the small talk was in lieu of more quarreling. Weary of both, she gave him a small smile. "Only family members and pre-approved friends are allowed upstairs, so we have to say goodbye here." As she thought on something, she laughed softly.

"What's funny?"

"It occurs to me that this is our third goodbye today. At the hospital this morning, Nate's office, now here."

"May be a Guinness record."

"May be." As she looked into his eyes, her smile faltered. "I take back what I said a minute ago about the crashing airplane."

"Don't worry about it."

"No, I want to say... This wouldn't be happening if it weren't for you, flying last night when no one else would. Thank you, Rye."

"You already said it."

"I'm saying it again."

He negated the need for the additional gratitude with an uneasy roll of his shoulders.

The elevator arrived. Before the door opened, he tensed as though expecting someone to pounce out of it. But the cubicle was empty. He placed his hand on the door to hold it open.

"Twenty-four hours to spare," he said.

"But I'm going to start the drip right away."

He bobbed his chin. "Good luck. I'll know it got Violet well when you get famous."

"That's not why I'm doing this."

"I know."

"Don't leave thinking that."

"I don't."

There was so much more she wanted to say, but the more she said, the less talkative he became. "Take care, Rye." She went up on tiptoe and kissed him chastely on the cheek.

But as she was pulling away, he clamped his free hand over the back of her head, and kissed her as though his life depended on it. It was hungry, and hard, and over almost before she realized it had happened.

He pushed her into the elevator. "For a long time, I'm gonna wish I'd gotten inside your clothes."

He released the door.

When it reopened on the third floor, Brynn's lips were still throbbing, and Rye's parting words echoing in her mind. Later, she would dwell on what might have been between them, if only things had been different. If only he and she had been different. But there was more to regret than she had time for now.

She started down the corridor. The doors to all the private quarters were shut. No one was in the snack room or the communal parlor. As she got closer to the room at the end of the hall, butterflies took flight in her tummy, not because of the risk she was taking, but because of the joy she was about to bring to Violet and her family.

She tapped lightly on the door. The attendant on duty opened it and stepped out into the hallway. "Dr. O'Neal."

Brynn smiled pleasantly and acted as though she always showed up here looking completely exhausted and disheveled, dressed in yesterday's clothing. "Hello, Abby. How was your Thanksgiving? Did you have to work all day?"

"No. I came on at four this afternoon. How was yours?"

She smiled wanly. "Not at all customary."

"I'm surprised to see you here tonight."

"I wanted to check on Violet, ask what kind of day she had."

The young woman's smile wavered. "Oh. I thought you would have heard."

*8:01 p.m.*

Rye stood staring at the elevator door long after it had shut out his last look at Brynn. He didn't move away until his cell phone vibrated. It was Dash.

Rye answered querulously. "Is this my wake-up call?"

"You in bed?"

"Yeah."

"How's the hotel?"

"To be honest, haven't really noticed. It's got a rack. That's all that matters."

"And you're in it?"

"Isn't that what I said?"

"Yeah, but you're lying."

Rye was surprised that Dash knew that, but he tried to act annoyed. "You're having me tailed, or what?"

"Do I have reason to?"

Rye swore silently. "Okay. Busted. Why're you calling? Another job?"

"No. I just hung up from an enlightening chat with a Deputy Sheriff Williams."

"Wilson?"

"Whatever."

Rye put his back to the wall and rested his head against it. "What did he want? That mess in Howardville has been cleared up."

"He wanted to know did I know where you were, because he ain't in Howardville, and that 'mess' hasn't been cleared up at all. He found blood on the floor of a parking garage in downtown Atlanta, and has a movie of you doing a Jackie Chan impersonation on a kid with a knife."

Rye pinched the bridge of his nose hard enough to bring tears to his eyes. "Fuck, fuck, *fuck!*"

"Guess that answers if it's true or not."

He could feature the workout Dash was giving his cigar. For this occasion, he might have lit it. "Listen, Dash, I don't know why Wilson called you—"

"Only contact they had for you."

Rye thought of his parents, and his stomach bottomed out. "You didn't give Wilson any next-of-kin info, did you?"

"Hell, no, I played a regular dunce. But I'd kinda like to know what I'm covering you for. Felony or a misdemeanor?"

"Vengeance. That kid with the knife was the one who zapped me with the laser."

"Figured that might be it. But how was it that he was your ride to Atlanta?"

"Wilson knew about that?"

"Oh, yeah. The man's a wizard. He knows all about you and the lady doctor shacking up in a low-rent cabin, about these two heavies hauling you outta there in a black Mercedes, and delivering you to Dr. Lambert. Who, Wilson said, was none too happy to learn that she had lied to him, obviously so she could run off with you again.

"They know that's how come she lied because Wilson and APD have another movie of you, this one of you and Dr. O'Neal rendezvousing in the parking garage. Not all that tenderly, though. Wilson said it looked to him like she was reluctant to go with you at first, but that you succeeded in luring her out."

"Hardly luring."

"What would you call it? Coercing? Strong-arming? Kidnapping? If I was you, I'd settle for luring."

Rye ignored everything except the fact that Wilson and Rawlins had tracked Brynn and him to Atlanta. If they had security camera video of what had taken place on the third and ground levels of the garage, it probably wouldn't be long before they got the tag number of the Uber car that had taken them to the hotel.

"Dash, did you give Wilson this phone number?"

"No."

"Or tell him about the hotel you booked for me?"

"Played dumb about everything. Are you at the hotel now?"

"No."

"Huh. I thought maybe you and the doctor were availing yourselves of—"

"No."

"Then where are you?"

Rye didn't respond.

Dash said, "You're not going to tell me diddly, are you?"

"If Wilson comes back to you and applies pressure, you can truthfully say you don't know anything."

"Just tell me if you're okay. You were the one bleeding in that garage."

"The guy cut my hand, but not bad. I got my revenge."

"You didn't castrate him."

"Next worst thing. I'm done there."

"That altercation, that's all this deputy has on you?"

"I swear."

After a significant pause, Dash said, "Not to his way of thinking."

Rye had never heard Dash speak in such a solemn tone. "What's his way of thinking?"

"He didn't lay it out, but he dropped hints."

"Like?"

"Like the condition of the man from the airstrip has been downgraded from guarded to serious."

Rye groaned. "Brain bleed?"

"Wilson said his heart's gone wonky."

"How bad?"

"They don't know yet. But Wilson wants to talk to you again."

"As a material witness or a culprit?"

"Didn't say, but he threw out the word 'manslaughter' and let it hover."

Rye rubbed his brow. "What else?"

"He dropped a bombshell of a name on me."

"Let me guess. Senator Richard Hunt."

In a gruff and angry undertone, Dash said, "What the fuck, Rye? You couldn't make an enemy who has a little less clout?"

"It's too long a story to tell now, Dash, and it has nothing to do with me except that the shitheads who wrecked your plane and tried to scrub me are on Hunt's payroll."

"What's a senator got against you?"

"Wasn't about me. It was about the cargo."

"Wilson kept referring to that black box. What's with that?"

"You won't hear it from me."

"Then you'll never climb into another of my cockpits!"

"Until tomorrow."

He could hear Dash's fuming breathing, the squishy chomping on his cigar, but by the time he spoke again, he'd calmed down a bit. "What about *her*?"

He could only be referring to Brynn. "*Nothing* about her, all right?" Dash waited him out. Rye glanced at the elevator, then added softly, "I'm done there, too."

Dash didn't say anything, and when the silence became uncomfortable, Rye yielded and spoke first. He asked if he was still booked on the flight to Columbus the following evening. Dash confirmed that and asked Rye what he intended to do in the meantime.

"Wilson and Rawlins—that's his partner—don't have anything on me, but they could delay me getting out of here tomorrow night. I'll stay under the radar until my flight. I need the bunk time anyway."

"How long's it been?"

"Long." Before Dash could tear into him about his lack of sleep, he said, "My phone's almost out of juice. I'll check in with you in the morning."

"You still want the first thing that comes up?"

"You read my mind."

He clicked off and started down the empty corridor, his boot heels striking loudly in the hollowness. The guard was absorbed in what he was watching on TV.

Even more so than before. Because when he heard Rye approaching, he turned around. A wide, proud grin spread across his otherwise basset hound face. "Hey, look. I'm on TV."

When Rye reached the table, he stopped. "What?"

"News was delayed on account of a ball game, but see?"

The guard chuckled as he pointed himself out on the screen, which showed a wide shot of a moderate crowd of people. Rye recognized the backdrop as the courtyard he and Brynn had walked through only minutes before, the building in the background.

The guard stood out in the crowd because he was in uniform when everyone else was wearing civilian clothing or white lab coats.

Rye had difficulty making sense or lending credibility to the voice-over commentary. The captions superimposed across the bottom of the screen seemed just as nonsensical. But, gradually, he began to piece together a story that filled him with disbelief and anguish.

The guard said, "I guess I shouldn't be lettin' on about myself, when it's all about Violet. Sweet kid."

He was talking to himself. Rye was already running back toward the elevator.

# Chapter 21

*8:08 p.m.*

The light above the elevator indicated that it was still on the third floor. For the second time in three hours Rye opted for the fire stairs. He climbed, taking several at a time, rounded the landings without slowing, and burst through the door marked "THREE," winded but wild to find Brynn.

The long and empty hallway stretched both left and right. He ran several yards in one direction, didn't spot anyone or hear voices behind the closed doors, reversed direction and ran the other way until he reached the last room, where light shone into the hall through the door standing ajar.

He pushed it open and went in. There was a hospital bed, empty except for a pink, well-worn stuffed bunny lying on the pillow. Under the window, a twin bed, the linens stripped from it and piled in a bundle on the bare mattress. Coloring book pages of ballerinas taped to the walls.

Rye registered all this within a second.

Brynn and a young woman with a name tag clipped to her scrubs were standing before a wall-mounted flat-screen TV, watching the same news story Rye had seen a portion of downstairs.

Hearing him huff up behind her, Brynn turned her head. Her face had been leached of color; her expression was stark with despair. He moved to stand beside her in a show of support, but he didn't touch her, aware of the other woman's curiosity over his sudden appearance.

The news story ended with a wrap-up from the smiling anchorwoman. "Senator and Mrs. Hunt certainly made it a memorable Thanksgiving for little Violet and her family, hey, Mark?"

The co-anchor looked into the camera through moist eyes. "They certainly did. What an inspiring and heartwarming story for Thanksgiving night. And the story isn't over. We'll have coverage of Violet's homecoming for you on our morning program."

He went on about it being a day to count blessings and spread happiness to those in need of cheering, that everyone should take the Hunts' example to heart. Rye's stomach turned. Since Brynn appeared to be hypnotized by the anchor's blather, he plucked the remote from her hand and muted the audio.

The name-tagged woman regarded him with uncertainty. "Are you with Dr. O'Neal?"

Brynn roused herself. "I'm sorry. Abby, this is...uh...my... friend."

He hitched his chin. "Hi."

Abby said hi back, then, "Is everything all right, Dr. O'Neal?"

Brynn placed a reassuring hand on the young woman's arm. "Yes, of course. Fine. I'm just more than a little surprised that I wasn't consulted before all this took place." She motioned toward the TV. "Who signed Violet out? Dr. Lambert?"

"No." The doctor she named must've been familiar to Brynn. She gave an absent nod. "I would like to have been notified, so I could be here to wish Violet a safe journey home."

"It all happened so suddenly," Abby said with a genial smile. "No sooner had I come on duty than the TV vans started pulling up outside the gate. I'm told that only the administrator was given a heads-up, and barely fifteen minutes before the Hunts themselves arrived in a long white limo. They intended for it to be a surprise, and said that it wasn't about them, it was about Violet."

"Leaving one to wonder how the TV stations knew of it in advance," Brynn said.

Abby shrugged. "They're such a high-profile couple, I guess it's hard for them to keep anything under wraps."

"The limo might have been a giveaway," Rye said. He admired Brynn's ability to maintain her forced smile when he felt like smashing something.

Brynn asked, "Was it ever explained how Violet came to be chosen for this—"

"Farce."

"—honor?" Brynn asked, talking over Rye's angry whisper.

Abby's lips formed a moue of sadness. "I heard the senator telling one of the reporters that they wanted to do this for a child who was seriously ill, but well enough to withstand the trip." She laughed softly. "Of course the travel was streamlined for her. They made it hassle-free for Violet and her mother."

"Yes," Brynn said, keeping her smile pasted on, "they literally rolled out the red carpet for them."

The news vans had caravanned behind the Hunts' limousine to a private landing strip where the couple's Gulfstream had been waiting to fly Violet and her mother to Tennessee for a reunion with her father, brothers, and beloved dog, Cy.

Cameras had captured the red carpet–white glove treatment extended to them by the two pilots and flight attendant, as well as the fond farewell hug that the senator and his wife had bestowed on a smiling Violet and her tearfully grateful mother.

The end of the poignant story had shown the Hunts' jet soaring off the runway into a rainy sky. The two stood arm-in-arm on the tarmac beneath an umbrella, waving until the plane's blinking lights disappeared into the clouds, which was the fade-out shot that had brought tears to the anchorman's eyes.

"Violet has more surprises in store," Abby informed them in a hushed, happy voice. "Elsa from *Frozen* is scheduled to visit her at home tomorrow. Violet is also going to receive a new iPad, with all her favorite apps already downloaded, and a TV for her bedroom." She chatted on, unaware of how appalling this was to Brynn.

"Mrs. Hunt is even prettier in person than she is on TV. Her suit was just okay, but her shoes were to die for."

Before Abby could expand on wardrobe, Rye clasped Brynn's elbow and said in an undertone, "We need to get out of here."

Brynn must've picked up on his urgency and the reason for it. She said to Abby, "We're due at a party. I only wanted to stop by and say a quick hi to Violet."

Rye steered her around, out of the room, and down the hall toward the elevator. She went without protest.

Abby fell into step with them. "As close as you are to Violet and her family, I'm sure they would welcome a call from you. And she'll be back on Tuesday."

Tuesday. Days past the GX-42's expiration.

"Yes," Brynn said. "Her next radiation treatment is scheduled for Wednesday." She worried her lower lip. "No matter how streamlined the trip, her autoimmune system is so weakened, I worry about infection. Severe fatigue."

"I overheard Mrs. Hunt say that the flight crew has the weekend off, but they'll be flying Violet back. And she's being safeguarded. Violet's doctor in Knoxville was put on notice. A medical team supervised by him will be on standby the whole time she's there. The senator insisted on that. Violet's welfare is his top priority."

Brynn and Rye exchanged a look.

"It's a shame you got here too late to see her off."

Quietly, Brynn said, "Much too late."

"I need to get back to work," Abby said. "Have fun at your party."

She started back down the hall. Rye watched her until she reentered Violet's room. As they drew abreast of the elevator, he noticed that the ground floor button was lighted, indicating that someone had summoned it. It could have been anybody. But the hair on the back of his neck stood on end, and he trusted that instinct. He wheeled Brynn around. "Hurry."

She reacted without question as he towed her toward the fire stairs and rushed her down them. When they reached the first floor, he opened the door a crack. No one was at the elevator or in the corridor. The guard was still hunched over the television, his back to them. "Is there another way out?"

"An emergency exit on the other side of the building."

"Will an alarm go off if we open it?"

"I have the code to disarm it."

"Lead the way."

They slipped through the door without drawing the guard's notice and walked as rapidly and as silently as they could. Rye continued looking over his shoulder, checking the fire stairs door they had just come through. His ears were attuned for the ping that would signal the arrival of the elevator.

They rounded a corner at an intersection of hallways. The emergency exit was at the far end of one. He and Brynn jogged toward it. Brynn punched in the code on the keypad, and a lock released with a loud metallic click. No alarm blared when Rye depressed the metal bar and pushed open the heavy door.

He ushered Brynn out ahead of him and, after one last look behind him, followed her. He waited only long enough to hear the reassuring click of the door relocking, then grabbed her hand and took off in a dead run.

*8:18 p.m.*

Abby emerged from Violet's room with her arms full of bedding, but drew up short in fright. A tall man was standing just beyond the door. "Mercy, you startled me."

"I'm sorry," he said. "Didn't mean to."

"Can I help you? Only family is allowed—"

"Oh, I know. The guard said. But I'm Dr. Lambert's driver tonight. He didn't want to get out of the car in the rain, so he sent me in to see if Dr. O'Neal was here. He needs to consult with her about a patient. Sure enough, when I asked the guard, he told me she came in not long ago."

"She was here. You just missed her."

"By how much?"

"I'm surprised you didn't meet them in the elevator."

"Them?"

"I guess he was her date. They were on their way to a party. If it's an emergency, I can call her and tell her to come back. I have her number."

"That's the problem. Dr. Lambert has been calling her phone for over an hour. He thinks it must be on the fritz." He held up a slip of paper with a telephone number handwritten on it. "Is this the number you have for her?"

She pulled her phone from the pocket of her tunic and accessed her contacts. "That's it."

"Do you by chance have another?"

"Only the number of her answering service."

"Dr. Lambert tried that. They struck out reaching her, too. Her phone's battery must've run completely dry." He started backing away and gave her a smile. "Sorry about scaring you."

Until he turned and started walking away, Abby hadn't noticed a second man waiting at the elevator. He wasn't a heart-stopper like the one she'd talked with. He had shifty eyes and looked ill-kempt even in his dark chauffeur's uniform. She thought this face looked battered, too, but that could have been a trick of the lighting.

Abby couldn't fathom why Dr. Lambert would need two drivers.

Then again, knowing Dr. Lambert, she figured he needed one for himself and another for his ego.

*8:22 p.m.*

The hospital complex was a sprawling campus. The concrete arteries connecting the various buildings were lighted like the Vegas strip. The rain helped to blur the lights, but it also kept the sidewalks free of other pedestrians, making Rye and Brynn that much more conspicuous. They covered a lot of ground in a short span of time, but not so much that Rye relaxed his vigil.

He kept them moving at a clip while staying on the lookout for the black Mercedes. He didn't know positively that Goliad and Timmy were on their trail. But if they weren't already, they or someone of their ilk in the Hunts' employ would be soon. The first place they'd look for Brynn would be where she would have expected to find Violet.

Spotting a taxi leaving one of the main buildings, Rye said, "I'll flag it down. Don't dawdle." He dropped Brynn's hand and took off in a sprint. When she caught up to him, he was holding open the back door; they scrambled in.

"Where to?" the driver asked.

"Just drive," Rye said. "She needs a minute. Got some bad news about her cousin."

"Any particular direction?"

"Just drive."

Grumbling, the driver sat forward and drove away. For the first half mile, Rye watched out the rear window, but didn't detect a tail.

"Are we being followed?"

"I don't think so. But I could be wrong."

Brynn pushed back her hood. Passing headlights gave him fleeting glimpses of her face. He couldn't tell if the watery streaks on her cheeks were tears, rainwater, or reflections of trickles on the windows. Regardless, her expression was telling. She was devastated.

"They knew all along that I would attempt to steal the drug for Violet," she said. "As proved by the timing of that grotesque display. They staged it while we were making the drive back from Howardville."

"Even before you ran out on Lambert, the Hunts had hedged their bet by getting Violet out of reach."

"Worse, they made sure I can't get to her. Her homecoming will be televised. Which means more media in Tennessee. Lights, cameras." She placed her fingers against her temples and pressed hard. "I was mentally prepared to cross the line of ethics. I knew the risks and was willing to take them. But I would rather not have a spotlight on me when I did."

"You could call Mr. and Mrs. Griffin." Brynn had never revealed to him Violet's surname, but there was no need for confidentiality any longer. Following the news story, everybody knew their name. The Hunts had made sure of it.

"Call, tell them that you have the GX-42," he said. "If you got up there before eight p.m. tomorrow, they would send Elsa packing and let you carry on."

"Would they, Rye? Now? With the spotlight shone on them? I'm not so sure. The risks would be greater for them, too."

"What if it was your kid?"

She gave a rueful smile over his repetition of her question. "I would send Elsa packing."

"I'm betting they would, too."

"But even if they did, there's a medical team on high alert. With Violet's welfare being the senator's 'top priority,' she will be closely monitored." Looking defeated, she said, "The Hunts covered all the bases."

"Do you think Lambert was behind it?"

She considered it, then shook her head. "If Nate had known about the televised spectacle they had planned, he would have been at the center of it. More than likely he's irked over being excluded." She lapsed into thought, then said, "This has her stamp on it."

"The wife with shoes to die for?"

"She's the senator's mama bear. She's also an excellent promoter. A winner." She laid her head back against the seat and closed her eyes. "They fought dirty, but they won. As a physician, I can't let this dose go to waste. I'll deliver them the vial tonight. Humble myself and admit to a temporary loss of reason. Something. I'll make nice. Uphold my Hippocratic oath. My conscience will be clear, and I'll no longer be looking over my shoulder for Goliad and Timmy."

"They're not the only ones on your tail."

His tone brought her eyes open. She gave him her full attention.

"I had a call from Dash."

He related the conversation. Even knowing that her brain was sluggish with exhaustion and desolation, he didn't spare her the details. She needed to be made aware of everything she was up against.

"He didn't elaborate on Brady's condition?"

"'Heart's gone wonky.' That's all Wilson could tell him." He paused. "Did you hear the rest of it, Brynn?"

"Goliad and Timmy. Wilson and Rawlins. All after little ol' me. I never wanted to be this popular."

"The deputies are on the wrong track, but at least they're doing their job. Everybody else is after the drug." He resettled, turning toward her slightly. "Can I toss out one thought?"

"Will it be helpful?"

"It might crystalize your thinking."

"Then, please."

"Okay, say you deliver the drug to the Hunts. Humble yourself. Make nice. All that stuff you said. What happens after you give it to him?"

"His disease goes into remission, doesn't recur, he'll live a longer and healthier life."

"But will you?"

"What?"

"Are you sure they'll call the dogs off?"

"Once the GX-42 is in his system, what would they hold against me?"

"Betrayal. You would have given it to Violet if they hadn't gone out of their way to prevent it. They don't strike me as forgiving types, Brynn. And since your plan to give it to Violet was foiled, what's to keep you from blowing the whistle on the whole thing?"

"I couldn't do that without admitting my own culpability."

"But Senator and Mrs. Hunt would have a whole lot farther to fall. Talk about a spotlight. You could shine it right on them, and that isn't the glare they would want to be caught in."

Her eyes seemed to plumb his. He held steady. This had to be her decision.

In a quiet voice, she said, "What you're intimating is that, no matter which patient gets the drug, I face exposure, censure, possible peril."

"Those are bigger words than I would use, but, basically, yeah."

"So it comes down to—"

"You know what it comes down to, Brynn. You already said. Worst-case scenario? You had the means to try to save Violet and didn't." He touched the pocket of her coat that contained the vial. "As long as you're in possession of the game ball, you're winning."

She looked at him for a few seconds longer, then said in a rushed voice, "If I could get on a flight to Knoxville tonight, I could be on the Griffins' doorstep first thing in the morning."

"Amidst media."

"But the Griffins would welcome me with open arms. I'm

sure of that. I could lay it all out to them. They may say no to the GX-42, but at least they'll have been given a choice. If they agree, we'll devise a way for me to do the infusion."

"If they say no?"

"I'll bring it back to Richard Hunt."

"By eight p.m.?"

"I bet they would cancel their flight crew's weekend off."

He checked his watch. "With the mess the airlines are in, there probably won't be a flight tonight."

"I'll rent a car."

"Are you up to making that drive?"

"How long will it take?"

"However long, you were up all night last night and only got a short nap today."

"One way or another, I'm going." She leaned forward and said to the driver, "Take us to the airport, please."

The driver grimaced into the rearview mirror. "Traffic on both interstates is going nowhere fast. If you're trying to make a flight—"

"Do your best," Rye said.

The driver shot him a resentful look. "This thing doesn't have wings, you know."

Rye huffed a laugh. "Yeah, I know. But I've got a twenty in my pocket that can be yours on top of the fare, plus the expected fifteen percent, if you stopping bitching and drive. But don't take the exit to the main terminals. Take the one just before it."

Brynn said, "Back way?"

"Back alley."

"What's there?"

"Lots of porn."

# Chapter 22

———◦◉◦———

*8:58 p.m.*

Delores ended the call with a decisive tap on her phone screen. "They missed them by minutes."

Nate, still seated at the desk where she had assigned him a place, ran his hand over the top of his head. Richard gripped the rolled armrests of the easy chair in which he sat, an evident attempt to keep himself from flying into a rage.

Only by an act of will did Delores keep her voice steady as she recounted for them everything Goliad had told her. "According to him, they must have used an emergency exit. It's the only way they could have gotten out of the building unseen. He doesn't know if they left the premises on foot, or if they have transportation now, but either way, they disappeared. He's spent the past twenty minutes cruising through the complex in search of them."

"Did you give Goliad her home address?"

"He's on his way there now. But she would be a fool to go home, and she's no fool, which has become all too obvious." She turned to Nate. "How could you have let her out of your sight before checking the box to be certain that the vial was in there?"

"She didn't sneak the drug while I was with her," he exclaimed. "Blame your two watchdogs. They were with her for hours. You should be castigating them, not me."

Delores hugged her elbows, running her hands over her upper arms in agitation. To a large extent, Nate was right, but she'd be damned before admitting it. Besides, who was *he* to correct *her*? He was getting way above himself.

"Well," she said, "we can be glad we made that preemptive strike. The girl is hundreds of miles away, surrounded by media and medical personnel. Dr. O'Neal can't get to her. But we must get to Dr. O'Neal." She checked her wristwatch. "Need I remind anyone that we now have less than twenty-four hours to start the infusion?"

She went to Richard's chair, bent over the back of it, and hugged him from behind. "We've been under shorter deadlines, darling." She kissed the top of his head, then turned to Nate. "What was the pharmacologist's last stand on sneaking another vial?"

"He's unbending. The offer of more money didn't faze him. And, he, uh, raised another sticking point." He left the desk, went to the bar, and helped himself to three fingers of their best scotch.

Delores said, "Well?"

Nate shifted his gaze to Richard, who sat contained, but rather like a volcano building up pressure before an eruption. Delores recognized the signs. Nate did not. He faced Richard squarely.

"During our last conversation, the pharmacologist used the word 'transparency.' More than once."

"In what context?" Richard asked.

"The upcoming Senate committee hearing. I believe it's scheduled for week after next?" He sipped his drink, cleared his throat. "The opioid crisis has created a rush—many fear a dangerous rush—to put treatment drugs on the market. This has placed the commissioner of the FDA and the heads of several pharmaceutical companies in the hot seat to defend their haste. You're sitting on that committee, Richard, as an outspoken critic of the accelerated testing, and as a banner carrier for enforcing stricter regulations."

"You're telling me things I already know, Nate," he said. "And the crisis I'm most concerned about *tonight* is the one taking place *in this sitting room*." To emphasize the last four words, he made stabbing motions toward the floor with his index finger.

"I understand, of course," Nate said. "But, you've been advocating a 'clamp-down' on the sponsors of experimental drugs, especially those covered by the Orphan Drug Act. You're quoted as saying it's not 'cost effective' to spend millions on developing a drug when relatively few patients will benefit from it. As you know, GX-42 falls into that category."

He paused to let all that sink in, although Delores had gotten his point, and so had Richard.

Nate swirled the scotch in his glass. "This has created a moral dilemma for the pharmacologist. He's conflicted over providing it to you, when you're on a soapbox demanding budget cuts that would curtail its testing. To paraphrase him, it's like you want to squeak in under the wire before limitations, heatedly endorsed by you, are implemented."

Richard's fingers turned white with tension around the armrest. "To a man of integrity, as, according to you, this scientist is, I can see where that might create a moral dilemma."

"Well, then—"

"But you have no integrity, Nate." He leveled his fiercest glare on him. "How dare you take the high ground. Do not speak to me about moral dilemmas, or transparency. In short, do not fuck with me again."

Those reverberating words were punctuated by a buzzer, signaling someone at the estate entrance gate. "Media, no doubt," Delores said. "Trying to follow up today's story about that girl. The housekeeper will take care of it."

She picked up her gold lighter and fiddled with it, turning it end on end as she began to pace. "For the time being, let's assume that the pharmacologist is a lost cause. Where would Brynn O'Neal have gone, Nate?"

"I—"

"Excuse me, Senator, Mrs. Hunt." The housekeeper was standing in the open doorway. "A Deputy Don Rawlins is at the gate. He says it's important that he see you."

Nate covered his face with both hands. "Don't these clowns ever give up?"

Delores spun around to confront him, demanding, "What could they want with us?"

"I have no idea," Nate said. "When they saw me out of the parking garage, they were eating humble pie for wasting my time."

Turning to the housekeeper, Delores said, "Tell them that we've retired—"

Richard cut her off. "Let them in." The housekeeper withdrew to carry out the order. Richard said to Nate and Delores, "Information is power. Let's see what they have to say. Maybe they've uncovered something useful to us about Dr. O'Neal or the pilot."

Nate downed his scotch. Delores checked her hair and lipstick in the wall mirror and was standing in her "senator's wife pose"— feet in fourth position, hands clasped at her waist—when the housekeeper led the two officers into the sitting room.

"Gentlemen," Delores said, smiling. "Excuse our informality. We weren't expecting company. Other than our dear friend Nate Lambert, whom I understand you've met."

Hats in hands, they introduced themselves by name and politely shook hands with her and Richard. "An honor, sir," Rawlins said. He looked over at Nate. "Doctor."

Wilson's greeting was equally uncordial toward Nate.

Turning on the charm, Delores motioned the two officers into chairs and played hostess. "I know from Nate that you've had an awfully long day. It can't have been much of a Thanksgiving for either of you. Would you care for something? I can offer you all the leftover turkey sandwiches you can eat."

They smiled as expected, but declined the sandwiches as well as an offer of pie. "Just coffee, please," she said to the housekeeper. "I think we could all do with that." She perched on the arm of Richard's chair and placed her hand on his shoulder. "I think the senator and I are missing a link here. What brings you?"

Richard said, "You know my stance on supporting law enforcement officers. How can we help you?"

Wilson took the lead and consulted a note he'd made on his cell phone. "We have a Georgia license plate number we'd like confirmed as being registered to Mrs. Hunt. Black Mercedes." He read off the number.

Delores looked at Richard, and he at her, and then both turned to the deputies. She said, "I have no idea."

"Nor do I," Richard said. "We're not personally responsible for the upkeep of the automobiles we own and use, either here or in Washington."

"This car was in Howardville this morning."

"Oh! Then that must've been the car Goliad drove up there," she said.

"Goliad have a last name?"

She laughed. "I'm sure he does, but I've only ever known him by the single name. I'm sure his full name is in our employee files."

"I'd like to have his full name when you can get it for me, please."

"Of course. He's signed off for the night, but I can get it to you first thing tomorrow."

"Did he get a parking ticket in your town?" Richard asked with his most diplomatic smile. "If you're here to collect the fine, I'm happy to pay."

Wilson forced a laugh. The other one, who in Delores's opinion had a pugnacious face, didn't crack a smile.

The housekeeper wheeled in a serving cart. The next few minutes were spent pouring and serving everyone's coffee to their liking.

When the housekeeper left, Delores picked up the conversation. "We sent Goliad up to Howardville to ensure that Dr. O'Neal would make it back to Atlanta safely. She was on an important errand for us."

"Yes, the doctor explained the errand, but didn't tell us on whose behalf it was."

"But I wouldn't, would I?" Nate asked, at his most snobbish. "Patient confidentiality."

Not put off, Rawlins said to him, "Concerned as you are over that patient, I thought you'd be at the lab running tests on those time-sensitive blood samples, trying to match...what was it? Cell markers?"

"I dropped the samples at the lab on my way here. I wouldn't want to impose a tedious explanation of the matching process on Senator and Mrs. Hunt."

"I'm sure they appreciate that consideration," Rawlins said. "You ever locate Dr. O'Neal?"

"No. I'm almost glad I haven't. I'm very upset with her. Terribly disappointed."

"For not overseeing the tests with you?"

"Among other things," Nate replied and gave a delicate shudder.

Richard set his cup and saucer on the small table at his elbow. "Nate has told us about Dr. O'Neal's seeming infatuation with the pilot and their ill-timed interlude this morning."

Wilson said, "They left the rendezvous spot with your Goliad and another man."

"Who would that be?" Pretending ignorance, Delores looked to Richard for clarification.

"A new man Goliad has taken under wing to train," he said to the deputies. "I believe his name is Timmy. I don't know his last name."

She waved her hand as though those details didn't matter. "This is so out of character for Dr. O'Neal. Ordinarily she's so stable, entirely devoted to treating that sweet little girl, and in pursuit of every possible avenue for her survival."

The two deputies looked at each other. Wilson came back to Delores. "Sweet little girl?"

"Dr. O'Neal and Nate's patient." When the two officers gave Delores blank stares, she looked at Nate with perplexity and a trace of asperity. "Even without divulging Violet's name, I was under the impression you had explained everything to these gentlemen."

Delores could have slapped him. He just sat there like a ventriloquist's dummy, his mouth opening and closing but nothing coming out.

Fortunately, neither of the deputies was paying attention to him. They were looking at her and Richard. Wilson coughed behind his fist. "Excuse us, senator, Mrs. Hunt. We had surmised that these blood samples were being tested for one of you."

"Oh," she said on an exhalation. "No. Richard and I are blessed with good health." She let her smile falter. "Sadly, not so for Violet. I learned of her situation through one of the foundations that Richard and I support. We wanted to do something meaningful for her and her family."

"Why don't we play them the DVR?" Richard suggested. "That will explain things."

"We had just as well make some use of it." Her smile to the deputies was modestly apologetic. "We wanted to keep this between us and the girl's family, but the media got wind of it. There's no longer a need to protect her identity."

Richard used an iPad on the end table to turn on the flatscreen fitted into a bookcase. The DVR had been paused at the place in the newscast where the story of Violet began.

The deputies watched with interest, and, when Richard paused the recording on their private jet disappearing into the clouds, the two looked justifiably embarrassed. Wilson said, "Very generous gesture."

"Thank you. She's had it rough and deserves some happy days." Richard came to his feet. "If that's all, Del and I have had a long day, too."

Both deputies stood up. Wilson threaded his hat through his fingers. "That's not quite all, senator."

With visible but contained impatience, Richard divided a look between the two.

Rawlins said, "We've still got a man up in Howardville who was attacked last night." Turning to Nate, he said, "We'd like to ask Dr. O'Neal a few more questions about what happened out there at the airport."

Nate said, "Granted, Brynn has been indiscreet today, but she isn't the sort to knock a man unconscious."

"But he's the sort."

"Mallett?"

Rawlins nodded.

"Then I suggest you look for him," Nate said. "We don't even know that he's still in Atlanta, or that they're together."

Delores watched the deputies for their reactions to Nate's lie.

Rawlins said, "Oh, they're together, Dr. Lambert. After she abandoned you, things got interesting in that parking garage." He turned to Delores. "First, Mallett had a run-in with your Mercedes-driving friend and his second."

"My goodness," she said on a shocked gasp. "Richard, did you know about this?"

"Of course not."

Rawlins continued. "After the encounter with Mallett, security cameras show Goliad and the other guy driving out in the Mercedes. Also shows Mallett and Dr. O'Neal hooking up several minutes later in her parking space and leaving together on foot."

"It seems that this Mallett is at the center of all the bloodshed," Richard said.

"I shudder to think of him with Dr. O'Neal," Delores said. "Do you think she's in danger? He obviously has a violent bent."

Nate chimed in. "There's no doubt in my mind that he injured that man at the airfield."

"Maybe," Rawlins said. "We can't figure a motive, though. And Dr. O'Neal may be moonstruck, but I can't see her covering for Mallett for something as serious as an assault."

"Has the poor victim described his attacker?" Delores asked.

"He was struck from behind."

"What a pity. I hope he recovers soon."

Nobody responded to that. Then Wilson said, "Well, we've taken up enough of your time. Please notify us if you see or hear from either of them."

There were handshakes all around and promises to share information should any become available. Delores herself walked the officers to the door and saw them out, then returned to the sitting room, went straight to the bar, and poured a drink.

"Just when we need to be our most surreptitious, Brynn has got these yokels nipping at our heels," Nate groused. "I could kill her."

"That's certainly an option," Richard said. "But we have to find her first. You know her better than we do. You see her almost every day. Have you thought of where she might have gone? What resources she has at her disposal? A second home? A second car? A roadmap to Violet Griffin's house in Tennessee?"

Compared to the near shout on which he'd ended, Delores's tone was soft and perfectly controlled. "You made a blunder, darling."

"A colossal one," Richard said. "When we trusted Dr. O'Neal."

"When you mentioned bloodshed."

Richard's gaze snapped to hers.

"The deputies hadn't said anything about blood. How would we know there had been bloodshed unless we knew about his knife fight with Timmy?"

*9:37 p.m.*

Wilson and Rawlins climbed into the SUV. They waited until they were clear of the gate and underway before Wilson looked over at Rawlins. In unison, they said, "They're lying."

# Chapter 23

———◆———

*9:41 p.m.*

The taxi driver hadn't been exaggerating about the amount of traffic on the interstate highways. It took longer to get to where they were going than Rye had anticipated, and when he assisted Brynn from the back seat, she looked at him as though he had lost his mind.

The neighborhood was dicey, bordering on sinister. Streetlights had either burned out or been shot out. The few enterprises still in operation were closed for the night. Most had metal grills protecting their windows and doors from break-ins. The street was shuttered, dark, and best avoided.

But since Rye didn't like either their taxi driver's beady eyes or his attitude, he asked him to drop them two blocks shy of their destination. Grudgingly Rye tipped him the promised extra twenty, for which he received no thanks. He waited until the taxi's taillights disappeared around a corner, then drew Brynn into the recessed entrance of an abandoned store.

"You're out of luck. The place is shut down." She brought his attention to the faded "For Sale" sign taped to the door. "Has been for some time now, looks like."

"This isn't where we're going. I didn't want the cabbie to know our final destination."

"*I* don't know our final destination."

"Remember that beach bar you and your friends went to? I told you there was a hangout like it near every airfield in the world."

"We're going to such a place?"

"Couple of blocks from here. Rough neighborhood. Rough and rowdy bar."

"Lots of pornography."

"You'll see. But if you want to fly to Tennessee, you've got to go where the flyers are."

"There's an international airport within shouting distance. It has lots of airplanes and pilots to fly them."

"It also has passenger manifests, TSA checkpoints, and ID requirements. If anyone having, say, congressional authority, checks to see if you're on a flight—"

"I hadn't thought of that."

"Richard Hunt will. He'll check the car rental outfits, too."

"So what do I do?"

"You let me broker you a deal with a private pilot."

"Forgive me for pointing out the obvious."

"I can't fly you, Brynn. Even I have limits. I wouldn't get into a cockpit again until I've had some sleep."

"I've never chartered a flight. How much will it cost?"

"Depends on the aircraft. But I won't let anyone take advantage of you. I'll get you a fair deal."

"It will probably put my credit card over the limit."

"You shouldn't put a charge on your card, anyway. I'll call Dash. He'll cover it. You two can settle up later."

"He would do that?"

"He'll gripe, but he'll do it. What do you say?"

She sighed, looked around, clearly in a quandary.

He put his hands on his hips. "Decide, Brynn. Do we do this or not? Your call."

She deliberated for another second or two, then said, "I'm not committing to it yet, but you dismissed the taxi, and the chances of getting another on this street are slim to none. I guess as long as we're this close to the hangout, it wouldn't hurt to look into a charter."

"Wait." He caught her arm before she could move away. "One more word of caution. The place will be full of guys who'll take one look at you and see fresh meat. Most will be drunk, uncouth, talking raunchy."

"I can handle that."

Her flippant dismissal amused him. He drawled, "Is that right?"

"I wasn't raised in a convent."

"No, but have you ever been groped by a flyboy? They don't fool around. No time for subtlety. He'll be flying out in an hour or two. Gotta get it while he can." He put his hand on her ass and pulled her to him, tilted his head, and lowered his lips to hers.

"No." She pushed him away, but her hands stayed flat against his chest inside his jacket. "What if you *had* slept a solid eight hours, Rye?"

He didn't say anything.

"No answer. Answer enough." She dropped her hands and stepped back. "That was going to be a goodbye kiss, wasn't it? Once you pass me off to the next flyboy, you'll make your grand exit."

"As a favor to you! That's what you said you wanted. Never to see me again. Remember?"

"Exactly. So why bother with kissing? I didn't even ask for your help."

He wanted to kiss her now more than ever, if only to prove that he could and still leave without a backward glance, without regret. The problem was, who would he be proving it to? To her? Or himself?

He should be sleeping. He should be long gone. Yet here he was, lending expertise and assistance in an effort to fix her problem. Any decent person would do the same, if not for Brynn, for the sick kid.

He would see this through and then split with a clear conscience. But if Brynn could do without kissing, by damn so could he. "You want to get to Tennessee?"

"You know the answer to that."

"Then you need to move on it before half the population of Atlanta, plus Wilson and Rawlins, are breathing down your neck. If you don't favor this plan, fine. You don't want any more of my help? Even better." He sliced the air with his hands. "I'll see you as far as the main airport, and we'll go our separate ways from there. But make up your mind."

She crossed her arms over her center, toed a dead weed in the wide crack in the sidewalk, looked at the barred windows, and reread the "For Sale" sign.

When her eyes reconnected with his, she said, "How graphic is the pornography?"

*9:53 p.m.*

To Brynn the noise level was raucous, but Rye, shouting directly into her ear in order to make himself heard, said, "It's Thanksgiving. Light crowd."

With an unbreakable grasp on her elbow and a proprietary demeanor, he steered her around tables where groups of men huddled over beer mugs and plates piled high with carbohydrates.

Billiard balls clacked amid whoops of triumph and curses of defeat. *Top Gun* was playing on a TV larger than Brynn's living room wall. Music was piped at a deafening level through scratchy overhead speakers.

There were only a handful of women in the place, all younger and less modestly clad than Brynn. Nevertheless, she received her share of speculative once-overs, whistles, and leers.

Rye headed toward a table on the periphery, which was a bit more secluded and where the lighting was dimmer. It was occupied by two men whose nachos had been reduced to crumbles. On the table was a collection of empty drinking glasses. Rye leaned down. "I'll buy you a round in exchange for the table."

They looked up at him, ogled Brynn, and one said, "Two rounds."

"Done."

With nudges and winks, they wished Rye good luck, then left them. As they sat down in the vacated chairs, Rye said, "I recommend sticking to the basics like a cheeseburger and fries, or nachos."

"What else is on the menu?"

"Sides."

"What are they?"

"Chili and jalapeños."

"I'll take the cheeseburger. No sides."

He signaled a passing busboy and, as he was clearing the table, Rye said, "Couple of cheeseburgers, please."

"I ain't the waiter."

Rye gave him a pained look. "Give me a fuckin' break and bring out two cheeseburgers, okay?"

The young man looked even more pained. "Fries?"

"What do you think? And two Cokes."

"Bourbon in those?"

Rye shook his head. "I may be flying tomorrow."

"Rum?"

Rye laughed. "Straight Coke."

After the young man moved away, she said, "You seem right at home."

"Yep. And I know how the system works. Wait here. Keep

your head down. Don't make eye contact, or he'll take it as encouragement."

"Who?"

"Pick one, any one."

He left the table and waded his way to the bar, where he motioned the busy bartender over. He paid for the drinks of the two men who'd given up their table, then conferred privately with the bartender.

Brynn read the names and dates and vulgarities carved into the tabletop.

Rye returned. "I put a bug in the bartender's ear."

"He'll find a pilot for me?"

"He won't have to. The pilot will find us."

"That's the system? You put the word out and see who comes around?"

"Basically. But don't be scared. Whoever winds up taking you will have met my qualifications. He won't be a rookie."

"Thank you."

"Save it for when you're on your way."

She took a look around. "You were teasing me about the porn."

"No, I wasn't." He indicated the wall nearest their table.

She looked at it, then realized that every inch of wall space was covered with pictures of airplanes. Every era of aviation was represented, so was every type, shape, color, and size of aircraft.

Rye said, "I call it 'plane porn,' because it's what every guy in here gets off on."

"Flying."

"Flying." He handed a five-dollar bill to the busboy, who had returned with their food and drinks.

They doctored their burgers using the condiments grouped into a beer six-pack in the center of the table, then dove in hungrily. When Brynn came up for air and took a sip of her drink, she said, "Why do you love it so much?"

"Tabasco?"

He'd poured a puddle of it onto his plate, but she knew he was using the quip to dodge giving her an answer. "Why do you love flying so much?"

"Early exposure, I guess. Most of my growing up was done on Air Force bases."

"Was your father a pilot?"

"He had his license, but flying bothered his ears. Pulling Gs made him sick."

"He didn't have the stomach for it."

He responded to her joke, but then his smile relaxed into a thoughtful expression. "He didn't have the—" Coming up empty, he made a gesture of dismissal.

She ate one last French fry, then moved the plastic plate aside and wiped her hands on a paper napkin. "Didn't have the what?"

"I don't know."

"Yes you do."

He dabbed the last bite of his burger into the pool of hot sauce, but returned it to his plate without eating it. He took a drink, shifted in his seat, turned to see if perhaps the bartender had forgotten him. When he finally resettled and his gaze lighted on her, she said, "Rye, this may be the last private conversation we ever have. Make it count."

"Why?"

"Because, it's been roughly twenty hours since you knocked me to the ground. That was the high point. Since then it's been one calamity after another. Aren't I entitled to take away something meaningful from this experience?"

"You turned down a grope and a damn good sloppy kiss in the making."

She held his stare.

He relented by exhaling a deep breath as he leaned back in his chair. "Thing of it is, I don't know how to explain it, any more than I know how to explain my fingerprints. They've always been there, and so has the obsession for flight. It goes beyond liking it, or even loving it. It's…" He paused, searched for the word, and again drew inspiration from his fingerprints. "Ingrained."

He must have thought that she would comment, or thank him for enlightening her, and that would be the end of it. But she continued to watch him with a listening aspect.

Eventually, he continued. "For as far back as I can remember, I wanted to be up there. I'd spend hours on end as close as I could get to a runway, watching the planes take off. One after the other. Over and over. I never tired of it. Envied the guy in the pilot's seat. All the time thinking, 'God, I can't wait to do that.'"

He looked toward the ceiling as though seeing open sky through it. Coming back to her, he said, "To this day, for that last nanosecond before I pull back on the yoke, I savor the anticipation of taking off. I still can't wait."

Her eyes glossed over with tears, but she sniffed them back. "Now, was that so hard?"

"Not very poetic."

"You're wrong." She spoke with emotional huskiness, but even above the cacophony, she knew he heard her.

He sat forward and braced his elbows on the table. "Okay, Dr. O'Neal, your turn. Why did you become a doctor? Did you answer a call to serve your fellow man?"

"Something like that. My mother died when I was very young. Before I understood about incurable illnesses, I was angry at the doctors for not making her well. Wasn't that what doctors were for?"

"You wanted to do better than they had."

"I suppose that factored in, early on at least. But becoming a doctor was also—"

"Excuse me?"

She and Rye looked up at the man who'd interrupted them.

He was around Rye's age, but cleaner cut, with hair worn short, and a smooth shave. His Hawaiian print shirt was tucked into his jeans. A Levi's jacket was slung over his shoulder, hooked on his index finger.

"Rye Mallett?"

Rye shot the bartender a vexed look. "I told him no names."

"You're in need of a pilot to fly this lady to an as-yet-undisclosed destination ASAP. Is that right?"

"You instrument rated?"

"Yes."

"How many hours do you have flying IFR? And what kind of plane is at your disposal?"

"I'm not applying."

Rye's tone turned testy. "Then what?"

"There's a cop asking around the pool tables if anybody's seen you and a lady fitting this one's description. Said the police are canvassing all the probable places for you to charter or rent a plane."

"Shit!"

"So, that resonates?"

"Yeah. It resonates," Rye muttered.

"What did y'all do to tick off Atlanta PD?"

"You don't care what we did, or you wouldn't be over here warning us."

"Was it short of killing somebody?"

"Way short. In fact, she's a doctor who's trying to save a life and running out of time to do it. Security cameras in a parking garage have me trying to teach some manners to an asshole who came at me with a knife. His package is gonna need an ice pack for several days, but he's still breathing."

The explanation seemed to satisfy the other man. He pulled on his jacket. "The cop went into the can, but he won't be long. I'll walk out with her, like she's my date. The cop has a picture of you taken off a security camera. I got a glimpse of it. It's blurry, can't tell much, but doesn't hurt to be careful, so use my cap."

He passed Rye a Braves ball cap. Rye put it on and slid off his bomber jacket.

"Good call," the man said. "Jacket's cool as shit, but it's part of your official description. Meet you outside." Addressing Brynn, he said, "You ready, sweetheart?"

He came around and held her chair.

Brynn looked at Rye with full-blown panic, not only because the police were conducting an official search for them, but because they didn't know this man from Adam, and she was being handed over to him. Regardless of the stance she'd taken earlier, she didn't want Rye to abandon her *now*.

"Are you coming?" she asked.

"Right behind you," he said. "Now go!"

She stood up, unsure her trembling legs would support her. The stranger placed his arm across her shoulders and propelled her toward the exit. But as soon as they had cleared it, she drew to a halt. "I'm not going any farther without Rye."

"I'm trying to help, I swear."

"Why would you?"

"Rye Mallett? Are you kidding? He's a legend."

Just then the legend exited the bar. He spotted the police unit parked off to one side and reclaimed Brynn by grabbing her hand. "Thanks, buddy. I owe you, but we gotta split."

"Where's your car?"

"Don't have one."

"Damn, man. Come on." He motioned for them to follow as he led them through the mazelike parking lot where lined spaces had been ignored. When they reached his car, he unlocked it with a fob and opened the back seat door.

Rye said, "No farther until I know who the hell you are."

"Jake Morton."

Then he saluted Rye.

# Violet

———◦◉◦———

I get to sleep in my own bed tonight. It has softer pillows than at the hospital. They call it a hotel, but who are they kidding? It's really a hospital, just without bright lights. Only sick people stay there. I'm on the floor for kids with cancer. Mom and I stay there while I get radiation. I hate radiation. But I don't have to think about it again till Wednesday.

I get to be at home for four nights, or maybe five. Mom said she wants Dr. O'Neal to be the one to say when I should go back. Dr. O'Neal wasn't there when I got sent home.

Here's what happened. I was taking a nap. I woke up when people came in my room. One was a man who is a senator. His wife's name was Mrs. Hunt. She had red lipstick and blond hair. They talked to me in soft voices, and smiled the whole time, and she said I was adorable. He patted my shoulder and told me I deserved a medal for being so brave.

Does he think I'm a soldier? He must be really dumb.

When I whispered that to Mom, she shushed me and said she would explain later, but she never got to, because the senator's wife wouldn't stop talking except when she had her picture

taken. She asked me if I was excited about being on TV. I said,
"Yes, ma'am," because Mom was looking at me with her "Use
your manners" face. Mrs. Hunt told me to wave to the cameras,
so I did, because I didn't want to make her mad. She acted like
the boss of everybody.

There was a couch on the airplane for me to lay on. I didn't
throw up. The lady in the dark blue dress brought me a ginger
ale. I didn't drink all of it. She kept asking me if I wanted something else, but I didn't.

When we got off the plane, more people were there to take
pictures. We rode home in a long white car like when we drove to
the airplane. Two policemen went ahead of us on motorcycles.

Lots of people were in our yard. They were taking pictures,
too. I was too tired to wave this time. I only wanted to see my
dad. He ran out the front door and down the steps and hugged
me. He had to pick up Cy and hold him because he was barking
at the TV people.

My room has lots of balloons in it. My brother popped one.
Daddy told him to settle down.

The doctor—not Dr. O'Neal, my first doctor—came in and
checked me over. A nurse is spending the night in our house.

Everybody left my room except Daddy. He sat on the bed.
He asked me about the airplane ride. I told him about the couch
and the ginger ale. He rubbed my head and told me he could
feel hair growing back, but I know there's none there. I smiled
anyway.

He leaned down and kissed my cheek, then wished me good
night and told me to rest because tomorrow was going to be a
big day. He left before I could see that he was about to cry. He
thinks I don't know that he cries sometimes, but I do. Kids are a
whole lot smarter than grown-ups think.

I can hear my brothers in their room. They're fussing over a
video game. Mom and the nurse and now Daddy, too, are having cake and coffee in the kitchen. They moved Cy's bed to my

room. He's asleep in it. Since I got sick, he's the only one who has stayed normal and doesn't treat me different.

Daddy told me I was in for a big surprise tomorrow. I think it's that Dr. O'Neal will be here when I wake up. I wonder if the senator and his wife got her permission to send me home. If they didn't, she's going to be mad, because, more than anything, she wants me to get well.

I sure hope I do. If I die, she's going to be so disappointed.

# Chapter 24

*10:22 p.m.*

When Rye was saluted, he fell back a step as though he'd been struck. "Cut that shit out."

Jake Morton smiled amicably. "Okay. But climb in. I'll take you anywhere you want to go."

"Thanks all the same," Rye said, "but I won't be responsible for getting you into trouble."

"I'm not leaving you, Mallett. Non-negotiable." Jake glanced beyond them toward the bar. "That cop won't be peeing forever."

Relenting, Rye gave Brynn a nod. They all got into the car, Brynn and Rye in back. Jake wasted no time putting several blocks' distance between them and the bar, then asked where they wanted to go.

Rye said, "Just take us over to the airport. Drop us outside baggage claim. Somewhere near the taxi line."

Jake said, "Seriously, name the place. I'll take you."

"Can't do it," Rye said. "Someone might have seen you leave with us. If you're asked later, you can honestly say you left us at the airport. After that, you don't know."

"Is this business with the police that serious?"

"No. But her patient is."

Jake looked at Brynn in the rearview mirror. She said, "I can't discuss it, but it really is a life-or-death matter."

Jake gave a solemn nod. "Airport it is."

"You fly?" Rye asked.

"Oh, yeah. I have a Bonanza."

"Sweet."

"Mine's older, but refurbished. Put in a new engine two years ago. I was off today. Hadn't been for the fog, I would've taken her for a spin."

"What's your day job?"

He laughed. "Flying." He named the freight carrier he flew for.

Brynn and Rye looked at each other. He raised his eyebrows as though asking her if Jake was their man. She was about to nod yes when Jake said, "I fly at zero zero thirty. Quick round trip to KC. Back by breakfast."

Which meant that he wasn't available tonight, and Brynn realized she was disappointed. She liked Jake Morton. She got a sense that Rye did, too.

He asked, "How did you know me? Have we crossed paths?"

"I was in Afghanistan same time you were."

Rye tensed up, the change in him drastic enough for Brynn to feel. Jake kept talking. "I flew C-130s in and out of Bagram. Troops. Pallets of water. Jeeps. You name it. Didn't fly into the worst of the shit like you did, but I heard all the stories. Never thought I'd get to meet you."

Rye turned his head away and looked out the window, saying in a subdued voice, "Thanks for your help tonight."

"No problem. I consider it an honor."

The airport traffic was more congested than usual, but Jake inched his car toward the curb, then lurched into a space left by a departing minivan. Rye opened the back seat door on the passenger side. "Don't bother getting out, Jake. We need to hustle."

"Understood." Seeing that Rye was about to remove the ball cap and give it back, he said, "Keep it, but I would like to shake your hand." He stuck out his hand over the seat back.

Rye reached forward and they shook.

Jake said, "There's not a flyer in the world who wouldn't understand how you felt. Also not one in the world who wouldn't buy you a beer. In a heartbeat."

Rye held his gaze for several beats, then said brusquely, "Take care of yourself."

Brynn scooted over and got out. Rye shut the car door, tapped the roof twice, and Jake drove away.

The encounter had started and ended with such abruptness, it seemed surreal, but Brynn knew that the parting exchange between the two men had been significant to each of them. Brynn wished she could ask Rye about it, but this wasn't the time or place.

Police were everywhere.

Fortunately the officers were overwhelmed by the motor and pedestrian traffic and were industriously keeping it under some semblance of control. Trying not to draw attention to themselves, she and Rye joined the taxi line, shuffling forward a few feet at a time.

"I'm sorry," she said.

"For what?"

"You were eager to wash your hands of me."

"Yeah, well, you're stuck with me, too."

"I could still rent a car and drive myself to Knoxville."

"You could. And watch for Goliad and Timmy to show up in the rearview mirror. Or, because you'd be on the lookout for them, it would probably be a pair of new players. You wouldn't see them coming before it was too late."

"The Hunts wouldn't order my execution, Rye."

He snickered. "For what's inside your coat pocket? Get real, Brynn. Young women disappear all the time. You'd be publicly mourned by Lambert, but he would console himself with his influx of cash. Hunt would have his GX-42, and your life would be written off as a small cost of doing business."

"That's cynical."

"That's life. Bad guys thrive. Good ones die."

She wondered if he was referring to war buddies. "Who, specifically?"

"Let's hope not Brady White."

Heeding Jake's advice, he wasn't wearing his jacket, but he patted down one of the pockets and took out his cell phone. He asked Siri for a number and had her call it for him. Brynn listened in.

"Howardville Community Hospital. How may I direct your call?"

"I'm a friend of Brady White's. I heard he'd taken a downturn. Can you give me an update on his condition, please?"

"I'll connect you to the OR. You can speak to the charge nurse."

"He's in surgery?"

"If…if you'll hold, sir, I'll check to see what his status is. Please stay on the line."

Rye disconnected and said to Brynn, "This morning the lady in the ER wouldn't tell me anything. This one tried to keep me on the line. Which means they're tracing the calls."

"At least we know Brady is still alive."

"That's something. That's huge. But we still have the problem of getting you to Violet."

"I'm open to ideas."

"First, we acquire new phones." With sleight of hand, he silenced the phone he'd just used and dropped it into a nearby trash can. "Sooner or later that number will be attributed to me by the Howardville SO. Which means it will be fed to Wilson and Rawlins, and they'll share it with the Atlanta PD. If they track it, they'll be looking for me here, while I'm somewhere else. *If* I can get this frigging line moving."

He looked toward the front of it, as though calculating how long it would be until their turn. He was still wearing the ball cap, which kept anyone except Brynn from seeing how his eyes were constantly sweeping the crowded area, looking for a sign that they'd been spotted by someone in uniform.

"What are you thinking of doing?" she asked. "Returning to the hotel?"

He shared his concerns about security cameras getting the license plate number of the Uber car they'd taken from the garage to the hotel. "But I don't have a choice except to go back. I left my flight bag behind."

He gauged the length of the line again. "We're sitting ducks here. What we really need to do is scare up some wheels. We got lucky with Jake, but guardian angels don't come around that often, and using taxis and hiring cars is risky."

"Do you know anyone who would lend you a car on short notice, late on Thanksgiving night, without asking too many questions? Someone you trust? Fellow doctor? A girlfriend? Boyfriend?"

She shifted her gaze away from him.

"Welllll," he said. "That was like a puff of cold air on an aching tooth. There's a man in your life?"

"Past tense."

She tried to avoid looking at him directly, but he followed the evasive motions of her eyes. "Husband?"

"We weren't married."

"But a serious relationship."

"We lived together for a while."

"Huh." His eyes were shadowed by the cap's bill, but she could sense their intensity on her face. "Your recent kissing ban. Is it because of him?"

With heat behind it, she asked, "If he can help us, does it matter?"

He turned aside and muttered something she thought it was

probably just as well she didn't catch, then came back to her with an indifferent shrug. "When you have a dead stick, you look for somewhere to land, and anyplace will do."

*10:47 p.m.*

"So you're Timmy."

The former gang member stood accused before a very harsh judge. Richard Hunt looked at him with scorn.

Delores had to agree that Timmy did make for a sorry sight, especially standing beside Goliad, who, as usual, looked handsome and was in total command of himself. Timmy was listing to his left, and his face bore gruesome evidence of the beating he'd received from Rye Mallett.

"This first job was an audition of sorts," Richard said. "I'm not impressed by your performance so far. People who work for me in this specialized capacity do so under the radar. Stealthily. Do you even know what that word means? It means they don't commit reckless and stupid acts that bring hillbilly deputies to my home."

"Yes, sir."

Goliad stepped forward. "Timmy acted impulsively, sir, but in self-defense."

Timmy jerked his head around and practically snarled at Goliad, "And you just stood there like a stump and let him have at me!"

"Because I'm too smart to get in the way of a knife," Goliad returned calmly.

Delores stepped in. "Gentlemen, this finger pointing is getting us nowhere, and it's taking up precious time that we do not have. The only thing I really want to hear is that you have located Dr. O'Neal."

"I'm sorry, ma'am, but no, we haven't," Goliad said.

Richard cursed under his breath.

Head down, arms folded, Delores made a circuit of the room, then stopped in front of Timmy. "Will you excuse us, please?"

He cocked his head warily, his ears practically twitching like an animal sensing a predator. "What for?"

"Because I believe you need an Advil, and the housekeeper has some in the kitchen." Delores gave him her sweetest smile. "Goliad will be along in a moment."

Timmy's eyes narrowed. He knew he was being dismissed, but he didn't have much choice except to go quietly. He was already on quicksand with Richard.

"Which way?"

She motioned him through the double doorway. "Stay left. You can't miss it."

He gave Goliad a resentful glance over his shoulder, but he went as told. Delores pulled the doors closed behind him.

Richard asked Goliad, "How much does he know about this situation?"

"Because doctors are involved, he guessed that the contents of the box were medical-related. But he doesn't know any more than that."

"Keep it that way," Richard said. "You're the only person in our entire organization that we've entrusted with the seriousness of the situation. We must get that drug from Dr. O'Neal."

"I understand."

"I think we should pull Timmy off the detail," Richard continued. "For the time being, anyway. He's a loose cannon. If his particular talents are called for later, we know where to find him."

"I agree," Delores said without hesitation. "Knife fights? Jesus. I don't care how provoking that pilot was." To Goliad she said, "Make it sound like we're worried about his injuries. Tell him to take the rest of the night off and go to bed. You'll call him tomorrow to see if he's fit to come back to work."

"Yes, ma'am."

Richard said, "Now to the other matter. Where the hell is Dr. O'Neal?"

Goliad braced himself before answering. "We've looked in all the logical places. Her office. The areas of the hospital where she works. Her house. It's locked up tight. We tried tracing her phone. No luck this time. I'm sure she—more likely Mallett—saw to that."

"Nate gave you a list of her close acquaintances."

"Reached about half of them," Goliad said. "Told them I'd found her phone and was calling her contacts in an attempt to return it. I asked if she had a getaway, lake house, someplace where she might be spending the holiday. No to all that. Only one car is registered to her, and we know where it is."

"Anything on the father?"

"Long list of O'Neals with criminal records. I've got people trying to make a connection, but that will take some time."

"I could kick Nate for not getting his name out of those deputies," Delores said.

Shortly before Goliad and Timmy had arrived, Nate had slunk out, leaving the task of finding his wayward colleague to them. Not that his contributions had been of much help, and his unsolicited editorial comments had begun to grate on Delores.

"If we asked the deputies for her father's name now, it would raise red flags," Richard said. "Besides, I doubt she'll remain stationary. She'll be trying to get to the girl."

"I've got hackers checking airlines and car rental companies," Goliad said. "Neither her name nor Mallett's has shown up anywhere. And," he said, drawing a breath, "there's another complication."

"Great. Just what we need," Delores remarked.

Goliad looked at her apologetically before explaining. "I've got snitches all over the city with their ears to the ground. One picked up on an Atlanta PD officer asking around for them at a bar out near the airport where pilots of Mallett's caliber hang out."

"Atlanta PD?" Delores asked.

"Thanks to Timmy and the knife fight," Richard said.

"Probably," Goliad replied somberly. "Last thing we want is for me and police to overlap in our pursuit of Dr. O'Neal. Everybody knows who I work for. Something happens to her, it could come back to you."

Richard dragged his hands down his face. "So where does this leave us?"

"I continue looking, but keep it discreet. Hope something turns up."

"With absolutely no guarantee that anything will before time runs out."

Goliad raised his hands at his sides in a gesture of helplessness. "Until something breaks, I don't know what else to do, sir."

Delores had been making aimless circuits around the room but following every word of the discussion. She said, "We can't depend on something breaking. Since it appears that Dr. O'Neal has gone undercover, we must do something to bring her out."

"Like what?" Richard asked.

"I don't know. But someone had better arrive at an idea. And soon." Turning to Goliad, she said, "Take Timmy to whatever rock he sleeps under, then come right back. I want you here if you get a bite from any of the hooks you've baited. Richard and I are dead on our feet. We're going to sleep for a while. You can stretch out on the sofa in the den."

"I won't be long." Goliad headed for the door.

Delores fell into step behind him and said to Richard, "I'll see them on their way. Would you like something from the kitchen?"

"I'm fine."

She and Goliad left the room together. Timmy was nowhere in sight. She drew Goliad to a stop. "I'm glad we have a moment alone," she whispered. "There's something you don't know that I feel you should."

She told him about Richard's gaffe of mentioning bloodshed

to the deputies. "We weren't supposed to know anything about that fight. In fact, we both pretended to be shocked when they told us about it. Maybe they didn't catch the slip."

Goliad frowned. "Safer to assume that they did and are now wondering why you lied to them."

She slumped. "That's my greatest worry. That's why I needed to tell you." Looking contrite, she added, "We dump everything on you, and rely on you far too much."

"Not at all."

"No, we do. I can tell that you're as exhausted as we are, but you're so dedicated. We don't take your loyalty for granted, although I'm afraid there are times when you might think we do. The truth is, I don't know what we would do without you, Goliad."

Lightly, she rested her hand on the placket of his shirt. "I don't know what *I* would do without you." Stepping closer, she said, "I'm not entirely trustful of Timmy. Honestly, I'm a little afraid of him. I won't go to sleep until I know you're back and under our roof."

"I'll get back as soon as I can."

"Are you sure you'll be comfortable enough on the sofa?"

He swallowed audibly. "Yes, ma'am."

"Good night, Goliad."

"Good night."

She slid her hand off his shirtfront and turned away, smiling to herself. Fearing banishment and permanent separation from her, he would never act on his desire. He would rather suffer in agonizing silence and be able to remain near her and in sight of her than do something impulsive that would cause his severance.

He would never touch her, but every once in a while, Delores reminded him of just how much he wanted to.

# Chapter 25

———⊰●⊱———

*11:11 p.m.*

Rawlins pulled the SUV to the curb and cut the engine. Neither he nor Wilson moved as they regarded the dwelling. The street was dark and silent; the only sounds were the ticks of the motor as it cooled. No interior lights were on that they could see. There was a porch light, but it wasn't on, either.

"What do you think?" Wilson asked.

"Won't know until we check it out."

"I'm so tired, you may have to goose me to get me out of this seat."

Rawlins snorted. "I'll pass."

He opened the driver's door and alighted. Wilson groaned as he pushed open his door and got out. Together they went up the walk to the sheltered front door. Rawlins pressed the bell, and they heard it chime.

He rang it twice more before a light came on inside, then the overhead porch light nearly blinded them when it was switched on. Door locks were unfastened, and then the door was pulled open.

Standing barefoot behind the screen door, wearing a white

266

t-shirt and red flannel pajama bottoms with penguins on them, was Wes O'Neal. He said, "I didn't do it."

Wilson smiled. "Been a long time, Wes."

"I've lost track. Where'd all your hair go to?"

He asked it with such good humor, Wilson didn't take umbrage. "How are you getting on these days?"

"Up till two minutes ago, I was sleeping with a clear conscience. Can't imagine what brought you all the way down here from Howardville. I haven't been up there in a coon's age. Whatever's missing, I didn't take it. I've gone straight."

"Mind if we come in?"

"Why?"

"If you've gone straight, you've got nothing to worry about."

Wes seemed to debate it, then flipped up the hook lock on the screen door. Its hinges squeaked when he pushed it open. Turning his back to them, he went ahead to switch on a lamp.

The living area was separated from the galley kitchen by a Formica-topped bar with one barstool. The small, round dining table had two mismatched chairs. On the table was a chessboard, a game seemingly in progress. Taking up most of the floor space was a recliner, an ugly maroon leather monstrosity.

"I don't have much company, so seating is limited," Wes said, claiming the recliner for himself.

"Nice chair," Wilson remarked.

"I didn't steal it."

"You've gone straight."

"That's not the reason. I couldn't carry the damn thing." Wes rubbed his hands up and down the padded arms. "I got it at a yard sale. Paid cash. I have a job. Working nine to five at the Walmart."

"Stocking shelves?" Wilson asked.

"Spotting shoplifters."

Rawlins guffawed. "The fox guarding the chicken coop."

"Which is why I'm good at it." Squinting up at Rawlins, he

said, "I can't remember your name, but I recognize your face. Football player for Clemson, correct?"

"That's right. Don Rawlins. My rookie year with the Howardville SO, I arrested you for B and E. Auto parts store."

Wes grinned. "Charges were dropped. The owner had told me I could borrow some jumper cables. He didn't tell me I had to wait until he opened the next morning to pick them up."

Wilson chuckled. Rawlins failed to see the humor. He looked like he was about to face off against Alabama for the national championship. He said, "Mind if I take a look around?"

Wes spread his arms wide. "Knock yourself out. What you see is about it. Bedroom and bathroom through there." He pointed at an open doorway. "My bathrobe is hanging on the back of the door. Bring it, please. It's chilly in here."

With over-politeness, Rawlins asked, "Anything else?"

"Thanks for asking. My slippers should be at the side of the bed."

Rawlins turned and stalked off.

Wes came back around to Wilson. "He's a barrel of laughs. What's he looking for, anyway?"

"Just checking things out."

Under his breath, Wes said, "Pull my other one."

Wilson walked over to the table where the chess set was. "Who're you playing?"

"Myself mostly."

"Do you cheat?"

"Of course."

Wilson pulled one of the chairs from beneath the table and turned it around so he would be sitting facing Wes. When Rawlins returned, he shook his head at Wilson to indicate that Brynn O'Neal wasn't hiding in the back rooms. He dropped the slippers in front of Wes's chair and tossed the robe at him, then sat down on the barstool.

Wes pushed his arms through the sleeves of his flannel robe. "Better. Now, what brought y'all?"

"We're here about Brynn."

Wes's smile vanished. "Oh, Lord." He slapped his hand over his heart and fell sideways, catching himself on the arm of the recliner.

Wilson swiftly assured him that she was fine. "At least to our knowledge, she's all right."

Wes, his hand still on his heart, took several restorative breaths. "This isn't a next-of-kin call, then?"

"No. Didn't mean to give you that idea," Wilson said. "I'm sorry."

"Well, you should be. You scared the hell out of me." Wes pushed himself upright and puffed out his cheeks as he exhaled. "If nothing's happened to her, then what's going on?"

"We're not sure what's going on, Wes, and that's the God's truth. But I'll tell you as much as we know."

Wilson began with the crash of the airplane that Brynn was scheduled to meet. Her father listened without interrupting. Wilson could tell he was dismayed by the bizarre sequence of events, and by the time Wilson related those of the past few hours, Wes was in obvious distress.

He swiveled his head around to Rawlins as though hoping he would deny it all, or tell him it was a joke, then came back to Wilson. "Y'all are saying she's gone missing?"

"We're saying that the circumstances are murky. She lied to her colleague about who she was meeting down in the parking garage. Security cameras caught her leaving with that man Mallett."

"Whose reputation is shady at best," Rawlins added.

The twinkle in Wes's eye turned to a glint. "If he hurts her, I'll kill him."

"If it's any comfort to you," Wilson said, "we don't get a sense that he would physically harm Brynn. In fact, if I were to guess, I think he's protecting her from those two men on Hunt's payroll."

"Wait. You said Hunt sent them up to Howardville to see that

Brynn got back safely with that box. Why would she need protection from them?"

Rawlins took over the explanation. "We get the feeling that there's more going on with the senator and Mrs. Hunt than meets the eye."

"Well, no shit, Sherlock. He's a politician."

"Yes, but our speculation is that there was something else inside that box besides blood samples."

"Such as?"

"We don't know. But, whatever it is, if it belongs to Richard Hunt, and your daughter has made off with it, then—"

"Hold it right there," Wes said. "I am—was—a thief. I own up to it. But Brynn? Never."

"That may be true, but her actions today are questionable, and she's made herself inaccessible. Her cell phone goes straight to voice mail, and she hasn't checked in with her answering service. We've looked for her in every likely place she might be taking refuge."

Wes plopped back in his chair, clarity dawning on his wrinkled features. "Oh, I see. Now I get why you're here. You thought she came running to Papa?"

Wilson assumed an edgier tone. "Have you seen her, Wes?"

"No."

"Talked to her?"

"No."

"When was the last time?"

"Two years ago. Three, maybe."

That jibed with what Brynn had told him the night before.

"I can't remember when it was exactly," Wes continued. "Sometime before my last incarceration. She'd finished her residency and was affiliated with the hospital. Doing good for herself."

"Was she working with Dr. Lambert at that time?"

"Never heard that name before you said it a minute ago.

Brynn talked about her work, but only in general terms that I could understand."

"Did she refer to a patient named Violet?"

"Don't remember her talking about any patient. Why?"

"Little girl, seven or so now. She's very sick. Seems to be special to Brynn."

Wes raised his shoulders. "I wouldn't know. And, anyhow what's this got to do with what's gone on today?"

"You watch TV tonight?" Rawlins pointed out the archaic model in the corner.

"It's busted."

"Huh," Rawlins said. Then, with a bead on Wes, he said, "You have no idea where your daughter might be? With a friend, maybe?"

"Maybe, but I don't know any of her friends."

"If she's in trouble, and you're holding out—"

"I'm not!"

Rawlins came up off the barstool. "You expect us to believe that you haven't seen or heard from your daughter in *years*?"

Wes glowered. "I'm a crook, not a liar."

Wilson interrupted their exchange before it became more contentious. "Calm down, Wes."

"My ass, I'll calm down." He popped up from his chair. "You wake me up, tell me Brynn's in danger from hit men at the beck and call of a senator, who I'd bet good money is crookeder than me. She's in the company of a...a...bush pilot, who's a lightning rod for trouble. Why aren't y'all out combing the city for her instead of grilling me?"

Wilson stood. "Do you have a phone, Wes?"

"Doesn't everybody?"

He and Wilson exchanged phone numbers. "I'm sorry we upset you, Wes. I hope there's a logical and harmless outcome to all this. Rawlins and I may be overstepping, completely wrong about the Hunts, Dr. Lambert, all that."

"But you have a hunch that something's not square."

"A strong hunch," Wilson said. "And somebody's got to answer for the assault on Brady White. Now I don't know if Brynn is guilty of wrongdoing or not. But there are a lot of questions pivoting around her. So far she's failed to provide us with straight answers."

"You're making Brynn sound like a criminal on the run."

Wilson said, "Well, just before we got here, we got a call from the office. Myra. Remember her?"

"Sure, sure. What?"

"A call came into the Howardville hospital from a man asking about Brady White's condition. People answering the hospital lines had been asked to get as much info as they could from anyone calling about him. Lady got flustered." He told Wes the gist of the conversation. "He must've smelled a rat. Hung up."

"Or he could've been a friend who heard what he wanted to know."

"Possibly. Except that we got the number, passed it on to local departments, and the phone the call came from was found in a trash can at the airport. Which is a trick that somebody on the run would pull to throw us off their trail."

"Brynn would never think to do that," Wes said. "Me? Yeah. But not her."

"Mallett would." In his bad-cop voice, Rawlins said, "If she contacts you, we need to know immediately. If you harbor her or Mallett, your parole officer will be the first person I call."

Wes scowled at him. "Don't threaten me, Clemson. I'm not afraid of jail. Find my girl, make sure she's safe. That's all I care about." He opened the front door. "Now get out of here and get to it."

Wilson paused on the threshold. "You have my number, Wes."

"Yeah, yeah." Once Wilson was through the door, Wes latched the screen and slammed the door. Locks snapped.

The two deputies walked back to their SUV. Wilson said, "I don't think he had a clue about any of it."

"He seemed genuinely upset," Rawlins said, then chuckled. "And actually took offense when I questioned his truthfulness."

"That's Wes," Wilson said. "He's a crook, not a liar."


*11:23 p.m.*


Wes turned off lights as he made his way back to his bedroom.

As soon as he cleared the doorway, an arm came out from behind the door, hooked his throat in the bend of the elbow, hauled him up against a hard chest, and applied choking pressure to this windpipe.

"Not one word," he was told in a growl.

With his air cut off, he couldn't have uttered a peep. He wouldn't have even if he could. He was crooked, not courageous.

From the corner of his eye, he saw a dark form—a woman, if his eyes weren't deceiving him—at the window that overlooked the front yard. She was peering through a slit in the blinds.

Wes was about to run completely out of air by the time she said, "They're gone."

The arm around his throat relaxed, then let go. He rubbed his Adam's apple, croaking, "Brynn?"

"It's me."

"Are you all right?"

"Yes, I'm okay."

She walked toward him, gradually taking shape as she got closer. He could see her a little better when the guy turned on the bathroom light, but he kept the door open only a crack.

For the first time in years, Wes saw his daughter's face, and, even as deeply shadowed as it was, he was struck by how beautiful she was. Like her mother. She looked tired and a little worse for wear, although she didn't appear to be injured.

They'd been out of touch since their last parting, which had been acrimonious. Despite what the deputies had concluded,

Wes truly hadn't expected her to seek him out. But here she was, and he couldn't think of anything to say.

When it became obvious by the lengthy silence that she couldn't, either, he said, "So you did come running to Papa."

"Only because I was out of options." She was assessing his appearance, as he was hers. "Why penguins?"

He pulled the baggy legs of his pajama bottoms out to his sides as though about to curtsy. "They were markdowns at the store."

"You really work for Walmart?"

"I go in two hours early tomorrow on account of Black Friday. It'll be a zoo, but I don't work the crowd. I spend my shift up in a security booth that's got all these video screens. On the lookout for shoplifters."

"You know all their tricks."

"Most. I'm a bit rusty. Thieves have gone high tech. But so has catching them."

"Is that why you've gone straight? Fear of getting caught never stopped you before."

"Hmm. Still bitter, I see."

"Your sense of humor may charm everyone else, but it was lost on me a long time ago," she said coolly.

Wes harrumphed and turned around to confront the tall form silhouetted by the bathroom light. "You're—"

"The bush pilot."

Wes looked him over and snorted with disfavor. "From what I hear, you're the source of my daughter's troubles."

"You've got it backwards. Until I flew cargo for her last night, life was good. It's been fucked up ever since. So, as warm and tender as this family reunion is, can we move on to why we're here?"

"Which is what?"

"We need a getaway car. What can you steal?"

# Chapter 26

*11:27 p.m.*

The pilot tipped his head toward Wes. "This is the *man*?"

"Well, he is," Brynn said.

"The one you lived with."

"In a serious relationship. Just as I said."

"Yes, but you deliberately led me to believe—"

"I can't help that you jumped to the wrong conclusion."

"Like hell."

Wes had been following the exchange with interest. Brynn seemed to suddenly remember that he was there. She mumbled an introduction. "This is Wes. Dad, Rye Mallett."

Wes said, "Can't say that it's been a pleasure so far."

"My sentiments exactly."

"Was crushing my windpipe necessary?"

"Might've been. I wasn't taking any chances."

Sounding put out with both of them, Brynn asked, "Is coffee a possibility?"

While Wes was making coffee, Mallett went around to all the windows in the living area and made certain that the blinds were tightly drawn. He also checked the bolt on the front door.

275

When the coffee was ready, Wes and Brynn sat down at the table across the chessboard from each other. Mallett perched on the barstool. Mallett's eyes were as watchful as a hawk's. Or as a pilot's, Wes supposed. Seek-and-avoid. Wasn't that the aviation phrase? He was also alert to every sound.

Wes recognized the symptoms of feeling cornered and restless. He figured Mallett wasn't new at getting out of scrapes. He looked the type.

"How did you get in?" Wes asked him.

"You taught Brynn a trick or two about housebreaking."

Wes turned to her. "You came through the window?"

"Just like you taught me."

Wes was pleased. "Then I guess I did something right by you. Cops inside. You didn't make a sound. Good work."

She didn't acknowledge his praise. "We came by taxi, but had the driver let us out a few blocks from here. We walked the rest of the way, saw the sheriff's SUV at the curb, and the two deputies on your porch. We went around back to wait until they'd left. Your bedroom window was open about an inch."

"After sleeping in a cell block for years at a time, you appreciate breathing fresh air."

"Rawlins didn't notice the raised window when he came into the bedroom. It was open just enough so that we could hear your conversation."

"Was everything he and Wilson told me the truth?"

"More or less," Brynn replied.

"Which? More? Or less?"

"Neither Rye nor I harmed the man at the airport. We're actually very worried about him."

"I believe that. What's the 'but'?"

"But I do have something that Richard Hunt perceives as his."

Wes slumped. "Your mother died afraid of this very thing."

"Of what thing?"

"Afraid that you had gotten the gene, and that one day it would manifest itself."

Brynn sighed. "Relax, Dad. I didn't inherit your bent for stealing."

"I don't steal," he said. "I just—"

"Take stuff that doesn't belong to you," Mallett remarked.

Wes shot him a look. "Not out of meanness, or envy, or greed. Nothing like that. Just…"

"Just…?"

"Convenience."

"I see. Thanks for the clarification." Mallett raised his coffee mug in a mock toast.

Wes went back to Brynn. "What do you have that the senator perceives is his?"

"I can't tell you."

"They could cut out my tongue before I'd rat you out."

"I know that. But the less you know, the better for you. I don't want to get you into trouble." She looked at Mallett with annoyance. "Never mind what Rye said. We don't want you to steal a car for us. But if you have one we could borrow, it would be a big help."

"Does it have to do with that sick little girl the deputies mentioned?"

Brynn gave a small nod. "Please don't ask me for more details than that."

"Okay. But based on what Wilson and his partner told me, you're not just dodging them. You've got some much rougher characters after you, too." He pointed his chin at the cuts on Rye's left hand. "The fight in the garage?"

"Timmy," Mallett said. "He's a twisted kid with lots to prove."

"Meaning dangerous."

"High-octane dangerous."

Wes rubbed his hand across his mouth and chin. Focused on Brynn, he said, "Sweetheart—"

"Don't call me that."

"Fair enough. But please listen to your old man. Sometimes you've gotta raise your hands and walk out from cover. Surrender. Giving yourself over to the authorities is never a preferable choice, but sometimes it's the only smart one."

"I'm not surrendering."

"Technically it wouldn't be a surrender. Wilson only wants you for 'questioning.' That doesn't mean arrest. He gave me his number. Why don't I call him, get him back over here, y'all sit down together and—"

"No."

"Brynn—"

"No! I can't turn myself over to them. Not now, anyway. Not yet."

"Okay, okay. You want time to think about it. I get that. Say, first thing in the morning."

She shook her head. "Even if they cleared me, I can't afford the time it would take to sort out everything. I'm racing the clock."

"Clock? What clock? There's a deadline?"

"A crucial one."

"Then all the more reason for you to stop the clock. Call Wilson now. Maybe if you cut a deal, gave him and Rawlins something on Hunt in exchange for—"

"No." She scooted to the edge of her seat. "I listened to you, now you listen to me. In spite of what it looks like, I'm doing a good thing. I swear to you on Mother's grave."

"But you can't tell me what it is?"

She shook her head.

"Rawlins acts tough, but Wilson is a reasonable person. I bet he would understand if you explained—"

"Possibly when it's over, I will. But not before."

"How come?"

"Because they could stop me."

"Maybe not. Convince them your motives are honest."

"You're not listening. Guilt or innocence isn't the issue. It's *time*."

"Sweetheart, Brynn, I've got experience with these things. I know the approach that cops respond to. Let me—"

"You can't help with his, Dad, and, anyway, you have to go to work."

"I can skip work."

"I wouldn't let you do that."

"But—"

"You're wasting your breath," Mallett said.

Wes turned to him. "It's my daughter and me talking here. I'll ask you kindly not to interrupt."

Mallett said, "She's not turning herself in, and neither am I. And every second she spends arguing with you about it is squandering time better spent." He came off the stool. "Yes or no on the car? If it's no, we're leaving."

Wes looked between the two of them, saw the resolution in both their expressions, and realized that it was two against one, and he was the odd man out. He looked at Brynn with a frown of consternation. "I couldn't talk you out of dating that wild Hendrix boy, either."

"And I survived him."

"Yeah, but look where you are now." He gestured toward Mallett. "He's a step or two down, you ask me. But"—he sighed—"you've got my car for as long as you need it."

She didn't hide her relief. "Depending on how things go, it could be several days before I can return it. How will you get to work?"

He pointed to the chessboard. "A greeter at the store is a friend of mine, lives in the neighborhood. We ride together every now and then. Pick up a pizza on the way home. Share it over a game of chess."

"He won't mind the inconvenience?"

"She." Reading the surprise on Brynn's face, he chuckled. "I'm a thief, not a monk."

She reached across the table and touched his hand. "Thank you."

He acknowledged her thanks with a nod, then heaved another sigh and slapped his thighs as he came to his feet. "What state do you want to be from?" At their quizzical expressions, he said, "We need to swap out the license plates."

Turning, he walked toward the bedroom, saying over his shoulder, "If y'all are going on the lam, you've got a lot to learn."

*11:39 p.m.*

Wes had always kept an "emergency kit" somewhere in the house. His present one was in the crawl space under the floorboards of his closet floor. In the old trunk, they found several license plates that hadn't expired, a variety of new cell phones still in their boxes, a Ziploc bag stuffed with cash, which Brynn and Rye declined, and a prison-issue toiletry kit, which she claimed.

With Mallett's help, Wes got all the floorboards back into place. Brynn excused herself and took the small dopp kit into the bathroom with her, and Wes and Mallett returned to the living area where they plugged in the phones to charge.

Wes sat down in his recliner. Rye took one of the chairs at the table, tilting it onto its back legs, propping himself at an angle against the wall.

"She looks done in," Wes said.

"Both of us are sleep-deprived."

"You're welcome to stay here till morning, get some shut-eye."

"You heard Rawlins. If they were to come back and find us here, you'd be in trouble with your parole officer. Besides, she needs to get on her way."

"To?"

Mallett shook his head. "If Brynn didn't tell you, why do you think I would? My loyalties lie with her."

"Of course," Wes said, nodding. But he questioned whether loyalty was the only foundation for their solidarity. Sparks flew every time the two looked at each other, and even when they were avoiding eye contact, there was a simmering awareness between them.

Wes idly scratched his armpit. "You two didn't meet until last night?"

"That's right."

"Hmm."

"What?"

"Nothing." He situated himself more comfortably in the recliner. "Just, you got awfully wrapped up in her problem."

"Too wrapped up." Mallett was looking cornered and restless again. "But that ends soon. She gets gone, I'll be out of it."

"Brynn will go her way, you'll go yours."

"Yep. Just a day later than scheduled."

"It's been quite a day, though."

"You can say that again."

"You and Brynn gonna stay in touch?"

"No. Better for all concerned."

"Especially you."

Mallett's green eyes narrowed a fraction. "You're damn right."

Wes gave him a critical once-over and snuffled. "You think you're too good for my girl?"

"Other way around."

"I hear ya." Wes took a deep breath and let it out slowly. "She's too good for me, too."

"That's plain enough." Mallett looked around the shabby room. "She was desperate, or she wouldn't have come here. She wants nothing to do with you."

"She tell you that herself?"

"Didn't have to."

Wes gave Rye a sad smile and said softly, "Son, you've got it wrong."

"How's that?"

Wes reached over, picked up a bishop from off the chessboard, and rolled it between his palms. "Brynn had it tough growing up. All the odds were stacked against her, but she put her shoulder to it, and worked like the devil to achieve what she set out to do. When she became a doctor, got her position in the hospital, no daddy was ever prouder than me."

He paused, studied the chess piece, noticed that the paint was wearing thin in spots. "I didn't want to be an embarrassment to her, something in her life that had to be explained or made excuses for. I didn't want her having to claim kin with an old con." He tipped his chin down and looked at Rye from beneath his brows. "Was me, not Brynn, who stipulated that she have nothing to do with me."

Mallett held his gaze as he slowly lowered the front legs of his chair to the floor.

Their stare held until Brynn came out of the bedroom.

Mallett looked at her and said quietly, "Time to go."

*12:04 a.m.*

Once they were underway in Wes's second- or third-hand compact, little was said for the first fifteen minutes.

Brynn stared out the passenger seat window, tracking rivulets of rain as they formed and streamed down the glass. Following the path of one with her fingertip, she broke the silence. "He seemed well, don't you think?"

"I don't know what he was like before."

"Before, he was just as he was tonight. Unchanged except for a little more gray hair and an inch or two around his middle."

"He's been hitting the pizza with his lady friend."

Brynn gave a wistful smile. "I've never known him to have girlfriends."

"Hard to work them in between parole and his next stint."

"I suppose. And then there was me," she said. "I must've cramped his love life, too."

Neither spoke as Rye passed an eighteen-wheeler throwing up enough spray to engulf the small car. Once the truck was behind them, he asked, "Why do you lead people to think it was you who turned your back on him?"

"I don't do that."

"Yes, you do. Or at least you don't correct them when they assume that's the case. How come?"

She turned her head and looked at him. "You don't want to know anything about me or my life."

"How many times are you going to throw that up to me?"

"Don't snap at me. I'm only upholding the rule set by *you*."

He didn't say anything to that, but his jaw tightened, and so did his grip on the steering wheel. The rest of the trip was made in silence except for the rain beating a relentless cadence against the roof of the car.

When they reached the hotel, a neon sign above the entrance to the parking garage informed them that it was full. Rye, swearing under every breath, searched the open lot and pulled into the first available space he could find nearest the side door they'd used earlier.

In a stilted voice, she asked, "Before I go, do you mind if I come in, use the bathroom, get some snacks from the mini bar?"

"No. Sure."

They bleakly gauged the distance they had to cover in pelting rain. Neither was inclined to leave the shelter of the car. They stayed as they were for a full minute, then Rye said, "It's not going to get any drier."

They made a dash for the door. Just as they reached it, a

pair of headlights drew Rye's attention to the corner of the building.

A police car.

*12:26 a.m.*

He swiped their room's card key, shoved open the door, and pushed Brynn through. In their haste, she stumbled over his boots. "Rye? What?"

"Cop."

They ran down the long hallway, Rye frequently checking behind them, fully expecting to see officers in pursuit. But they made it to the end of the hall and out of sight around the corner. He bypassed the elevator and hustled Brynn through the door to the fire stairs.

She ran up them ahead of him, but with his hand at the small of her back, urging her onward. Over her shoulder, she said, "Maybe we should hide somewhere on the ground level until we can get back to the car."

"Can't leave my bag."

They reached the seventh floor. Rye cautiously opened the door. In both directions, the corridor was empty. He motioned Brynn through. They jogged toward their room.

When they got to it, Rye moved Brynn aside, went down on one knee and checked to see that the thread he'd pulled from the hem of the bedspread was still stuck between the door and the jamb. It was. He unlocked the door. Brynn rushed into the room. Rye checked the hallway once again, followed her in, and bolted the door.

"The thread?"

"I saw it in a movie," he said.

"As we left, you sent me ahead to hold the elevator."

"That's what I was doing. Good thing. Because as least we know no one has been inside the room." They'd left only the bathroom light on. "Don't turn on any more lights," he told Brynn as he checked the floor of the closet to make certain his flight bag was as he'd left it.

Then he moved to the window and peered through the crack between the wall and the edge of the drape. "Christ! Only one person, no one riding shotgun, but he's parked at the end of a row. Lights off. No exhaust from the tailpipe."

"Just sitting there?"

"Just sitting there."

"Maybe he has nothing to do with us."

"Maybe."

"It could be hotel security."

"Maybe."

"Dammit, Rye. Say something besides *maybe*."

"Well, sorry. That's the only answer I have at the moment. I don't know what he's doing there. What I do know is that he's got an unrestricted view of that side door."

She looked at the clock. "I should be on the road."

He absently acknowledged that as he assessed their predicament. "You can't get through that exit and to Wes's car without him seeing you. Do you want to chance it?"

"There's no 'or'?"

"Or you go through the lobby, out the front, flank him, and sneak around to the car."

"He may still see me."

"Another 'or' is to give it a while, see if he leaves. He could be taking a coffee break, and just chose that spot."

She gave it a moment's thought. "That's logical, isn't it? If he'd seen us, recognized us, he would have chased after us, wouldn't he?"

"Not necessarily. He could have called it in and is waiting for instructions on how to proceed, or for backup."

"Backup for us? We're not public enemies number one and two."

"Not to law enforcement. But that's how the Hunts would rank us, and I wouldn't put it past them to have cops on the take."

"So then...what do I do?"

"I think you wait a while, see what happens."

She slumped with disappointment, but without debating it further took off her coat, shook the rainwater off it, and hung it in the closet. He draped his bomber jacket over the desk chair so the leather would dry. He motioned toward the mini bar. "Something to drink?"

She shook her head.

He watched as she sat down on the edge of the bed and gave her a long, meditative look. Eventually she noticed. "What?"

"I do want to know about your life," he said. "About you and Wes. Tell me why you make people think you shunned him, when it was the other way around."

She looked prepared to refuse, then she looked resigned, then she looked away from him, and, in a barely discernible voice, said, "It hurts too much."

He checked the cop car. It was still there. Nothing else beyond the window was noteworthy except hard rain. He walked over to the bed and sat down on the end of it. "What hurts too much?"

"Rejection, and admitting to being rejected. So, I mislead people into thinking that I rejected him." She hooked a strand of damp hair behind her ear. "The deceit began early. Whenever Dad was in, I pretended not to care. Indifference was an easy and safe barrier to hide behind. I fooled everyone into believing that I was ashamed of him, when, in truth..." Her voice hitched. She took a breath. "When all I ever wanted was to be with him."

She paused, ran her hand over the duvet. "He told you the truth about why he steals," she said. "It was never about the booty, the gain. He rarely kept the things he took. They had no value to him.

"What he loved was being a rapscallion. The challenge for

him wasn't to avoid capture, but to make friends with those who put him behind bars. Living as the town 'character' was more important to him than living with me."

She looked down at her hand where it rested. "I must have inherited my mother's hands. Slender, long fingers. Dad's hands have wide, stubby fingers." She gave a soft laugh. "He had a time of it, wrestling my hair into ponytails, which as often as not were lopsided. He cursed tiny buttons that wouldn't go into their buttonholes."

The light from the bathroom cast half of her face in shadow, but Rye could see how pensive her smile was.

"Once, I picked a bouquet of wildflowers and needed a vase to put them in. Rather than steal one, which I expected, he painstakingly glued sequins onto a Mason jar. By the time he finished, the flowers were wilted, but I put them in the vase anyway. I still have it. It's the ugliest thing you've ever seen. But it's the dearest thing I own."

She choked up, but recovered quickly. "Before tonight, the last time I saw him, he told me that since I was all grown up and doing well, it was time we cut ties and got on with our separate lives. We had been separated so many times before, you would think I had become immune.

"But I no longer had the resilience or faith of a child. I couldn't cling to a naïve hope that things would change, get better, that he would miss me enough to want me with him. Because that separation was voluntary, mandated only by him, it hurt much more than all the others combined."

She sat for several seconds, then left the bed and went into the bathroom. "Did you see a hair dryer in here?" A few seconds later one was switched on.

Rye got up and checked outside again. "Damn it." The police unit hadn't gone anywhere. The officer could be sleeping through his shift. Or guarding that door. He had no way of knowing, and the only way he could test it was to show himself.

The hair dryer went off. Brynn came out, her hair still only partially dry. She was briskly rubbing the ends of it with a towel. "Still there?"

"Yeah. But there's no sight of anyone else, which means he didn't call for the cavalry or they would have been here by now."

"Do you think it's safe for me to leave?"

"Unless he's manning a post."

She bowed her head and rubbed her forehead. "I can't fail at this. I can't."

"Hey." Rye went to her, took the towel from her hand, and dropped it to the floor. "You're not going to fail. We'll figure a way. You'll get to Violet with time to spare."

She raised her head and looked at him with damp, imploring eyes. "Do you promise?"

"I have every faith in you." Then he continued forward, his footsteps unchecked. She had no choice but to back up until she was against the wall. He placed both hands above her head and on either side of it.

"What's this about?" she asked.

"Sharing body heat." He bumped her middle with his.

She dropped her head forward and left it to rest against the center of his chest. "Look, Rye, exhaustion made me nostalgic. I told you a boohoo story, but it wasn't designed to make you feel sorry for me."

"Then feel sorry for me."

She raised her head. "What for?"

He lifted a strand of hair lying against her chest and rubbed it between his thumb and fingers. "Because I've been wanting you for almost twenty-four hours, and I'm tired of it."

She swallowed, said huskily, "You've passed on several opportunities."

"Best I recall, the last time I made a move, you pushed me away and enforced a kissing restriction."

"It was intended to be a goodbye, so why should you care?"

"I wanted that kiss."

"You'd said you didn't have designs like that on me."

"Well..." He moved in closer, the bump graduating to a meshing. Her placed his hands at her waist and began gathering up her sweater. He took it slowly, giving her time to object, slap his hands away, stop him in any fashion. She didn't.

He leaned in to whisk his lips across hers as he continued to raise her sweater until it cleared her chest. Her arms went up. He pulled it over her head and let it fall where it would.

She lowered her arms, but otherwise didn't move. He took advantage of her passiveness to drink in the sight. The slender column of her neck, the shallow triangle at its base, a bosom made for pillowing. Her bra was the color the sky turns right before the first star comes out.

He placed the fingertips of both hands on her collarbones, traced their width to the bra's shoulder straps. "I believe that's what I said. What I can't believe..." He lowered the satin strap, dragging it down her arm with painstaking slowness until the cup of her bra caught on her nipple. "...is that you took me serious."

He moved his hand to the under curve of her breast and pushed it up, then lowered his head and placed his mouth on the swell above the twilight-colored fabric. He kissed it open-mouthed and with leisurely sweeps of his tongue, before gently sucking the skin.

She made a purring sound as her body went lax. Her head was back, her eyes closed. She was biting her lower lip. He whispered, "Is that permission to continue?"

She opened her eyes and, clasping his head firmly between her hands, brought it to hers. Their mouths came at each other hungrily. This was no coy kiss. Her tongue was giving and receiving, and the way she drew his in was as erotic as hell.

The caveman in him was awakened with a vengeance. He wanted to claim her mouth, possess it, and to inflict pain on every other man who'd had so much as a sampling of it. He wanted to kill the wild Hendrix boy.

He reached around and unhooked her bra. It dropped between them, then fell away. When next he put his mouth to her breasts, he covered a nipple. It was hard, ripe with arousal. She arched up, offering him more. He teased, he tugged. Pleasuring her became his sole purpose in life.

Until her hands moved to his fly and started working open the metal buttons. She was deft. In a matter of seconds, she had him in hand, almost stopping his heart, but not curbing the male instinct to thrust.

Which he did. Into her firm grasp. The pressure she applied was perfect. The skin-to-skin friction was so incredible that, by the time she'd worked her way up to the tip, it was drum-tight and damn near bursting. Her thumb made a pass across the slit, pressed.

"Jesus, Brynn," he gasped. "Stop. Stop." He moved her hand off him.

"You're pushing me away again?"

He tried to laugh at the absurdity of that question, but he was breathing too hard. "Hell no. Fuck no. Take off…" He couldn't even finish but gestured at her remaining clothes.

Holding his gaze, she sat down on the bed and pulled off her boots and socks, then stood up and removed her jeans. She pulled back the bedcovers and lay down, thighs demurely together.

Between them was a pastel patch of lace that was expanding Rye's veins with raw lust. He loved the thing. He wanted it gone.

He managed to undress and wrangle a condom out of his wallet, then crawled onto the bed, parted her thighs, and settled between them. Holding her hips between his hands, he planted a solid kiss on that tantalizing terrain between navel and sex. It deserved more attention. Adoration. It warranted a shrine.

But some other time.

He dipped his head lower and brushed the triangle of lace with his lips, back and forth several times. Then, with Brynn working at the panties as urgently as he, they were finally cast off. Again, he forgot how to breathe. She was beautiful.

His fingertips grazed the delta of soft hair, then he slid his hand between her thighs. His fingers dipped into warm honey, into her, then went deep and stroked. Her hips came off the bed. She fitted her mound into his palm and ground it against the heel of his hand with a feverishness that matched his.

He withdrew his hand and stretched out on top of her. He kissed her neck, ravenously, but a bit awkwardly, as he fumbled with the wrapper and got the condom on.

Then—God, finally—he pushed into her in one long, un-interrupted glide, until he was completely, solidly embedded. Seized again by a primal possessiveness, he clamped the slender cord of her neck between his teeth and held it for several heart-beats, then raised his head and looked down into her face.

Her cheeks were flushed. Catching the dim light, her eyes shone silver as they looked into his. Breath rushed past her lips, made swollen and red and damp from kisses.

"Pride be damned," she whispered. "I wanted this. I wanted this."

Sliding her hands down to his butt, she secured him inside her even deeper and began a sinuous belly dance under him. The rhythmic curl and tilt of her hips started a throb in his cock that would have been painful if it hadn't felt so damn good.

With his nose, he pushed her hair aside and placed his lips against her ear so that she would hear every panted word, each curse, praise and blessing, every syllable of the sex-talk chant that urged her toward her orgasm, and his inarticulate, mating growl when he allowed himself to come.

The only thing he wished he could take back, the one thing he wished he hadn't said where she could hear it, where *he* could hear it, spoken on a serrated sigh as he sank onto her in sweet repletion: *Brynn.*

# Chapter 27

———⊰⊱———

*12:37 a.m.*

N ate had gone home.

He had the uneasy impression that the Hunts couldn't have cared less.

Earlier this week, Richard and Delores had pleaded tearfully with him to stick his neck out and smuggle out the dose of GX-42. "Name your price. Anything," Richard had told him. "Get me the stuff that will beat this thing."

Delores had been almost too emotional to speak, but her brimming eyes had implored him. She'd managed to croak, "You're our only hope, Nate."

So much for her worship. Tonight they'd looked at him with cool disdain and distrust, as though it had been hc who had double-crossed them, not Brynn.

*Brynn.* Trusted colleague and conspirator, she had yielded to the final choice of the recipient with disappointment, but also with an unbending devotion to this chancy move they were making as a team. It was now obvious to Nate that she had wanted the inevitable fame of a medical pioneer.

Jonas Salk. Christiaan Barnard. Nathan Lambert.

He had envisioned GX-42 ultimately being named for him. Never in his fantasies had it been Brynn who achieved such heights.

Arriving at his high-rise residence building in Buckhead, he had relinquished his Jaguar to the parking garage valet and taken the soundless elevator up to the twenty-second floor. The view of the skyline from his living room was dazzling, but tonight it had been obscured by rain, and, in any case, Nate hadn't been in the mood to admire it.

He'd poured himself a neat whiskey. Usually, he limited himself to two drinks in an evening, and he'd had those in the Hunts' sitting room. He'd had the third in the hope that it would either induce sleep or, even better, relieve some pressure so that his mind could free-float.

In that semi-stuporous state sought by mad artists and drunken writers, perhaps he would be creatively inspired. His subconscious might devise a genius plan that would restore him to the Hunts' good graces and salvage this debacle before time ran out.

He'd finished the whiskey, gone through his routine bedtime preparation, turned off the lights, and had gotten into bed. But sleep had eluded him for more than an hour, and the alcohol hadn't evoked any brilliant ideas.

He'd finally slipped into a light doze when the building intercom buzzed. Initially he'd wondered if the buzzer had been part of a dream. When it went off again, he questioned why the building concierge would be calling him at this hour. If there had been a medical emergency with one of his patients, he would have been contacted on his cell phone. He decided to ignore the summons.

But it was persistent. He threw off his cashmere blanket and walked across the silk-and-wool-blend carpet to the box on the wall. He pressed the blinking lighted button and put annoyance behind his voice. "Yes?"

"I hate to disturb you, Dr. Lambert, but there's a man at the main entrance, demanding to see you. He says that he's been sent by a Mr. Hunt, that the matter is urgent, and that you'll know what it's regarding. Should I let him in?"

"Did he give you his name?"

"Goliad."

Nate's heart thumped. They'd found Brynn! And the GX-42. And Goliad had been dispatched to swiftly escort him back to the mansion.

"Send him up."

He slid his bare feet into his house shoes and pulled on his robe. He was hastily belting it when his doorbell chimed. He moved quickly through the apartment and eagerly pulled open the front door.

Then he recoiled. "What are you doing here?"

"Hey, doc."

Timmy planted his hand in the center of Nate's chest and pushed him backward as he sauntered into the apartment.


*12:39 a.m.*

In Timmy's world, reprisal wasn't merely expected, it was compulsory.

When someone was affronted, whether intentionally or not, the offender had better beware. The concept of forgiveness was unheard of. An insult was never forgotten. Grievances were long-lived and, if a person died before getting satisfaction for one, the grudge was passed down to his successors, heirs of hatred.

After tonight, Timmy bore Goliad just such a grudge.

The greaser hadn't lifted a hand to stop Mallett from almost unmanning him, and then later had stood silently by while Richard Hunt read him the riot act like he was a nobody. As he was driving Timmy home, Goliad had used a hard-ass, boss tone to tell him that if he wanted to continue working for the Hunts, he had better grow up, lose the chip on his shoulder, and get his shit together.

That was precisely what Timmy had done. Although, when Goliad issued that order, this wasn't what he'd had in mind.

When Dr. Lambert answered the door and saw Timmy, he looked like he might pee his pajama bottoms. Over the PJs he was wearing a robe made of some slick and shiny material.

Timmy fingered the lapel. "In this movie I saw a coupla years ago, a guy was wearing a robe just like this. Big black dude. Drug kingpin. He blew somebody's head off with a forty-five, point blank." He put the tip of his index finger against the bridge of the doctor's nose, jabbed it, and said, "Pow! He probably had to throw the robe away. Brains are hard to wash out."

The doctor blinked rapidly and nervously licked his lips. "Where's Goliad?"

"Last I heard, he was gonna crash on the Hunts' sofa." He strolled over to the bar, picked up the twenty-five-year-old special reserve scotch, uncapped it, sniffed it, then drank directly from the bottle.

"H... how'd you know where I live?"

"Goliad pointed the building out to me. I'm in training, you know. I need to know these things."

"Did you come alone?"

"Just me." Timmy spread his arms wide, the movement sloshing whiskey out of the bottle. "Oops." He looked at the splashes on the floor. "Reminds me. Down in the main lobby? How do they get the floor to glow like that?"

The doctor cleared his throat. "It's, uh, constructed of a translucent material and illuminated from underneath."

"Illuminated. Huh. Well, it's cool-looking."

"I don't think Goliad would appreciate your using his name to bluff your way into a private residence."

"No, he probably wouldn't." He cocked his head to one side and closed one eye. "I just figured it out."

"What?"

"What your head reminds me of. I've been trying to think of it, and it just now came to me. A suppository." He chortled. "I guess that's how you can keep it so far up your own ass."

Lambert pulled the belt on his robe tighter. "Why didn't Goliad come with you?"

"Because I didn't invite him." Casually and with confidence, he turned his back on the doctor. The douche wasn't going to do anything, but even if he stupidly attempted it, Timmy could see their reflections in the walls of glass that enwrapped the living room.

"This is some place. On a clear night, you must have a real nice view. Being up this high, I mean." He leaned forward slightly and looked at the street below. "Long way down. Long, long way."

"What do you want, Timmy? Has there been an update on Dr. O'Neal's whereabouts?"

"Not that I've heard. She's got great tits, doesn't she?"

"I haven't noticed."

Timmy barked a laugh at that and turned away from the window. "Why am I not surprised?"

That remark goaded the doctor into taking a G.I. Joe stance, which, with the shiny robe and all, was downright comical. "I'm compelled to report your coming here to the Hunts, by way of Goliad. I understand he's your supervisor."

"Know what he called me?"

"Sorry?"

"Goliad. I overheard him talking to one of the guys who chauffeurs the Hunts around. Goliad called me a cockroach."

"That was certainly unkind of him."

"Unkind?" Timmy laughed. "Highest compliment he

could've paid me. Know why? Because cockroaches have survived for kazillions of years because they're adaptable."

The doctor didn't say anything, just nodded.

"Well, see, I'm adaptable." He used both hands to point to his chest. "If a situation does an unexpected one-eighty on me, and things go to shit, I don't look back to see what went wrong and cry over it. No. I stay cool and keep my eyes forward." He made an arrow of his hand and aimed it ahead of him. "And—I swear, I've got the devil's own luck—the turnaround usually winds up working to my benefit."

With a maneuver he'd mastered over years of practice, he removed the switchblade from his sleeve and flicked it open. The doctor jumped like a rabbit. Flashing him a cunning smile, Timmy calmly began flipping the knife end over end, catching it by the handle each time.

"This brouhaha is over the lady doctor making off with the magic potion, or youth serum, or holy water, whatever it is, right?" He laughed at Lambert's startled expression. "I can see that you, like everybody else, thought I didn't know that, but how stupid would I have to be not to figure it out?

"I saw the paperwork Mallett had such a hard-on for. That metal box came from some pharmaceutical lab in Ohio. All hush-hush. Two doctors competing for possession of it. And a senator frantic to get his hands on it." He stopped the flipping and pointed the knife at Lambert. "What is it?"

Lambert's gaze was fixed on the switchblade. He probably couldn't work up a spit, but he eked out, "I'm not at liberty to say."

Timmy held his pose for a long time, then shrugged abruptly. The doctor flinched again. "That's okay," Timmy said. "I probably wouldn't understand your medical mumbo jumbo, and anyhow I don't give a fuck what it is.

"I just know that the Hunts want it, and want it bad. What do I want, you ask? I want to win their favor, get in good with them, suck that sugar tit that Goliad's had to himself all these years. The way to do that? Solve the problem."

The doctor's eyes shifted from the knife up to Timmy's eyes. "How do you propose to do that?"

"It's so simple, it's a mystery to me why nobody's thought of it." He laughed and took another swig of the whiskey.

# Chapter 28

*12:50 a.m.*

**B**rynn missed his weight on her, the tickle of hair against places where her body was smooth, the scent of his skin, the overall feel of him on her and inside her. The tumult was over, but she wasn't done savoring the aftermath.

With regret, she opened her eyes.

Rye lay facing her, perfectly still, staring at her as though he'd been waiting for her to come out of the post-orgasmic daze in which he'd left her. He touched her neck with the tip of his index finger. "Does that hurt?"

"No."

"I didn't mean to bite that hard."

"You didn't. My skin bruises if you look at it hard."

"Any bruises from last night when I held you to the ground?"

"One." She rolled toward him so he could see her back.

He grimaced and gently stroked the spot just above her hip. "I'm sorry. I've been rough on you." As though talking to himself, he added, "I'm rough on everybody."

"The person you were talking to on the phone earlier?"

His eyes sharpened on her. He stopped caressing, but his sudden withdrawal was more than tactile.

"I came out of the bathroom just as you tossed your phone onto the dresser. You seemed upset."

He turned onto his back. "How much did you overhear?"

"'Love you, too.'"

He didn't say anything.

Brynn plucked at the hem of her pillowcase. "Wife?"

"No."

She let go a shaky breath. "A little late for me to be asking, but I'm relieved to know I didn't commit adultery."

"You're safe on that score. In fact, you're safe on every score."

He flung back the sheet and got up. Moving to the window, he checked the parking lot. "Our friend is still there."

The phone he'd gotten from her dad had been charging on the nightstand. He unplugged it and checked the readout. "Good to go. You'd better start calling anybody you trust with your new number." As he made his way toward the bathroom, he scooped his jeans off the floor.

Startled by his abruptness, Brynn sat up and held the sheet against her chest. "Are you coming back?"

"No. I'll keep a lookout. You want the bathroom first?"

She gave a small shake of her head and pulled the covers up to a more modest level. "You go ahead."

"I won't take long."

He didn't. She'd heard the commode flush. The shower ran for about ninety seconds. Several minutes later, he came out. He was wearing his jeans; his hair was still wet. He didn't look her in the eye. In fact, he didn't look at her at all.

He picked up his shirt, went to pull it on, and noticed that the sleeves were inside out. He flapped the shirt to shake loose the bunched fabric. "Why don't you sleep for a while. If he leaves, I'll wake you up."

"You should sleep, too."

"Heard that already. From Dash."

"You talked to him?"

"Texted him while I was in the bathroom. Sent him my new phone number."

"Has he heard anything more from Wilson?"

"No, and I asked."

"Maybe they're responsible for the car outside."

"If they had tracked us here, we would know it. They wouldn't be covert."

She thought so, too, which made her even more leery of the policeman outside. Wilson and Rawlins were a threat, but they were restricted to abiding by the law. The worst they could do was detain her and prevent her from getting to Violet in time.

A corrupt lawman posed much more danger, as did Goliad and Timmy, who were lawless and would go to extremes on behalf of Richard Hunt. She only had to look at Rye's left hand to be reminded that they could strike with violence. "You never put anything on those cuts."

"They're fine." One of the sleeves was still bedeviling him.

"Stop fighting with that. If you won't lie down, at least sit down."

"Why are you nagging me?"

"Why are you acting like an ass?"

He stopped wrestling with the shirt and threw it down. "Because it would be a shame to ruin a really great fuck with stupid and pointless conversation."

She held his stare for a moment, then rolled to her other side and tucked the covers beneath her chin. "If our cop hasn't left within an hour, I'll take my chances and sneak out. You'll enjoy that. You'll be free of me."

He muttered a curse. Then, "It was my mom."

She turned toward him. "What?"

"That's who you overhead me talking to."

Brynn came up on her elbows.

He maintained an arrogant stance, as though spoiling for a fight. "Anything else you want to ask?"

"Where does she live?"

"Outside Austin. On a lakefront lot. Dad has a bass boat and goes fishing almost every day. He's a cliché. Bores you blind with stories about the big ones that got away."

"How was their Thanksgiving?"

"Good. Except for my newest nephew. He's teething."

"How old is he?"

"I don't know, Brynn. I've never seen him."

"Why not?"

He didn't say anything, just gnawed the inside of his cheek. He went to the window and peeped out again, but she thought that was an excuse to turn away from her.

"Why don't you go home?" she asked.

"I never know what my schedule is going to be."

"Does your mother fall for that excuse?"

He came back around, his eyes angry, so she knew she'd struck a chord. However, rather than demur, she pressed. "What causes you to twitch in your sleep, Rye?"

*"Twitch?"*

"Yesterday morning in the cabin, while we napped, several times you woke me up, jerking, talking unintelligibly."

"Sorry. You should have nudged me."

"What disturbs your sleep? And why can't you land? That is, land and stay for any length of time."

"I'd rather be in the air."

"So you've said. You love flying. It's an obsession. It's in-grained." She paused and looked at him meaningfully. "It's also your escape. From what?"

He checked his wristwatch, then placed his hands on his hips. "Are we done yet?"

"Jake told me you were a legend."

"Vlad the Impaler was a legend. Ted Bundy."

Refusing to buy into the act of indifference he was staging, she persisted. "Jake's a liar? You didn't fly into the worst of the shit?"

"Stories get exaggerated. They take on a life of their own."

"True. But they have some substance."

"Believe as much or as little as you want to."

"I believe you could fly for anybody. So why do you fly for Dash-It-All and the like?"

"What's wrong with it?"

"Nothing. But there's little prestige."

"Screw prestige. I like my kind of flying."

"Why?"

"Because most of the time, I can fly alone."

"Why do you prefer that?"

He bent down closer to her so she wouldn't miss his point. "I don't have to talk to anybody."

"About what happened over there?"

"Over where?"

She just looked at him, and she outlasted him.

He rubbed the back of his neck and tilted his head from side to side, popping the vertebrae. But that didn't relieve the strain. Still vexed, he opened the mini bar, took out a beer, and carried it over to an easy chair near the window. He looked outside and swore softly, indicating to her that the police car was still there.

He plopped down, yanked the pull tab, took a drink from the can. "You want to hear a nice bedtime story? Too bad. This ain't it."

She sat up and raised her knees, wrapping her arms around them.

He began with an air of boredom. "This is the story about the pilot of a C-12. Know what that is?"

"Obviously an airplane."

"Military version of a King Air. They're used for personnel and cargo transport, troop support, rescue, surveillance. They serve variable purposes, depending on which branch of the military is using them, and what for. A C-12 can be the food truck. An ambulance. Sometimes a hearse."

He studied the can of beer in his hand, took a drink from it. "Anyway, that particular day, two C-12s were to fly a squadron of fighter pilots, plus their commanding officer, and some support personnel, out of Bagram. They'd been there for a couple of days, attending a briefing on where some badass Taliban who needed taking out were hiding up in the Nuristan province. We were flying them back to their base.

"Wasn't the worst of shit by any means. Duck soup, really. Scheduled to take off at sixteen hundred, but as happens in military life, the commander's meeting ran long, things got pushed back, so I thought I'd get some sleep while we were waiting.

"Next thing I know, the other pilot was waking me up, saying the planes were on the tarmac, they'd been put through pre-flight, and a lot of traffic was coming in, so the tower was telling us to get the lead out. I grabbed my gear. 'I'll be there soon as I take a leak.'

"He said, 'They assigned me to the first ship in line. That new bird.' He told me the squadron and commanding officer were already aboard. 'You get the economy flight, Mallett.' The second plane was older, not as tricked out. It was hauling light cargo and the support personnel. He gave me a mock salute on his way out. 'You snooze, you lose.'"

Brynn's throat began to tighten. She folded her hands together and placed them against her lips.

He drained the beer and set the can with deliberate care on the table at his elbow. "A sidebar here. You know how you can buy the same brand of blue jeans, same size, same style, but each pair will fit just a little different from the others until you work them in?

"Planes are the same. Aircraft can be identical. Same model, same configuration, cockpit panel, all the same. But each plane has its quirks. I'd flown that new plane a dozen times or more.

I'd turned in a squawk list to the—" He paused when he saw her puzzlement. "Oh. Squawk list. A list of those quirks I mentioned.

"Mechanics hadn't gotten around to checking them out, and the other pilot hadn't seen the squawk list. He'd also never flown with the copilot, which isn't necessary, but it helps to have some hours with the other flyer in the cockpit."

"I climbed into the captain's seat of the second craft. Copilot saluted me. More smack talk about me flying the VW instead of the Rolls. The two planes taxied. The first one took off."

He hesitated. Took several breaths. "Soon as it got airborne at full takeoff power, I realized that he was having control problems. One of the items on my list was that new plane's yoke. It was sticky. You had to pull back on it firmly but smoothly. Then you'd be fine."

He was miming the motions, pulling both fists toward his chest.

"The pilot didn't know that, so when he felt that minuscule amount of resistance, he panicked and overcompensated, pulled back hard. I was yelling at him through my headset, 'Too much! Too much!' But he nosed up too fast, too steep, went practically vertical and stalled. He couldn't correct it."

Tears were stinging Brynn's eyes, but she blinked them back without moving, not wanting to distract him from finishing.

"What was really weird?" he said. "It was so damn graceful, the way it arced over before going into the nose dive. It was like watching an Olympiad in slow motion." He gave a humorless laugh. "Tanks were full, of course. The fireball was spectacular." He sat forward and put his elbows on his knees, digging his thumbs into his eye sockets.

Brynn didn't say anything for a time, then, "If you had been flying it, could you have corrected it?"

He lowered his hands. "That's the point of the story, Brynn. If I'd been flying it, there would have been nothing to correct. Thirteen people died because I nodded off." He looked at his palms as though seeing blood on them. "I knew all those pilots. They were great guys. The best of the best. Such a fucking waste."

"You think the least you could have done was to die with them?"

He raised his head and looked at her with vehemence.

"That's is, isn't it?" she asked softly. "That's the issue. You didn't die that day."

"I beat the odds."

Nodding slowly, she said, "But if you fly long enough, often enough, in conditions that are risky enough, the odds will begin to stack against you until eventually..."

"My number will come up."

Even having guessed that was his mind-set, she made a mournful sound of dismay. "You *want* to die?"

"Not die," he said, "just...just not have to live with this anymore."

She searched his haunted eyes. How could she respond in a way that would reverse his thinking, reset his reasoning, relieve his guilt, or console him to some extent, any extent? Nothing came to mind. "I don't think anyone, except yourself, can help you with this, Rye."

"I didn't ask for anyone's help. I don't want anyone's help."

"You would rather suffer alone."

"And not have to talk about it."

"That must be awfully hurtful to people who care about you."

"It is."

"Is that why you've shut yourself off from your family?"

He stood up and turned his back to her. "From everybody."

From her, certainly. His lovemaking had been passionate. He'd whispered stirring things she had taken as sincere because he hadn't said them to woo her. She had already been wooed. But the instant the intimacy had shifted from the physical to the emotional, he had detached himself.

She wanted to go to him now, hold him close, and tell him how she hated that he suffered this continuous anguish. But knowing that her attempted comforting would be rebuffed, she stayed where she was.

At the window, he said, "No change. He's still there, and it's still pouring. What do you want to do?"

She looked at the clock. It was almost one-thirty. "Honestly, now that I've been prone, I don't think I could endure the drive. I would be a danger to myself and anyone else on the road. I would arrive at five-thirty or thereabouts. Would it be fair to the Griffins to barge in at that hour and hit them with all this?"

"That's up to you. Whenever you say you're ready, I'll take on the guy outside to get you out of here."

She glanced toward the window. "He hasn't bothered us, and no one else has come along. Why don't we rest? Just for a few hours. I could leave at dawn, present myself at a reasonable time of morning, and still have hours to spare."

He looked at the bed. "I could use a nap. I can't promise that I won't twitch."

"But I promise that I won't talk."

He gave her a wry smile. "Deal." He walked over to the bed, managed the sleeves of his shirt, and pulled it on. He picked up his new phone and the card key, then switched off the bathroom light. "Go to sleep. I'll be right back."

"Where are you going?"

"To call Dash."

"What for?"

"I forgot to tell him something when I texted before. Don't let anyone in but me."

The door closed behind him.

# Chapter 29

*1:22 a.m.*

Goliad pulled his car up beside the police unit and motioned for the officer to lower his window. He gave Goliad a mock salute.

Goliad asked, "Have you seen them?"

"Neither coming or going."

"Room number?"

"Seven oh seven. It's on this side. Third window from the south corner. Drapes are closed. If there's any light on, it's feeble. Hasn't changed since I got here. No motion. So can't say for certain if they're in there or not."

"I'll be in the row farthest from the building," Goliad told him. "Stay here until further notice. Let me know if you see anything." He passed the cop an envelope of cash through the car windows, then drove away and found a parking space that provided a view of the entire building.

After tucking Timmy in for the night, he had returned to the Hunts' house and, through the house intercom, told Delores that he was back. She'd thanked him. They'd exchanged good nights.

But Goliad hadn't availed himself of the sofa.

For one thing, her husky whisper telling him how much safer she felt with him nearby had left him with an erection, which he suffered frequently. Tonight, she had touched him, making his desire even more rampant. It consumed him. It was demoralizing and potentially destructive, but he was helpless against it.

Countless times he'd considered leaving, getting away from her entirely. He could easily find lucrative employment. With his experience, he would be a valuable asset to a Mexican drug cartel. He'd lived all his life on the U.S. side of the border, so he understood the *norteamericanos'* way of life and how to maneuver in it. He spoke flawless English without a trace of a Spanish accent. He would have his choice of jobs.

Yet he stayed. His unrequited love for Delores was torturous, but he would endure it if only to be able to see her on a near-daily basis, to watch her move, to hear her voice. A smile, a word of gratitude from her was like a caress.

The only permissible way for him to express his love was to serve her with unqualified loyalty. So instead of resting on the study sofa, he'd continued his quest for Brynn O'Neal and Rye Mallett. He'd made follow-up calls to his snitches and offered more substantial bribes to law officers on the take.

None had had anything to report. A canvass of hotels and motels hadn't yielded a guest named either Mallett or O'Neal. But Goliad recalled the phone conversation Mallett had conducted while in the car and reasoned that a room might have been booked for him by the company he was flying for.

After ten minutes on Google, he had obtained the legal name of the owner of Dash-It-All. He'd begun calling hotels and motels within a reasonable distance of Hartsfield-Jackson, asking to be connected to the guest room of Mr. Dashiell Dewitt.

On the sixth call, he'd gotten a strike. The hotel operator had put him on hold while she rang the room, but Goliad had hung up before the call went through and instead phoned a beat cop who was notorious for taking graft.

The police officer had gone to the hotel, told the desk clerk that Mr. Dewitt had reported that a rifle was missing from his car, which had been parked on the hotel parking lot. It was emphasized to the clerk that, in light of recent mass shootings, law enforcement took weapons matters seriously. He must follow up with Mr. Dewitt immediately. The clerk had willingly given him Mr. Dewitt's room number and had advised him to use a side door.

The officer had passed all this information along to Goliad, who had told him to park near that door and to report to him any sightings of the couple immediately.

Acting on the new information, Goliad had called in a replacement to take over watch duty at the mansion and, alone, had driven to the hotel.

The gloom and rain reduced visibility, but he applied his binoculars to the designated window. It was as the cop had described to him: drapes drawn and the room looked dark.

But then, an infinitesimal flicker at the edge of the drapes. A motion so subtle and short-lived that if he had blinked he would have missed it.

He lowered his binoculars and smiled.

He debated calling the Hunts and informing them of this latest development but decided to wait until he could report that he had the drug in his possession.

*1:26 a.m.*

Rye stepped out into the corridor, leaned against the door, and pressed the back of his head into the hard surface. He felt weaker, more shaken, more unbalanced now than he had last night after the crash.

That hadn't been his fault, but the blame for this was solely on him. He had let it happen. He had made it happen. Knowing it was a mistake, he had touched Brynn anyway, and, God, it had been good, moving inside her. Terrifyingly good. Because, when he came, he'd been all in: body and mind. Heart.

And, as if that hadn't been cataclysmic enough, he'd then poured out his soul, revealing to her aspects of his torment that he'd never spoken of to another human being.

Twenty-four hours with her, and he'd broken all his self-imposed rules:

*No bonds. No involvement. No one.*

He had fibbed to Brynn. He hadn't forgotten to tell Dash something in a text. The truth was, he hadn't replied to Dash's last question. He saw now that Dash had repeated it, adding a few blue words to emphasize his need of an answer. *R U still flying for me tomorrow night?*

Up until a few minutes ago, Rye had been unsure of his answer. The plan had been for him to see Brynn off on her way to Knoxville, wish her well, and that would be it.

But he couldn't abandon her. He simply couldn't. It wasn't because they'd had fantastic sex, or because he'd opened up to her about his personal tragedy. It was because there were still people who could stop her, and he wanted Brynn to get what she'd strived for. He wanted Violet to have a shot at life.

Even after seeing Brynn safely to Tennessee, he would have hours in which to reach Columbus. If commercial service couldn't get him there, he would charter a plane out of his own pocket. He wouldn't let Dash down. He would fly that load of Roman Red. He wouldn't alert Dash to his change of schedule, though, not until it was too late for him to do anything about it. If he told him now, he'd have a conniption, and Rye didn't need the argument.

He tapped in *Affirmative.*

The reply came immediately. *Not that glad to hear from you. I was hoping you were asleep.*

*About to be. Will ck in tmo.*

Tomorrow, after he was sure that all had worked out well for Brynn and he'd told her goodbye.

But first he had to get through the rest of the night without reaching for her.

*1:32 a.m.*

Brynn used the time Rye wasn't in the room to take a quick shower. She came out of the bathroom wrapped in a towel, but she decided it would be presumptuous of her to return to the bed naked, given Rye's mood.

While in search of her undergarments, she noticed Rye's bomber jacket hanging on the back of the chair. It was odd to see it without him. The jacket was as much a part of him as the growth pattern of his scruff.

She ran her finger along the edge of the collar. The leather was crinkled and scoured. It showed its age, but in a good way. Like the squint lines at the corners of Rye's eyes.

Unable to resist, she dropped the towel, lifted the jacket off the chair, and slid her arms into the sleeves. It was too large and heavy on her frame, but the silk lining against her bare skin was seductive and felt wonderful.

She was examining one of the nicks on the sleeve when the door was pushed open and Rye strode in. When he saw her, he stopped dead in his tracks. The door closed on its own.

Brynn was petrified by embarrassment. "I'm sorry. I just...You're obviously very fond of this. It must have special significance. I don't know...I don't know what possessed me. I shouldn't have touched it, much less..."

"Stop." He walked past her on his way to the window.

He didn't report a change, so she assumed the police car was still there. He turned back to her, closed the distance between them, and took hold of the jacket with a fist on each side of the zipper. He rested his forehead against hers. "Once this is over, I'm off again."

"I understood that the first dozen times you told me."

"But, dammit, Brynn."

"What?"

Raising his head, and looking her up and down, he whispered, "How did you know that this is my favorite fantasy?"

"It is? Since when?"

"Since I walked in that door."

With a groan, he stamped his mouth over hers, slanting it to the perfect angle. The forceful thrust of his tongue was no less thrilling and exciting than it had been the first time he'd kissed her. More so, if that were possible. It reignited her craving for his mouth, his hands, him.

She pushed off his shirt, then folded her arms around the back of his neck, clinging. He slid his hands inside the jacket, his palms coasting over her breasts before he placed them on either side of her waist and pulled her with him as he backed up to the end of the bed and sat down.

Holding her in front of him between his legs, he nuzzled her breasts, dabbed at her nipples with his tongue, nipped at the area around her navel with his teeth. His tongue drew spirals in the hollows beneath her hip bones.

When he started to move lower, she responded to the gentle guidance of his hands as he parted her thighs, wider, until his soughing breath caressed her, then the brush of his lips, the wet heat of his open mouth, the sweeps and swirls and strokes of his tongue.

She gasped his name, clutched his hair. His mouth was merciless, unpredictable, eliciting unexpected flares of feeling that stole her breath. When an orgasm was only one caress away from shuddering through her, she angled his head away. "Not yet."

She placed her hands on his shoulders to steady herself, then pushed him back onto the bed. In the process of scooting toward the head of it, he unbuttoned his jeans and worked them past his hips. Brynn straddled his legs. The feel of soft denim against the insides of her thighs was incredibly erotic. She relished the sight of his heaving chest, the drastic dip of his taut stomach beneath his rib cage, and his sex, pulsing with vitality, the tip already glossed.

He panted, "If you don't ride me, there is no God."

Smiling, she combed her fingers up through the fan of light brown hair on his chest as she bent over him and took him into her mouth. Sensations aroused by his elementally male scent and taste were intensified by the low animal sound of pleasure that vibrated through his entire body. She drew on him until he huffed her name and tugged her head up by handfuls of her hair.

"Now." He took himself in hand, so that when she stood on her knees, he guided himself into her. As she sank down on him, he released a long exhale. Through the squint she was coming to identify with him, he looked at her with thrilling, possessive greed. "Damn, this is hot."

His thumbs stroked the channels at the tops of her thighs; then he reached around and claimed her bottom with strong hands that lifted and lowered her as she rubbed herself against his hardness, creating the friction that rendered almost unbearable pleasure.

Their motions grew increasingly fast and urgent. He jack-knifed up, burrowed his face into the open jacket, and sucked her nipple into his mouth. He worked his fingers down between them where they were joined, gathered moisture on the pads of them, then feathered, pressed, encircled. Again, again, and again until she came apart.

Her orgasm was long and intense. While aftershocks continued to ripple through her, he lay back down and carried her with him. Then, with his hands splayed over her bottom, grafting her to him, he thrust high and came.

Brynn lay limp and motionless on his chest, feeling his fingers sifting lazily through her hair, listening to his heart beating against her ear, until she fell asleep.


*2:14 a.m.*


A short while later, she moved off him. He mumbled sleepy protests and tried to hold her, but she extracted herself, took off his jacket, and laid it at the foot of the bed. With a groan, he got up, checked the window. "I hope the bastard's uncomfortable."

He shucked his jeans and got back into bed.

She pulled the covers over them and snuggled against his side, his arm cradling her head, their legs intertwined under the covers.

She kissed his pec and touched his nipple with the tip of her tongue. He gave a grunt of approval. "Should we set an alarm?" she whispered.

"I'll wake up."

"You're sure?"

"Um-huh."

She resettled and was almost asleep, and thought he was, when he mumbled, "What happened with the wild Hendrix boy?"

She snuffled a laugh. "Whatever brought that on?"

"Just wondering if I have to hunt him down and kill him."

"He's spared. Nothing happened. We never even went out. I just let Dad think so."

"How come?"

"To get his attention."

He'd been lying with the back of his head on the pillow, eyes closed. He opened them now and tipped his head to look into her face.

She gave a small shrug. "It worked for a week or so."

He studied her for a moment, then stroked her lips with his fingertip. Without saying anything more, he turned her away from him and fit her into the curve of his body. He lay his arm across her. Heavily. Holding her close.

# Chapter 30

*5:32 a.m.*

I can't believe this." Delores angrily disconnected her phone, ending another unsuccessful attempt to reach Nate. "I feel like I'm operating in a vacuum."

"Coffee?" Richard asked.

She snapped a no, and then instantly ameliorated her tone. "I'm sorry. I don't mean to take my distress out on you."

"I'm as anxious as you are, Delores. More so. I'm the one with terminal cancer."

She fell back as though he'd inflicted a mortal wound.

He ran his fingers up through his hair. "Now I'm sorry. Lashing out at each other is counterproductive, a waste of energy. Let's try to keep calm. All right? We don't know that anything catastrophic has happened."

"We don't know that it hasn't, either. Where is everybody?"

They'd awakened almost simultaneously and, in robes and house shoes, left the master suite. The housekeeper wasn't due to report to work for another two hours. Delores had asked Richard to get the coffee started while she checked in with Goliad.

Except it wasn't their trusted facilitator she had found in the study. Asleep on the sofa was their chauffeur, snoring like a warthog. She'd startled him awake with a loud and imperious, *Where is Goliad?*

That was just one of the million-dollar questions among many. Where was Nate? What was he doing? When he'd taken his departure last night, he'd said he was going home to try to sleep for a few hours, but had insisted they contact him immediately if they received news of Brynn.

Delores had been periodically calling him for the past half hour. All the calls had gone unanswered. Goliad had inexplicably left the house, destination unknown, and wasn't answering his phone. She was furious with both of them.

She'd declined coffee, but Richard poured her a mug anyway and added the two packets of raw sugar she preferred. He slid it toward her across the eating island. She sat down, took one sip, and then sprang up again.

"On the most critical day of our lives, everybody has abandoned us."

"Goliad must have given the chauffeur a reason for calling him to watch duty."

"He told him to come immediately, that he had to leave without delay. He didn't explain why. To him or to us," she added with irritation. "How many times have we told him to keep us informed? How hard is it?"

"Maybe the matter wasn't important enough for him to disturb our rest."

"But important enough for him to tear out of here?"

"Delores, please stop prowling. Sit down, drink your coffee."

She slapped her hand on the granite. "Stop being so damn calm."

"One of us has to be," he said, raising his voice for the first time. "What good is becoming hysterical doing you? Or me?"

She sat down on the barstool and reached across the island

for his hand. "I'm not hysterical, I'm frightened." She glanced at the clock. "It's now less than fifteen hours until Nate must begin the infusion, and nothing toward that is happening."

"You've jumped to that conclusion. On what basis? A few missed telephone calls, for which there are dozens of logical explanations."

"I disagree. Ordinarily, perhaps, but not today. Nate knows his future is riding on this. Typically when one of us says jump, he asks how high. Now, he's ignoring my calls? That's worrisome, Richard. What if he's become sympathetic to Dr. O'Neal's cause?"

"He wouldn't."

"I've lost all faith in him."

"I think that's premature."

"Or overdue," she murmured.

"You were the last to speak with Goliad last night. What was said?"

"I told him how much safer we felt when he was around. And what does he do? Posts a chauffeur in his place. He knows better than to leave us in the lurch. Where did he go?"

"Maybe one of his many informants came through with a tip on Dr. O'Neal's whereabouts, and he had to act on it immediately, before she eluded him again. Wouldn't you rather him be in hot pursuit than giving you moment-by-moment play coverage?"

"Right now, I would appreciate both." She sipped her coffee, thought for a moment, then picked up her phone again and punched in a number.

"Who now?" Richard asked.

"If Goliad has Dr. O'Neal in his sights, and he's in hot pursuit, he will have taken Timmy along."

*5:35 a.m.*

Timmy's cell phone ring was an obnoxious rap beat. He looked at the readout and winked at Nate as he answered. "Good morning, Mrs. Hunt."

Nate's chest caved in, although he wondered how he could shrink into himself any further than he already had shrunk over the past four hours. Timmy had given him barely time enough to switch out his nightclothes for a suit and tie before manhandling him out of his condo.

At Timmy's insistence, they'd eschewed the sleek, swift elevator and boarded one lined with quilted furniture pads that the building's maintenance personnel used. Timmy had asked him what level of the parking garage his car was on. He pushed the bright orange button designating the second level. The elevator began its creaking descent. Nate had feared that when they reached bottom, he would be DOA, cocooned in one of the furniture pads.

But he'd still been alive when Timmy prodded him through the deserted garage to his car and told him to drive. Timmy had gotten in on the passenger side, giving a long wolf whistle in appreciation of the Jag's interior.

Nate had driven from the garage as instructed, and thus the worst hours of his life had begun to unfold.

Occasionally consulting a map on his phone, Timmy had given him directions. Driving conditions couldn't have been worse. They drove through downpours that caused Nate to hydroplane. The only advantage to the inclement weather was that traffic was minimal, enabling Nate to keep half his attention on the jackal in his passenger seat.

He'd kept his panic at bay only by telling himself that if Timmy had wanted him dead, he would have bled out by now on his living room floor. Or he'd have been a splatter on the sidewalk below his twenty-second-story window. Or he'd be gasping for his last breath in the trunk of his car.

Timmy wouldn't have had him dress up if he was going to kill him.

Or had he just been making him casket-ready?

Gruesome thoughts such as that had compelled him to do exactly as Timmy had ordered, without argument, every mile of the journey, the destination of which had eventually become apparent.

Knoxville, Tennessee.

The rain had been relentless, and the farther north they went, the harder it fell. The topography turned hillier. The forested summits wore cowls of rain clouds and fog. They'd been a half hour out of Knoxville when Timmy had yawned, stretched, and scratched his crotch.

"Next exit has a Mickey D's. I'm hungry."

Nate had taken the exit, arrived at the McDonald's, and pulled into the drive-through lane as told. Timmy had ordered a breakfast sandwich and coffee. Nate had declined food, and the last thing his nerves needed was caffeine. He'd ordered an orange juice, which, for some reason, Timmy had thought funny.

After picking up their order at the window, Timmy had told him to pull over and park. He'd done so. Timmy had devoured the sandwich with the dining manners of a hyena and had just relaxed against the seat to savor his coffee when his cell phone broadcast that auditory assault.

Now, having learned that it was Delores calling, Nate didn't know if that was a good thing or bad. Should he feel elation and relief, or dread and fear? Should he shout out a plea for help? Or would that incite Timmy to slit his throat then and there?

Cowardice won out. He said nothing, only sagged a little deeper into the driver's seat and listened to the one-sided conversation.

"Goliad?" Timmy said. "No, why? Huh. Well, ma'am, I can't tell you. He dropped me off at my apartment last night, told me to take a pain pill and rest, that he would contact me on an as-needed basis. Haven't heard from him since." There was a pause, then, "Dr. Lambert? Oh, now him I can help you with. I'm looking at him."

Nate heard Delores's exclamation of surprise, heard her passing the information along, presumably to Richard.

"Where are we?" Timmy said, repeating her question for Nate's benefit. "A half hour or so from Knoxville, noshing some chow, killing a little time, don't want to get there too early."

Delores rattled on for about thirty seconds, but she was talking too fast for Nate to catch what she was saying. When she ran out of breath, Timmy said, "If you'll allow me, I'll explain, Mrs. Hunt. See, after I got home last night, I didn't go straight to bed like Goliad advised.

"No, I started thinking this situation through, and it was like a light bulb came on above my head. You know, like in a cartoon? Or maybe it was a vision from God. Anyway, it occurred to me where that sick little girl—the one I saw on TV with you and the senator? Well, I figured out where she fit into this big picture. She's in competition with you to get whatever it is that Dr. O'Neal made off with. Tell me if I'm wrong."

There was silence at the other end of the call. Or, if Delores had spoken, her response had been too softly spoken for Nate to hear.

Timmy continued in a breezy manner. "I got to thinking that shuttling her out of state just wasn't far enough. You and the senator stopped short. If the lady doctor took a mind to drive up here like we did, and there was no longer any competition for whatever she's got that you want, then..." He paused, but there was nothing but silence at the other end of the call.

"If you're as smart a lady as I think you are, Mrs. Hunt, you're catching my meaning. The only sure way to win this race is to rub out the competition, wouldn't you say?"

Nate's stomach heaved. Gorge filled the back of his throat with a citrus sting.

Although he hadn't heard either Delores or Richard speak a word, Timmy said, "You can thank me later. Oh. On the outside chance I hear from Goliad, I'll tell him you're waiting on him to call you."

With that, he disconnected and laid his phone aside. "Man, my ass is sore from sitting too long." He arched his back, rolled his shoulders, cracked his knuckles. "Pull back around to the drive-through. I'm gonna have one of those breakfast parfaits."

Nate stayed as he was, gaping at him. "Are you insane?"

"They're good. Honest. Crunchy granola. You ought to try one."

Nate's chest was so tight with desperation, he could barely push sufficient air across his vocal cords. "You're going to 'rub out the competition'? You're going to kill that child?"

"No!" Timmy laughed, and then laughed harder. "Hell, no. Is that what you thought? No, I'm not going to." The obscene laughter stopped abruptly. Timmy leveled soulless eyes on Nate. "You are."

# Violet

———◆———

It's morning and it's raining.

I had to get up early on account of it's my special day, and Mom said we needed to get a move on.

I can't have a regular bath because of my IV. I get bed baths. Most times nurses give them, but this morning it was Mom. I'm wearing my favorite gown. It's pink and has a sparkly crown like a princess on the front.

Daddy stayed home from work because it's my special day.

My brothers had to get up early, too, and they're mad because they have to wear church clothes, and my oldest brother said he shouldn't have to because it wasn't *his* special day, and Daddy told them to cut out the whining.

I don't blame my brothers a bit for being mad, and nobody asked me if I wanted a "special day."

The nurse who spent the night left and another one came to take her place. Her name is Jill. She has a thousand braids with a thousand beads in them. She's young. Her sneakers have flashing lights around the bottoms, and she said that if I played my cards right, she might get me some like them. My older brother said she was cool, and I think so, too.

I got a present. It's a new iPad Mini. My brothers tried to hog it.

The doctor came. He's nicer than Dr. Lambert, but not as nice as Dr. O'Neal.

Dr. O'Neal's mom died when she was little. That's what made her want to become a doctor. She doesn't have a husband or kids. I asked her how come, and she said she's been too busy trying to make people well. What that really means is that she hasn't found the right man to marry. I'm sure glad she doesn't want to marry Dr. Lambert. Gross.

One time she told me she needs my help to cure a lot of people with the same cancer as me. I told her I hoped I didn't let her down. She gave me a fist bump, and then an extra long hug.

I'll know when she comes because I can see the whole front yard through the window in my bedroom. But the only people out there now are the TV people. They're sitting in their vans because of the rain.

If Dr. O'Neal is the surprise for my special day, she hasn't got here yet.

# Chapter 31

---

*6:32 a.m.*

Rye woke up, unwound himself from Brynn, and eased out of bed. He went directly to the window and looked out. "Brynn."

She didn't stir.

"Brynn."

"Hmm?"

"The police car's gone."

She sat up and pushed hair off her face. Any other time, he would have paused to admire how adorable she looked, but he was hastily pulling on his clothes. "He's gone," he repeated. "Maybe it was just some poor underpaid cop sleeping through his shift. Get dressed. I'll get coffee."

He pulled on his jacket, then leaned down and gave her a quick kiss.

"Milk, no sugar," she called after him.

None of the vending machines on the seventh floor dispensed coffee, so he took the main elevator down. It emptied him into the jam-packed lobby. Travelers initially held up by the fog had been further delayed by the successive bands of torrential rain.

People were sleeping on any surface they could stake claim to, some sitting with their backs to the wall, heads drooping. A young mother, looking frazzled and at wits' end, was trying to shush her mewling infant.

The dawn was gray, and with almost an hour to go until sunrise, the lobby remained in semi-darkness, making it difficult for Rye to avoid the prone forms on the floor. He made it to the adjacent dining room without stepping on anyone. Kitchen staff were setting up the breakfast buffet. He was relieved to see that the coffee bar was already in service.

He was filling a disposable cup from an urn when a young man shuffled up beside him. Rye's glance caught him in mid-yawn. His clothes were rumpled. He was unshaven and bleary-eyed. Which was why Rye was surprised when he perked up upon seeing him and said, "Mr. Dewitt, good morning."

Rye now recognized him as the harried clerk who had checked him in yesterday. He hadn't thought the young man would remember him. "Morning." Not wanting to engage, Rye concentrated on filling a second cup from the dribbling spigot.

"Did your rifle turn up?"

*Rifle? What was he talking about?* Rye couldn't fathom. But the guy had addressed him by Dash's name, so he hadn't mistaken him for someone else. Rye played along. "Uh, yeah."

"Wasn't stolen, then?"

"No, I'd left it. At my in-laws' house."

"Glad to hear it. We don't like property to go missing off our parking lot."

"No worry. All good."

Rye, mind churning, moved aside to place lids over the two cups of coffee. The young man took his place at the urn. He said, "The policeman must've been relieved to hear that. These days, any lost weapon is cause for alarm."

"Got that right."

"I'm sure that's why he didn't want to wait for morning to talk to you. Gotta commend his diligence. What time was it last night when he went up to your room?"

"I don't remember exactly."

"Around one, one-thirty, wasn't it?"

"In that neighborhood."

The clerk's unwitting revelations were starting to take the shape of a disturbing scenario. Rye carried on conversationally, so it wouldn't sound like fishing. "Surprised me that he came up to the room unannounced."

"Really? He said you were expecting him. He'd just forgotten your room number." Looking worried now, the young man said, "I hope you weren't already in bed."

"No. I was up." Rye gave him a quick grin and raised a coffee cup in each hand. "Getting cold. Have a good one."

"You're only booked for one night. Checking out today?"

"Immediately."

This time, Rye didn't carefully pick his way across the littered lobby. He walked quickly and with purpose, chucking the two cups of coffee into the trash can at the elevator. He and Brynn wouldn't have time to drink them.


*6:44 a.m.*


The slamming door brought Brynn running from the bathroom. She took one look at Rye and asked, "What?"

"You ready?"

"Boots."

He pulled his flight bag from the floor of the closet and tossed it onto the side of the bed. "Someone—a cop—told the desk clerk a story about Mr. Dewitt's missing rifle. I think—"

"Who's Mr. Dewitt?" Responding to the haste with which he was gathering up his belongings from the bedside table and dumping them into the duffel, she crammed her feet into her boots.

"Dash. Somebody smart got his name and used it to track us here. Doesn't sound like Wilson and Rawlins. They would have knocked and announced themselves."

"So the policeman—"

"Was probably working for the other faction, keeping an eye out for us."

Boots on, she yanked her coat from a hanger in the closet. "Where is he now?"

"Don't know. But I'm not waiting around to ask." He shouldered his flight bag, went to the door, and put his hand on the knob. But there he paused, reached for her hand, and pressed Wes's key ring into it. "Listen. I don't know what we might encounter on our way out. But whatever happens, you get away from here. Drive like a bat out of hell. Understand?"

"Do you think—"

"I don't know, but if I'm detained, for any reason, in any way, you run to Wes's car and head for Tennessee."

"I can't leave you."

"You can. You will. You've got to get to Violet. If you don't, everything we've been through won't count for shit. You've got to make it, Brynn."

A protest was forming on her lips. He stopped it with a quick but potent kiss, then repeated, "You've got to make it."

Gazing into his eyes, she nodded with full understanding.

He checked the peephole, then opened the door, and, pulling her along behind him, turned to his left.

He ran smack into Goliad. Rather, into the bore of Goliad's pistol.

*6:47 a.m.*

The man had to have been hiding in the recess between the door of their room and the one next to it. He was alone. Rye asked, "Where's your buddy? The one who kept vigil?"

"I sent him on his way, figuring you wouldn't come out as long as he was there."

"Smart." Then, in as droll a tone as Rye could muster, he said, "You had just as well put the gun away. You're not going to shoot me."

"I'd be doing the world a huge favor."

Rye chuckled. "Couldn't agree with you more. But you don't know which one of us has what you came after."

That gave Goliad pause.

Rye cocked his eyebrow. "See? You shoot one of us and grab the other, you may be grabbing the wrong one. In which case, you've got a body that you have to take time to search, while whichever one of us you didn't shoot is raising a hue and cry. In a hotel overflowing with potential witnesses. Security cameras all over the place."

Rye shook his head. "Outcome of that scenario is capture and life in prison for you. It's the same dilemma you faced in the cabin, except that this is more problematic. You don't have your sidekick, and there are seven stories between you and escape. No, Goliad, you're too smart and careful to do something dumb like that.

"You would be identified within minutes. In no time, your connection to the Hunts would be discovered, and then you'd really be screwed in any number of ways, and I can think of a dozen without even trying very hard. But the first of them is that killing me won't guarantee that you'll obtain the life-extending elixir for the senator, which is what they sent you to do, and I don't think they would forgive a fuckup of that scope."

Rye eyed him steadily. Goliad's obsidian eyes didn't blink. Rye said, "The real reason I know that you won't shoot either of us? If you were going to, you would have by now."

He knew better than to credit himself with talking Goliad out of shooting him. Goliad had realized the difficulties involved even before Rye had rattled them off to him. So, no, he didn't fire the pistol, but neither did he pack it away.

He turned it on Brynn. "Where's the stuff?"

Before she could answer, Rye said, "One more thing. Another deterrent that you should think about."

Goliad looked at him.

All glibness gone, Rye said, "If you hurt her, *I will kill you*, and I don't care how many witnesses there are."

Goliad's eyes narrowed fractionally, but he shifted his gaze back to Brynn. "Your boyfriend here, I had just as soon see dead. But I don't want this to end badly for you, because you seem like a caring lady, and I admire that."

"Thank you."

"Just give me the drug, I leave, you go on about your business."

"The drug *is* my business."

"And this is mine," he said, tightening his grip on the pistol.

She drew a steadying breath. "You know that Senator Hunt has much more time. The progression of his cancer—"

"I don't make these choices."

"But you should," she stressed. "Did you watch the news story about Violet? If so, you saw how temporary she is. This is her only hope."

"Give me the drug."

He spoke with the slow, precise emphasis that Rye associated with him. The Hunts' stranglehold on him was unassailable. It superseded compassion and human decency, perhaps even his own moral convictions. Regardless of how passionate and persuasive Brynn's appeal, this man wasn't going to be swayed.

She looked at Rye as though asking what she should do. He blinked in a way that said, *Better hand it over.*

To Goliad she said, "It's in my coat pocket. Don't shoot me for reaching for it."

He gave a nod, then held up a hand to halt her. "You," he said to Rye, "move back ten feet, put your bag on the floor, turn around and raise your jacket and shirttail."

"You think I'm carrying? What would be the point? I haven't replaced the clip you took."

"Now, Mallett."

Rye looked at the other man with consternation, but did as told, and showed Goliad his waistband all the way around. When they were facing again, Goliad told him to keep his hands up and away from his body, which he did.

Goliad made a motion to Brynn, who unzipped her coat pocket, and took out the bubble-wrapped package. "It's sensitive to light and heat, and any exposure to bacteria would be—"

"I'll be careful." Goliad extended his hand.

Startling them all, a door opened a short distance away, and a housekeeper pushed a rattling cart into the corridor. In a singsong voice, she wished them a cheerful good morning.

Taking Goliad completely off guard, and shocking the hell out of Rye, Brynn went around Goliad and walked briskly toward the woman in the pink uniform. "I'm so glad you arrived when you did. We used all our towels last night. May I please have some extras?"

Without waiting for a response, Brynn lifted several from the stack on the cart and then broke into a sprint. Both Goliad and Rye charged after her, but Goliad had a ten-foot head start.

The housekeeper flattened herself against the wall in fright. As Goliad passed her, he one-handedly hauled her cart into the middle of the hallway. Running full out, Rye barreled into it, knocking it over and scattering everything it carried. He hurdled piles of fresh laundry and rolls of toilet tissue.

Brynn's intention had probably been to take the fire stairs, but just as she drew even with the elevator, the bell above it dinged. She heaved the stack of towels toward Goliad. He batted them down, stumbled over them, kicked them aside as he chased after her.

The elevator doors opened. Brynn stepped in. Goliad, pistol held close to his side and out of sight, got in behind her. Rye put on a burst of speed and slipped in between the two closing doors.

He crowded in behind Goliad to make room for himself, because there were five other people in the elevator: a silver-haired couple looking annoyed for having been herded to the back; two teenage girls wearing earbuds and staring into their phones; a heavyset man in shorts and flip-flops.

Affably, he bellowed to the newcomers, "Morning, folks. Headed down to the buffet? The biscuits and gravy are tops. Grits, too."

The teenagers continued to peck on their phones without looking up. The older couple smiled politely, but neither spoke. Brynn was on Rye's left, huddled in the corner of the elevator, as though trying to go unnoticed. She didn't speak. Rye thought she might have been holding her breath.

Goliad turned around to face out. Rye had kept his back to the door, so he and Goliad were now eye to eye. With everyone else in the cubicle unaware, Rye poked the short barrel of his pocket pistol into Goliad's stomach. The man's eyes registered surprise, and his abs contracted, but he didn't react so that anyone else would notice.

Rye whispered, "I was just fooling about the clip." During the chase down the hallway, he'd managed to retrieve his pistol from the pocket of his bomber jacket. Last night he'd loaded it with the spare clip he carried in his flight bag.

Given the close quarters, there was no way he could verbally communicate with Brynn. He couldn't have advised her anyway, because he had no idea what Goliad planned to do when the elevator doors opened. Raise his gun hand and commence a shootout? That seemed unlikely, but Rye couldn't dismiss the possibility.

Brynn had forced Goliad's hand. He had proposed a peaceful settlement where nobody got hurt. But it had to be clear to him now that she wasn't going to surrender the GX-42 without a fight.

Whatever Goliad did, Rye would have only seconds in which to process it and react correctly, or people could die. But years of pilot training had taught him to do just that.

Goliad's method of problem-solving was more stolid.

Giving Rye the advantage here.

He hoped.

The elevator stopped. The double doors behind him began to open. Brynn once again seized an opportunity. Wraithlike, she slipped around behind Rye and cleared the doors before they had even opened all the way.

"She wants those biscuits while they're hot," the flip-flop man said around a booming laugh.

Rye pretended that Brynn had pushed against him on her way out. He fell forward into Goliad, throwing him off balance. "Sorry, man." The apology was for the benefit of the others in the elevator, but he jabbed Goliad's middle with his pistol for emphasis before whipping around and running after Brynn.

Rather than trying to navigate the crowded lobby, she'd headed down the long corridor that came to a dead end at the side door they'd been using. When she reached it, she looked back to ensure that Rye was behind her before she pushed through the door to the outside. By the time Rye got to the door, he saw her through the glass, splashing across the parking lot in a mad dash toward Wes's car.

His relief was short-lived.

Before he could depress the bar to let himself out, Goliad caught up to him, grabbed him by the collar of his jacket, hurled him against the wall, then landed a punch in Rye's diaphragm that robbed him of breath. It also hurt like bloody hell, but not as bad as a bullet would have. Goliad still didn't want a firefight, especially not after a terrorized housekeeper had witnessed their race down the hallway.

But bare hands could be just as deadly as guns if one knew how to apply them. Goliad outweighed and outmuscled him. Rye couldn't bring him down. Not in a fistfight, not by swapping swings. So he folded his arms across his midsection and, with a grunt of pain, bent double.

Then he came up beneath Goliad's chin with his head. Goliad's teeth clacked, his head snapped back, and when he brought it upright, Rye's hands were folded around his pistol, the short barrel pressed up against the soft underside of Goliad's jaw.

Rye wheezed, "Drop the gun."

Goliad's weapon landed with a dull thud on the carpet near their feet.

Still raspy, Rye said, "Why don't you just back off and let the kid have the drug?"

"Because she's not who I work for."

"Stubborn son of a bitch."

With the hilt of his pistol, Rye rapped Goliad hard, right on the bridge of his nose, then pivoted and pushed through the door. Rain and cold air blasted him in the face, but it felt good. It cleared his head in time for him to leap backward, out of the way of an oncoming, speeding car. Wes's car. Brynn behind the wheel.

The car skidded to a stop inches from him. In his haste to get the passenger door open, he nearly dislocated his shoulder. Brynn accelerated before he'd pulled in his right leg. Through the glass exit door, he saw Goliad down on one knee, holding a hand to his face.

Rye and Brynn didn't speak until they were out of the parking lot, up the ramp onto the freeway, and speeding along in the outside lane. By then, Rye had almost regained his breath. "Tell me you still have it."

"I still have it."

"Intact?"

"Yes."

He laid his head back and closed his eyes. "That's what matters."

"You matter, too. Are you in pain?"

"I'll live."

"Goliad?"

"Not as pretty as he used to be. He'll need a nose job."

"But he's all right?"

"Nothing life-threatening, and he'll recoup, so we're on borrowed time. Not only him to worry about, though. All my talk about security cameras? Wasn't crap. Our altercation won't go unnoticed. Somebody will get the plate number on this car. Make and model, too. It could get back to Wes." He raised his head and looked over at her. "Damn, I hate that, Brynn."

"Believe me, he's been in tighter spots."

"Yeah, but I've never put him in one before." He thought for a minute. "Drive to Walmart."

"Dad's Walmart? Why?"

"When I switched out the license plates, I put his under the carpet in the trunk. I'll put them back on, then we'll leave his car and let him know where it's parked. If somebody comes looking for it, they'll find him at work, and his car on the lot of the store."

"Thanks for thinking of that."

"I don't want him to get into trouble."

"Neither do I, but without the car, how will we get to Tennessee?"

He leaned forward and looked up through the windshield at the torrential rain and bottom-heavy, opaque clouds. "We fly."

# Chapter 32

———◆———

*7:20 a.m.*

They exited the freeway and pulled into a self-operated car wash, which wasn't doing any business today. Brynn pulled into one of the bays. In a matter of minutes, Rye had replaced the original plates on Wes's car.

He was just getting back in when his cell phone rang. "Only one person has the number," he said to Brynn as he fished the phone from the front pocket of his damp jeans. "Hey, Dash."

"I've called you three times."

"I silenced the phone after our last text so I could sleep. You'll be glad to know I got several hours. I'll be fresh for the flight this evening."

"I gave the job to somebody else."

Rye, disbelieving what Dash had just said, shot a look toward Brynn, then mumbled an excuse to her, got out of the car, and walked several yards away. There was no way Dash could know about his change of plan. He was still expecting Rye to fly on the passenger flight from ATL that evening.

"The schedule is tight, but not *that* tight. I told you I would make it, and I will."

"It's not about the schedule, Rye." He paused. Sighed. Swore. "The FAA office in Atlanta called me at the butt crack of dawn. Seems those two deputies from Howardville wiggled their way up the chain of command and finally got to the top dog there. The upshot is that after talking to them, he's thinking the accident report you called in yesterday morning was inaccurate and incomplete."

"I told him I would send a full report and photos when the weather cleared. It hasn't."

"Yes, but you fudged on the amount of damage done to the craft and—"

"It was dark and foggy. I couldn't see my hand in front of my face, much less accurately assess the damage."

"No mention of a laser."

"I didn't want to say anything about it until I could do so without getting everybody in a tizzy."

"He got in a tizzy when he heard that the crash had put a guy in the hospital."

"It didn't! The crash occurred at least a mile from where Brady White was attacked. When I called in the accident report, it hadn't been confirmed—and still hasn't been—that the crash and the assault on him are related."

"Yeah, well, that isn't washing with the FAA. And now the NTSB. Those deputies sowed seeds of doubt about the degree of your involvement in a felony. The feds want to hold a party at the crash site, and they want you to be the guest of honor."

*Fuck!* "When?"

"Tomorrow morning. Nine sharp. You're to meet them at the sheriff's office in Howardville. Since you've been dashing hither and yon, keeping yourself unreachable, it fell to me to inform you."

Nine sharp on a Saturday morning. Over a holiday weekend. A crash with no fatalities and no injuries to anyone on board or near the craft. The feds were taking this seriously. Wilson and Rawlins must've laid it on thick. "Okay."

"You'll be there?"

"I said okay."

"Okay. After they've eyeballed the plane for themselves, heard your explanation, they'll make a determination on what action to take."

"Action? Like fine me?"

"Could be."

"Suspend my license?"

"Rye, listen—"

"*Revoke* my license?"

"I don't think they'll take it that far. Even if they issued a notice of intention, you could demand a hearing, and when all the facts came out, you'd win. But, until that time, I can't use you."

"You're shitting me."

"Pains me, but I have to protect my business. And you know how word spreads like wildfire through the aviation community. You may have trouble getting work from other outfits.

"In fact, my advice is that you waste no time contacting the highest ranking FAA official there in Atlanta. Apologize for not making yourself clear when you called the agent yesterday. You were thinking of him, didn't want to spoil his Thanksgiving. You're willing and eager to cooperate with the investigation. Win the guy over before you even meet with him. And, until this is smoothed over, and you're cleared, don't fly again."

*Don't fly. Don't fly. Don't fly.*

The threat of it alone made Rye's blood run cold. "Dash. This is an unfair and unfounded overreaction. Even during my two tours in Afghanistan, I never had so much as a hard landing. Since I've been flying, never a bobble until this. Not one close call."

"No one questions your flying ability, Rye. But your head's not on straight." His lowered pitch gave the words more heft. "It hasn't been since you got back. Now, I'm sorry for coming down hard on you, but that's the truth, and you know it. That incident in Afghanistan has eaten at you until you're beginning to scare even me, and I don't scare easy."

"You're the one who sent me out on Wednesday night."

"I know, and I've regretted it ever since. That crash. I even wondered—"

"I knew what you wondered. And fuck you. It was caused by a laser beam being shone into my eyes, not the fulfillment of a death wish."

"I already told you I believe you."

Rye was aware of Brynn watching him through the car windows, worry etched on her face. He turned his back so she wouldn't witness him begging. "Don't ground me, Dash."

Dash swore again. "You think I take pleasure in it? You're the best flyer I know. But you need to sort yourself out. You need to sort out this mess with the agencies. Until you do, I've got my own interest to protect."

Rye stared out at the rain, unseeing, dismay and anger warring inside him. Anger won out. "You know what? So do I. You owe me for my last three jobs. Put my check in the mail."

"Don't be like this."

"No, I changed my mind. Send it Fed Ex."

He clicked off. When the phone rang almost immediately and he saw Dash's name, he silenced it, but it vibrated in his hand for a long time. He didn't get back into the car until it stopped.

"What's happened? What did he—"

An abrupt shake of his head cut Brynn off. "Give me a minute." More gently, he added, "Please."

He sat there, tapping the phone against his chin, considering his choices. They boiled down to two. Do as Dash advised, kiss the agencies' asses, and, until things were smoothed over, don't fly? Or, forever grieve another death he possibly could have prevented?

His career was in jeopardy. But so was his soul.

"Screw it," he muttered and motioned for Brynn to start the car. "To Walmart."

While on the way, he pulled a business card from the inside breast pocket of his jacket and began to tap in the number printed on it. Brynn asked, "Are you calling Dash back?"

"No." Rye hadn't intended to keep the card that had been pressed into his palm during a strong handshake, much less use the contact fewer than twenty-four hours later. "I'm calling Jake Morton."

*7:38 a.m.*

Walmart's parking lot was filled to capacity with diehard Black Friday shoppers undaunted by the weather. It took Brynn a while to find a parking space. Then she called Wes and asked how his day was going.

He described the bedlam inside the store. "Three shoplifters. Two fistfights. One overturned display. And five more hours till my shift's over."

She told him where his car would be when he got off work. "Fifth row in on the west side. Second car. Thank you for letting us use it."

"You said it could be a few days before you got it back to me. Mission accomplished?"

"Dad, you're truly better off not knowing."

"In other words, no. Are you safe? Just tell me that much."

She thought about Goliad, handguns, a chase through a hotel, a narrow escape.

"I'm safe."

"Mallett still with you?"

"Yes."

He snorted. "Then you're not safe."

"On the bright side, I could be on the lam with the Hendrix boy."

"By comparison, that hoodlum is looking a lot better." He sighed. "Leave the car key in the ignition. It'd be a lucky break for me if somebody stole the clunker."

"Bye, Dad. Thanks again."

"Brynn? Call me. If you ever get a hankering to."

"If you'll stay out of trouble."

He laughed. "Fair terms."

He had taken a baby step toward reconciliation. To protect herself from heartbreak and disappointment, she wouldn't plunge headlong into reestablishing a relationship with him. She would approach with caution. But it was a start that made her smile as she disconnected the call and placed his key ring beneath the driver's floor mat.

Rye asked, "Has he nabbed any shoplifters today?"

"Three so far. By the way, he thinks I would be better off with the wild Hendrix boy."

"He's right."

"He's concerned for my safety."

"He should be. I about had a heart attack when you took off running down the hallway of that hotel. You should have given me warning."

"What would you have done?"

"I don't know." Holding her gaze, his aspect changed. He reached across and stroked her cheek, then pressed the pad of his thumb against the corner of her lips. "You also should have given me warning about forgetting a condom the second time."

She took a small, swift breath. "Yes, I should have, but I wasn't thinking of—"

"Me, either,"

"—that. For the first time ever."

"Me, too."

Neither moved or said anything, only looked at each other with searching eyes, a taut silence stretching between them.

The spell was broken by two quick toots of a car horn. Jake had pulled in behind them. They had no choice except to brave the rain. Rye held the back seat door of Jake's car for her; he got in front. Shaking rain out of his hair, he thanked Jake for meeting them on such short notice. "How was your flight?"

"Business as usual."

"I didn't know if you'd be back this early or not."

"Barely. Haven't been home yet." He was still in uniform, except that he'd loosened his necktie.

"You up for a quick round-trip flight to Knoxville?"

"Now?"

"Soon as we can get wheels up. We'll pay you, of course."

"It's not the money," Jake said. "Hell, I would do it gladly. But I have to fly again this evening. Rules say I need eight hours in the sack."

"I know all about rules," Rye grumbled. "They're killing me."

"I could provide taxi service if you still need it."

Rye shook his head. "No, if you can't fly us yourself, what I really need is your Bonanza."

# Chapter 33

———⊰⊙⊱———

*7:49 a.m.*

Jake was taken aback, but he didn't respond to Rye. He concentrated on getting them out of the congested parking lot. He sped across a heavily trafficked boulevard and pulled up to a restaurant that didn't open until five o'clock. They had that lot to themselves. Jake put the car in park but left the motor running.

"You need my plane? You got it."

"Not that simple." Rye looked at his wristwatch. "This negotiation needs to be quick, but let me emphasize that you should think hard before agreeing."

Then Rye laid out the basics of the situation. "We need to fly to Knoxville. I'm omitting the details for your own protection. Less you know, the better."

"I picked up on that last night. Save the explanations. You've got the loan of my plane. You only had to ask."

"Not a loan. I pay you."

"Cover the gas, that's all."

"If you don't let me pay for it, no deal. It needs to be a charter."

"You can return me a favor sometime."

"I'll do that anyway, but I'm paying you." He paused. "Shames me to say it, but the FAA and NTSB are on my case."

"What the hell?"

"Nothing official yet, but they're conducting an investigation."

"Into what?"

"What I consider to be a minor crash. Their opinion may differ. I wasn't drunk, wasn't using drugs, wasn't *running* drugs. I'm not breaking the law now, only outrunning it to avoid a tie-up that Brynn doesn't have time for."

Rye looked over his shoulder at her before continuing. "I know your offer to help is earnest, Jake, and I appreciate it. But these aren't small considerations. If lawmen come looking for us, don't stick your neck out. Tell the truth. I was licensed, instrument rated, my money was good, and that's all you asked. Tell them you sensed we were in a jam, you just didn't realize how serious it was."

"How serious is it?"

"Serious. Because here's the other thing. We've crossed swords with people in high places, and they have knee-crackers and throat-slitters at their beck and call. I shit you not." He held up his left hand so Jake could see the cuts across his knuckles.

"I'm lucky the fingers are still attached. So, if someone who doesn't have a badge comes asking after us, lie your ass off. Don't challenge a thing they say. You're as dumb as dirt, as innocent as the day you were born, you never heard of us."

"What happens when you get to Knoxville?"

"As far as you're concerned? Nothing. I fly your plane back. It should take only a few hours to cover the round trip." He took a breath. "Look, Jake, any other time, I wouldn't ask a stranger—"

"I'm a stranger to you; you're no stranger to me."

Rye chuffed a bitter laugh. "About that legend stuff, I'm not the guy you think I am, not the man you heard stories about, most of which were barracks bullshit. The hero doesn't exist. Never did. But I swear I can fly the plane, and I'll return it to you in one piece, not a scratch on it."

"I'm not worried about the plane. It's the two of you. The thought of cutthroats being after you—"

Rye interrupted. "If you're feeling any hesitation, say no. Don't do it."

"I'm not saying no. I only wish you'd let me help more."

"The help we need is the use of your plane."

Jake turned to Brynn. "Life or death, you said."

"Yes. And time is running out."

He looked at Rye. "Another rescue?"

Rye hesitated, then said, "Something like that."

"You always did volunteer for the most dangerous missions. And that's not barracks bullshit. It's a matter of record."

Rye didn't say anything to that.

"You've got my plane," Jake said.

Rye reached across the console. "Thank you."

As they shook hands, the other pilot gave a dry laugh. "Don't thank me. I just flew in from KC. Have you looked at the radar?"

*8:28 a.m.*

Jake rented hangar space at an FBO twenty miles west of Atlanta. It was controlled, but Rye would be the only pilot flying in or out any time soon.

When the three of them came in, dripping rainwater, two corporate jet pilots waiting out the weather were sprawled in armchairs in front of a TV, watching a football game being played someplace where the sun was shining. The woman at the desk was engrossed in a paperback novel.

Brynn and Rye stayed in the background while Jake explained to her their determination to take off, despite the weather. Brynn overheard the words "Family medical emergency" and "may be their last chance to say goodbye."

Rye filed his flight plan. He and Jake put the plane through its preflight check. Because of the rain, Jake arranged for them to board inside the hangar and have the plane towed out.

When all was ready, Brynn hugged Jake goodbye. "You're doing a tremendous service. Some day I'll tell you all about it."

"Good luck with your patient."

Rye thanked him again, but issued a final word of warning. "Remember what I told you. If anyone comes around asking, cover your ass."

Jake slapped him on the shoulder and wished them a safe flight.

On their taxi, rain bombarded the windshield. Poised at the end of the runway, Rye reached over and squeezed Brynn just above her knee. She jumped. He smiled over her startled reaction and spoke above the engine noise. "Scared?"

She shook her head.

"Liar."

He'd noticed her white-knuckling the edge of the copilot's seat. Although the cockpit view of the elements was intimidating, she preferred sitting beside Rye to being in one of the four passenger seats behind the cockpit.

Solemnly, Rye looked directly into her eyes. "Brynn. This is what I do."

His confidence calmed her. "I wouldn't be here with any other pilot."

He held her stare, then verbally acknowledged the clearance he'd received in his headset.

She recalled what he'd told her last night in the bar about the anticipation he felt before each takeoff. *I still can't wait.*

When he gave it the throttle, she experienced the same level of exhilaration.

*9:12 a.m.*

Goliad would rather have taken another drubbing than return to the Hunts' mansion with nothing to show for his efforts except failure.

The housekeeper admitted him into the house. "They've been waiting for you to show up. They're having breakfast. I'll tell them you're here."

Dispassionately, she asked if he would like an ice pack for his nose. It was swollen and red and, unless he underwent corrective surgery, would probably be permanently misshapen. But he declined the ice pack. Swelling nose and eyes were the least of his worries as he made his way to the sitting room of the master suite, where private meetings were customarily conducted.

He didn't have to wait long before Richard strode in, Delores close behind. She was immaculately dressed, perfectly groomed, but, as during any high-stakes situation, the air around her seemed to crackle with her unique brand of energy.

The senator walked straight up to Goliad, his expression demanding. "I gave your disappearing act the benefit of the doubt. I told Delores to relax, that you must be hot on the trail of Dr. O'Neal. But here you are, and no doctor."

"I located her, but she managed to get away."

"What about that?" Richard asked of his nose.

"Mallett. With the help of a corrupt cop, I tracked them to a hotel. It was late. Since nothing happened overnight, I saw no reason to disturb you. This morning, I intercepted them as they were leaving." He described the encounter. "I hoped to talk the doctor out of it without creating any trouble."

"Obviously she didn't go for that idea."

"She saw an opportunity to run, and did." He told them

about getting caught in the elevator. "There was nothing I could do until I closed in on Mallett at the exit. He stunned me. By the time I got outside, all I could see were their taillights. I didn't get a plate number on the car."

"'There was nothing I could do'?" Delores repeated. "I don't accept that, Goliad."

"There was nothing I could do without the risk of implicating you, ma'am. Or you, senator."

"I would have denounced you," Richard said. "That's always been our agreement. If you're caught committing a crime, you're on your own."

"That's still our agreement," Goliad said. "On any other day, I would have shot both of them up there on the seventh floor. If caught, I would have expected you to disavow any knowledge of it. Today, however, I thought you would rather avoid any and all dealings with the police."

"He's right, Richard," Delores said. "Investigators would have linked him to us like that." She snapped her fingers. "We can't have any more policemen showing up at our gate, asking questions, probing. Today of all days, discretion is essential."

"Discretion?" The senator turned to her. "That's a curious word to use in light of what's happening as we speak."

"That's foolproof, darling. The inevitable will happen. It has no connection to us, except in recognition of our timely benevolence to the dying child and her family. It's the best press we could possibly hope for."

Goliad could feel the tissue around his eyes getting puffier by the minute. His nose was throbbing. The discomfort was distracting, but that's not why he was having trouble following their thread. "I'm sorry. What am I missing?"

Delores smiled up at him. "While you were chasing after Dr. O'Neal through a hotel, a better plan was hatched and implemented."

"By who?"

"Of all people," she said with a light laugh, "Timmy."

Goliad looked between them to make certain that they were serious, that he'd heard correctly. Last night, they had treated Timmy like a leper they couldn't wait to get out of their home. Now, they looked smugly pleased with him.

Richard consulted the clock on the mantel. "We should be hearing soon."

"Hearing what?" Goliad asked.

Delores said, "That our problem has been taken care of."

*10:02 a.m.*

The weather around Knoxville was no better than it had been in Atlanta, but Rye made a perfect landing through ponderous rain at a municipal airport located on the fringes of the bedroom community in which the Griffins lived. As at the other airfield, there was little activity. At one end of the lobby, two men were playing cards. Another was asleep in a chair.

An older man was manning the desk. While Rye conferred with him, Brynn called an Uber car to take them to the Griffins' home.

"He'll be here in five to seven minutes," she told Rye when he rejoined her. "You have time for this." She passed him a cup of coffee.

"Thanks. Did you call the Griffins?"

"I've wrestled with it, but decided not to."

"Still afraid that letting them know will jinx it?"

"Silly, I know."

"Not silly. Pilots are superstitious, too." He took a sip of coffee. "Once there, you'll be ready to roll?"

"Mr. and Mrs. Griffin signed the consent forms when we applied for compassionate use, but I'll go over everything with them again." She began explaining the steps she would take but broke off when she noticed that Rye was listening with only half an ear. She was stuck with a sudden realization. "You're not coming with me."

He looked down at her half-empty cup. "Finished with that?"

Dumbly she handed it to him. He carried it along with his over to a trash can. When he came back he said, "No, I'm not going with you. But I'll stick around here until I've heard from you that you're inside the house and that all is good."

"You have plenty of time to make that flight to Columbus this evening."

"No rush to make that." He told her the extent of his last conversation with Dash. She was flabbergasted. "Why didn't you tell me?"

"I needed some time to absorb the shock."

"I could tell when you got back in the car that his call had made you angry."

"At first," he admitted. "But I can't really fault Dash. This could impact his livelihood."

"You meet with the accident investigators tomorrow?"

"Early. They're not screwing around. It's up to them to decide how reckless and irresponsible I was."

"You weren't reckless and irresponsible."

"They may think otherwise."

"This is serious, then."

"Serious. Not life-threatening."

"But it is, Rye. It's threatening to *your* life."

He held her gaze, then shifted it beyond her. "There's your ride."

She put her hand on his arm. "Please come, Rye. I want to talk to you some more about this."

"What good will talking do?"

"All right, we won't talk about it. Just come. You only have to stay long enough for me to introduce you to Violet and her family. They'll want to thank you."

"No thanks necessary."

"I understand completely that you want to get Jake's plane back, but surely one hour won't make a difference."

"That's not what you've been telling everyone else."

"I haven't slept with anyone else!"

Then she was struck with another realization, this one like a slap to the face. She gave a mirthless laugh. "Of course. What's wrong with me that I didn't catch on sooner? It's *because* we've slept together that you are so eager to part ways."

He didn't say anything, only assumed a familiar air of impassivity.

"Or could it be that you're afraid to come face-to-face with a sick little girl? Afraid that you might actually be touched, experience a human emotion, *feel* something?"

"That's not why."

"Then why?"

"This is your show, Brynn. Go be the star of it."

She covered her heart with her hand. "Oh, that's very sweet. You're staying away for my sake." She dismissed that notion with another sardonic laugh. "Why don't you admit it? You're a little glad that you have that meeting tomorrow morning. It gives you a good excuse to cut and run."

"I just don't see the point of dragging this out."

"Nor do I," she snapped. "I have a life to save, and it isn't yours. You're a lost cause. You're hell-bent on flying straight into the heart of guilt and unhappiness. Until the day it kills you. Well, have at it." She motioned toward Jake's plane out on the tarmac. "Don't let me hold you up any longer."

*10:09 a.m.*

She pushed through the door and didn't look back. She got into the car. It drove away.

Someone behind Rye snuffled. "That went well."

He turned. One of the pilots who'd been playing cards was standing behind him, grinning. Apparently he'd overheard at least some of what Brynn had said.

"Fuck off." Rye nudged him aside and ignored the epithets muttered in his wake as he walked toward the pilots' lounge. His cell phone dinged, indicating he'd gotten a text. It was from Dash. *Didn't give your number, but IMPORTANT u call!!!* The message was followed by a phone number.

Rye didn't feel like talking to anybody, but if one of the federal agents was trying to reach him regarding tomorrow's meeting, he figured he should start sucking up now. He dialed the number.

"Rawlins."

"Oh, fabulous," Rye said. "My day is officially made."

"Don't hang up."

"Name me one good reason."

"We impressed on your pal Dash how important it was."

"What did you threaten him with? A shakedown by the FAA and NTSB? Thanks for that, by the way. If they revoke my license, if they even suspend it, I'm going to make your life a misery."

"Do you want to hear this or not?"

"Probably not."

"I think you will. It's about Dr. Lambert."

As though asking after an old friend, Rye said, "How is Nate?"

"That's the point, wiseass. He pulled a disappearing act similar to Dr. O'Neal's. Not at his office. Not at the hospital. Hadn't even checked in. Last place Wilson and I saw him was at the Hunts' estate. Called it. Housekeeper told us they'd been trying to reach Lambert, too."

"Are you getting to the good part? Soon, I hope?"

"Lambert owns a condo in a ritzy high-rise. We checked with

building staff. The doctor had a visitor late last night. Identified himself as Goliad."

"My, my. He gets around."

"Yes, he does. We learned through APD about the fracas at the hotel early this morning."

"Damn security cameras are taking the fun out of everything."

"We retrieved your flight bag."

"Thanks. Bring it to the meeting tomorrow morning."

"Wilson's motioning me to hurry this along."

"I owe him a drink."

"Dr. Lambert's guest last night wasn't Goliad."

Rye sensed from Rawlins's shift to a no-nonsense tone that a clever comeback would be inappropriate, that the deputy had finally gotten to the good part. "Who was it?"

"We've got him on video, but it's jerky. So I'm sending you a text of the description the concierge gave us."

Within seconds, the text came through. He went back to Rawlins. "Timmy."

"Timmy. He escorted the doctor out of his condo. They left together in the doc's car. Watching the security video, you don't get a warm fuzzy."

Rye rubbed his forehead. "I'm no cheerleader for Nate Lambert, but this doesn't sound good."

"That's what Wilson and I thought, too. Now—and here's why we're calling you. Local TV station here aired a news story this morning about the little girl who was shuttled off last evening to—"

"I know about it."

"Figured you did. Look at your text again. This is a freeze frame taken off the telecast. The reporter is doing a stand-up outside the little girl's house up there in Tennessee. Got it?"

The picture appeared on his phone. "Yeah."

"Look behind the reporter."

There stood Nathan Lambert. Unmistakably. Beside him and slightly behind him was Timmy.

Rye's heart stopped, then began thudding. "I gotta go."

"Is Dr. O'Neal there, Mallett?"

Rye hesitated.

"*Mallett?* Is she there?"

"On her way to the house." Where Timmy was.

"Where are you?"

"An airport. Just flew her in. Have y'all got people...? A... the sheriff's department here you can notify?"

"And tell them what?"

"Jesus, I don't know, tell them—"

"About a box, empty except for blood samples? About your run-ins with Goliad, your unexplained abductions of Dr. O'Neal, a senator's somewhat strange but so far legal behavior? What do we tell them? Huh? It all feels criminal, but what's the crime? Time you shared with us, don't you think?"

"I will. But not now. Get people moving toward the Griffins' house."

"Based on what?"

"No time, Rawlins. Just move on it!"

"Beyond Brady White's heart giving out during surgery—"

"Wait! *What?*"

"You didn't know? He arrested on the table. They worked on him for ten, twelve minutes—"

Rye clicked off and slid down the wall onto his haunches. This blow hurt worse than when Goliad had slugged him. Anguish squeezed his chest so tight, he thought his breastbone would crack.

He could see the photo on Brady's desk of him and his family. Brady smiling up at him from his hospital bed. Marlene saying, *He couldn't wait to meet you.*

He pressed the heels of his hands against his eyes to block the images.

No time to think about it now. He had to get to Brynn.

Brynn, whom he'd pushed away.

Straight toward Timmy.

He tapped in the number of her new phone. No answer. No voice mail. "Shit!"

He surged to his feet and bolted from the lounge, running like a madman from room to room, looking for the pilot he'd swapped expletives with. He found him studying a radar monitor.

Breathless, Rye said, "Dude, sorry about what I said earlier. Do you have a car here I can borrow?"

# Chapter 34

*10:39 a.m.*

During the twenty-minute drive from the airfield to the Griffins' neighborhood, Brynn's cell phone rang almost continually. There was never a name identifying the caller, so it could only be Rye. She didn't answer. Why rehash the quarrel, when the outcome would be the same? As he'd said, why drag it out?

But not even her personal heartache could suppress her happy anticipation of delivering the good news to Violet and her parents. She felt a flutter of excitement as she neared their home.

The hours she'd spent researching, studying, struggling with doubt, commiserating with Violet's parents, arguing with Nate were about to culminate in the best way possible: Violet would be reprieved, possibly saved.

The driver stopped at the corner at the end of the Griffins' street. "Mind if I let you out here? There's a lot going on up there. It'll be hard for me to turn around."

"This is fine."

She was carrying nothing except what was in her coat pockets as she started up the incline toward the house. A minivan, presumably belonging to the family, occupied the driveway. TV vans were parked end to end along the curbs on both sides of the street.

Also parked in front of the house were two limousines.

And, last in line, Nate Lambert's Jaguar.

Upon seeing it, Brynn stopped. There was no mistaking that it was his car. She parked hers next to it every day in the garage of their office building.

There could be only one reason he was here, and that was to get the drug away from her before she administered it to Violet. Why hadn't she foreseen this? He would have predicted that, once she learned Violet had been sent home, she would follow. He had beat her here.

But she had a strong advantage over him. Dr. Brynn O'Neal was Violet's overseeing physician. Both the child and her parents had utmost faith in her. When they learned that she was here, and why she had come, they would be overjoyed.

Nate couldn't very well tell them that he was denying the drug to Violet so he could give it to his patient. He wouldn't arm-wrestle Brynn for ownership of it. He was hamstrung. There was nothing he could say or do without exposing his perfidy.

*As long as you're in possession of the game ball, you're winning.*

Bolstered by Rye's words, she continued walking toward the house at the end of the cul-de-sac. Blocking the sidewalk, hunkered beneath umbrellas, was a congregation of neighbors, whose curiosity hadn't been dampened by the weather.

She was still some distance from them when, out of their midst, Nate appeared. As he made his way toward her, he didn't look like his cocksure and overconfident self, however. Without an umbrella, hood, hat, or raincoat, he looked bedraggled and panicked.

"Nate?" She said his name aloud, but she was actually talking to herself, puzzled by his uncharacteristic demeanor.

"He's a little wound up."

The statement came from so close behind her, she felt the

speaker's breath in her hair. She turned quickly to find herself face-to-face with Timmy. He was wearing a rain jacket, the hood up.

He said, "Unless you want to get cut, don't do anything stupid."

She looked down. The tip of a slender silver blade was pressed against her coat at waist level. "I won't do anything stupid."

"More's the pity." His evil grin made her shiver.

Nate reached them, near hyperventilating, wringing his hands, almost in tears. "Brynn. Give me the drug."

"It should go to Violet, Nate, and you know it. Your name is on that exemption application for her as well as mine. You know she's—"

"For godsake, it's too late to argue about it," he said, his voice cracking. "Give it to me or—"

"Or he offs the kid."

She looked at Timmy with misapprehension. "What?"

"Since Lambert here seems to have lost the power of speech, I'll explain," Timmy said. "The situation is this. If you don't give the potion to Dr. Lambert, he's going to push air into the kid's IV. If she's dead, she no longer needs the drug, right? Right. Freeing it up for you-know-who."

Flabbergasted, she turned to Nate. "He's not serious."

"Deadly serious. Give me the drug."

Brynn's mind was reeling. "Have you seen the family? Violet?"

His head wobbled a yes. "She's all right. Rather tired. Listless. But happy to be at home. I . . . I . . . " He cast a nervous glance toward Timmy. "I asked to examine her more thoroughly after . . . after . . . "

"Elsa," Timmy said. "She's in there now putting on a show. Off and on, you can hear her singing. She and the mayor got here at the same time. Separate limos."

Nate was breathing as though he'd climbed Everest without oxygen. "When the special guests arrived, everyone else was invited to wait outside. Me included."

"You're waiting for the program to conclude so you can go back in and do what this psychopath said? You're going to murder that child?"

Her voice had risen. Timmy, grin in place, said through clenched teeth, "Pipe down, doc."

She looked behind her. No one was paying them any mind. The attention of all the media people and other onlookers was focused on the front of the house in order to see the celebrities when they came out. Alerting any one of them to trouble without Timmy's knowledge would be impossible.

She came back around to Nate and looked at him with unmitigated disgust and condemnation.

His lips trembled. "He came to my apartment!" he said, spraying spittle. "Issued veiled threats. Forced me to drive him up here."

"On the Hunts' orders?"

"I thought it up myself," Timmy replied.

"He talked to Delores around dawn," Nate said.

"And she sanctioned this?"

"Yes. No, no. She didn't say anything, just hung up."

Nate knew as well as Brynn what that indicated. So did Timmy. When she looked at him, he said, "Bosses are pleased as punch."

"You haven't got the drug yet."

"About that, my patience is wearing real thin."

Nate moaned her name in a pleading tone. "Please do as he says. Richard will get the drug as he was supposed to all along. This will be over."

"For Violet, certainly."

"Either way, it's over for her."

"You would actually kill her?"

"That's just it! If I don't—"

Timmy smacked his lips. "Violet and me are friends. Like this." He crossed his index and middle finger.

Brynn was horrified. She turned to Nate. "You let him get near her?"

"I didn't have a choice! He threatened to cut off my ear."

"He introduced me as his personal assistant," Timmy said. "I did a magic trick for Violet. She laughed at my knock-knock jokes. Nobody will suspect a thing if I return to her bedroom. She's wearing a pink nightgown. Has a crown on it."

Brynn thought she might be ill, but she took a defiant stance. "You kill a child in her own bed. How do you propose getting away with it?"

He snickered. "I won't have to worry about that, because you're not gonna let that kid die. We all three know that. You wouldn't risk calling my bluff, would you now?"

No, she wouldn't. She recalled Rye telling her dad that Timmy was a twisted kid with a lot to prove.

Nate pulled her from her disturbing thoughts. "Did the family know you were coming, Brynn?"

She shook her head.

"Had you told them we acquired the drug?"

"No. I didn't want to build up their hopes and not deliver."

"Then neither Violet nor her parents will ever know what she missed out on. And, possibly, compassionate use will be approved for her before the new regulations are enforced."

"New regulations?"

Realizing his slip, he said, "We can discuss it later."

"Nate, damn you. What?"

In rapid and broken phrases, he explained about the upcoming Senate committee hearing on experimental drugs and clinical trials.

"And Senator Hunt's position on the clamp-down?"

Nate's abashment said it all.

"So this is the only dose available now, and more than likely the only one for the foreseeable future."

"Now that's a damn shame." Timmy nicked her coat with the tip of his knife. "Give it up."

"Brynn, for heaven's sake," Nate groaned. "You've lost. Lose gracefully."

"Or lose your life," Timmy said.

She scoffed. "You wouldn't kill me in front of all these people."

He moved with the speed of a striking snake, creating a slice in the fabric of her coat from one side seam to the other, deep enough to expose the fiber insulation. "See? I would. The next cut will open up your pretty, smooth belly. I could have you stuffed into Lambert's Jag and bleeding out before anybody noticed."

He had made a believer of her. Her heart was in her throat. She'd lost her capacity to breathe. Sensing her surrender, Nate began patting down her pockets while she stood frozen in fear.

He located the bubble-wrapped vial and took it out.

Timmy astounded them both when he snatched it from Nate and tossed it up like a baseball, catching it in midair. "Be careful with that, you idiot! Give it to me," Nate demanded, holding out his hand.

"I'll keep it."

"I would rather safeguard it myself," Nate said.

"Do you have a knife?"

"Knife? No."

"Then shut up."

Nate backed down and watched with uneasiness as Timmy tucked the vial into an inside pocket of his rain jacket.

"All right, we've got it, let's go." Nate glanced at his watch. "It's elevenish now. That puts us back at three, three-thirty. Time enough."

"You and I will ride in the back seat." Timmy grabbed Brynn by the arm and began pulling her toward Nate's car.

*"Brynn!"*

As one, she, Nate, and Timmy looked toward the source of the shout. Rye still had one leg inside the back seat of a car stopped at the corner. He clambered out, slammed the door shut, and began running toward them.

"Christ," Nate moaned. "All we need. He's a jinx."

Renewed hope surged through Brynn.

With feline swiftness, Timmy executed an agile move that brought him to Brynn's side, the blade of his knife pressed into her left armpit.

"Stop right there, Mallett." He spoke softly, but in a voice that, in itself, sounded lethal.

Rye halted with such suddenness, inertia pushed him forward. He nearly lost his balance.

Timmy said, "I'll slice off her tit, then stab her in the heart. It'll burst like a balloon."

Rye said, "You wouldn't live to brag about it."

"Let's try it and see."

Brynn's breath gusted out. "I'm all right, Rye."

"So far," Timmy said. "But she won't be if you don't back off."

"Your face looks like hell, Timmy," Rye said. "What color are your balls this morning?"

"I owe you for that."

"I agree. You want to use your knife, come after me. Let Brynn go."

Brynn could see herself and Timmy reflected in the lenses of Rye's sunglasses. She reasoned he was wearing them so Timmy couldn't tell exactly where he was looking. Brynn intervened. "There's no need for another fight."

"Why's he holding a knife on you?"

"He's got the drug, and wants to make sure that it gets to the senator."

"That's right," Nate said, his self-importance reasserting itself. "As was the original plan. This nonsense was totally unnecessary, Brynn. None of this would have happened if you had left well enough alone." To Timmy, he said, "Let's go. It's a long drive back."

Calmly, Rye said, "Why don't you all fly back with me?"

"I don't think so, ace," Timmy said. "I already saw you crash."

Brynn's knees had gone weak with relief at his suggestion. Ignoring Timmy's remark, she said, "That's a wonderful idea. Don't you think so, Nate?"

His gaze ricocheted among them, landing on Timmy. "It is a good idea. It would save hours. But we don't need him to fly us. The Hunts' jet is available."

"But not the pilots," Brynn said.

"What?" Nate asked.

"Abby, at the outpatient hotel? She told Rye and me last night that they were off duty until they fly Violet back on Tuesday."

Rye said, "That's right. She did."

"Then I guess it's you, or a four-hour drive," Nate said.

Timmy still looked reluctant and distrustful. "You got a plane big enough?"

Rye made a show of sizing him up and finding him lacking. "Big enough for you."

Nate pressed his argument. "Time-wise, it would give me a wide comfort zone I wouldn't have if we drive back. After all this, you don't want to disappoint the Hunts by being late."

Timmy capitulated, but said to Rye, "No funny stuff, or your girlfriend dies."

*11:22 a.m.*

The pilot whose car Rye had asked to borrow had repeated his words back to him: "Fuck off."

Rye had to call for a car. It had arrived in under four minutes, which had seemed like hours. The drive to the address Brynn had given him earlier had also seemed unending, and then, when he arrived, he wondered just where the hell the police were. He'd expected the area around the Griffins' house to look like an armed camp with Timmy in custody for kidnaping Lambert.

But apparently Wilson and Rawlins had dropped the ball. They hadn't notified their local cohorts.

Instead of a huge police presence, Rye had been met by a terrifying tableau that had almost caused his own heart to burst. He and God hadn't been on speaking terms for a long time, and Brady White's death had all but severed the fragile connection. Nevertheless, Rye found himself praying that Brynn would somehow get through this unharmed.

It was a lot to pray for, considering that Timmy was the threat. He overcompensated for his meager physicality with meanness and spontaneity. He had remembered Rye's Glock and had made him produce it and drop it into the street drain, discreetly, so not to draw the notice of the crowd of gawkers in the Griffins' yard.

There had been an instant, when the pistol was in his hand, that Rye had considered aiming it at the center of Timmy's forehead and pulling the trigger, but he wasn't sure he could do that before Timmy poked Brynn. With reluctance, he'd dropped the handgun through the grate.

Now they were all in Lambert's car, en route to the airport, where Jake's plane awaited. Lambert was driving, Rye was in the front passenger seat, Timmy and his knives were in the back seat with Brynn.

"How long is the flight?" Lambert asked.

"Around an hour. Depending."

"On what?"

"Weather. Air traffic around Hartsfield. Atlanta control may keep us in a holding pattern for—"

Nate interrupted. "We can use the Hunts' airstrip."

"Private airstrip?"

"It's in a pasture behind their house," Timmy offered. "Goliad showed me."

"How long is it?"

"How should I know? Long."

"Well, depending on the type of aircraft, the length of the runway is rather important to making a safe landing."

Timmy laughed. "You know all about how wrong that can go, don't you?"

Rye wondered if it was just his imagination, or if Timmy's laugh had sounded forced, uneasy.

Nate said, "The runway accommodates their private jet."

"Then we'll be okay," Rye said.

"But if you don't even know where the runway is, how will you know where to fly?" Timmy asked.

"GPS. All I need to program it is the airstrip's identifier."

"I'll call Richard and Delores from the airport," Nate said. "They'll give you whatever you need. They'll probably roll out a red carpet for us when we get there."

He smiled across at Rye as though all was right with the world again. Rye could barely restrain himself from decking him.

He looked out the passenger window into the side mirror and angled his head so he could see Brynn through the back seat window. She was staring out at the waterlogged landscape, looking deep in thought. He and she hadn't had an opportunity to exchange a single word privately.

He wanted to tell her he was sorry for letting her go to the Griffins' alone. No, for *forcing* her to go alone. If he'd been with her, she wouldn't be in danger for her life, and Violet might even now be getting the infusion.

He had a lot to make retribution for. That seemed to be the pattern of his life these days.

When they reached the airfield, Jake's plane was the only one on the tarmac. "That's the plane?" Timmy said.

"That's it."

"It looks old."

"It is. Has a new engine, though."

"What happened to the old one?"

"Flamed out, I guess."

Timmy must have realized that Rye was baiting him. He instructed Nate to let him and Brynn out at the entrance. "Don't want the lady to have to walk through the rain." As he claimed Brynn's arm and propelled her forward, he looked over his shoulder and taunted Rye with a wink.

Brynn kept her head forward.

Nate parked in the visitors' parking lot. Looking around, he said, "I hate to leave my car here. I hope it will be all right."

"I don't think you need to worry about it."

"It could get stolen."

"I don't think you need to worry about it," Rye repeated. "Once you give the senator that drug, you're dispensable. Haven't you figured that out yet?"

Rye could tell by Nate's whey-faced expression that the prospect hadn't occurred to him, but Rye figured it would preoccupy him from now on. He got out and ran through the rain toward the building. Nate came along behind.

Everyone who'd been there earlier had cleared out except for the older man working the desk. Recognizing Rye, he waved him over. "You're not thinking of taking off in this, are you?" He pointed to his television screen where a Doppler radar map showed a wide band of red.

Rye swore.

"They've been doing weather bulletins, one after another," the man told him. "Better wait it out."

Rye didn't see a way to communicate to him the trouble they were in without endangering all of them, the older man included. If he raised an alarm, called 911, some or all could be dead or injured long before the police arrived.

Brynn would be the first casualty. Timmy kept her at his side. His knife was no longer visible, but Rye didn't trust that. Timmy could access it in a flash.

Not only was she Timmy's hostage, so was the vial of GX-42. In any kind of altercation, it could be damaged or destroyed.

Rye walked over to the group. "We're going to have to wait out a line of storms."

Naturally, Nate argued. "But the whole point of flying was to beat the clock."

Rye motioned for him to look out the wall of windows. Just since they'd entered the building, conditions had worsened. Jake's plane was being slashed by rain and buffeted by high winds.

"If you want to drive through this," Rye said, "you'd better get going. Tack on an extra hour to the trip."

Nate gnawed his lower lip with indecision. "How long do you think this weather will last?"

"Let's look."

Rye led them into a room where a counter held an array of computers, all tuned to weather-reporting stations. He sat down in front of one. "We're here, and we're going there," he said, pointing out the two spots on the map. "This line of storms stretches between those two points, almost solid. Red means bad. Purple's worse. There's hail in this," he said, touching another spot on the screen.

"I've flown in worse," he said, speaking over his shoulder at Nate, who was hovering. "I'd willingly take off with you and him," he said, inclining his head toward Timmy. "But Brynn would stay. I don't care if you die. I don't care if I do. But I wouldn't risk her life, especially to benefit yours." Lambert puffed up, but Rye ignored that and said, "So what's it to be, Lambert? Your call."

"It's my call," Timmy said. "We wait it out."

He pushed Brynn down into one of the folding chairs lined

up against the wall, sat in the one beside it, and linked their arms together.

*12:13 p.m.*

Brynn resented the cheerfulness with which Nate phoned the Hunts.

In a chipper voice, he said into his phone, "I have good news and bad news." In carefully guarded language he informed them that the rather drastic measure Timmy had proposed proved to be unnecessary.

"Dr. O'Neal surrendered what we came after. She is returning with us. Mr. Mallett is flying all of us back, landing on your airstrip. The bad news? We're waiting out a rainstorm before taking off." He listened, then said, "Yes, it was a coin toss, but we all agreed that flying there would take less time."

Nate listened, occasionally murmuring *splendid* or a synonym of it. "Perfect. Mr. Mallett needs the... what was it?"

"Identifier," Rye said.

It was given to Nate, who relayed it to Rye. "They're also asking when we'll be there."

"The flight will take an hour at most, once we take off, and if the weather cooperates. It may not be a straight shot. May have to go around some storms, which will add time."

Nate promised to text the Hunts just before they took off. He disconnected and announced, "Goliad will be there to pick us up."

"Oh, I look forward to that," Rye said.

With the same degree of sarcasm, Nate said, "And Richard and Delores look forward to meeting you. They've heard so much about you."

No sooner had he said that than his cell phone rang. "They must have forgotten something." He checked the LED. "Oh, it's Mrs. Griffin."

Brynn's startled reaction was to try to stand and go to him, but Timmy yanked her back down. "Let me talk to her, please," Brynn said.

"I'll handle it." Nate answered with his name, then listened. "Yes, yes, she was there. She wanted to see Violet, of course, but didn't want to interrupt Elsa's performance."

Brynn listened with a sinking heart as he explained that no sooner had Brynn arrived than she'd received word that one of their patients had an emergency. "We were summoned to return to Atlanta immediately. Dr. O'Neal regretted being unable to see Violet before we left."

He listened, then said, "She mentioned that her phone has been malfunctioning. I'll tell her that you tried to call. I'm sure she'll be in touch with you as soon as she's able. Now, I really must go, Mrs. Griffin."

He hung up abruptly. When it became apparent that he wasn't going to volunteer anything, Brynn asked, "How did they know I was there?"

He cleared his throat. "Violet saw you through her bedroom window."

Brynn wilted. "Was she upset that I didn't go inside?"

Not quite meeting Brynn's eyes, he added, "I'm sure she'll be fine. The nurse on duty seemed quite capable."

"She's got the mutt to keep her company."

Given the way Rye looked at Timmy after that remark, Brynn thought Timmy either very brave or a reckless fool.

After that, the wait began. Time, which had passed so quickly, now crawled. If not for Timmy, Brynn wouldn't have minded the slowdown. She no longer had the GX-42, but she knew where it was. She remained only miles away from Violet. There were eight hours to go until the infusion had to be started. And Rye was with her. Those factors kept her hope alive.

But Timmy kept her plastered to his side, out of Rye's reach, and within earshot of himself and Nate. She'd been unable to communicate privately with Rye, although, often, the way in which he looked at her was more potent than mere words. His gaze evoked memories of shared frustration, anger, and passion. Depending on the memory, her emotions dipped to the lowest ebb or soared.

She had spent less than two days with him, and yet he had generated more anguish and joy than she'd experienced with any other person in her life.

Except possibly Violet.

How could that be?

She loved Violet.

Timmy kept them confined to the small room. At one point the desk attendant had come to the door, suggesting that they would be more comfortable in the lobby. Rye had thanked him but told him that they all had an interest in the movement of the storms.

Timmy watched him walk away. "That old man should keep his curiosity to himself."

"He's just being hospitable," Rye said.

"Meddlesome," Timmy grumbled.

Rye and Brynn exchanged a look. They were afraid for the man.

Nate was too absorbed in his own dilemma to be aware of the undercurrents. He paced, keeping one eye on the clock, the other on the radar screen. He pestered Rye with questions. "Once the storms move through, we can take off right away?"

"After I file my flight plan and put the plane through pre-flight."

"Why can't you file the flight plan now? Get that out of the way."

"Because if you don't take off within two hours of your ETD, your IFR flight plan expires. I'd have to file another."

"You're saying it could be another two hours!"

Rye used the toe of his boot to indicate the radar screen. He was leaned back in a desk chair, hands stacked on top of his head, feet propped on the counter. Brynn wasn't deceived by his seemingly relaxed posture. He was coiled to spring if necessary.

"I'm not in charge of the weather. Anytime you want to go, we'll go. But the condition still holds. Brynn stays here."

"No, no, Delores was very glad to know that she'll be along."

*So she can gloat*, Brynn thought.

Timmy, who was watching the radar screens, said, "We'll wait till there's no more red."

That didn't occur until almost two o'clock.

# Violet

---

D r. O'Neal left without coming inside!

When I saw her walking toward the house from the end of the block, I was so excited. I *knew* she was going to be the special surprise Daddy told me about.

But I couldn't say anything when she got here because Elsa was singing, and it would have been rude to interrupt the song. Everybody made a big deal of Elsa when she got here. "Look, Violet, it's Elsa!"

Don't they know that I know Elsa isn't real, and that this is just a lady dressed up to look like her? But she was nice and asked me questions about other stuff besides cancer. I just wish she hadn't been singing when Dr. O'Neal got here.

There were a lot of TV people in the way, but I saw Dr. O'Neal on the sidewalk talking to Timmy.

He's Dr. Lambert's friend, but I don't think Dr. Lambert likes him much, and I don't, either. His jokes are stupid, and he didn't fool me with his magic trick. My little brother could have done it better. I didn't like Timmy being in my room. He stood too close to the bed and fiddled with my IV line. Nobody is supposed to touch it except nurses like Jill.

Dr. Lambert checked my chart and asked Jill some questions. Mom asked why he was here instead of Dr. O'Neal, and he said she wasn't working the holiday weekend, but that was a fib, because she got here just after he told us that.

I don't think she was glad to see Dr. Lambert and Timmy. While they were talking, she kept shaking her head. Dr. Lambert took something out of her coat pocket. Timmy grabbed it and didn't give it back.

Then this other man came running up to them. He's the same age as Dr. O'Neal, but the jacket he had on looked really old. The sun's not out, but he had on sunglasses, too. Mostly, though, he didn't look at anything except Dr. O'Neal.

He got mad when Timmy pushed Dr. O'Neal into the back seat of a car and got in behind her. I think the tall man wanted to sit by her, but he had to get in front with Dr. Lambert.

After Elsa left, I told Mom that Dr. O'Neal had been outside. She asked me if I was sure. I told her over and over, *Yes I'm sure*, and asked if she thought cancer had made me blind? She told me to watch my mouth, but she called Dr. O'Neal anyhow to tell her to come back. Dr. O'Neal didn't answer her phone, so Mom called Dr. Lambert, and he said Dr. O'Neal had to leave on an emergency.

I started crying.

I think they gave me a special day because I'm going to die. I wish I had seen Dr. O'Neal instead of Elsa.

# Chapter 35

———=◦◉◦=———

*1:57 p.m.*

**N**o more red," Nate announced. "Not in the direction we're going."

Rye had been aware of that for more than half an hour. Heavy rains still threatened, and there was a low ceiling, but the hazardous elements had moved past. He'd kept the information to himself in order to delay their flight for as long as possible.

Because once they took off, any hope for Violet would be lost. Brynn knew that, and Rye felt her pain. After that call from Violet's mother, her despondency was palpable.

He had tried to figure out a way to distract Timmy, overpower him, something. But he'd been unable to devise a plan of attack that wouldn't result in injury or worse for Brynn. Now, time had run out.

He lifted his feet off the counter and took a closer look at the nearest computer monitor. "Yeah, I think we're good to go." He reached for his cell phone.

Timmy sprang to his side and halted him after he'd made only a few taps on the screen. "Who are you calling?"

"Flight Service in Atlanta."

"What for?"

"To file my flight plan." He held up the form he'd already filled out.

Timmy snatched the sheet from him and scanned it. "What's all this mean?"

Rye pointed out the various blocks. "Type of plane. Aircraft ID. These letters stand for this airport, place of departure. Destination. You heard Lambert give me that. Estimated time of departure, 1930 Zulu. Two-thirty, to you. Estimated time of flight, one hour. Airspeed, altitude, amount of fuel. Number aboard, four souls."

"Souls?"

"Industry speak. You know, in case you crash and die."

He'd determined that Timmy had a fear of flying. He planned to milk it. Petty revenge, maybe, but he would derive some enjoyment out of making him squirm.

Timmy looked over the form again, then handed it back to Rye and chinned toward his cell phone. "Okay, call. But I want to hear who answers."

Rye shrugged, tapped in the toll-free number, and held out his phone to where Timmy could hear. A male voice answered, "Leidos Flight Service."

Rye raised his eyebrows inquisitively. Timmy nodded another okay, but carefully monitored everything Rye said as he repeated exactly what he'd printed on the flight plan. When he got to the end he said, "Total souls aboard, four. Three normal. One lost soul named Timmy."

Timmy gave him the finger.

The man on the phone wished Rye a nice flight. "Nice?" Rye said. "I'll say. Private strip. Being met by a personal aide, maybe even a red carpet. This is tall cotton for a freight dog like me."

The guy chuckled. "I recognize the identifier. Tall cotton for anybody. Have fun."

Rye looked at Timmy. "I can hardly wait."

*2:27 p.m.*

Rye put the plane through its preflight check, then motioned the others out of the building. They filed across the tarmac. As Rye handed Brynn in, he whispered, "Brady didn't make it out of surgery."

The news was another blow to her, and she reacted to it as such. He would have postponed telling her, except that it was crucial she understand that Brady's dying had been a turning point for him. He murmured, "I'm all in."

"What's going on?" Timmy said from behind them.

"Her seat belt's stuck." Rye fiddled with it as he whispered, "I won't bail on you again. Not until this is over. One way or another." He pressed her hand. He wanted to kiss her. Badly. Instead, holding her gaze, he gave the seat belt a tug. "That should do it."

He pointed Lambert into one of the other passenger seats. After he climbed aboard, Rye closed the double doors. "I have to go first," he told Timmy as he stepped onto the wing.

"No way in hell."

Rye stepped back down. "Pilot's seat is on the left. So either I go in first, or I have to crawl over you, or you take the pilot's seat and fly the plane."

Grudgingly, Timmy stepped aside. As soon as Timmy boarded, Rye reached across him.

"Hey!" Timmy whipped out a knife.

"I have to make sure the door is shut properly," Rye said. "Unless you're okay with being the first one to fall out if you didn't do it right."

Timmy leaned back so Rye could reach the door, but he kept the knife unsheathed, tapping the flat of the blade against his thigh. After making sure the door was secure, Rye strapped himself in.

Timmy said, "Don't try anything tricky."

"Or what? You'll knife me? Killing the pilot wouldn't be a very smart move, would it?"

"No, which is why I would knife your girlfriend instead. Not kill her. Just make her bleed a lot."

Rye didn't respond to that. But as the plane lifted off the runway, he said, "Oh, hell."

Timmy looked at him with alarm. "What?"

"I forgot to take my meds."

*4:04 p.m.*

As Rye had predicted, he had to dodge several storm cells, which had added time to their flight. Their descent had been bumpy, but he executed a smooth landing and was now taxiing toward the far end of the runway, where, through the window of the plane, Brynn could see a vehicle waiting. It looked like something used by the Secret Service.

Nate lamented the sad state of his designer suit, which was only semi-dry after having been rained on. "I hate to arrive in this soggy condition."

Brynn couldn't stomach Nate's vanity in light of her defeat, which was a solid and unrelenting pressure against her heart. Throughout the entire ordeal, she had clung to the premise that until the drug was coursing through Richard Hunt's bloodstream, there was still a chance for Violet to get it. Her optimism now seemed incredibly naïve. How could she possibly have succeeded against such a juggernaut?

Even worse than being vanquished was knowing that Violet felt abandoned by her.

When they reached the end of the runway, Rye turned the plane around, so that the right side, on which they would deplane, was facing the long, black SUV. Goliad was standing beside it. As soon as Rye killed the engine and the propeller began to wind down, Goliad approached the plane. He opened the doors to the passenger cabin from the outside, looked in, and motioned Nate out. He alighted with a bounce in his step.

Brynn ignored the hand Goliad extended to assist her down, and climbed out on her own. Timmy walked down the wing from the copilot's seat.

Rye came last. When he reached the ground, he squared off with Goliad.

After assessing the damage he'd done to Goliad's face early that morning, he said, "I hope that hurts as bad as it looks."

Goliad withstood Rye's goading with characteristic stoicism. "I would enjoy repaying you, but Senator and Mrs. Hunt are waiting."

"Then let's get going." Rye took only one step toward the SUV before Goliad flattened his hand firmly against his chest. "You're not coming."

Brynn's pulse spiked. She looked at Rye with alarm and could tell that he didn't like that arrangement any more than she did. "Lambert said the Hunts were looking forward to meeting me."

"Lambert was wrong."

"I beg your pardon," Nate said. "Delores told me herself—"

One baleful look from Goliad shut him up. Going back to Rye, Goliad said, "This runway is private property. The Hunts reported your landing to the sheriff's department, who reported it to the local FAA office. Turns out, the agency is already familiar with you. You're meeting with an investigator tomorrow about that crash up in Howardville. Add this trespassing matter, and you have a lot to answer for. Starting now."

He tipped his head. They all looked in that direction. A police car was speeding up the intersecting road toward them, lights flashing.

Rye whipped off his sunglasses and took a step toward Goliad. "You gotta be kidding."

"Kidding? No. The FAA didn't think it was funny, either. You can't charm, trick, or talk your way out of this one, Mallett. You're over."

The squad car, with the sheriff's department seal on the side, came to a halt beside the SUV. Two uniformed deputies got out. As they approached the group, one said, "Rye Mallett?"

"Me."

"We've been looking for you since last night. Had people chasing all over the city, running down cell phones in trash cans and such. And here you are, landed in our backyard."

The second deputy said. "More accurately, the *senator's* backyard. He's filed a formal complaint of trespassing."

"And I filed a flight plan," Rye fired back.

"We know. We called the flight service ourselves soon as we saw you touch down. The guy you talked to remembers you bragging about the red carpet treatment you'd get upon arrival."

"My point exactly. The Hunts knew I was coming."

"But without invitation," the deputy said. "They've got their own jet and two pilots on staff." He gave Rye a scornful once-over. "Why would they resort to using your services?"

"This is absurd!" Brynn exclaimed. She spun around to Nate. "You know this is a farce. You made the arrangements. Do something, say something."

His eyes were cool, calculating. "At your urging, I agreed to fly with him, Brynn. But I don't know anything about aviation rules and regulations. If he's in violation of them, that's hardly my fault."

She stared at him, aghast. "In good conscience, you can't let his happen, Nate."

But apparently he could. Goliad motioned him toward the SUV. "The Hunts are waiting for you, Dr. Lambert." Without an instant of hesitation, Nate strutted to the vehicle and climbed up into it.

Goliad took Brynn's elbow. She jerked it free. "I'm not going."

"The Hunts requested to see you," Goliad said. "Specifically."

"I don't give a damn what the Hunts requested. *Specifically.* I'm not leaving until this matter is settled. Rye flew to this airstrip with the Hunts' full knowledge, permission, and gratitude."

The two deputies looked at each other, then came back to her. One said, "That's not what we were told, miss."

"Then they lied. Mr. Mallett didn't do anything wrong."

Goliad moved closer to her. "Maybe your father would vouch for him."

The veiled threat, softly spoken, hit Brynn like a freight train. Her lips parted, but only a thread of breath escaped. No words.

Goliad added, "A deputy could be dispatched to pick him up. His parole officer would be notified, of course." Through the slits of his swollen lids, his eyes were implacable.

She looked at Rye and made a gesture of helplessness.

"It's okay. Go. I can take care of this."

"But—"

"Don't stick your neck out for me. I'll be gone tomorrow anyway, remember?" To punctuate that, he put his sunglasses back on, blocking her from seeing into his eyes. Despite his softly spoken words as he buckled her seat belt, this was another shutdown, another goodbye.

Goliad took her arm again, and this time she didn't have it within herself to resist. She got into the SUV. As Timmy scooted in beside her in the back seat, he said, "Ohhh. You gonna miss him?" He made smooching noises close to her ear.

She ignored his mockery. To respond, even with as little as a dirty look, would require energy she no longer had. Her fighting spirit had been drained dry.

*4:17 p.m.*

Rye would have fought tooth and nail to keep Brynn out of that SUV, if not for Goliad's threat regarding Wes. Whether Brynn admitted it or not, she loved the scoundrel. She had looked stricken at the thought of him and his parole being placed in jeopardy.

Rye knew if he acted unmoved and detached, she would believe it. He could tell by her hurt expression that he'd been convincing. He would apologize later. First he had to get through to these deputies that he'd been set up and that Brynn's situation was precarious.

As the SUV pulled away, he turned to them. "Have you talked to a Deputy Wilson or Rawlins? From Howardville? They're up to speed on what's really happening here. Dr. O'Neal may be in danger."

"In danger from *you*. We know. That's why the Howardville SO put out a BOLO on you two last night after you abducted her from a garage."

"Abducted? No. Listen. A lot has happened since then. Brynn's life was threatened today. That little guy, looks like a fox? He's been holding her at knifepoint all afternoon. Lambert is in just as much danger, only he can't see past his own ego. No love lost between him and me, but I'm afraid for him, too. I just didn't let on now because—"

He broke off, realizing that, for all the reaction he was getting from them, he had just as well have been speaking a lost language. Neither appeared alarmed by what he was telling them. Neither had even blinked. That's when it hit him: They were on Hunt's under-the-table payroll.

If he implicated the senator in any wrongdoing, he would be taken straight to lockup. He would be denied even his one phone call. The lock on his cell would corrode before he was released. That's why Goliad had said *You're over* with such succinct confidence.

Rye scanned the horizon. No cavalry was coming over the hill. The pine tree–lined road intersecting the runway was empty. He was on his own.

One of the deputies went through the motions of being an honest cop and consulted his notes. "You're not the registered owner of this plane, Mr. Mallett."

"A buddy loaned it to me."

"Did he? Because we called the owner. Jake Morton? He said, yeah, he let you charter it, but with reservations. Didn't know much about you."

"I told him not to..." Rye stopped himself.

"What?" The deputy moved in closer. "Told him not to what?"

Rye said nothing else. Jake hadn't trusted these guys, either. He'd only done what Rye had advised, but that advice might very well hang him now.

"Did Mr. Morton know you planned to fly his plane, unauthorized, to a private landing strip belonging to a U.S. senator?"

"No. It was a rushed, last-minute change of plan. But it wasn't 'unauthorized.' I believe the arrangements were made through Mrs. Hunt. Maybe she forgot to inform the senator."

"Close as they are, I doubt that," one of the deputies said. "Besides, it's not like Mrs. Hunt to forget anything, much less something that threatens their personal security."

Rye didn't comment, afraid that whatever he said from this point would soon reach the ears of the Hunts, placing Brynn in even greater peril.

One of the deputies asked him if he was armed.

"No."

"A Glock is registered to you. And you have a CHL."

"Y'all have gathered all this intel on me in only a couple of hours? You've sure been industrious."

"We feared for the senator's safety."

"You think I look scary? What about the two guys in the black suits?"

"The little guy is new, but we're well acquainted with Goliad."

"I'm sure you are."

"Nice guy. Solid."

"Hmm." Solid as the kickbacks he doled out.

He was patted down despite his denial of being armed. One of the deputies said, "We'll continue this conversation at the department annex."

"I promised to return Jake's plane tonight."

"Sorry, that's a promise you'll have to break."

"From here, the flight to the FBO where he hangars it will only take about twenty minutes. You can pick me up there."

One snuffled a laugh. "We let you get back in that cockpit, what's to keep you from taking off for Timbuktu?"

"Fuel capacity."

The quip didn't go over well. One of the deputies unsnapped his holster and curved his hand around the grip of his pistol. "Are you going to give us a hassle, Mr. Mallett?"

He raised his hands. "No hassle, but how about this? One of you flies over there with me."

"And become your hostage?" Both scoffed. "I don't think so."

"No. Swear to God—"

"Hands behind your back."

"Seriously? You're really arresting me?"

One pulled out flex-cuffs. "You have the right—"

"Don't do this. Please. I've got to be in Howardville tomorrow morning at nine sharp. I can't miss that meeting, or I could lose my pilot's license."

"You should have thought of—"

"Wait a goddamn minute!" Rye shouted when one secured both his wrists behind his back. "I can't leave my buddy's plane unsecured."

They ignored all his protests and finished reading him his rights as he was roughly escorted to their car and pushed into the back seat. "You're making a terrible mistake." The car door was slammed in his face.

They drove away from the landing strip. When they rounded the same bend in the road that Goliad's SUV had taken a few minutes earlier, Rye got his first look at the Hunts' mansion.

Sitting atop a hill, it looked as impregnable as a castle. The dense cloud cover had created a premature dusk, which had activated the strategically placed landscape lighting around the house, bathing it in an incandescent glow.

*Freaking Camelot*, Rye thought. Complete with treachery within.

Brynn was up there. Inside. Doing what? Making her profound apology to the Hunts for her subterfuge? No. No way. Not Brynn. She wouldn't grovel, but she would honor her professional oath and assist Lambert if he asked her to. She had told Rye she wouldn't let the precious, single dose of GX-42 go to waste, even if Violet wasn't the one to benefit from it.

But what really concerned Rye was what would happen to Brynn afterward. He had warned both her and Lambert that once the drug was inside Richard Hunt's system, he would be more determined than ever to safeguard the secret of his illness and how he'd schemed to get the drug. The only way to guarantee that the secret would never get out would be to permanently silence anyone who was privy to it.

Rye's blood ran cold. He had to get to Brynn.

Once again, he tried appealing to the deputies. "Listen, guys, there's a whole lot more at stake here than you realize. Lives are on the line. Dr. O'Neal and Nate Lambert are—"

He was cut off and hurled against the far door when the

deputy who was driving gave the steering wheel a sharp turn to the right in order to avoid a head-on collision with a vehicle in the opposing lane that crossed the center stripe.

The deputy overcorrected to keep from plowing into the ditch, but managed to straighten out as he stood on the brakes. The squad car went into a rubber-burning, fishtailing skid before coming to a jarring stop on the narrow shoulder.

The other vehicle backed up and came alongside the squad car. The darkly tinted driver's window came down. Rawlins's bellicose face appeared in the opening.

# Chapter 36

—➤◆◄—

*4:51 p.m.*

Goliad ushered Nate and Brynn into the mansion through the front door. Timmy came in behind them.

"I know the way." Nate struck off in an impatient and self-important stride toward the sitting room in the master suite.

With no enthusiasm whatsoever, Brynn followed.

She had been here twice before, the first being when Nate and she had explained to the couple the application process for compassionate use of an experimental drug, and then again when Nate had laid out his plan to bootleg a single dose.

"For a price," Brynn remembered him saying. At the time, she had thought only in monetary terms. Now, she was thinking of the real price: Violet's life.

She entered the sitting room through a set of double doors. Tall, handsome, and imposing, Richard Hunt stood in the center of the room beneath a chandelier, waiting for Nate and her to approach him.

The senator shook hands with Nate and told him he was glad to see him. "Likewise," Nate gushed. "It's been a day, to say the least."

The senator's American-eagle gaze moved to Brynn. He took in her dishevelment with obvious disdain. "Dr. O'Neal."

With an equal shortage of warmth, she said, "Senator."

Standing beside her husband, Delores looked as radiant as a blushing bride. Her cashmere sweater and wool slacks were the color of cream and so well tailored, they looked as though they had been poured over her shapely figure. Her blond mane was shiny, her makeup impeccably applied, jewelry expensive but understated.

The frostiness in her gaze belied her smile. "Dr. O'Neal. I understand that you journeyed all the way to Tennessee today to see Violet."

"Yes."

"Such an adorable and precocious little girl. Was she enjoying the special day the senator and I arranged for her?"

The woman's saccharine tone made Brynn want to grind her teeth. "I don't know." She looked at Timmy where he stood sentinel with Goliad in front of the double doors, now closed. "I was waylaid before I could see her."

"What a pity. A wasted trip, then."

Delores executed a graceful turn to welcome Nate with a quick hug and air kisses on both cheeks. Then she reached for her husband's hand and clasped it between hers. "*Finally*. Let's do this, for godsake."

An IV pole had been positioned at the side of an oversize easy chair. Aimed toward it was a video camera already mounted on a tripod. Ancillary lights had been placed around the room, but, after looking through the camera, Nate decided he liked the warmer, cozier, non-clinical nuance created by lamplight alone. He dimmed the chandelier.

The camera set-up belonged to the Hunts, but Nate was both star and director of the video that would document what he referred to as "this monumental moment in medical history."

Brynn was happy to be excluded. Even if he had invited her

to share his limelight or to comment on camera, she would have declined.

The entire scene disgusted her. She felt like a stage prop in a surreal play, and wouldn't have believed it was actually happening if she couldn't feel Goliad's unwavering dark stare on her. It was as though he'd been commissioned to see to it that she didn't try to abort the infusion. If she made an attempt, he would stop her.

Days in advance, Nate had brought in all the apparatus he would need. A portable table had been set up for his use. He draped it and the senator's chair with sterile sheets. He pulled on a pair of latex gloves, snapping them against his wrists. He inserted the IV shunt into the vein in the bend of the senator's elbow.

Delores laughed and said, "We have everything except the drug. Who has it?"

Timmy sauntered forward and took it from his inside pocket.

Upon seeing the small familiar bundle, Brynn's heart clenched.

Delores reached for it first and held it against her cheek, then handed it to her husband, who said, "There were times when I doubted this moment would ever come."

Brynn watched as Richard passed it along to Nate. He tore away the bubble wrap and set the vial on the table next to a syringe.

Then, for the benefit of the camera, he explained what would take place next. "It's remarkably easy. I will inject the syringe of GX-42 into this bag of a compatible IV fluid. It will take approximately an hour to drain the bag. After infusion, GX-42 goes to work."

He expounded on the remarkable results achieved on laboratory animals. In greater and more scientific detail than she had used with Rye, he explained how the drug worked, and projected that it would be a breakthrough in the treatment of hematologic cancers.

A rumble of thunder drew Brynn's attention to the shuttered window. The sky had turned dark, although it was only a little after five o'clock, not quite sundown. She wondered if Rye was already airborne.

Nate was putting his heart and soul into his speech, touting himself as a pioneer, willing to gamble on the drug's efficacy when it hadn't yet been officially FDA-approved for clinical trials. "Yet, at tremendous risk to my professional reputation, I did what I believed was right for my patient."

Brynn was curious as to who would ever see this video except Nate himself. How much satisfaction could he derive from viewing it in private and celebrating his accomplishment alone?

The Hunts had been such sticklers for keeping the senator's cancer under wraps that Brynn was surprised they had consented to Nate's recording at all. Weren't they the least bit worried that his ego would compel him to share it with colleagues whom he perceived as competition?

She looked over to where the senator sat in his chair, primed to receive the infusion. His wife sat on an ottoman near him. Each appeared to be listening, but like people who were trapped at a banquet with a boring after-dinner speaker at the podium.

Nate was so caught up in his own elocution, he didn't realize that their interest was marginal at best. They were indifferent to what he was saying into the camera.

Suddenly, Brynn recalled Rye's cautionary words about what would happen after Richard Hunt received the drug.

*Are you sure they'll call the dogs off?*

She now realized why the Hunts looked complacent and smug, and were comfortable with Nate making the recording. So many factors would prevent him from ever exploiting it. First, he wouldn't have access to it. The camera belonged to them. But even if Nate did somehow obtain it, he would be hesitant to share it. With his overblown speech, he had hanged himself. Lastly, if he ever was foolish enough to threaten to expose them,

Richard and Delores wouldn't be beyond taking measures—extreme measures—to ensure that he didn't.

The skin on the back of Brynn's neck prickled. She looked again at the picture-perfect couple. Their attentiveness to Nate was feigned. He wasn't their focus.

She was.

Nate picked up the syringe. "Are we ready?"

"Not quite." Delores gracefully stood. "This is such a personal moment for Richard and me. I wondered if we might clear the room."

"Excellent idea," Nate said. He turned to Goliad and Timmy. "Gentlemen. Allow us some privacy, please."

Delores looked at Brynn and smiled. "She goes with them."

*5:18 p.m.*

Deputy Wilson helped Rye from the back seat of the squad car and warned him to keep his mouth shut.

Rawlins took the other two deputies aside and began by apologizing for nearly running them off the road. "I was afraid he would get away again." He thumbed toward Rye over his shoulder.

He told them that the trespassing allegation would be added to the list of those they had on him, but that they needed Rye in Howardville in the morning and asked that he be remanded into their custody. "We, the FAA, and NTSB have got first dibs on him."

The deputies weren't swayed. The negotiation went back and forth for several minutes while Rye tried his best to look contrite. Eventually Rawlins won out. Still handcuffed, Rye was packed into the back seat of the SUV. Rawlins started the motor but let it idle as they watched the other car disappear behind a rise.

Rye was the first to speak. "What took you so fucking long?"

"We were halfway to Howardville," Rawlins said. "Took time to turn around. It was pissing rain, and you've got your nerve to complain."

"I was beginning to think you hadn't understood my cryptic message."

"How'd you pull it off?" Wilson asked from the passenger seat.

"Three-way on my cell phone. I went to recent calls, called you back with one tap. As expected, Timmy got suspicious, stopped me there. When he gave me the go-ahead to call the flight service, and I got them on the line, I merged the calls. He didn't notice. I was afraid you'd start blabbing into the phone, and I'd be blown."

"No, the message came through."

"I packed as much info as I could into that conversation about the flight plan, hoping you'd catch on."

"We understood."

"I thought you might have ignored me again. Why warn me about Timmy and Lambert being at the Griffins' house if you weren't going to send help?"

"We tried," Wilson said. "Full explanation to local PD took a long time. It finally reached the brass, but they were squeamish. They knew that when their officers showed up there, they would be on TV. Didn't want to get a bad rap for busting up the dying girl's party with the mayor, organized by a senator.

"By the time they mustered enough guts and manpower and sent a unit out to the house, there was no sign of any of you. Didn't know what airport you were at, or what plane you'd flown. Couldn't track your cell phone or Brynn O'Neal's. I'm sure you have yourself to thank for that. Tried Dr. Lambert's, but with the weather—"

"Okay, okay, that's history," Rye said. "Thanks for showing up here. Those two who arrested me are dirty. They work for Hunt.

Come on, Rawlins. Get going." He nodded toward the steering wheel.

"Get going where?"

"To the Hunts' place. We've got to get Brynn out of there."

The two exchanged a look before Rawlins turned back to him. "Look, Mallett, Wilson and me played your phone game, drove all the way back here and saved you from a couple of cops on the take, only so you could send us to fetch your girlfriend? Does she even want to be fetched? Or is she glad to be rid of you?"

Rye leaned forward. "She's no doubt glad to be rid of me, but she's in trouble. Timmy? Why do you think I dropped his name? He was holding a knife on her while I was playing that *phone game*! We gotta move it. Now!"

Neither leaped into action. Wilson said, "We know Richard Hunt and his wife to be liars. We caught them in one about your altercation with Timmy. But Hunt is still a U.S. senator. Last time we showed up at his house, we left with our tails between our legs. We won't go busting in again until we know why."

"There's no time to explain," Rye said. "It'll take too long."

"Then you'd better get started," Rawlins said, folding his thick arms across his chest. "From the top, and don't leave anything out. Otherwise, we're not going anywhere except back to Howardville, and we're taking you with us."

Rye looked at the clock on the dash. Twenty-five minutes past five. He'd been separated from Brynn for more than an hour. An eternity. Timmy needed only a tenth of a second to kill her.

Rye started talking and made each word count.

He told it straight, even admitting to ways in which he'd tried to confound them. He told them about the GX-42. He told them about meeting Jake in the bar and how he had come to his and Brynn's rescue, twice.

"Leave him alone," Rye said. "He didn't know I was going to 'trespass' in his plane. He saw a pilot in trouble, he helped out. He would've done the same for any other aviator."

"I doubt that," Rawlins remarked. "You said he was star-struck."

"I said no such thing."

"Implied it. You said he'd heard of you in Afghanistan."

"Airmen with time on their hands talk," Rye said in a mumble, turning his head aside to look out the passenger window. It was raining again. The sky had turned stormy. He could no longer see the house on top of the hill.

Rawlins said, "Myra dug a little deeper on you and uncovered the details of what happened over there, learned about the crash of the plane you were supposed to be flying."

"Myra's a jewel."

"Is that what's the matter with you?"

Rye turned back to look at Rawlins. "Who said anything is the matter with me?"

Rawlins gave him a look. Wilson coughed behind his fist.

Rye cussed under his breath. "Okay, I carry around some shit; doesn't everybody?"

"Way we heard it, you weren't responsible."

"Felt like it. I know I'm responsible for Brady. Weren't for me, he wouldn't have been there that night."

"He doesn't hold it against you. In fact, he wants to see you again tomorrow when you're in town."

Rye's heart bumped. He looked at Rawlins. Was the deputy baiting him? He turned to Wilson.

"Brady's doing good," he said. "Stable condition."

Rye turned back to Rawlins. "You asshole! You told me he died during surgery."

"I told you he arrested. They worked on him, got him back. You hung up on me before I finished."

Rye's ears were ringing. "But he's okay?"

"What part don't you understand?" Rawlins said.

"Look, you son of a bitch, I've been dying a little myself over thinking that Brady was dead."

"Well, he's not." Rawlins made an impatient motion. "Go on with your story."

"Haven't you heard enough?"

"What about Wes O'Neal?"

Rye sighed. "We got to his house while you were still there. He loaned us his car." He paused, looked between them, and then admitted to switching out the license plates. "That's hardly worse than a parking violation. Don't go after him. He's trying to make a go of it." Again, he split an anxious look between them. "Can we roll now?"

"You've told us everything?"

"Yes, dammit."

Everything except that he and Brynn had made love.

*Made love?*

He would review the terminology later, and in private. Right now, he had to impress upon them the potential danger she was in. "Y'all don't like me. I get it. I royally fucked up your Thanksgiving.

"But Brynn is a dedicated doctor who's been giving it her all, putting her reputation on the line, putting up with *me*, trying to save the life of a kid with blood cancer. Now if that sounds like criminal activity to you, God help you. But it sure as hell doesn't sound like it to me."

"According to you, Hunt's getting the drug."

"Right now."

"So, that's what they were after. Everybody will be happy. What do you think is going to happen to Dr. O'Neal? She'll be disappointed, maybe, but why do you think she's unsafe?"

"Because she tried to keep Hunt from getting it. He and the missus aren't going to take that betrayal lying down. Plus, they can't afford for anybody to find out about this. Any of it. Goliad is faithful to a fault. He'll do whatever they tell him, including making sure that nobody lives to tell of it."

Wilson looked skeptical. "I can't see them actually ordering a person's murder."

"Bet you'll change your mind if Brynn and Lambert turn up dead."

Wilson said nothing to that.

"Even if that isn't the plan," Rye continued, "there's Timmy, and Timmy is frigging psychotic. He may do something without being told to. For the hell of it. There's something off about him, but I can't nail it."

"He's a street kid with an attitude," Rawlins said, "but, so far, all we've got on him is his fight with you. And honestly, if you'd hit me in the face with a fire extinguisher, and I'd had a knife…"

"Okay, Rawlins, point made, but—" Rye gnawed his lower lip. "That first night, in your office, I asked you why I would want to beat up Brady after he'd talked me down through the fog. Remember? You had no answer to that."

"Okay."

"Okay. So here's a question that I don't have an answer for. If Timmy was up there to guarantee that Brynn returned with the drug that I was flying in, why in hell did he use that laser on me and risk a crash? What was his motivation?"

"Doesn't need motivation," Rawlins said. "He's psycho. You said so yourself."

"I guess." Rye put his back to the door and began rubbing his wrists together, chafing against the unbreakable flex-cuffs. "But then today, when I offered to fly them back to Atlanta, shave off hours to get the drug to Hunt in time, Timmy didn't jump on the idea. He's scared of flying. That was real, but it's like he didn't…"

He stopped, squeezed his eyes shut, and concentrated. "Like he didn't care whether we got it back in time or not." Suddenly he had it. "He wanted to crash me. Destroy the plane, destroy the drug. Right?" When neither said anything, he repeated it. *"Right?"*

"Why would he want to destroy it?"

"I don't know. But I'm going to find out." By now, he was in a desperate struggle to get out of the flex-cuffs. "Get these god-damn things off me. I'm going up there."

"I told you, we can't go barging back in there without—"

"Fine. You stay. I'm going."

Hands still bound, he groped for the door latch and lifted it. The door swung open. He tumbled out backward and landed hard on the pavement.

# Chapter 37

———◀◉▶———

Goliad pointed Brynn toward an upholstered bench against the wall outside the sitting room from which she'd been expelled. "Why don't you sit there while we wait?"

"I'd rather stand."

"Sit down. Please."

She sat.

Timmy took up a slouched position against the opposite wall. He produced a knife from wherever it had been secreted, exposed the blade, and began nonchalantly flipping it into the air, letting it turn end on end several times before catching it by the hilt.

Brynn tried to ignore him, but his pastime was unnerving.

Goliad must've thought so, too. He said, "Cut it out."

Timmy stopped and pushed away from the wall. "I'm hungry. Is that old lady who works in the kitchen still here?"

"She was given the rest of the day off."

Timmy made a face. "Well, I'm gonna scrounge."

"Not now. They may need us."

"I'm hungry, man. I've been to Tennessee and back."

Goliad considered it, then said, "Don't be long."

Timmy ambled off in the direction of the kitchen.

Through the wall behind her, Brynn could hear muffled conversation in the sitting room but couldn't understand what was being said.

"Is that drug going to cure him?"

Goliad's question surprised her. Up till now, he hadn't expressed any interest in the outcome of all this.

"The prospect is very good," she replied. "No one will know for certain how effective it is until it's tried."

Goliad nodded thoughtfully. "The little girl, is she going to suffer? At the end, I mean."

"Not if I can help it. But there's nothing I can do about her family's suffering."

He stared at Brynn, then glanced toward the kitchen. "I'm going to check on him. Don't go anywhere. I don't want to have to hurt you."

He left. Brynn checked the time. Only a few minutes had elapsed since she'd been banished from the sitting room, but it seemed much longer than the hands on her watch indicated. She wondered how far along Nate was in the process.

Had the syringe of GX-42 already been injected into the IV solution?

*5:34 p.m.*

When Goliad entered the commercial-size kitchen, Timmy was sitting on the countertop, bumping his heels against the cabinet door below, eating a banana. Goliad motioned him down. "Back to work."

Timmy hopped off the counter and did a hook shot with the banana peel into the sink. He wiped his mouth with the back of his hand. "You hang around 'cause you want to fuck her, don't you?"

Goliad, who had already turned away, came back around. "What?"

"The boss lady." Timmy made an obscene gesture with his tongue.

Goliad's swollen face turned dark with anger.

Timmy chuckled and tapped the corner of his eye. "I see these things. I know."

"You don't know anything." Goliad turned again to leave.

"There you're wrong. I know you're never going to get in Delores's panties. And I also know where a kidney is. Right about here."

He jabbed a stiletto into the right side of Goliad's back all the way to the hilt. Goliad arched up and back. He staggered as he turned to face Timmy, who bugged out his eyes and whispered, "Boo!"

Goliad dropped to his knees in front of him, then fell face-down onto the polished tile floor. Timmy said, *"Adios, amigo."*

Bending over Goliad, Timmy placed a hand in each of his armpits and dragged him across the floor, grunting. "Like a sack of cement."

The walk-in pantry was enormous by most standards, but it barely accommodated Goliad's large form. In order to get out after pulling Goliad in, Timmy had to carefully step around him.

He left his knife sticking up out of Goliad's back. It was acting as a plug. He didn't want to have to mop up a gulf of blood when he came back later to dispose of the body.

*5:35 p.m.*

Nate gaped at Delores. "What do you mean, you want to do it?"

"Exactly what I said. I want to inject the drug into the IV bag."

Richard said. "Brilliant, darling. I love that idea."

She leaned down and kissed him lightly on the lips. "We've come all this way together. I want to take an active part."

"As you should. Nate?"

"I don't think it's a brilliant idea at all."

"What matters is that Richard and I do." Not even deigning to look at Nate, she stroked her husband's cheek.

Nate sputtered, "But you're not medically qualified."

"It's not brain surgery. How hard can it be?"

"It's not hard, but you don't know how."

Delores turned to him. "Do you?" she challenged. "Don't you have nurses to take care of the menial tasks while you're busy being stupendous you?"

"I—"

"Have you ever, over the course of your career, done this before, Nate?"

He wet his lips. "Not since I was an intern." He glanced nervously toward the camera.

"Don't worry about how this is going to look in your silly video," Delores said. "We got what we needed from you, didn't we, Richard?"

"*Needed* from me?" Nate asked, his voice going thin.

Richard said, "I think Delores is referring to your florid admission of breaching professional ethics."

Nate's jaw loosened. He opened and closed his mouth several times, without sound.

"Not that you need to worry about it getting out," Richard continued calmly. "You were never going to leave this room with that video."

"No. No, of course not. I didn't intend to. I was making it for you only. And posterity."

Delores snickered as she walked over to the camera and turned it off. "It's superfluous now. And so are you, Nate." She popped a pair of latex gloves from the box on the table and pulled them on. "Tell me what to do. More to the point, what *not* to do to screw up, and then leave me to do it."

*5:37 p.m.*

Timmy returned from the kitchen alone.

Brynn's spine stiffened. "Where's Goliad?"

"Still in the kitchen."

"Why?"

"He's having a snack." He came to stand directly in front of her.

She stood up. "I may get something to eat, too."

He did a sidestep to block her path. "How come I get the feeling that you don't like me?"

She assumed her haughtiest expression. "I can't bear you, for a multitude of reasons. In fact, you make my skin crawl."

He gave a soft whistle. "Listen to your smart-mouthin'."

"Get out of my way."

He shook his index finger inches from her face. "You were shagging that pilot, weren't you?"

Before she could form another putdown, he was thrust forward with such force, Brynn had to leap out of the way to keep him from falling into her. As it was, he landed flat on his face, the thick rug saving his forehead from splitting open.

Rye, who'd sneaked up behind him and kicked him in his lower back, planted his boot on the back of Timmy's neck, pinning him down. Leaning over him, he whispered, "If you utter a sound or move, I'll break it. Swear to God, your skinny neck will snap like a wishbone." Coming upright, he said, "Brynn, pat him down. Hurry." Only then did she realize that Rye's hands were bound behind him.

Without thinking twice about it, she dropped to her knees. Timmy looked at her out the corner of his eye, clearly terrified. He believed Rye's threat. *She* believed it.

Timmy lay perfectly still as she searched his pockets. She found a knife in one.

"Check his ankles."

A scabbard was strapped to his right one, a small knife in it.

"Cut these things off me," Rye said.

Ordinarily, strong clippers were needed. Timmy's knives were kept razor sharp. The first one Brynn applied cut through the tough plastic.

Rye said, "The reason he tried to crash my plane? The drug was never supposed to make it here."

For a split second, Brynn's eyes remained locked with Rye's, but needing no further explanation for the moment, she ran to the double doors and burst through them.

Delores was about to uncap the vial.

"No!" Brynn lurched forward and rammed her shoulder into Delores. Knocked off balance, Delores careened against the IV pole, knocking it over and, in the process, dropping the vial.

Brynn caught it before it hit the floor.

"Give me that!" No longer beautiful and composed, Delores came at Brynn like an enraged she-cat. Brynn backpedaled away from her, quickly putting the vial behind her back and out of the other woman's reach.

"Once the vial was opened, what were you going to do with it?" Brynn asked.

"No use lying." Rye's voice stopped whatever Delores was about to answer.

She spun around to find Timmy being held, his hands behind him and shoved up between his shoulder blades in Rye's unyielding grip. Rye held one of Timmy's own knives at his throat.

His punky arrogance had vanished. The young man's eyes were wide, wild, mortally afraid. He squealed, "Tell him, you bitch."

"Brynn, what are you doing?" Nate asked. "What is going on?"

Richard Hunt had stood, looking from Rye and Timmy, to his wife, to Brynn, who still clutched the vial in her fist behind her back.

Delores was the first to compose herself. She addressed Rye. "No doubt you're Mr. Mallett. Such a pleasure to finally make your acquaintance."

"I doubt it. Why did you have him try to crash me?"

"What a ridiculous notion."

Rye shoved Timmy's hands up higher between his shoulders. Brynn heard his shoulder sockets pop. Timmy hollered in pain. "You lying bitch." Timmy rolled his eyes back toward Rye. "She paid me ten grand. She wanted the airplane to crash and burn. But it didn't, and that started all this. Yesterday, she told me to get the drug here, no matter what, so—"

"Of course I told him that," she said, still speaking smoothly and reasonably. But Brynn detected a tension in her phony smile. "I was making every effort to save my husband's life."

"Yeah?" Rye nicked Timmy's throat, drawing blood.

That spurred Timmy to begin to babble. "She said to get it here so she could destroy the drug herself. That's all there is of it, right? She didn't want Hunt to get it. She said Goliad was too loyal to her husband to double-cross him. If Goliad had known what she was going to do, he would have stopped her or told her husband. So she hired me."

Delores's fists were clenched at her sides. "Shut up!"

Brynn, breathless with disbelief, looked at Nate. He had nothing to offer. He had backed into the wall and had one hand held over his mouth, whimpering. Richard Hunt's gaze was trained on his wife.

In his deep, melodious voice, he said, "Delores?"

"They're all lying, Richard."

"Are they?" The senator was seething. "Goliad!" he shouted. "Where the hell is he?"

"Brynn." Rye spoke her name sharply. "Out. Now!"

"Not with the drug." Richard took a step toward her.

"Hold it, senator!" Rye said. "You touch her, and you're gonna have a lot to explain to the media. Police are on their way here. And don't rely on Lambert to lie for you. To save his ass, he'll sing like a canary."

Brynn hastily rounded the portable table, giving no regard to Nate, who whined her name as she passed him.

When she reached the open doors, Rye thrust Timmy forward and sent him sprawling at Delores's feet. Then he banged the double doors shut, grabbed Brynn's hand, and ran with her across the wide entry foyer into the formal dining room where a pair of French doors stood open.

"This is how I got in," he said as he pulled her along behind him. "We gotta hurry. Wilson and Rawlins are on my tail."

"Where are they?"

"Their SUV got stuck in a ditch when Rawlins was turning around to chase me down."

"There's more to that story."

"Much."

He approached the vehicle she recognized as the one that Goliad had used to transport them from the private landing strip. "Goliad," she said. "Where is he?"

"Can't be far," Rye said.

"Are the keys in the truck?"

"With luck."

The fob was in the cup holder. They scrambled in. Rye left the lights off as he sped down the lane to the main road. When he reached it, he turned right toward the landing strip.

*5:44 p.m.*

Timmy came unsteadily to his feet and, standing before Richard, pointed a finger at Delores. "She paid me. She didn't want it to get to you. She said that a plane crash would look like an accident. Then when that pilot—"

"Enough!" Richard barked. "I get the picture."

Nate was dismayed to find himself in this situation. When, where, had it all gone wrong? This was supposed to be his moment of triumph. Confounded by Delores's deceit, he said, "You wanted it destroyed? All along? Why?"

Beneath her husband's incendiary glare, she drew herself up, not with shame over having been found out, but with defiance. She shook back her hair. "For sixteen years, I've made all the important decisions. If it wasn't for me, prodding you, pushing you, politicking for you, you would still be peddling tin houses. I was the locomotive, Richard. You were a cattle car I dragged along.

"Well, it was my turn. Publicly I would have mourned your death. 'How horrible. He was so strong, so vital. Who could have predicted a rare blood cancer would bring him down? Mrs. Hunt is prostrate with grief.'

"That's what they would have said." She laughed. "But then, after the lavish funeral I would throw you, they'd be saying how brave I was to assume your place, your seat in the Senate. This is what Richard Hunt would want and expect from his widow, to take up the torch and carry on." She smiled beatifically. "And it wouldn't be too long before they forgot all about you."

Following her dumbfounding monologue, Nate braced himself for Richard's reaction, one with an impact equal to an earthquake, a lightning strike, another big bang. Therefore, it astounded him when a smile spread slowly across the senator's face.

When he spoke, his voice didn't rumble with righteous wrath. Rather, it was soft and laced with sympathy. "How naïve of you, Delores. Did you honestly think that I didn't know what you had planned? If Dr. O'Neal hadn't come in when she did and taken that vial from you, I would have. I knew what you were about." He cast a glance toward Timmy. "Did you actually believe that I would allow you to put this urban vulture on the payroll without thoroughly vetting him myself?"

She laughed. "You were oblivious."

"If it makes you feel better to think that," he said with a shrug. "Every kiss, caress, tear, avowal of how much you loved me, all lies."

"You didn't know! You couldn't have known."

"You're not nearly as good at deception as you think you are. As it turns out, I'm far superior."

She tossed her hair again. "What difference does it make now who was the better deceiver? You can't tell anyone about this or you incriminate yourself, just like that redneck pilot said. I have the video that proves your compliance in our little scheme. You're not going to show it to anyone. Not when you're so outspoken on imposing stiffer FDA regulations. Exposing this scandal would irreparably cripple your crusade.

"So," she said, spreading her arms at her sides, "we'll put this behind us. Our marriage will go on as before. In due time, I'm sure Nate can procure another dose of the GX-42."

Richard looked at her with a sympathetic smile. "Impossible, darling."

"With enough money, anything is possible."

"It has nothing to do with money. We won't go on as before because you'll be dead, killed by the man who loved you."

"You would never kill me."

"True. But he will."

He nodded toward the doors, which had been silently pulled open by Goliad. He stood with a pistol in hand.

Timmy gaped at him stupidly. "You're dead."

Goliad fired a straight shot through the center of Timmy's forehead. He never felt it.

Delores looked at Goliad and exhaled his name in appeal.

"You have no honor." The bullet went through her heart. She dropped.

Goliad lowered his arm. The pistol fell from his hand to the floor. "I'm sorry, sir," he said to Richard.

The obsidian eyes that, to Nate, had always looked disturbingly lifeless did actually blink out an instant before his body collapsed. The hilt of a knife was sticking up out of his back.

*5:50 p.m.*

Heedless of the rain and the absence of headlights, Rye never took his foot off the accelerator between the mansion and the runway, steering with one hand, holding his cell phone to his ear with the other. He filed another flight plan. "Two souls on board." He completed the call just as they reached the end of the landing strip.

Sheets of rain slashed against the SUV. He glanced over at Brynn. "Weather's not ideal, but we'll punch through it at about eight thousand feet. You okay with that?"

"Yes, just get me there. Can we make it?"

"We'll make it."

"In time?"

"We'll make it," he repeated with emphasis. "But better we do this in the dark until right before takeoff. Can you see your way to the plane?"

She could barely make out its shape in the darkness. "I'll find it."

"You go first," he said. "I'm right behind you."

She flipped up her hood, but it did her little good against the deluge. She was out of breath and shivering with cold by the time she reached the right side of the craft. Rye caught up with her there.

He went first, opened the door on the copilot's side and got in, then heaved himself into the pilot's seat. Brynn climbed in behind him. He reached across her to make sure the door was locked. "Buckle up."

He put on his headset and started the engine. His hands seemed to do a dozen things at once, moving competently and assuredly. He used only the plane's taxi light as he steered it to the far end of the runway and turned it around.

"I have clearance," he said and looked over at Brynn. "Ready?"

"Ready."

He flipped on the plane's lights, used the PTT button to light the runway, then gave the plane the throttle.

A pair of headlights flashed on at the far end of the runway. The vehicle came speeding straight toward them. Rye stamped on the plane's brakes, and, simultaneous to that, his cell phone rang. The vehicle kept coming and didn't stop until it was twenty yards from the nose of the plane.

Swearing liberally, Rye whipped off his headset and answered his phone. "Rawlins, is that you?"

"Shut her down."

"Not a fucking chance. Get out of my way."

"You tampered with evidence and fled the scene of three homicides."

"What are you talking about?"

"The bloodbath at the mansion."

"Know nothing about a bloodbath."

"Lambert called in a 911. Those two deputies who arrested you were the first responders. Three dead. Timmy, Mrs. Hunt, Goliad."

"Jesus." He looked across at Brynn, who had overheard and appeared as stunned as he.

"Lambert told them you two were there. They called us. We had a hunch where you had run off to and volunteered to stop you. I repeat. Shut her down."

"Nobody was dead when we left. That we knew of."

"Good, you can tell the detectives that."

"When I get back."

"You can't leave."

"I'm getting Brynn to Tennessee. Tonight. Now."

"You're going to play chicken with me on this runway?"

"It's not a game to me. I'm flying this drug to a dying kid."

"I get that. But if you go, you'll be digging yourself into real deep shit."

"Yeah? Well, I've got a propeller at about the level of your thick skull. You decide who's in deeper shit here. You or me?"

Brynn heard Wilson saying something in the background. Rawlins cursed.

"There's not time to debate this, guys," Rye said. "That little girl is lost if we don't go now. Make yourselves useful. Have a police escort meet us. Brynn will text you the name of the airport."

"Can't let you go."

"Hell you can't! Say you missed us. I won't be gone long. Soon as I drop Brynn off, I'll fly right back. I'll surrender myself. Undergo interrogation. Spend the night in lockup. Take a lie detector test. But for right now, get the hell out of the way."

"How do we know you'll be back?"

"I give you my word."

"And I'm giving you the finger," Rawlins shouted into the phone.

Rye sighed. "Figured that if you caught up to me, you'd be a prick, so I left something for you in the driver's seat of that SUV. It's your guarantee that I'll be back."

"What is it?"

"My pilot's license."

# Violet

*7:37 p.m.*

Whean I saw the blue-and-white lights flashing outside my window, I thought it must be an ambulance coming to take me to the hospital because my special day with Elsa and the mayor had tired me out.

Honestly, I wish I could have watched *Frozen* on my new TV with Cy, and my brothers, and Mom and Dad. The mayor's breath wasn't nice, and Elsa didn't sing as good as the one in the movie. But she was nice and didn't talk about cancer and how adorable I am. If I have another special day, I hope they bring Taylor Swift or Alicia Keys.

After the mayor and Elsa left, and all the TV people in the yard went home, I didn't feel good.

Mostly I was sad over Dr. O'Neal leaving without even saying hi.

There's another nurse now instead of Jill. She doesn't have braids or shoes with lights on them.

Daddy fed my brothers pizza and sent them to their room to watch a movie. He and Mom keep checking on me. By now, I can tell when they're just plain worried, and when they're *really* worried. They're *really* worried.

411

I heard Mom say to Daddy, "I was afraid this would happen. But Senator and Mrs. Hunt were so generous and kind to do it."

"How could you say no?"

"I couldn't, but..."

That's all I heard. I think they went into the kitchen and called an ambulance.

But now I see that the lights aren't on an ambulance after all. It's two policemen on motorcycles and a police car. Have they come to take us back to the airplane with the couch in it? Will we fly back to Atlanta tonight?

I hope not, because I'm really tired. And I want to sleep in my room with Cy another night. I don't want to cry. When I cry it makes everybody feel bad.

*Wait.* Dr. O'Neal is getting out of the back seat of the police car! She came back!

The tall man in the old leather jacket came back with her. But not Timmy and not Dr. Lambert, and I'm glad.

Dr. O'Neal and the man are jogging up the walk. Mom and Daddy have gone out to meet them. Mom is hugging Dr. O'Neal. Daddy shakes hands with the tall man.

I think he must be a good friend of Dr. O'Neal's, because they get into each other's personal space a lot, but they never say excuse me.

Mom wants them to come inside, but the man is shaking his head no. I think he's saying something about the police car, because he's started walking backward toward it. Dr. O'Neal is pulling on his hand, like she doesn't want him to leave. But he keeps shaking his head.

Mom hugs him. Daddy shakes his hand again, using both hands, and then they come back inside.

Dr. O'Neal and the man just stand there looking at each other, and then they sorta crash together, and hug each other tight, and start kissing like people do in the TV movies that are inappropriate for young audiences. Seriously? I know grown-ups kiss and make babies.

Dr. O'Neal scoots closer to the tall man until they're touching all up and down. Maybe she wants to marry him. But if they do get married, I hope their kids don't get cancer.

When they quit kissing, he gives Dr. O'Neal a little push toward the porch.

He starts walking toward the police car. Dr. O'Neal turns and runs up the walk.

I hear the front door open and close. She's talking in a hurry to Mom and Daddy. Now they're all coming to my room really quick. Dr. O'Neal is the first one in. Her cheeks are pink, and she's breathing fast like she's been running. There's a big tear in her coat. You can see the stuffing. Her boots have mud on them. Her hair needs brushing.

But I don't care. I'm so happy to see her.

But she looks even more happy to see me.

# Epilogue

———◦◦◦———

*Six weeks later*

Using the familiar old-fashioned room key, Rye let himself into the cabin, but stopped short on the threshold when he saw Brynn sitting on the end of the bed.

This first sight of her since he'd told her goodbye at the Griffins' house sent his heart into arrhythmia, making it difficult to appear cool. But he tried to act nonchalant as he stepped inside and shut the door.

"Do you come with the cabin now?" He took in the familiar burlap lampshades, paint-by-number artwork, the striped bedspread. "Must say, you spruce up the decor."

"Thank you. I wasn't sure you would recognize me."

His brows went up as he shrugged off his jacket. "I recognize that biting tone."

"Sorry. I didn't mean to start right in."

"Hmm. You were going to work up to telling me what a bastard I am?"

"Oh, I'll get there."

He came even to where she sat and propped his butt against

the dresser. "I've only seen you in one set of clothes, so you do look different."

She laughed softly. "I have cleaned up a bit since I last saw you."

He would have bet his bomber jacket that he remembered how much he liked her face, but the wager would have lost him his prized possession. Even his most vivid memories of her paled in comparison to the living, breathing version.

She was wearing a slender black skirt and high-heeled boots. Her pale gray sweater was thin, not bulky. It clung to her breasts, which he knew were a perfect fit in his palms.

He gave a soft cough. "Marlene tell you I was coming today?"

"She called to inform me a few days ago. Said she hoped I was free. I think she's matchmaking."

As though the idea of Marlene White playing Cupid was amusing, he made an effort to smile. It didn't quite work. "She didn't know where I was staying."

"No. I played a hunch."

"You talked a key out of the pothead?"

"I played him, too."

"I bet." He looked her over. "That getup. He'd have to be a monk to hold out, and probably not even then."

She blushed over the compliment but didn't acknowledge it. "How was Brady's flight?"

This time his smile was automatic. "He was like a kid at Christmas. I gave him control a couple of times. I swear, it was so much fun to watch him having so much fun. We flew over this wide-open pasture in a valley. I banked, came around for a second pass, went in real low, almost like I was going to do a touch-and-go, then climbed out steep. Brady—" Catching himself, he stopped.

Her expression was knowing, a trifle smug. "How nice that you can give him such a treat, but remain detached and uninvolved."

He looked down and studied the toe of his boot. When he raised his head, he met her steady gaze head-on. "It was great."

She didn't gloat over his admission. Her victory lap came in the form of a soft smile. "I know today meant a lot to both of them."

"It meant a lot to me."

After a brief but weighty silence, she asked if he and Dash were on speaking terms again.

"Yeah. He was in a tight spot. I forgave him."

"You were the one in the tight spot. How'd it go with the FAA, the NTSB?"

"Good. Wilson and Rawlins helped."

"They met you when you got back that night?"

"At the hangar when I returned Jake's plane. They delivered me to the detectives who were investigating the crime scene at the Hunts'. I was questioned."

"I was deposed in Knoxville the next day."

"I owned up to 'subduing' Timmy in order to protect you. Wilson and Rawlins vouched that neither of us was there to witness the shootings, so we didn't know how it played out after we left.

"They also explained the medical emergency that you and I were responding to. Lambert confirmed it. The police were much more focused on Senator Hunt, who kept changing his story. Still, it was hours before they freed me to go.

"Rawlins, Wilson, and I barely made the nine o'clock meeting up here, but we did. We trooped out to the crash site. I talked the agents through what happened. You, me, Lambert all attested to Timmy's confession about trying to crash the plane. I was cleared. Investigation closed."

Her face lit up with her smile. He found himself looking at her mouth. He longed to dab the corner of her lips with his thumb. His tongue.

He dragged his gaze back up to hers. "How's Violet? Is the drug working?"

"No negative side effects. Her latest blood test shows a marked increase in healthy blood cells. The cancer hasn't spread. We're holding our breath, but it looks good."

"That's great news, Brynn."

"You can drop the surprised act," she said dryly. "Nate told me you've called him three times to ask about her."

"I wanted to know."

"No need to get defensive, Rye. I didn't accuse you of anything except being a kind and caring human being. I appreciate your concern, and so do the Griffins. You certainly had a vested interest in Violet's prognosis. It would be nice if she could thank you personally."

Dodging that, he said, "To hear Lambert tell it, Violet's turnaround was due to him and his genius."

"Nate is obnoxious and unlikable—"

"That doesn't begin to cover it."

"—but he also did the research along with me. He put in the long hours, too. He's entitled to take credit."

"No more than half."

She gave a modest shrug and became reflective. Voice quiet, she said, "You nailed it, you know."

"What?"

"To some extent, I was doing it for me. Not for acclaim. Not to become famous, but to—"

"Live down being a convict's kid."

"You saw that."

He shrugged. "Little bit. Anyway, it's not a sin."

"No doubt my mother's death contributed to my ambition. But when I was most ashamed of my last name, the loftiest goal I could conceive of was to become Dr. O'Neal."

"Doesn't matter why you did it, Brynn. Matters that you did."

Her saw her throat work with emotion. "Well, the important

thing is that Violet's improvement will open up clinical trials for other patients."

He gave her a thumbs-up. "Way to go, Dr. O'Neal."

God, he loved when she blushed.

"Did Nate tell you the irony?" she asked.

He shook his head.

"The morning following the infusion, I called my answering service for the first time since I'd checked out on Thanksgiving eve. They'd been unable to call me because...well, you know.

"Anyway, there were three calls designated as urgent. I didn't recognize the name or number. It turned out to be a member of the FDA review board who was considering the compassionate use of GX-42 for Violet.

"The board member had seen the news story about her and recognized the name. She spent hours Thanksgiving night calling other members of the board. By morning she had a consensus. They approved the application for Violet and gave it emergency status."

He laughed. "No shit?"

"No shit. I'd been given leave to use the drug immediately. I didn't breach ethics after all."

"I'll be damned. Shining the spotlight on Violet actually worked against the Hunts."

"That's the irony. And Richard Hunt is in the worst kind of spotlight. He's got so many spin doctors spinning, he still can't keep his stories straight. The latest is that Goliad was jealous of Timmy and obsessed with Delores. It's a muddle."

She leaned back, propping herself up on her hands. When she crossed her legs, a split on the side of her skirt opened. It took a moment for her words to register.

He said, "I doubt anyone will ever know the whole of it. Hunt will continue to lie and maneuver. Postpone. "

"Meanwhile fighting for his life," Brynn said. "Secretly he's undergoing chemo and radiation, but that only buys him time.

According to Nate, he still refuses to apply for the exemption for fear of disclosure. He says that's all the media would need to ruin him.'"

Another lull ensued. Rye remained fixated on the several inches of thigh visible above her boot. He wanted to start there and kiss his way up.

Before he embarrassed himself, he refocused. "How's Wes?"

"He caught a shoplifter the other day."

"That's what they pay him for."

"Yes, but he let her go without reporting her. She had three children under three years old, and was shoplifting a home pregnancy test. Dad thought she deserved a break."

They shared a smile, but after a moment hers turned wistful. She sat up straight and cleared her throat. "The other day, Violet asked me about the man in the old leather coat." She cut a glance toward his bomber jacket where he'd draped it over the back of a chair. "Seems she saw us kissing outside her house. She asked if you were my boyfriend." She waited a beat before saying, "I told her no."

He didn't say anything, but shifted his position against the dresser, telling himself it was because that spot on his butt had gone numb.

Brynn continued, "I told her no because I could never fall for a man who shuts people out. Strangers. Even people who care about him. I told her that no matter how attractive he was, or how amazingly good sex with him was, or how he'd been willing to sacrifice his pilot's license—the thing he values above everything else—in order to save her life, I couldn't pine for a man who takes off in an airplane, indifferent to whether or not he'll safely land."

She looked down at her open palm and dusted it with the other. "Knowing how others would grieve the loss of his life, it's selfish of him to have such careless disregard for it. I asked Violet why in the world a sane woman would want a man like that."

"No sane woman would," he said. "He sounds like a loser."

"That's just it. He's not."

"You were supposed to be building up to calling him a bastard."

"What good would it do?"

He pushed off the dresser and went over to the window. He flicked the tacky drape open. It was cold out. The wind was brisk. But the sky was crystal clear, not a cloud in sight. It had been a perfect day for Brady's flight.

"I knew a guy like that," he said. "He was a sullen and self-centered son of a bitch. Thought he had problems. Thought life wasn't worth living. He was carrying around all this crap over an accident, an airplane crash. Thirteen people died. Anybody would be sick over that.

"But the thing with him was, he was conceited enough to think that somehow he could've prevented it. That he could've overturned aviation physics, or outsmarted fate, karma, the alignment of the stars, God's will, whatever, when, stripped down to basic fact, it was their time."

Keeping his back to Brynn, he looked up at the sky through the window. He'd been wrong: There was a small cloud drifting past, caressing the crest of a hill.

He took a deep breath. "Anyway, this guy thought he should have died that day, and, because he didn't, he waited for another opportunity. Sure enough, one night, when he really had no business flying, he lost control of his aircraft.

"Odd as it seems, he didn't just let it crash and death take him. Instead, he fought like hell to survive. Odder still, the crash turned out to be the best damn thing that could have happened to him. It shook him up. Woke him up.

"Over the course of a couple of days following it, he came to realize that maybe there was a purpose to his still being around. A reason for him not to have flown that C-12 that day. Maybe he could help save a kid's life. Or give a thrill ride to a guy who couldn't fly himself. Who knows why things turn out the way they do?" He braced his hands on the windowsill and lowered his head between his hunched shoulders.

In a husky voice, Brynn asked, "What happened to him?"

"He cleaned up his act. Some. He'd made a new buddy who flies for a freight carrier. Big, slick outfit. They need experienced pilots. He's considering it. A necktie is required, but he'll have a permanent address, and the pay is good. Good enough for his buddy to afford to have his own plane, and he's always hoped to own one himself.

"He spent Christmas with his family. Held his nephew. He went so far as to firm up a date for a return visit. Told his folks he might bring somebody along, if they didn't mind."

"Who?"

"Aw, there was this girl. Woman, rather. Quite a woman. Smart. Sassy. Took no shit. Thick and silky hair. Eyes the color of fog. Or rain when moonlight shines through it. A body that made him want to take his time, go slow, make it last, hold back. Or speed the hell up. Christ, just looking at her made his mouth water. Once, he got so lost, he forgot a condom, came inside her." He shook his lowered head. "Before that, he'd thought nothing could top being airborne."

He paused, ran his hands up and down the front of his thighs. "But, he blew it."

"How?"

"He was a coward. Kept pushing her away. Shut her out."

"What was he afraid of? Involvement?"

"Too late for that. He was sunk the minute he tackled her and saw her face for the first time. No, what he was afraid of was that she would see him for what he was, and tell him to stay the hell out of her life.

"But the poor sap held out the hope that one day she would show up unexpectedly. He sort of hoped that if that happened, she wouldn't be as desirable as he remembered, that he wouldn't want her any more. Instead, it was all he could do to keep his hands off her."

Nothing was said for a time, then Brynn said with exasperation, "You'll fly through zero visibility and a mile and a half of thunderstorms, but you won't walk across ten feet of ugly carpet? You are a coward."

He turned and cocked his head to one side. "What? Oh. You thought I was talking about *me*?"

She ducked her head and laughed, then looked up at him again, challenge in her eyes.

He sighed. "You're gonna make me come after you, aren't you?"

"If you want me, it's required."

In two long strides, he was cupping her shoulders, pressing her back onto the bed, settling atop her as she stretched out beneath him. He pushed his hands up through her hair, clasped her head, said, "I want you," then fused his mouth to hers. Though it was broad daylight, they kissed with the unleashed desire reserved for the dark.

He couldn't get enough of her, of feeling her breasts moving against his chest, her breath rushing across his lips with excitement and happiness, both evident in her glistening eyes when he finally raised his head and looked into them.

"We've known each other for less than two full days," he said. "This could be the worst mistake you ever make, Brynn."

"I'll take my chances."

Reaching under her sweater, he unhooked her bra, then put his hands inside the cups, reshaped her breasts with gentle squeezes, tweaked the hard tips, then bared them to his seeking mouth.

She ground the back of her head against the mattress. "I could kill you for putting me through the torture of the last six weeks."

He fanned his tongue over her nipple.

"But don't stop that," she groaned and began to paw at the buttons on his jeans.

He pulled her sweater over her head. She wiggled off the loosened bra. He tore open the buttons of his shirt and lay on her again, skin to skin, their hearts thumping together, their breaths ghosting between their lips, eyes locked.

He slid his hand into the slit of her skirt, caressing her inner thigh to the top, then into her panties, his fingers separating, stroking, slipping inside. She clenched around his fingers, tilting her hips toward him in an appeal for more, even as she worked her underwear down her legs and off.

She opened his fly. He swelled against the fist she made around him. He could feel his pulse pumping hot and thick against her palm, her fingers. Pulling his hand from beneath her skirt, he spread her moisture over the head of his cock. "Guide me in."

With his hands under her bottom, he lifted her. She planted him snugly just inside her. She squeezed, and he moaned her name. He pulsed, and her breath hitched. Then a strong, swift thrust embedded him. They held there for the endurance of a deep, soulful kiss.

Then, in perfect synchronization, they began to move.

———◆———

Day faded into dusk. Twilight gave way to full darkness. The passage of time went unnoticed.

They languished in bed, eyes and hands and mouths overindulging in what they'd been able only to sample six weeks earlier, when the pace, even for lovemaking, had been hectic.

The water in the shower turned cool before they got out. When they returned to the bed, he put his bomber jacket on her. Lying facing her, he rested his cheek on one hand and, with the other, opened the jacket.

Lazily, he toyed and teased until her eyes were lambent, her lips parted, her skin flushed with arousal.

He told her he might replace the existing lining of his jacket with a new one, a painting on silk of her, posed just that way. He nosed her hair aside and whispered directly into her ear, "Knowing you're wet."

She said that changing his prized jacket sounded like serious business, like permanence. "Won't you get tired of me?"

He eased her onto her back, settled in the cradle of her thighs, and rubbed against her to demonstrate how much he wanted her yet again, as badly as before.

"You know what I told you about the feeling I get right before every takeoff?"

"You can't wait?"

He smiled.

# Acknowledgments

Special thanks belong to two people who assisted me throughout the writing, rewriting, rewriting, rewriting, and editing of *Tailspin*.

Robert Newton, friend and private pilot, talked me through all the flight sequences—numerous times. Add to all those conversations the countless emails from me to him, asking "just one more question," so many that he says I should be able to solo by now! Not true, but if I got anything wrong, the blame is mine, not his. Thank you, Bob.

I owe a huge debt of gratitude to my beloved sister, Lauri Macon, who tackled the mind-boggling subject of orphan drugs, and how they're developed and tested. Her thorough and meticulous research acquainted me with NLA101, a drug already in clinical trials in Europe. My GX-42 is based on it but is entirely fictitious. Let's hope not for long.